T0339130

Stories for the Years

Stories for the Years

LUIGI PIRANDELLO

TRANSLATED FROM THE ITALIAN BY VIRGINIA JEWISS

YALE UNIVERSITY PRESS ■ NEW HAVEN & LONDON

A MARGELLOS
WORLD REPUBLIC OF LETTERS BOOK

English translation and translator's introduction copyright © 2020 by Virginia Jewiss. The stories in this collection are a selection of those published in Italian as *Novelle per un anno* by Bemporad (vols. I–XIII, 1922–1928) and Mondadori (vols. XIV and XV, 1934 and 1937). Most of the stories had been previously published in Italian magazines and newspapers.

Yale University Press books may be purchased in quantity for educational, business, or promotional use. For information, please email sales.press@yale.edu (U.S. office) or sales@yaleup.co.uk (U.K. office).

Set in Electra and Nobel types by Tseng Information Systems, Inc.
Printed in the United States of America.

Library of Congress Control Number: 2019956866
ISBN 978-0-300-15096-4 (hardcover : alk. paper)

A catalogue record for this book is available from the British Library.

This paper meets the requirements of ANSI/NISO Z39.48-1992 (Permanence of Paper).

10 9 8 7 6 5 4 3 2 1

CONTENTS

TRANSLATOR'S INTRODUCTION

Luigi Pirandello (1867–1936) is best known for his plays, for which he was awarded the Nobel Prize in Literature in 1934. A prolific, restless writer, he also published novels, poetry, essays, and translations. Yet throughout his long literary career, the short story was always the genre to which he returned. He published his first story when he was seventeen, and hundreds more over the years, including one the day before he died. Others appeared posthumously, making for about two hundred and fifty in all. And *what* stories! Simultaneously heartbreaking and humorous, these hauntingly beautiful tales display a lyricism and naturalism largely absent from his philosophically driven theater. The Pirandello we meet here is a master storyteller, with an ear for dialogue, an eye for revealing details, and a keen sense of the crushing burdens of class, gender, geography, and mores. Archetypical figures lend some stories a folkloric quality, while animal characters cast others almost as fables. Still others recall the Italian literary movement of *verismo* or realism, or continue the long tradition of the burlesque. The narrative range is vast, yet the stories all share an extraordinary depth of psychological observation. Many of the themes will be familiar to those who know his plays, but the stories surprise us with their variety and emotional insight, and humanize the grand questions acted out in his works for the stage.

In Pirandello's most famous play, the groundbreaking *Sei personaggi in cerca d'autore* (*Six Characters in Search of an Author*), six characters from an unfinished play interrupt the rehearsal of another play and demand to act out their story, or in other words, to live. This bold work of meta-theater, which premiered in 1921, upended conventional notions of author, actor, and audience, dramatized the tension between life and art, and revolutionized the very concept of theater. The play's central themes—identity, self-creation, art's falsifying necessity—percolate through all of Pirandello's works, but it is in his short stories that they receive the most tender treatment. In these ironic, often bitter tales the author truly animates his concept of *humor*, which, as opposed to comedy, moves the reader beyond laughter to reflection and compassion.

Many of the stories are set in Sicily, the author's birthplace. The arid terrain, isolated villages, and noxious sulfur mines seem to map the fragile interior world of his characters. Others, set in Rome—where Pirandello moved in 1887 to study, and where he later took a job as a professor of Italian literature at a women's teaching college—grapple with the erosion of tradition and the ills of modern urban life. Rich in picturesque detail, these stories preserve a memory of an Italy that is long gone, but their appeal is far more than as period pieces. Their recurring concerns—solitude and betrayal, the rigidity of social conventions, madness, disappointment, financial ruin, old age, suicide, and untimely death—still speak to us today. The scorned lover, the despondent widow, the intransigent bureaucrat, the pompous lawyer, the wretched peasant, the frustrated priest, the lonely mother, the rebellious child: freed of the confines of formal theatrical production, Pirandello's characters here take center stage, exposing the general human condition in all its fatalism, injustice, and raw beauty. As a whole, these works offer a devastating yet deeply compassionate vision of life, which the author presents without moralizing.

Every story is jewel-like and precise in its expression. Take, for instance, "The Cat, a Goldfinch, and the Stars," in which a pet bird encounters a neighbor's cat. The title, with its jarring combination of definite and indefinite articles, foreshadows an inevitable tragedy. The bird that to a pair of elderly grandparents is *the* goldfinch—it belonged to their beloved granddaughter, now dead—to the cat is simply *a* goldfinch. The old couple's hopeless anthropomorphism, which sees in the goldfinch the embodiment of their granddaughter's spirit, is an expression of love and a longing for meaning in a meaningless world. Yet their fundamental humanity cannot but clash with the cat's pure feline instinct. Both humans and cat are blameless, for they act in keeping with their natures, the irreconcilability of which is, for Pirandello, the essence of tragedy. The domestic drama, amplified to cosmic proportions through the framing device of the unseeing stars, transforms this seemingly simple story into a devastating reflection on man's desire to soften the cruelty of the world. The grandparents' insistence on meaning, like the text's suggestion of metaphor, unravels under the aloof gaze of the satiated cat, who may be the only unconflicted being in all of Pirandello's works.

Pirandello's prose style shapes his arguments. In "The Cat, a Goldfinch, and the Stars," the repetition of key nouns and phrases implies fixed identities, while the deliberate inversion of subjects and objects articulates the dangerous slippage between bird, girl, and grandparents. Narrative compression heightens the story's fatalism: the cat does not make his appearance until the final paragraphs, and the denouement comes swiftly, matter-of-factly, yet is compounded by ambiguous pronouns when clarifying nouns are called for. From the very first lines, incomplete sentences, ellipses, and unanswered questions force the reader to do the work of making connections: "A stone. Another stone. A man goes by and sees them side by side. But what does this stone know of the one next to it? Of the water, or the gully where it flows?"

Pirandello's deliberate ambiguities and dynamic syntax present notable challenges to the translator. Italian allows for equivocation, which is central to this story, through its allowance for implied subjects, whereas English requires them to be explicit. Furthermore, word order in Italian is relatively free, allowing Pirandello to craft such masterfully confusing phrases as "No, non la vicina, il gatto, il gatto voleva uccidere il vecchio"—which, on first reading, could be taken to mean: "No, not his neighbor, the cat, the cat wanted to kill the old man." Logic, rather than language, makes us invert the words and restore order—such as it is—to the drama: "No, not his neighbor but the cat, the cat the old man wanted to kill." And yet the first reading harbors its own sardonic truth, as the reader will see.

Another animal story, "The Revenge of the Dog," opens with a beautiful, almost mystical description: "Without knowing how or why, one fine day Jaco Naca found himself the owner of the whole sunny hillside below the city, from which there was a magnificent view of the open countryside, of hills and valleys and plains, and in the distance the sea, far away, after all that green, blue on the horizon." The sentence unfurls as does the view, and the eye moves pleasantly across the gently sloping landscape of words. Here it is not ambiguity but rhythm that most demands the translator's attention, for the next sentence, even longer, but unrelentingly choppy, establishes a jarring contrast that sets the tone for the entire story:

> Some three years back, a foreigner, with a wooden leg that creaked at every step, had appeared, all in a sweat, at a farmhouse in the narrow, malaria-infested valley of Sant'Anna, where Jaco, yellow with fever, shivering to the bone, and ears buzzing from quinine, worked as a farmhand; the foreigner announced that a thorough search of the records had led him to discover that that hillside there, which until then was believed to be without an owner, actually belonged to Jaco: if he were willing to sell him part of it, for some still rather vague plans of his, he'd pay the official appraisal.

The harsh jerkiness of all those short phrases simultaneously introduces onomatopoetically the wooden-legged foreigner and the sickly Jaco Naca, and also foreshadows the divisive fate of the gentle landscape and its inhabitants. The action oscillates between the sunny hillside and the miserable little valley, "narrow as a grave," recalling the moral landscape of Dante's *Divine Comedy*.

The classical epic is also evoked. The three-part "Donna Mimma," recasts the classical journey of education in a feminine key and maps it onto the confines of Sicily. We follow a beloved midwife who is forced to leave her small village to study in distant Palermo, in order to earn a diploma for the profession she has been practicing successfully for years. During her absence, Donna Mimma is replaced by a "little coquette from the Continent"—in other words, a young woman from northern Italy. The Italian *smor-fiosetta*, as Donna Mimma scornfully calls her new adversary, combines the older woman's disdain for independent, modern women with typical Sicilian distrust of non-Sicilians. The contest between the two women conveys the fierce tensions between Sicily and the mainland, setting wisdom against knowledge, experience against education, and capturing all the bewilderment and frustration of old age. It also charts the sort of devastating concessions required to unite this deeply divided nation. Ancient folk wisdom is sacrificed to science, humanity gives way to bureaucracy, and "progress" crushes tradition. But—as with so many of Pirandello's plotlines— things prove not so straightforward. The primeval power of Sicily pushes back, giving birth to a creative, cynical compromise.

Sicily's peculiar spirit is epitomized in one of Pirandello's best-known stories, "The Jar." It opens with the abundance of a particularly good harvest and tells us much about old ways of gathering and pressing olives. But nature's generosity quickly cedes to man's parsimony and litigiousness. A broken earthenware jar, intended to store olive oil, pits its owner, a wealthy, quarrelsome landholder, against a clever, taciturn inventor of a mysterious glue. What follows is a battle of wills between bad-tempered Don Lollò, a violent man with "wolfish eyes," and Zi' Dima, "a crooked old man, with crippled, gnarled joints, like the stump of an aged Saracen olive tree." The clash of these caricatures makes for one of Pirandello's most burlesque tales. For an Italian audience, it also brings to mind the bawdy story involving a jar in Giovanni Boccaccio's *Decameron*, Pirandello's primary inspiration for this story and for his entire collection. Yet lurking beneath the comic tone is all the injustice of a feudal agrarian society. The broken jar and the effort to repair it hint at the inadequacy of the law to make amends for centuries of exploitation, and lead to a catastrophic yet darkly comical resolution in which rashness proves more effective than deliberation, and the laws of nature triumph over the laws of man.

Echoes of Pirandello's own life can be discerned in many of the challenges his characters face. Pirandello was acutely aware of Sicily's linguistic and cultural provincialism, as well as its compelling yet vulnerable traditions, unique history, and independent spirit. The thesis he wrote for his degree in Romance Philology was on the dialect of Girgenti, as his hometown of Agrigento was then known. (Ironically, he wrote it in German, having transferred to the University of Bonn after clashing with a Latin professor at the University of Rome.) Born in the final years of Italy's struggle for unification known as the Risorgimento, Pirandello was raised by parents actively involved in forging the new nation. His father fought together with Giuseppe Garibaldi in the 1860 Expedition of the Thousand, and his mother's family was part of the nationalist movement that opposed Bourbon rule. Italy's fraught political history of papal and foreign domination is remembered in stories such as "The Brazier," and contemporary events inform other stories: "When You Understand" registers the trauma of World War One, in which Pirandello's son fought and was taken prisoner, while "A 'Goy'" offers a bitingly ironic and sadly prescient perspective on war.

Pirandello's own political trajectory traces the contours of Italy's struggles over national identity. Declaring himself "apolitical," he nevertheless became a Fascist National Party member in

1924; theatrically tore up his party card in front of the party secretary in 1927; then allegedly gifted his Nobel Prize medal to the Fascist government, to be melted down to help fund the imperialist conquest of Ethiopia. Pirandello's personal life was also marred by upheaval and disappointment. Financial ruin devastated his family after sulfur mines that his father had invested heavily in were destroyed by floods. His beloved wife, Antonietta Portulano, suffered such a serious psychological setback that he eventually committed her to an asylum. His writing became a refuge and a financial necessity. (A 1973 *New York Times* profile noted that she became "expensively insane.") Her delusional jealousies and Pirandello's own guilt haunt "Mrs. Frola and Her Son-in-Law Mr. Ponza," which posits a strange yet sympathetic questioning of, and resignation to, madness.

In 1922, Pirandello began gathering his short stories into a collection he called *Novelle per un anno* (Short Stories for a Year). His ambitious plan of writing 365 stories—one for each day of the year—was never completed, but his title and preface make it clear that Pirandello conceived of them as part of the great short story tradition. Yet unlike the fourteenth-century *Decameron*, Giovanni Boccaccio's collection of one hundred stories, or the earlier Middle Eastern collection of tales known as *The Thousand and One Nights*, both of which Pirandello refers to in his preface, *Novelle per un anno* lacks a frame or other structuring device. Pirandello's determination to make a collection and his simultaneous refusal to make sense of it through some sort of unifying or organizing element is itself a manifestation of one of his dominant themes: life is chaos, and any control we believe we exercise over our lives is merely an illusion.

The one element that does unite his collection is his preface, which was to have been included in every volume, had his own life story not come to a close before his year of stories was complete. In it, Pirandello records his original vision: one impossibly large tome binding together all 365 stories — or short of that, twelve volumes of thirty or so stories each. Neither one was realized. So I have decided to honor Pirandello's wish for one volume of thirty stories, to restore an element of elusive calendrical fantasy to his work. The title I have given the volume, *Stories for the Years*, remembers Pirandello's title while emphasizing the timelessness of his tales. My selection was guided by my own wish: to celebrate Italy's greatest modern playwright as one of its most extraordinary storytellers. Having read and taught these stories for many years, I am delighted to share this collection of my favorites, many of which have never been translated into English before.

Virginia Jewiss
Rome, 2019

I am gathering all the short stories already published in as-sorted volumes, along with many others, previously unpublished, in a single collection entitled *Short Stories for a Year*. A seemingly modest move that, on the contrary, is perhaps overly ambitious, if one recalls that other collections of this sort, some of which are quite famous, have, by ancient tradition, been named for nights or days.

In keeping with the idea that this title suggested to me, I would have liked the entire collection to be bound in a single volume, one of those monumental tomes that fell out of fashion for works of literature quite some time ago. My publisher (and the reader will easily understand why) chose not to satisfy my wish, and instead advised me to divide the collection not into the twelve volumes of thirty or more stories each that I had resigned myself to requesting, but into twenty-four. Which, for anyone willing to ponder it, may lead to some not unhelpful reflections on the nature and necessities of our day.

I hasten to add that the stories in these twenty-four volumes are not intended to be linked explicitly to seasons, months, days of the year. A story a day, for an entire year, without any of them drawing their specific qualities from days or months or seasons.

Each volume will contain more than a few new stories. Of

those previously published, some have been revised top to bottom, others recast or retouched here and there. In short, they have all been reworked with long and loving care.

If only by the grace of this care, the author of *Short Stories for a Year* hopes that his readers will forgive him if they receive too much bitterness and too little joy from his conception of the world and of life, and will see in these many tiny mirrors merely a reflection of the whole.

L.P.

Stories for the Years

Without knowing how or why, one fine day Jaco Naca found himself the owner of the whole sunny hillside below the city, from which there was a magnificent view of the open countryside, of hills and valleys and plains, and in the distance the sea, far away, after all that green, blue on the horizon.

Some three years back, a foreigner, with a wooden leg that creaked at every step, had appeared, all in a sweat, at a farmhouse in the narrow, malaria-infested valley of Sant'Anna, where Jaco, yellow with fever, shivering to the bone, and ears buzzing from quinine, worked as a farmhand; the foreigner announced that a thorough search of the records had led him to discover that that hillside there, which until then was believed to be without an owner, actually belonged to Jaco: if he were willing to sell him part of it, for some still rather vague plans of his, he'd pay the official appraisal.

Rocks really, nothing more, with a tuft of grass here and there, which not even the sheep bothered to nibble as they went by.

Soured by the slow poison of disease that had destroyed his liver and consumed his flesh, Jaco Naca felt barely any surprise or pleasure at his good fortune, and sold the wooden-legged foreigner the better part of those rocks for a pittance. But when, less than a year later, he saw rising up on the hill two small villas, one more charming than the next, with marble terraces and stained-glass

verandas, the likes of which had never been seen in these parts—
such elegance!—each with its own pretty little flower garden, each
adorned with gazebos and fountains on the side facing the city,
and vegetable patches and pergolas on the side facing the sea; and
when he heard everyone commend, with admiration and envy, the
shrewdness of the cripple, who came from who knows where, and
who, with the rent from those twelve furnished apartments situated
in such a pleasant spot, would not only recoup his expenses in a few
short years but make himself a nice little bundle besides, well, he
felt cheated and deceived. The surly sluggishness that had allowed
him to endure misery and misfortune for so long, like a sick beast,
suddenly turned into rabid bitterness, and so, between violent outbursts and exasperated tears, stomping his feet, biting his hands,
and tearing his hair, Jaco Naca cried out for justice and revenge
against that swindling thief.

Unfortunately, it's often true that, in trying to avoid one problem, you run smack into an even bigger one. That wooden-legged
foreigner, to avoid the trouble of all those disturbing recriminations,
was rashly persuaded to slip Jaco Naca a little something extra, on
the sly, above and beyond the selling price: nothing much, but
Jaco Naca naturally suspected that that little something extra was
handed to him on the sly like that because the foreigner wasn't
completely convinced of his rights and wanted to placate him. Lawyers don't exist for nothing; Jaco Naca appealed to the law courts.
And so, while the few pennies he'd made on the sale went to cover
amendments and appeals, he devoted himself with rabid obstinacy
to cultivating what remained of his property: the very bottom of

the little valley, below the rocks, where the rainwater, coursing in wide rivulets over the rough, steep slope of the hill, had deposited a bit of soil.

People compared him then to a slow-witted dog who, having let a meaty leg of lamb be snatched from him, now furiously breaks his teeth on the bone abandoned by whomever enjoyed the juicy bits.

A miserable little vegetable patch, twenty or so equally miserable almond trees that still looked like stumps among the stones, had sprouted down in that little valley, narrow as a grave, in those two years of dogged labor; while up above, light and airy before the spectacle of countryside and sea, the pretty little villas sparkled in the sun, inhabited by rich people, who were naturally—or so Jaco Naca imagined—also happy. Happy, if for no other reason than for his grief and misfortune.

To spite those happy people and avenge himself thus on the foreigner, when there was nothing left to do, he dragged a big guard dog down into the ditch, tied him to a short chain, and left him there, night and day, dying of hunger, thirst, and cold.

"Cry out for me!"

■■■

During the day, when Jaco Naca, devoured by rancor, his eyes grim in his sickly, sallow face, hoed his garden, the dog kept quiet out of fear. Stretched on the ground, his snout resting on his front paws, at most he'd lift his eyes and let out a sigh or a long, whimpering yawn, practically dislocating his jaw in hopes of some bread crusts, which now and then Jaco Naca would throw at him, like stones, watching amusedly as the dog fretted whenever a piece rolled out of reach of his chain. But in the evening, as soon as he was left alone, and then the whole night long, the poor beast, so distraught, would howl and whine and moan so loudly, begging for help and mercy, that everyone in the villas would wake up and not be able to fall back to sleep.

From one floor to the next, from one apartment to the next, in the stillness of the night could be heard the grumbling, snorting, cursing, and fretting of all those people awoken from a deep sleep; the calls and cries of frightened children, the thud of bare feet, the shuffle of mothers' slippers rushing to and fro.

How could they possibly go on like this? Complaints rained down from all sides on the foreigner, who, having tried repeatedly, nicely and not so nicely, but in vain, to get that wretch to stop martyring the poor beast, finally advised his tenants to submit a petition, signed by everyone, to the city council.

But even the petition came to naught. The distance between the villas and the spot where the dog was chained up was in compliance with the law. If the depth of the little valley and the rise of those two villas made it seem as if the howling was coming from just outside their windows, well, that wasn't Jaco Naca's fault: he certainly couldn't teach the dog to bark in a manner more pleasing to their ears; if the dog barked, he was merely being a dog; it wasn't true that Jaco Naca didn't give him anything to eat; he gave him as much as he could afford; letting him off the chain was not even a consideration, because if he were loose he would go back home, and Jaco had to look after his interests, which cost him so much sweat and blood. A couple of tree stumps? Well, not everyone has the good fortune to become rich in the twinkling of an eye by taking advantage of a poor ignorant soul!

"Nothing, then? So there really is nothing to be done?"

On one of those nights when the dog had taken to howling even more woefully than usual at the cold January moon, a window in one of the two villas suddenly banged open and two shots rang out, one after the other, with a dreadful roar. The silence of the night, of countryside and sea, was jolted twice, upsetting everything; and in that general upset, what shouts and desperate cries! The dog's whining instantly became a furious bark, and many other dogs far and near joined in, barking on and on. In the midst of all that racket, another window opened, in the other villa, and the irritated voice of a woman and the shrill but no less irritated voice of a little girl shouted at the window where the shots had come from.

"Oh, good! Some courage you have! Shooting at a poor, chained beast!"

"Bad man!"

"If you're so brave, why don't you shoot his owner!"

"Bad man!"

"Isn't it enough for you that that poor dog is chained up there, in the freezing cold, dying from hunger and thirst? You have to go and kill him too? Some courage! Some heart!"

"Bad man!"

And with a rush of indignation, the window closed again.

But the other window remained open, the one where the tenant, who had probably expected his neighbors' approval, and instead had received the sharp rebuke of that irascible and biting feminine protest, still trembled from the violence he had committed. Really?

Really? He stood there like a madman for more than half an hour, bare-chested in the chill of the night, cursing not so much the damned dog that hadn't let him sleep for a month as the facile pity of certain women who, having the luxury of sleep during the day, can afford to lose some during the night without much harm, and what's more, with the satisfaction . . . ah, yes, with the satisfaction of feeling themselves tenderhearted, of sympathizing with beasts that steal sleep from those who slave away from morning to night. So he said, to keep from saying worse.

Talk in the two villas lasted deep into the night: heated discussions in every family, between those who sided with the man who fired the shots and those who sided with the woman who defended the dog.

They all agreed that the dog was insufferable; but they also agreed that he deserved compassion for the cruel manner in which his owner treated him. Except that Jaco's cruelty wasn't aimed merely at the beast, but also at them, whose sleep he stole by means of the dog. Calculated cruelty, openly declared revenge. Now, compassion for the poor beast undoubtedly played into the hands of that scoundrel who, by keeping him chained up and leaving him to die of hunger, thirst, and cold, seemed to defy them all, saying:

"So go ahead and kill him then, if you dare!"

Well then, they had to kill him, they had to overcome their compassion and kill him, so as not to give in to that scoundrel!

Kill him? But wouldn't that be unfair, making the poor beast pay for his owner's sins? Some justice! Cruelty upon cruelty, and doubly unjust, because, as they realized, not only was it not the dog's fault, but he was right to moan so! The double cruelty of that miserable wretch would be taken out on the beast if the people who couldn't sleep turned against him and killed him! But then again, if there was no other way to keep him from tormenting them?

"Careful now, ladies and gentlemen"—the owner of the two villas had appeared the next morning to admonish them, with his squeaky wooden leg. "For the love of God, let's be careful!"

Kill a Sicilian peasant's dog? Beware of even thinking such a thing! Killing a Sicilian peasant's dog means getting yourself killed, no doubt about it. Besides, what did he have to lose, that Jaco Naca? All you had to do was look him in the face—all that pent-up rage— to know he wouldn't think twice about committing a crime.

A little later, in fact, Jaco Naca, his face more sallow than usual and his rifle slung over his shoulder, showed up outside the villas. Since he couldn't be sure exactly which window the shots had come from, he muttered menacingly at them all, challenging whoever it was who dared try to kill his dog to come forward.

All the windows remained closed. All but one: that of Mrs. Crinelli, the tax inspector's young widow, the tenant who had come to the dog's defense. Little Rorò, the girl with the squeaky voice, Mrs. Crinelli's only child, her tiny face aflame and her big eyes sparkling, hurled herself at the railing and gave him a piece of her mind, tossing back the thick black curls on her proud little head.

When he first heard the window open, Jaco Naca readied his rifle in a rage. But then, seeing a little girl appear, he listened with a nasty grin to her bold invective, and when she finished, he asked bitingly:

"So who sent you, your papà? Well, tell him to come out then, you're just a baby!"

■ ■ ■

From that day on, the violence of conflicting emotions in the hearts of those people, on the one hand angry over lost sleep, on the other moved by the dog's wretched existence to a pity immediately checked by their fierce vexation with that despicable creature who turned the dog into a weapon against them, not only diminished the pleasure of living in those much-admired villas, but greatly embittered relations among the inhabitants, who, as spite compounded spite, soon came to open warfare, especially those two who had previously displayed precisely the opposite sentiments: the widow Crinelli and the school inspector Cavalier Barsi, who had shot at the dog.

People were saying that the ill will between them was not merely due to the dog. And that Cavalier Barsi the school inspector would have been more than happy to lose sleep at night if the compassion the tax inspector's young widow showed for him was even a fraction of what she had for the dog. People recalled that despite the repugnance the young widow had always shown for his squat, unattractive figure and clingy manner, as sticky as his greasy pomade, Cavalier Barsi had persisted in courting her, even when all hope was lost, almost to spite her, almost for the pleasure of being rejected, bitten until he bled, not only by the young widow but also by her daughter, that little Rorò, who looked at everyone with those big, sullen eyes, as if she lived in a world arranged precisely for the unhappiness of her sweet mamma, who suffered always and cried often, silently and seemingly for no reason. How much envy, how much jealousy, and how much spite factored into Cavalier Barsi the school inspector's hatred for that dog?

Now, every night in bed, mother and daughter, hearing that poor beast moan, would hold each other tight so as to suffer together those lengthy laments, waiting in fear that the window in the next villa would open and, under cover of darkness, more shots would ring out.

"Mamma, oh mamma," the little girl would wail, trembling all over, "they're shooting him! Hear how he howls? They're killing him!"

"No, dear, hush," her little mother tried to comfort her. "Calm down, dear, he's not going to kill him! He's too afraid of the mean man! Didn't you see? He didn't dare come to the window. If he kills the dog, the mean man will kill him. Hush, now."

But Rorò couldn't hush. For some time now, that poor beast's suffering had become an obsession. She'd be at the window all day, consumed with pity as she gazed at the dog down in the valley. She would have liked to go and comfort him, pet him, bring him something to eat and drink; and on the days when the mean man was gone, she would repeatedly ask her mother to let her go, pretty please. But her mother, fearing that the wicked man would turn up, and dreading that her little girl would stumble down the rocky slope, had never granted her wish.

But in the end she did, to spite Barsi, after he'd shot at the dog. At sunset, when she saw Jaco Naca head off with his hoe over his shoulder, she handed Rorò a napkin gathered at the corners and filled with bread crusts and leftovers from lunch, and urged her to be very careful and to watch her step on her way down the hill. And she would be watching from the window.

Many of the other tenants were also at their windows, admiring the courageous Rorò as she descended into that sorry grave to help the beast. Barsi was at his window as well. He followed the girl with his gaze, shaking his head and rubbing his rough cheeks, a hand over his mouth. All this ostentatious charity, wasn't it an out-and-out challenge to him? Well, fine: challenge accepted. That morning he had bought a poisonous paste to throw to the dog one of these nights, to be rid of him quietly. Tonight would be the night. Meanwhile, he stayed to enjoy the spectacle of all that charity, and all the loving exhortations the young mother shouted from her window not to get too close, he might bite, he doesn't know you.

The dog did, in fact, bark when he saw the little girl coming toward him, and, confined by the chain, leapt about threateningly. But Rorò, clutching the four corners of the napkin, kept approaching, certain that he would soon realize her good intentions. And there, the first time she called him, he started to wag his tail even though he kept on barking; and now, at the first piece of bread, he stopped barking. Oh, poor thing, poor thing! With what voracity did he gulp down those crusts, one after the other! But now came the best part . . . now Rorò, without the least apprehension, held out her two little hands, placing the napkin with the leftovers right under the dog's nose, and he, after eating them and licking the napkin for a long time, looked at the little girl first with astonishment, then with affection and gratitude. How she caressed him now, and with each caress she grew more reassured and happy that her friendship was returned: how many words of pity she said to him, she even kissed him on the head and hugged him, while her mother up above, smiling as her eyes filled with tears, shouted for her to come back up. But now the big dog wanted to play with the little girl: he crouched, then leapt friskily, heedless of the chain tugging on him as he squirmed and yelped, this time with joy.

Wasn't Rorò right to think that the dog kept quiet that night because she had fed and comforted him? They heard him bark only once, briefly, at a certain point, but then nothing. Of course, now that he was satiated and happy, he was sleeping. The dog slept and let the people sleep.

"Mamma," Rorò said, happy for the solution they'd finally found. "Again tomorrow, right, mamma?"

"Yes, dear," her mother replied, not fully understanding the question in her sleep.

And the next morning, Rorò's first thought was to look out the window at the dog who hadn't made a sound all night.

There he was, lying on his side on the ground, his four paws stretched out straight in front of him, how soundly he slept! No one was there, down in the valley, just—or so it seemed—a deep silence which, for the first time that night, had not been broken.

The other tenants, together with Rorò and her mother, were also astonished by the silence as they looked down at the still-sleeping dog, stretched out there that way. So it was really true? A little girl's crusts and caresses had performed a miracle, letting them all sleep, even the dog?

Only Barsi's window remained closed.

And since the wretched Jaco was nowhere to be seen, and maybe he wouldn't come at all that day, as was often the case, several tenants persuaded Mrs. Crinelli to give in to Rorò's wish to bring the dog breakfast, as she called it.

"But go slow, mind you," her mother admonished. "And then come right back up, no dawdling, okay?" she repeated over and over from the window, as the little girl took quick, cautious steps down into the valley, her tiny head bowed, smiling to herself at the festive welcome she expected from her big, sleeping friend.

Down below, behind a rock, crouched over and clutching his rifle, like a wild beast lying in wait, was Jaco Naca. The little girl turned and saw him, suddenly right in front of her, so close she barely had time to look at him with those big, frightened eyes of hers. The rifle cracked and Rorò tumbled backwards as her mother and the other tenants screamed, watching in horror as her tiny body rolled down the slope and into the big dog, who was still lying there, motionless, his four paws stretched out stiffly in front of him.

THE CAT, A GOLDFINCH, AND THE STARS

A stone. Another stone. A man goes by and sees them side by side. But what does this stone know of the one next to it? Of the water, or the gully where it flows? The man sees the water and the gully; he hears the sound of the water, and begins to imagine that it confides who knows what secrets to the gully as it flows by.

Oh, what a starry sky above the roofs of this poor little mountain village! Gazing from the rooftops to the heavens, you'd swear that the stars see nothing else tonight, so brightly do they shine.

And yet the stars know nothing of the earth.

These mountains? Could it be they don't know they belong to this village, which has been here for nearly a thousand years? Everyone knows their names: Monte Corno, Monte Moro. So how could they not even know they're mountains? And the oldest house in the village, could it not even know it stands here, forming the corner of this street, the oldest one in the village? Could that really be possible?

And so?

■ ■ ■

So go ahead and believe, if you like, that the stars see nothing but the roofs of your little mountain village.

I knew two old grandparents who owned a goldfinch. The question—how that goldfinch, with his bright, round little eyes, perceived their faces, his cage, or the house full of old furniture, or what he made of all their attention and loving kindness—never even occurred to them, so sure were they that when he perched on a shoulder and pecked at a wrinkly neck or earlobe, he knew perfectly well that what he perched on was a shoulder, that what he pecked at was an earlobe, and to whom the shoulder and earlobe belonged. Could it be that he didn't recognize them? Didn't know that the man was the grandfather and the woman the grandmother? And didn't know they loved him so because he had once belonged to their dead granddaughter, who had trained him so well—to perch on her shoulder, peck just so at her ear, and fly freely about the house?

A cage hung from the curtain rod, but he only spent the night there, and those brief moments during the day when he went to peck at his millet or drink a bit of water with those dainty little bows of his. His cage was like his palace, the house his vast kingdom. And often, perched on the dining room lampshade or the back of the grandfather's chair, he would dispense warbles as well as . . . a goldfinch, after all!

"Filthy thing, you!" the old woman would yell whenever she saw him do it. She ran around with a rag, always ready to clean up after him, as if there were a small child in the house who couldn't yet be expected to do certain things in the right way and in the right place. And she was reminded of her granddaughter, the grandmother was, the goldfinch reminded the old woman of the little girl, poor love. They'd done the same for her for a year, till then, like a good child . . .

"You remember, eh?"

And the old man: "Remember?" He could still picture her there in the house, such a little thing, only this high! And he would shake his head for a long while.

The old couple had been left alone with that little girl, an orphan, who'd lived with them since she was a baby. She should have been the joy of their old age, but instead, at fifteen . . . Yet the memory of her—wings and warbles—lived on in that goldfinch. And to think that at first it hadn't even occurred to them! They'd fallen into such an abyss of despair after the tragedy, how could they possibly have given any thought to a goldfinch? But he—the gold-finch, that is—he had come, all by himself, and had alighted gently on their shoulders, stooped and shaking with sobs, had cocked his head from side to side, and then, neck extended, had given a little peck on their ears, from behind, as if to say that . . . yes, something of her was still alive. He was alive, alive and in need of their attention, of the same love they had given her.

Ah, with what emotion had the old man taken him in his big hand and, sobbing, showed him to his elderly wife! What kisses were planted on that tiny head, on that cute little beak! But the goldfinch didn't want to be held, imprisoned in that hand; he squirmed with his little feet and head, and returned the old couple's kisses with pecks.

The old woman was absolutely certain that with his warbles he was still calling his little mistress, and that when he fluttered about from one room to the next, he was searching for her, searching un-ceasingly, unable to find peace without her. And that all those long trills were conversations with her: questions really, questions that words could not have expressed better, repeated three, four times in a row, questions that awaited a response and voiced his annoyance at not receiving one.

But how could that be, if it was also absolutely certain the goldfinch knew she was dead? If he knew, whom was he calling? And from whom was he awaiting a response to those questions that words could not have expressed better?

For goodness' sake, he's a goldfinch, after all! One moment he called her, another he mourned her. Right then, for example, as he sat all balled up on the bar of his cage, his little head tucked under, beak pointing upward and little eyes half-closed, could anyone doubt that he was thinking about her death? And sitting there, he'd let out meek little chirps every now and then—obvious proof that he was thinking about her, mourning her, grieving her. Those chirps were agony.

The old man did not contradict his wife. He was just as certain of it himself! Even so, he would quietly climb on a chair, as if to whisper some small word of comfort to that poor little suffering soul. And meanwhile, as if not wanting to see what he himself was doing, the man would open the spring door to the cage, which had closed shut.

"He's escaped, he's escaped, the rascal!" the old man would shout and, turning on the chair, would follow him, eyes smiling and hands spread in front of his face like a shield.

And so man and wife would bicker. How many times had she told her husband to let him be when he was like that, not to confuse him in his grief? There, did he hear him now?

"He's singing," the old man would say.

"Singing?" she would peck back at him with a shrug of her shoulders. "He's telling you every which way he can! He's furious!"

And she would rush to calm him. Calm him? The goldfinch would fly off and flit about the house. He was really annoyed, and with good reason: he must not have felt respected at times like that.

And this was the best part: not only did the old man swallow all his wife's rebukes without replying that maybe the goldfinch was chirping so mournfully because the cage door was closed, but, hearing her talk that way as she ran around after the goldfinch, he would start to cry. As the tears fell he would shake his head and say to himself: "Poor thing, he's right . . . poor thing . . . he doesn't feel respected!"

Of course he—the grandfather, that is—knew perfectly well what it meant not to feel respected. No one respected him, or his wife. They were ridiculed, both of them, because that goldfinch was all they lived for now. Poor old souls, condemned to keeping their windows always shut, and the old man, precisely because he was old and stayed inside and wept like a baby, condemned never to show his face outside again. But oh! He'd never been one to get his nose out of joint, and if someone somehow dared make fun of him, he was prepared to risk his life, as if it were nothing. (But what value could life have for him now?) Yes sir, for that goldfinch there, if anyone dared breathe a word to him. Three times, when he was young, he'd been within a hair's breadth of . . . right there, life or liberty! It didn't take much for him to see red!

These violent thoughts would make his blood boil every time, and he would get up, goldfinch often on his shoulder, go to the window, and glare at the windows of the house across the way.

The old man had no reason to doubt that those things across the way were houses, that those things were windows, with glass panes, balconies, flowerpots, and all the rest; or that those things above were roofs, with chimneys, tiles, and gutters, just as he knew who owned them and who lived in them and how. The problem was that it never once crossed his mind to ask what his house and those other houses across the way were to the goldfinch perched on his shoulder. Or to that magnificent white tabby cat all curled up on the windowsill across the way, eyes closed, basking in the sun. Glass? Roofs? Tiles? My house? Your house? My house or your house for that big white cat sleeping there in the sun? If he could get inside, they were all his! Houses? What are houses? Places where he could steal, or sleep more or less comfortably. Or pretend to sleep.

Did those two old people really believe that by always keeping the windows and doors shut, a cat, if he wanted to, couldn't find some other way to get in and eat that goldfinch?

And wasn't it also too much to expect that the cat knew that that goldfinch meant the whole world to those two old people because it had belonged to their dead granddaughter who had trained it to fly freely about the house? Or that the cat knew that the old man, who'd caught him spying intently through the closed windows as the goldfinch, carefree, flew around the room, had stormed over to the cat's owner to warn her that there'd be trouble, serious trouble, if he caught him there again? Where? when? how? owner . . . grandparents. . . . window . . . goldfinch?

And so one day he ate him—yes, the goldfinch, which to the cat was just like any other bird—after getting into the old couple's house—who knows how or when. The old woman—it was almost dusk—barely heard the cry, like a little squeak. The old man raced to the kitchen and caught a glimpse of something white darting by, and feathers scattered on the floor, delicate little breast feathers, which fluttered gently as he entered. How he hollered! His wife held him back, but in vain; he grabbed his gun and ran like a madman to his neighbor's house. No, not his neighbor but the cat, the cat the old man wanted to kill, right there in front of his owner; and seeing him sitting calmly on the sideboard in the dining room, he fired—one, two, three shots—shattering the dishes, at which point the neighbor's son, also armed, ran in and shot the old man.

A tragedy. Amid the shouting and weeping, the old man, dying, wounded to the heart, was carried home to his wife.

The neighbor's son fled to the countryside. The ruin of two households, confusion in the whole village all night long.

■ ■ ■

And the cat? The cat, a minute later, didn't even remember that he'd eaten the goldfinch, any goldfinch. And he certainly didn't realize that the old man had been shooting at him. One leap and the cat was gone. And now—there he is, all white on the black roof, sitting peacefully and looking up at the stars, which, from the dark depths of the moonless sky, do not—of this you can be absolutely sure—see at all the poor roofs of that little mountain village. But so brightly did they shine, you could almost have sworn that they saw nothing else that night.

A good year it was, even for olives. Robust trees, laden with fruit, which had all set earlier that spring, despite the fog that had weighed heavily on the blossoms.

Don Lollò Zirafa, who had a fair number of trees on Le Quote, his farm in Primosole, realizing in advance that the five old glazed earthenware jars he had in his cellar wouldn't be sufficient to hold all the oil from the new harvest, had ordered a sixth, larger one from Santo Stefano di Camastra, where they were made: a magnificent, big-bellied jar, as high as a man's chest, that would be a mother superior to the other five.

It goes without saying that he'd quarreled with the kiln owner about the jar. Was there anyone Don Lollò didn't pick a fight with? For every little thing, even for a small stone fallen from the walls of his property, even for a piece of straw, he'd shout for his mule to be saddled so he could dash off to the city and file a complaint. And so, with all those official stamps and lawyer's fees—a lawsuit here, a lawsuit there—and all those legal expenses to pay, he'd practically ruined himself.

People said that Don Lollò's lawyer, tired of seeing him appear two or three times a week, had, in order to get rid of him, given him a little book, similar to those used during mass: the law code. That way Don Lollò could rack his own brains searching for the legal foundations of all the lawsuits he wanted to start.

To poke fun at him, everyone with whom he quarreled used to shout: "Saddle the mule!" But now: "Consult your law book!"

And Don Lollò:

"I will, and I'll strike you down, you bastards, all of you!"

The new jar, which had cost him four *onze* in real money,[1] was placed in the fermentation shed until room could be found for it in the cellar. No one had ever seen a jar like it before. But it made a sorry sight there in that cave, which reeked of must and the raw, pungent smell that hangs in the air in dark, close places.

The olive harvest had begun two days earlier, and Don Lollò was in a rage; between the men who'd come to beat the olive trees and the mule-drivers whose mules were laden with manure to heap on the hillside for next season's bean planting, he didn't know which way to turn, whom to attend to first. He was swearing like a Turk and threatening to kill now this worker, now that, if one — even one — olive were missing, as if he'd already counted each and every one of them when still on the tree; or if every pile of manure were not exactly the same size. In a ratty white hat and shirtsleeves, his chest bare, his face all red and dripping with sweat, he ran here and there, roving with wolfish eyes and furiously rubbing his cheeks, which sprouted a new beard as soon as he'd been shaved.

Now, at the end of the third day, three of the tree beaters, entering the shed to put away the ladders and sticks, stopped in their

---

1. An *onza* is a gold coin minted in Sicily between 1732 and 1860.

tracks at the sight of that beautiful new jar, broken in two, as if someone, slicing its big belly with a clean cut, had lopped off the whole front part.

"Look, look!"

"Who could have done it?"

"Oh, mamma mia! What's Don Lollò going to say now? The new jar, what a shame!"

The first beater, more scared than the others, suggested they immediately close the door and leave as quietly as they could, leaning the ladders and sticks against the wall outside. But the second one said:

"Are you crazy? With Don Lollò? He's likely to think we broke it ourselves. Stay right where you are!"

He stepped outside, cupped his hands to his mouth, and cried:

"Don Lollò! Hey, Don Lollò!"

There he was, at the base of the slope with the manure haulers, gesticulating furiously, as usual, and every now and then pulling his ratty white hat so low over his eyes that it would get jammed on his neck and forehead. The final shimmers of twilight were already fading from the sky, and as the evening shadows brought sweet coolness and peace to the countryside, his gestures became even more furious.

"Don Lollò! Hey, Don Lollò!"

When he came up and saw the damage, he nearly went mad. He hurled himself at the three peasants. He grabbed one by the throat, pinned him against the wall, and started screaming:

"By the blood of the Madonna, you'll pay for this!"

When the other two, their weathered, bestial faces distraught, grabbed him in response, he turned his fury against himself, throwing his hat to the ground, pummeling his cheeks, stomping his feet, and braying as if mourning a dead relative:

"The new jar! Four *onze* worth of jar! Brand new!"

He demanded to know who broke it on him! It certainly didn't break by itself! Somebody must have broken it, for spite or envy! But when? And how? There was no sign of any violence! What if it had come that way from the kiln? But how could that be? It had rung like a bell!

As soon as the peasants saw that his initial rage had subsided, they began urging him to calm down. The jar could be repaired. It wasn't such a bad break. Only one piece. A skilled clay mender could fix it, good as new. Zi' Dima Licasi[2] was just the man. He'd discovered some sort of miracle putty, a closely guarded secret: a glue so strong not even a hammer could break it once it had set. So if Don Lollò wanted, Zi' Dima Licasi would be here tomorrow, at the crack of dawn, and in less than no time the jar would be fixed, better than before.

Don Lollò kept rejecting their advice: it was pointless, nothing to be done. But in the end he let himself be persuaded, and the next day, right at dawn, Zi' Dima Licasi arrived at Primosole, his basket of tools over his shoulder.

He was a crooked old man, with crippled, gnarled joints, like the stump of an aged Saracen olive tree. It was like pulling teeth to get him to say a word. Surliness was rooted in his very frame, misshapen as it was; as was his misgiving that no one could truly under-

2. *Zi'* means "Uncle" and is used as a term of respect.

stand or appreciate his worth as an inventor, amateur that he was. He wanted the facts to speak for themselves, Zi' Dima Licasi did. He had to keep his eyes peeled to make sure no one stole his secret.

"Let's see this putty of yours" was the first thing Don Lollò said after looking him up and down for a long time.

Zi' Dima, dignified, shook his head no.

"You'll see it in action."

"But will it do the job?"

Zi' Dima put his basket on the ground and took out a ball of tattered red cloth—a big, cotton handkerchief—which he proceeded to unfold slowly, everyone curiously looking on. When he finally produced a pair of glasses, the broken bridge and temples held together with string, they all laughed. Zi' Dima didn't care; he sighed and cleaned his fingers before picking up his glasses and putting them on. Then, with great solemnity, he set to examining the jar, now out in the farmyard.

"It'll do the job," he said.

"I don't trust just your putty, though," Don Lollò stipulated. "I want wire stitches too."

"I'm going then," Zi' Dima replied categorically, straightening up and throwing his basket of tools over his shoulder.

Don Lollò caught him by the arm.

"Going where? So this is how you behave with a gentleman? Would you look at him, acting like Charlemagne! You miserable pauper, you donkey's ass, I have to put oil in that jar, and oil leaks! Mend a mile-long break with nothing but putty? I want stitches. Putty and wire. I'm in charge here."

Zi' Dima closed his eyes, pursed his lips, and shook his head.

They're all the same! Denying him the pleasure of doing an honest job, a precision repair, and of demonstrating the quality of his putty.

"If the jar doesn't ring like a bell again . . ."

"I won't hear it!" Don Lollò interrupted. "Stitches! I'm paying you for putty and stitches. How much do I owe you?"

"For just the putty . . ."

"Sheez, you're stubborn!" Don Lollò exclaimed. "What did I say? I told you I want stitches. Fine, we'll settle accounts when the job's done, I don't have time to waste arguing with you."

And off he went to look after his men.

Brimming with rage and spite, Zi' Dima set to work. His rage and spite increased with every hole he drilled to thread the wire. His grunts, which accompanied the whirring of the drill, grew louder and more frequent, his face turned white with rage, his eyes narrowed with vexation. This first step finished, he hurled the drill into his basket and held the broken piece in place, to make sure the holes on both pieces lined up properly and were evenly spaced. Then, with a pair of pincers he cut enough lengths of wire for all the stitches, and called for one of the beaters to help him.

"Cheer up, Zi' Dima!" the peasant said, seeing how overwrought he looked.

Zi' Dima gestured angrily with his hand. He opened the tin can with the putty and, shaking it, lifted it heavenward, as if in offering to God, since men refused to acknowledge its qualities: then, with his finger, he began to spread it all along the broken edges. He picked up his pincers and the lengths of wire and climbed into the jar's open belly, ordering the peasant to set the broken piece in place, as he had just done. Before he began stitching, he spoke from inside the jar. "Pull, pull as hard as you can! See how it won't come off? Curses on those who don't believe it! Now bang on it, go ahead, bang on it! Does it ring, yes or no, even with me inside? Go on, go tell your boss!"

"Whoever's on top is in charge, Zi' Dima," the peasant sighed, "and who's on the bottom be damned! Come on, put the stitches in."

Zi' Dima set to stitching up the jar, threading each length of wire through two adjacent holes, one on each side of the joint, and then twisting the ends with his pincers. It took an hour to do the whole thing. He was sweating like a fountain inside the jar. As he worked, he grumbled about his ill luck. And the peasant, outside the jar, consoled him.

"Okay, now help me get out," Zi' Dima finally said.

But wide as it was in the belly, the jar was narrow in the neck. In his rage Zi' Dima hadn't noticed. Now, try as he might, he couldn't fit through the opening. And the peasant, instead of helping him, doubled up with laughter.

Zi' Dima was imprisoned in there, trapped inside the jar he himself had fixed, and that now, in order to get him out—it was the only way—would have to be broken again, this time for good.

Amid shouts and laughter, Don Lollò arrived. Zi' Dima was like a ferocious cat inside the jar.

"Get me out of here!" he was screaming. "Goddammit, I want out! Now! Help me!"

Don Lollò was stunned. He simply couldn't believe it.

"What? Inside? He sealed himself inside?"

He went up to the jar and yelled to old Zi' Dima:

"Help? What kind of help can I give you? You dumb old fool,

what have you done? Didn't you measure it first? Come on, try and get out: one arm first . . . like that! Then your head . . . come on . . . no, easy! Oh! Go back . . . wait! Not like that! Lower, lower . . . How in the world . . . ? And now, what about my jar? Calm down! Calm down!" he advised everyone, as if they were the ones about to lose their calm, not him. "My head is spinning! Keep calm! This is a new case. . . . My mule!"

He tapped the jar with his knuckles. It really did ring like a bell.

"Nice! Like new . . . You just wait!" he said to Zi' Dima, imprisoned inside.

"Go saddle my mule!" he ordered the peasant, and, scratching his forehead, mumbled to himself, "Well, just look what has happened to me! This isn't a jar, it's a tool of the devil! Stop, stop that right now!"

And he ran over to steady the jar, in which Zi' Dima was thrashing about like a caged animal.

"A new case, my friend, I need my lawyer to resolve it! I don't feel up to handling it myself. My mule! My mule! I'll go and come straight back, just be patient! It's in your best interest . . . and meanwhile, keep calm in there, easy! I have to look after my own interests. First and foremost, I'll do what it takes to defend my rights. But here, I'll pay you, for a whole day's work. Five *lire*, is that enough?"

"I don't want your money!" Zi' Dima yelled. "I want out!"

"You'll get out. But in the meantime, I'm going to pay you. Here, five *lire*."

He pulled the money out of his waistcoat and tossed it in the jar. Then, in a thoughtful voice:

"Have you had your breakfast? Bread and drippings, right

away! You don't want it? Throw it to the dogs then! All I care is that I gave you some food."

He ordered Zi' Dima to be fed, then mounted his mule and galloped off to the city. From his peculiar, ceaseless gesticulating, all who saw him thought he was on his way to join the madhouse.

Fortunately he didn't have to wait long to see his lawyer, but he did have to wait a good while for the man to stop laughing once Don Lollò explained the situation. All that laughter annoyed him.

"Excuse me, but what's so funny? You're not the one who's been swindled! That jar is mine!"

But his lawyer kept on laughing and wanted Don Lollò to tell him the story again, how it had all happened, so he could laugh all over again. "Inside, hey? He sealed himself inside?" And what was it that Don Lollò was proposing? "To ke . . . to keep him inside there . . . ha, ha, ha . . . ho, ho, ho . . . to keep him inside so as not to ruin his jar?"

"What, I'm supposed to ruin it?" Don Lollò asked, with clenched fists. "Adding insult to injury?"

"Do you realize what this is called?" the lawyer finally said to him. "It's called kidnapping!"

"Kidnapping? Who kidnapped him?" Don Lollò exclaimed. "He kidnapped himself! Why am I to blame?"

So the lawyer explained that there were two legal matters here. On the one hand, he, Don Lollò, must immediately free the prisoner so as not to be accused of kidnapping; on the other, the clay mender had to account for the damage he'd caused as a result of his carelessness or stupidity.

"Ah!" Don Lollò sighed with relief. "By paying me for the jar!"

"Not so fast!" the lawyer observed. "Not as if it were new, mind you!"

"Why not?"

"Because it was broken, obviously!"

"Broken? No, sir. It's fixed now, like new. Better than new, he even says so himself! And if I broke it again now, it could never be made whole again. The jar would be a loss!"

The lawyer assured him that this would be taken into consideration by making Zi' Dima pay what the jar was worth in its present state.

"In fact," he advised, "have him estimate the price himself."

"I kiss your hands," Don Lollò said as he rushed out.

When he got back, around evening, he found all the peasants making merry around the inhabited jar. Even the watchdog had joined in the festivities, jumping and barking. Zi' Dima had not only calmed down but even come to enjoy his bizarre adventure, laughing about it with the awkward gaiety of sad folk.

Don Lollò shoved everyone aside and peered into the jar.

"So! Comfy in there?"

"Very comfy! It's nice and cool in here, better than in my own home."

"Wonderful. Meanwhile, let me warn you that this jar cost me four *onze*, new. How much do you think it's worth now?"

"With me inside?" Zi' Dima asked.

The workers all laughed.

"Silence!" Don Lollò shouted. "It's one or the other: either your putty works, or it doesn't. If it doesn't, you're a cheat; if it does, then the jar is worth something. How much, though? You tell me."

Zi' Dima thought for a moment, then said:

"Here's what I say. If you'd let me repair it with just my putty, like I'd wanted to, I wouldn't have ended up inside here in the first place, and the jar would have been worth more or less the same as before. But now, with these ridiculous stitches, which I could only do from inside, how much could it possibly be worth? A third of the original price, more or less."

"A third?" Don Lollò asked. "One *onza* and thirty-three?"

"Even less, maybe, but not more."

"Well then," said Don Lollò. "I'll take your word for it. Give me one *onza* and thirty-three."

"What?" Zi' Dima asked, as if not understanding.

"I have to break the jar to let you out," Don Lollò replied. "And my lawyer says you have to pay me what you estimated it to be worth: one *onza* and thirty-three."

"Me, pay?" Zi' Dima laughed scornfully. "You must be joking! I'm going to rot in here."

And, with a bit of effort, he took his crusty little pipe from his pocket, lit it, and started puffing on it, blowing the smoke out the neck of the jar.

Don Lollò was piqued. Neither he nor his lawyer had anticipated this new situation, that Zi' Dima would not want to get out of the jar. Now what? He was on the verge of ordering "My mule!" again, but realized it was evening already.

"Oh, really? So you want to live inside my jar? You're all my witnesses! He doesn't want to come out, so as not to pay for the jar, but I'm ready to break it! Well, since he wants to stay in there, I'm going to sue him tomorrow for squatting, and for preventing me from using the jar."

Zi' Dima sent up another puff of smoke and then replied calmly:

"No, sir. I have no intention of preventing you from anything. Do you think I'm here for my own entertainment? Let me out, and I'll gladly evacuate. But pay . . . you've got to be joking, sir!"

Don Lollò, in a fit of rage, raised his leg and was about to kick the jar, but then thought better of it. Instead he grabbed it with two hands and, trembling all over, shook it hard.

"See how good my putty is?" Zi' Dima said.

"You crook, you!" Don Lollò roared. "Who created this mess, you or me? And now I'm supposed to pay? You can starve to death in there! We'll see who wins!"

And he stormed off, forgetting about the five *lire* he'd tossed in the jar that morning. For starters, Zi' Dima decided to use the money to celebrate with the peasants, who, having stayed on because of this strange story, were going to spend the night there, sleeping out in the open in the farmyard. One of them went to buy some things from a nearby tavern. The moon, as if on purpose, was so bright that evening it seemed like daytime.

At a certain point Don Lollò was awakened by a hellish din. He looked out his balcony onto the farmyard and saw a host of devils dancing in the moonlight: the drunken peasants who, hand in hand, were prancing around the jar, and Zi' Dima, inside, singing at the top of his lungs.

Don Lollò couldn't take it anymore. He rushed out like a mad bull and, before anyone could stop him, sent the jar rolling down the hillside with a shove. Accompanied by the peasants' drunken laughter, the jar rolled right into an olive tree and shattered.

■ ■ ■

Zi' Dima won.

DONNA MIMMA

I. Donna Mimma Leaves

When Donna Mimma, sky-blue silk scarf knotted loosely under her chin, walks down the sunny streets of her tiny village, it's easy to believe that her trim little figure, still unbowed and full of life though cloaked modestly in a long black shawl with a fringe, casts no shadow, not on the cobblestones of this little lane here, nor on the broad paving stones of the big piazza over there.

It's easy to believe because, for all the children—for all the grownups too, who, seeing her go by, suddenly feel like children again—Donna Mimma has an air about her that suddenly makes everything seem unreal: the sky paper, the sun a crimson sphere, like the star in the nativity scene. No sooner does she go by than the whole village, with its beautiful golden sun and beautiful blue sky, so new above those little old houses and those little churches with their squat little bell towers, and the little lanes and the big piazza with a fountain in the middle and the mother church at the far end, becomes like one big toy, the kind the Befana[1] brings. Each little toy piece—and there are lots of them, to be taken out, one by one, from the big oval box that smells deliciously of glue—is a house,

---

1. In Italian folklore, an old woman who brings gifts to children on the eve of the Epiphany.

with windows and a balcony, to be placed in a row or a circle, to make a street or the piazza; and this bigger piece here, with a cross and bells, is the church, and this one's the fountain, and around it go these little trees, with crowns of bright green wood shavings and little round bases so they won't fall over.

A miracle of Donna Mimma's doing? No. This is the world where Donna Mimma lives in the eyes of the little ones—the grownups too, who suddenly become little again as soon as they see her go by. Yes, little, because no one can feel grown up in Donna Mimma's presence. No one.

This is the world she conjures when she tells the children how she went to *buy* them, each one of them, far, far away.

"Where?"

Where? Oh, far, far away.

"Palermo?"

Yes, Palermo, with a pretty white litter made of ivory pulled by two handsome white horses without any harness bells, down street after long street, at night, in the dark.

"Why without any harness bells?"

"To not make any noise."

"And in the dark?"

Yes, but there's the moon at night, and the stars. But in the dark too, for sure! When you walk such a long way, for days and days, darkness falls as well. And on the way back, you always arrive at night, and ever so silently, so no one sees, no one hears.

"Why?"

Well, because a newly bought baby mustn't hear any noise. It would frighten him. He shouldn't even see the light of day at first.

"*Bought?* What do you mean, bought?"

With papà's money! Lots and lots of it.

"Flavietta?"

"Of course, Flavietta, more than two hundred *onze*. No, more, with these golden ringlets and this tiny strawberry of a mouth. Because papà wanted her to be blond and curly-headed, just like this, and to have big eyes that look lovingly at me, don't you believe me, my precious? Her eyes alone are worth that much, two hundred *onze!* You think I don't know, when I'm the one who bought her? Yes, Ninì too, of course. All of you, I bought all of you. Ninì was a bit more, because he's a boy. Baby boys always cost a bit more, my love; well, they work, boys do, so they earn a lot, just like papà. Did you know I bought papà too? Yes, I did. When he was just a little baby, of course! Still just a tiny thing! I brought him myself, on the white litter, in the night, brought him to his mother, dear soul. From Palermo, yes. How much for him? Oh, thousands, thousands!"

The children gaze in wonderment at Donna Mimma, at that pretty sky-blue silk scarf of hers, always new-looking, and at her hair, still shiny black, parted over her temples and twisted into two little braids that cover her ears, weighed down by massive teardrop earrings. They gaze at her oval-shaped eyes, at her delicate eyelids and her long lashes, at her finely veined button nose and her wide purplish nostrils, and at her slightly pointed chin, which sprouts a few curly metallic hairs. But she is shrouded in mystery, she is, this proper, little old woman, whom all the other women, even their own mothers, call Godmother,[2] and who, whenever she comes to

---

2. *Comare* means both godmother and midwife.

call, mamma's not feeling well, and then a few days later, another brother or sister appears, and Donna Mimma was the one to go buy the baby, with her litter, far, far away in Palermo. They gaze at her, their curious little fingers timidly touching her shawl, her dress, and well, yes, she really is a proper, little old woman, no different, it seems, from any other. But how can she go so far away then, with that litter, and how is it that she is the one who buys and delivers babies, just as the Befana delivers toys?

And so these little ones . . . —What? No, they don't know what to think, but somehow they sense in themselves a bit of the mystery that is in this old woman, who is right here now, whom they can touch, even, but who then goes so far away to get them, the babies, which means that they too . . . of course . . . in Palermo, but where? In a place she knows and they, being little, don't, though of course they must have been there too, when they were very tiny, if she went to Palermo to buy them . . .

Instinctively their eyes search for her hands. Where are Donna Mimma's hands? There, under her shawl. Why doesn't she ever show them? But of course! she never touches them with her hands. She kisses them, talks to them, gestures with her eyes, her mouth, her cheeks, but she never takes out her hands to caress them. It's strange. One of the more daring boys asks:

"Don't you have hands?"

"Good Lord!" Donna Mimma exclaims with a knowing glance at his mother, as if to say, "For goodness' sake, who is this devil of a boy?"

"Here they are!" she says, suddenly revealing two tiny hands in knitted half gloves. "What do you mean, I don't have hands? You little devil, you! Good Lord, what a question!"

Tucking her hands under her shawl again, she laughs and laughs, and pulls it right up over her nose, to hide her little laughs, which, God help us . . . "Good Lord!" she says, crossing herself. Can you believe the things that pop into a child's head!

Those hands seem made for molding the wax that the Baby Jesuses are made of, the ones placed on every church altar on Christmas eve, in a little basket lined with sky-blue satin. Donna Mimma understands the sacredness of her office. She senses how much piety there is in the act of birth, and so, in front of the children, she covers it with all the veils of modesty. And even when talking with the grownups, she never utters a word that might lift or lighten those veils; she speaks about it with lowered eyes, and as little as possible. She knows her role isn't always a joyous one, that often it's terribly sad, this welcoming into the world so many tiny beings who start to cry as soon as they take their first breath. It can be festive — even for the baby — to bring a newborn into the home of gentlefolk, though it's not always the case even there! But to bring them — so many of them! — into the homes of poor folk . . . it makes her heart weep. Yet for thirty-five years or so now, Donna Mimma has been the only one in the village to perform this role. Or, to be more precise, she was, till yesterday.

Now a little coquette from the Continent has arrived, twenty years old, *Piedmontese*. A short yellow skirt, a little green jacket, hands in her pockets like a man. The still-unmarried sister of a customs official. *Diploma from the Royal University of Turin*. Enough to make you cross yourself with both hands, good Lord, a girl with no experience of the world who nevertheless embarks on a profession like this! And such brazenness, you should see her! It's a miracle she hasn't written her profession on her forehead! A girl! A girl to whom such things . . . God, what a disgrace! Where does she think she is?

Donna Mimma can't reconcile herself to the Piedmontese. She looks the other way, and covers her eyes with her hand as soon as she sees her set foot in the piazza, hips swaying, head held high, hands in her pockets, the white feather on her velvet hat standing straight in the wind. And what a racket those insolent little heels of hers make on the paving stones: "Here I come! Here I come!"

She's no woman, that one, she's a devil! She can't be one of God's creatures!

"What? A sign?"

She hung a sign with her name and profession on her front door? And her name is . . . ? Elvira . . . what? Miss Elvira Mosti? Does it really say Miss? And what does *diploma* mean? Oh, the license. Licensed disgrace. Good God, can you believe such a thing? Who's going to call on that cheeky girl? And besides, what experience, what experience can she possibly have, if she is still. . . . In the name of the Father, the Son, and the Holy Ghost. The things you see these days, and in our village? Tsk tsk . . .

And Donna Mimma flaps her tiny hands in their knitted half gloves, as if seeing the flames of Hell licking around her.

"No, ma'am, thank you, coffee, no! Water, just a sip of water, I'm all discombobulated!" she says to her clients, whom she visits every now and then, or, as she says, pops in to find out if . . . no? nothing? It's in God's hands, ma'am, thanks be to Him, in heaven and on earth!

Donna Mimma is fixated on Elvira Mosti. Not that she's worried for herself, that the women might do her a wrong turn because of the Piedmontese. As if she could worry about such a thing, knowing what sort of women they are, with the fear of God in them, brought up proper right here in the village, and with respect for sacred things! Impossible . . .

But, oh Blessed Virgin, it's the thing itself . . . the scandal of it . . . what a dreadful girl . . . they say she talks like a carabiniere . . . that she pronounces all the dirty words, as if it were natural . . .

She's so overwhelmed by the obscenity of it that she doesn't notice the anguished embarrassment with which the women look at her. It's as if they have something to tell her, but can't find the courage.

The medical officer turned the other way today when he saw her go by. Maybe he didn't see her? But of course he saw her! He saw her and he turned the other way. Why?

A little later she discovers that that shameless girl went to see him at his house, together with her brother. To put in a good word for herself, of course. Who knows how she sweet-talked him, the way they know how to do, those awful foreign women who, in the big cities on the Continent, have lost the blush of modesty. And now this doting doctor . . . Diploma? What does a diploma have to do with it? Oh right, of course, because of her diploma! Really now, who doesn't know how these things go? A coy little smile, a little caress, and wicked men, like straw catching fire . . . these days even the old ones, no fear of God! What does a diploma have to do with anything? You need experience, that's what you need.

"Well, that and a diploma, Donna Mimma," sighs the pharmacist, with whom she has stopped to grumble.

"Do I have a diploma?" Donna Mimma exclaims with a smile, joining the fingertips of her tiny hands in their knitted half gloves. "Yet for the past thirty-five years, thirty-five, all of you are here because I'm the one who brought you, even you, Don Sarino, by the grace of God, my little ones! How many trips to Palermo I've made! Here, here, look here!"

Donna Mimma bends down and, in those two tiny hands that don't look strong but are, picks up a plump little boy who has stopped in front of the pharmacy, holding him up to the sun.

"This one too! And everyone else you see, all of them! I was the one who went to Palermo to buy you all, without a diploma! Who needs a diploma?"

The young pharmacist smiles.

"Okay, Donna Mimma, yes . . . you. . . . Experience, of course. . . . But . . ."

He looks at her, anguished and embarrassed, but not even he has the courage to help her see the threat that hangs over her.

Until a letter arrives from the Prefect's office in the capital, covered in seals and stamps, half printed and half handwritten, which, even though she can't really read it, she guesses is about the diploma she doesn't have, and that, according to statute such and such, paragraph. . . . She's still trying to decipher it when an officer appears to summon her in the mayor's name.

"His wife? Already?" Donna Mimma asks anxiously.

"No, the town hall," the officer responds. "There's a message for you."

"For me? Because of this letter?"

The officer shrugs his shoulders. "I don't know, come and you'll find out."

So Donna Mimma goes to the town hall, where she finds the mayor, all embarrassed. Donna Mimma went to Palermo to buy him too, and she went back to Palermo to buy him two sons, and would soon set out with her litter for a third. But . . .

"Look at this, Donna Mimma! See? Another letter from the Prefect's office, this one to us. Yes, about you. There's nothing to be done, I'm afraid. It prohibits you from practicing your profession."

"Me?"

"You. You don't have a diploma, dear Donna Mimma. It's the law."

"What law?" Donna Mimma exclaims, every drop of blood drained from her. "Some new law?"

"No, not new, no! But we . . . you were the only one here, for so many years, we knew you, we liked you, we had complete faith in you, and so we let it go. But we're in violation as well, Donna Mimma! These damn blasted formalities, see? As long as you were the only one . . . But now that other one has arrived. She found out you don't have a diploma, and since no one has been calling on her, see? She filed a complaint with the Prefect, and now you can't practice anymore. Or you have to go to Palermo, for real this time! To the university, to get a diploma too, like her."

"Me? To Palermo? At my age? At fifty-six? After thirty-five

years? They insult me like this? Me, a diploma? An entire village . . . But now I need a diploma to keep practicing? And to read and write? I barely know how to read! And to Palermo, me, who has never set foot outside this village? I'd get lost there! At my age? And all for that coquette there? I'd like to see her, with that diploma of hers . . . she wants to compete with me? And what can those professors teach me, when I can dress them up and down, the best of them, after thirty-five years of practice? I really have to go to Palermo? What? For two years?"

There's no end to it: a flood of angry, desperate tears, an on-slaught of halting, faltering questions. The mayor feels sorry for her, tries to comfort her. He lets her vent for a bit, then tries again. "Two years will pass quickly. Yes, of course it's hard. Teach you?! No! *Pro forma*, it's all just to get that piece of paper! So as not to let that dreadful girl win . . ." Then, like a good son, he accompanies her to the door and pats her on the back. Trying to cheer her up, to make her smile, he says, "Come now, how could you possibly get lost in Palermo, when not a day goes by without your making three or four trips there?"

Donna Mimma pulls her black shawl up over her sky-blue scarf and tightens it over her face, to hide her tears. That sky-blue silk scarf, children! The holy poetry of your birth is in mourning: Donna Mimma is going to Palermo, without her white litter, to study ob-structrics, and sepsis and antisepsis, extreme cephalic presentation, extreme breech birth . . . As decreed by law. Donna Mimma weeps, inconsolable. She barely knows how to read, she'll lose her way in the thorny science of those learned professors in Palermo, where she has gone so many times with the poetry of her white litter.

"Oh my good lady, my good lady . . ."

A heartbreaking lament, one that each of her clients, to whom she goes to give notice before her departure, hears. And in every home she kneels, and with tiny, trembling hands—she doesn't keep them hidden now—she caresses the children's little heads; inconsolable, she plants tears, together with kisses, on those blond and brunette curls.

"I'm going to Palermo . . . I'm going to Palermo."

The children look at her in bewilderment, they can't understand why she's crying so much about going to Palermo this time. They wonder if maybe this means something bad for them as well, for all the children still there, waiting to be bought.

And the mothers say, "But we'll wait for you!"

Donna Mimma looks at them, her eyes brimming with tears. She shakes her head. How can she accept such a tender untruth, she who knows all too well how life is?

"For two years, my good lady?"

Brokenhearted, she takes her leave, pulling her black shawl up over her sky-blue scarf.

II. Donna Mimma Studies

Palermo. It's evening when Donna Mimma arrives: that tiny woman in the immense piazza outside the train station.

Oh Jesus, moons? Is that what they are? Twenty, thirty of them. Is this a piazza? It's so big! Which way do I go?

"This way, this way!"

Dwarfed by all those buildings, giant nightmarish shadows

pierced with lights, blinded by the glare below and the illuminated streaks above, running down straight, endless streets; jostled by the hostile crowd, deafened by the hubbub crashing over her and the cars racing past her, dazed and utterly bewildered, Donna Mimma plunges into that infernal chaos in order to dislodge the dizzying disquiet inside her—the shock and stupor of the train ride, the first in her entire life.

Oh God, the train! Mountains, plains that move, turn, rush past, trees flying by, houses and distant villages flung about; and now and then the violent impact of a telegraph pole; whistles, jolts, the terror of bridges and tunnels, one after the other; dazzle and darkness, wind and suffocation in that clamorous tempest, in the dark . . . Jesus, Jesus!

"What did you say?"

She can't hear a thing, she doesn't know how to put one foot in front of the other anymore, so she clings to her nephew who has accompanied her—a young man, the standard-bearer of the family—master of the world he is, he can laugh and walk confidently, he knows his way around, he's been here before, two years of military service in Palermo.

"What did you say?"

Yes, of course, the carriage . . . what carriage? Oh, right, the carriage! How else is she going to get to the city, how is she going to walk all the way to the inn with that huge bundle of clothing under her arm?

Donna Mimma looks at the bundle: her whole life is in there, and she'd like to be in there too, bundled among her things under her nephew's arm, made of nothing but rags and the smell of laundry, so she wouldn't have to see, wouldn't have to hear anything more.

"Give it to me! Give it to me!"

She wants to hold the bundle close, so she can feel herself inside it. But her soul is outside, overcome by all these sensations that assault her from every side. Yes, she says, yes, but she doesn't really understand what her nephew is gesturing about.

Oh, sweet Jesus, why is he asking her? She'll do whatever he wants, she's like a poor little baby in his hands: the carriage, yes, the inn, yes, whatever he wants! Right now it's as if she's at sea in a storm, and taking a carriage is like grabbing onto a boat, getting to the inn like touching shore. She imagines, with terror, how, in three days' time, her nephew, after arranging her room and board, will return to their village, and how she will have to stay here, in the midst of all this bedlam, lost and alone.

■ ■ ■

They're in the carriage on their way to the inn when her nephew proposes they go see the fair in Piazza Marina.

"The fair? What fair?"

"The Fair of the Dead."

Donna Mimma crosses herself. Of course, tomorrow is the Day of the Dead, All Souls' Day! Donna Mimma has arrived in Palermo on November 1st, the eve of the Day of the Dead, she who had always come to Palermo to buy life! The dead, of course . . . But for children in Sicily, All Souls' Day is like Epiphany: the old Befana doesn't bring them toys on January 6; the dead bring them on November 2, so the grownups weep while the little ones rejoice.

"All these people?"

Lots and lots of them, no end in sight, so the carriages can't get through. All the mammas and papas, grandmothers, and aunts go to the Fair of the Dead in Piazza Marina, to buy toys for their little ones. Dolls? Yes, little baby sisters. Sugar puppets? Yes, little baby brothers. The very same little ones that for so many years, in the minds of the children in her faraway village, Donna Mimma came to buy at the Fair of Life in Palermo and brought back on her ivory litter. Toys, but real ones, with real, lively eyes, and real, delicate little hands, purple and clenched with cold. And a slobbering little mouth that weeps.

But now, Donna Mimma stares at the boisterous spectacle of that festival, more amazed than a little girl. She can't see how the dream of her mysterious journeys, as she would describe them to the children in her village, is now coming true, right here at the fair. And not only because, standing here amid the ear-splitting cries of vendors whose stalls glow with multicolored lights, the hissing and whistling and ringing, the multitude of sounds and the press of the crowd that spills endlessly into the piazza, her bewilderment grows along with her fear of the big city; but also because now she is the enchanted child. And because that air, which enveloped her in her little village, that fairytale air that followed her along the streets and into the houses, and that inspired everyone, big and small, to respect her because she was the one who brought the new babies from the mystery of birth into their homes, who brought new life to the old village, is gone. Cruelly stripped of her role, who is she now, here in the midst of the throng at the fair? A pathetic old woman, dazed and confused. They drove her from her dreamland, leaving her to shatter and disappear here, in the midst of this violent reality, and she no longer understands anything, doesn't know how to walk anymore, or talk, or look.

"Let's go . . . Let's go . . ."

Where? Away from here, out of this throng, it's easy to get out, with a bit of patience, slowly, slowly . . . But then? Finding her way inside herself again, as calm and confident as before, that will be hard: tonight the inn, tomorrow school.

■ ■ ■

At school, forty-two devils, all with the brazen air of young men in skirts, more or less like that awful girl who swooped down on her village from the mainland, practically wet their pants the first day she shows up, with her sky-blue silk scarf and her long black shawl with its fringe and lace pulled modestly round her. Oh, it's grandma! The old midwife from the fairytales, dropped out of the sky, who doesn't dare show her hands and keeps her eyes lowered out of decency and still talks about *buying* babies! They all stare at her, touch her, as if she weren't real, even though she's standing right in front of them.

"Donna Mimma? Donna Mimma what? Jèvola? Donna Mimma Jèvola? How old are you? Fifty-six? Aren't you a little young to be starting your studies! Already a midwife for thirty-five years? How? Illegally? How could they have allowed that? Experience? Oh, really! There's experience and then there's experience. Experience isn't everything, you'll see!"

And when Professor Torresi, whose task it is to teach general notions of theoretical obstetrics, enters the classroom, they introduce her, pulling her to the front with much laughter and noise.

"The grandma midwife, professor! The grandma midwife!"

Professor Torresi, bald and paunchy, but tall and handsome, like a cuirassier who has just dismounted his horse, a curly gray mustache and a large, hairy mole on one cheek (what a love! He pulls on it all the time during class, so as not to dishevel his mustache, which he carefully twirls upward), Professor Torresi, who has always been proud of his ability to instill discipline, treats those forty-two devils like fillies to be broken with spurs and riding whip. Nevertheless, he can't help but smile every now and then at some escapade of theirs, or better yet, chuckle slightly—reward for the adoration he feels. He'd like to cast a threatening look on their commotion, but when he sees that strange-looking old recruit before him, he wants to join in the fun.

He asks her how, having joined his class so late, she will ever figure things out. He has already—(*listen up! take your seats!*)—he has already spoken at length—(*silence, for heaven's sake! take your seats!*)—has already spoken at length about the phenomenon of gestation, from conception to birth; he has already spoken at length about the law of organic correlation; in the last lesson he covered occipital forehead and biacromial diameters, and today he is going to talk about transiliac diameters. What will she possibly be able to understand of such matters? Experience, fine. But what is experience? Listen up, listen up! (and Professor Torresi tugs the hairy mole on his cheek, what a love!): implicit knowledge, that's what experience is. And is that sufficient? No, and it never can be. Knowledge, in order to be sufficient, needs to go from implicit to explicit, that is, it must come out, come out, so that one may see clearly, gradually, and in every part distinguish, define, practically touch with one's hand, but with a seeing hand! Otherwise, knowledge can never become wisdom. Merely a question of names? Of terminology? No, the name is the thing. The name is the concept inside us of every thing outside us. Without a name there is no concept, and the thing remains inside us—blind, undefined, indistinct.

After this explanation, which leaves the entire class dumbfounded, Professor Torresi turns to Donna Mimma and starts quizzing her.

Donna Mimma looks at him aghast. It's as if he's speaking Greek. Forced to respond, she provokes such explosive laughter in those forty-two devils that Professor Torresi fears his reputation for discipline is at risk. He yells, bangs on his desk, calls them to order again.

Donna Mimma weeps.

When silence returns to the classroom, the professor, indignant, gives them a scolding—as if he hadn't laughed as well. Then he turns to Donna Mimma and scolds her too: it is a disgrace to present herself at school in such a state of ignorance, it is a disgrace to act like a little girl now, crying like that, at her age. Come on, there's no point in crying!

Donna Mimma agrees, nods her head yes, dries her tears. She wants to leave. The professor makes her stay.

"Sit down! And listen!"

Listen? She doesn't understand a thing. She thought she knew everything, after thirty-five years of practice, and instead realizes that she doesn't know a thing, not one single thing.

"Little by little, don't despair!" the professor comforts her when class is over.

"Don't despair, little by little," her classmates repeat, moved now by her tears.

■ ■ ■

But as that famous implicit knowledge Professor Torresi had spoken about starts making itself explicit, Donna Mimma—can she see more clearly now? anything but! Donna Mimma can't see anything anymore.

The idea of the thing, whole and compact, that before she had inside her, is now all mixed up, broken, crushed, lost in too many tiny details, each of which has a strange, difficult name that she can't even pronounce. How can she keep all those words in her head? But she tries: in the evening, she lights her oil lamp and hunches over her tiny table in her miserable little rented room, patiently sounding out the syllables in her textbook.

"Bi-bia-cro-bia-crom-i-al-biacromi-bia-cromial."

And so, at school, little by little, to her great surprise, she begins to recognize all those details, one by one and after countless attempts. Her exclamations are comic:

"But this . . . Good Lord, is that what it's called?"

Yet the reason for recognizing it, and for calling it that, with that particular name—that she simply can't see. The professor makes her, forces her to see. But then that detail breaks away even further from the whole and imposes itself on her, like some separate thing. And since there are so many details, Donna Mimma gets lost and can't find her way anymore.

It's a sorry sight when, during the practical obstetrics class in the maternity ward, the professor calls on her to demonstrate. This is what her classmates have all been waiting for, because this is the moment when she can show off her long years of experience. Of course! But the professor doesn't want her to do what she knows how to do, he wants her to say what she doesn't know how to say. And when it's time to do instead of say, he doesn't let her do it her way, the way she's always done all those years, when everything always went fine. No, she has to do according to the rules and precepts of science, point by point, the way he taught them to her. So if Donna Mimma throws herself into doing, he yells because she isn't observing precisely those precepts and rules. And if instead she holds back and strives to consider every precept and rule, well, then he yells at her because she gets lost and confused and can't manage to do anything properly anymore, can't find her old swift and confident precision.

But it's not merely all those details, and all those precepts and rules, that hinder her now. Something else, something far graver, something in her soul, is holding her back. It's as if she is suffering some horrendous violence that has been done to her, in the very place where she has always jealously guarded the meaning of life. It's more than she can bear, this crude spectacle, this baring of the role that for so many years she held sacred — because for God, every mother's shame and pain are the price of original sin — so she suffers and she would like to cover the spectacle with veils of modesty as much as possible, even in class. But no. All veils are cast off here. The professor throws them aside, cruelly tears off those veils, which he calls hypocrisy and ignorance. And he mistreats and mocks her, intentionally using obscene language. And those forty-two devils laugh unbecomingly at their professor's jokes, at his dirty words;

they laugh, with no restraint, with no respect for the poor patient, for that poor, miserable mother, lying there exposed the whole time, the object of study and experimentation.

Dejected, filled with shame and anguish, at the end of the day Donna Mimma withdraws to her little room and weeps, and wonders if she ought to quit her studies and return to her little village. During her long years of practice, she has put aside a nice little nest egg, which would see her through old age. She could live out her years peacefully, resting and watching contentedly all the little babies in the village, and the bigger ones, the little boys and girls, and the even bigger ones, the young men and women, and their mothers and fathers, all, all of whom she—the old midwife of the fairy tales—for all those years, knew how to bring into the world, without any rules or precepts. But that would mean giving in to that dreadful girl who at this very moment has undoubtedly taken her place in the village, bullying her way into every family. Could Donna Mimma stay there and watch, twiddling her thumbs? "Oh no, no!" She has to stay here, has to overcome her dejection, smother her shame and anguish, return to her village with her fancy diploma, and shout in that brazen girl's face that now she too knows all those things the professors say, that the mysteries of God are one thing, the work of nature another.

But her expert little hands . . .

Donna Mimma gazes sorrowfully through her tears at her little hands.

Will they still know what to do now, will they move like before? It's as if they're bound by all these new scientific notions. They tremble, those little hands of hers, but they don't *see* anymore. The professor has given Donna Mimma a pair of scientific glasses, but he has taken from her, forever, her natural sight.

And what will Donna Mimma do with those glasses if she can't see anymore?

III. Donna Mimma Returns

"Flavietta? But of course, my little miss, her too. What do you think? Why, in Palermo of course, with the ivory litter and papà's money. How much? Well, more than a thousand *lire*."

"No, *onze!*"

"Oh right, I said *lire*, but I meant *onze*, little missy, more than a thousand. Such a dear, correcting me! Here, I want to make you a kiss, dear! Another one . . . dear!"

Who is it who's talking like this? Well, look at her! The Piedmontese! The girl who two years earlier seemed like a man in a skirt, with her green jacket and her hands in her pockets. Jacket and hat have been discarded, and now she wears her hair like a country girl, and on her head, oh! the sky-blue silk scarf, loosely knotted under her chin, and a beautiful long calico shawl, with lace and a fringe. The Piedmontese! And now she too talks about *buying* babies, in Palermo, with an ivory litter and money from whom? From *babbo?*[3] Of course she says "babbo," because she speaks proper Italian, she does, just imagine! And she doesn't give them kisses, this one, she

---

3. *Babbo* is the Tuscan term for Daddy. For the narrator, both Piedmont and Tuscany are considered foreign, and much more cultured than Sicily.

makes them,[4] and she's all the rage with her Italian, and dressed like that, like a country girl: so charming!

"Pull the shawl tighter around your waist!"

"Yes, yes, like that."

"And your scarf . . . no, pull it down more in the front."

"And head up, like this!"

"Looser . . . a little looser under your chin, less tight . . . like that, good!"

She lowers her eyes modestly now, as she walks. And what harm is there if every now and then she gives a little mischievous glance, or a little smile shows off those adorable dimples on her cheeks. How sweet!

The wealthier mothers, hearing themselves called "madam" (My respects, madam! At your service, madam!), are all happy (poor things, with those big bellies). Happy that now, with the Piedmontese, it's as if they too knew how to speak proper Italian, as if they too were familiar with all the refinements and "civilities" of the Continent. But of course, because on the mainland, you know, it's customary to do this, and this . . . And then—you think it's nothing?—there's the satisfaction of having everything explained, step by step, as if by a doctor, with precise scientific terms that can't possibly cause offense because nature may be ugly, but my God, that's the way the Lord made it. So it's better to know how things really are, so you can act accordingly, take care of yourself, and then, when your back's to the wall, at least you know what you're suffer-

---

4. "Make a kiss" is not Italian but comes from the French "faire la bise."

ing from and why. The will of God, yes, of course, that's what the Holy Scriptures say: "in pain you shall bring forth children"; but is it disrespectful of God to study the wisdom of his ways? Poor ignorant Donna Mimma was content with the will of God. But this one respects God too, and what's more, she explains everything, how God wanted and decided the cross of maternity to be.

And the children, hearing that same marvelous tale, of moonlit voyages to Palermo with the ivory litter and white horses, told to them in such a different voice and style, are mesmerized because it actually seems as if it were being read to them, or that they were reading it on their own, in some beautiful book of fairy tales, and that the fairy has come to life before their very eyes. Does this pretty fairy really make those moonlit voyages to Palermo, does she really bring their new little brothers and sisters from Palermo? They gaze at her adoringly and say:

"Donna Mimma's ugly! We don't want her anymore!"

But the problem is that not even the peasant women want her anymore, because with them Donna Mimma was always in a rush, doing things without much ceremony, treating them as if they didn't have the right to complain about their labor pains, and all too often, if things went on too long, she'd rush off, all solicitous, to look in on some lady who was also in labor; while this one—such a love, and so beautiful, inside and out!—is always kind and patient, even with them. She doesn't make distinctions, so if a lady sends someone to have her come—quickly, quickly!—she responds politely but firmly that no, she can't come so quickly, because this poor woman is in her hands and she can't leave her. Just like that! Several times! And imagine, a girl who has never even experienced these pains knows and understands what they are, and tries to alleviate them, for rich and poor alike! She did away with her hat and her flightiness and all those airs she arrived with, so as to dress like them, like a peasant woman, with a shawl and a scarf, which look so darling on her!

Donna Mimma, meanwhile . . . What? With a hat on? Yes, hurry, go run and see! She has just arrived from Palermo, with a hat, a huge hat, like this, holy Mother of God, she looks like a monkey, like the monkey that dances on top of a little organ at the fair! Everyone rushes out to see her, all the children escort her home banging on pots, as if they were following the carnival granny.

"Really? A hat?"

Yes, a hat. Didn't she earn her university diploma, just like the Piedmontese? Two years she studied . . . and what studies! Look, they turned her hair white—it was still black when she left for Palermo. If the big doctor wants to quiz her now, she'll show him, he can't bewitch her with those magic spells of his anymore, because she knows how to say them now too, and even better than he does.

The hat? Oh, how small-headed and silly people in this village are! The hat is a right and a consequence of studying at the university for two years. Everyone there—all the women she studied with—wore one, so she did too.

Her profession—os . . . no, ob . . . obstreperics—it's not much different from being a doctor. The same thing practically. But doctors don't go around wearing a beret! Then why did she go to Palermo? Why did she study at the university for two years? Why did she get a diploma, if not to put herself on equal footing, in terms of studies and status, with the Piedmontese, who graduated from the University of Turin?

Donna Mimma is stunned. When she learns that the Piedmontese wears a scarf and shawl instead of a hat, she explodes. "Oh really? She took it off? And now she wears a shawl and sky-blue scarf? She does what? She says what? That she goes to Palermo to buy babies? With a litter? Traitor! Wicked girl! All to take food from Donna Mimma's mouth? Murderer! To get in the good graces of the ignorant people of the village? Wicked! Wicked! And the people . . . really! They accept this imposter, who used to go around saying it was foolishness and false modesty? Well then, if this brazen girl had to lower herself to become a village midwife, as she had been for thirty-five years, then why make Donna Mimma go to Palermo, make her study at the university for two years, to get a diploma? To have time to steal her place, that's why! To snatch the food out of her mouth, acting like her, dressing like her, saying the same things she used to say! Wicked! Murderer! Imposter, traitor! Oh, what . . . oh God, what . . . what. . . ."

Her blood rushes to her head. Still wearing her huge hat, Donna Mimma weeps with rage, wrings her hands, stamps her foot. Her hat flops to one side, and now, for the first time, a dirty word escapes her lips. No, she's not going to take her hat off, not ever. It's going to stay right here, right on her head. Out of defiance. The Piedmontese may have taken hers off, but Donna Mimma has put hers on, and she intends to keep it on! She has been to Palermo, she practically killed herself studying for two years, she has her diploma, and now she is going to set herself up right here in the village, not as the little midwife, but as the Ostrician with a diploma from the Royal University of Palermo.

Poor Donna Mimma. She's in such a rage pacing about her tiny living room that she says *ostrician*, and every object in her house seems to be staring at her dumbfounded because they expected to be greeted with joy and caresses after two years' absence. But Donna Mimma doesn't even see them. She wants to look the Piedmontese in the face, she says, she wants to see if—and out comes another dirty word—she has the courage to talk about ivory litters and buying babies in front of her; she wants to make the rounds of the village right now, without even a minute's rest, make the rounds of all the women in the village—with her hat on, yes sir!—to see if they too will have the courage, now that she has returned with her diploma, to treat her differently, all because of that stupid, skinny girl there!

But as soon as she steps into the street, there are those looks of astonishment again, those impertinent, ungrateful rascals who laugh and jest, who have forgotten just who welcomed them into this world.

"Dog faces! You little brats! . . . Sons of . . ."

They throw vegetable peels and pebbles at her huge hat, they follow her, making rude noises, leaping about her.

"Donna Mimma? Oh, look!" the ladies say, stopping to watch the comic, pitiful spectacle. Donna Mimma, with her huge, lopsided hat and her round eyes, all red with anger and tears, wants them to see the shadow of remorse in her, and in those round eyes of hers, red with anger and tears, she wants them to see her rebuke, her deep distress, as if they were the ones who'd sent her to Palermo to study, against her will, as if they were the ones who made her come back from Palermo wearing that huge hat, which, as the natural though excessive fruit of two years of study at the university, represents their betrayal.

Yes, my ladies, betrayal, because, if you wanted the kind of midwife that Donna Mimma was before, a midwife with a scarf on her head and a shawl around her shoulders, who told your children the fairy tale about the ivory litter and their little siblings being bought in Palermo with their fathers' money, then you should not have allowed her sky-blue scarf and her old fairy tales to be usurped by that brazen girl from the Continent who, coming from the university with a hat of her own, made fun of those things in Donna Mimma. You should have said to her, "No, dear, you made Donna Mimma study in Palermo for two years, you made her put on a hat so as not to be made fun of by brazen, flighty girls like you, and now you take yours off? And you put on a scarf and shawl and start telling that fairy tale about the litter, to take the place of the one you sent away? But for you it's all an imposture! Whereas for her it was natural to dress like that, to talk like that! No, dear, now you are betraying Donna Mimma, and just as you made fun of her before, with her scarf and shawl and her old fairy tale, now you'd have others make fun of her, with her huge hat and her obstetric science learned at the university." That, my ladies, is what you should have said to the Piedmontese. Or if you really do like her better, this "civilized" midwife who explains everything so well, step by step, how and how not to make babies, then make her put her hat back on, so as not to make fun of Donna Mimma who studied like a doctor and returned with a hat!

But you just shrug your shoulders, my ladies, and you make it clear to Donna Mimma that you don't know how to behave with the other one, who has already attended one birthing—yes, well, really well—and you're already committed for the next one . . . and so as not to compromise yourselves for the future, you say you hope to God that you've had enough of this cross you have to bear, no more children.

Donna Mimma weeps. She'd like to console herself a little with the children at least. She removes her scary black hat, hoping they will come near. But it's no use. They don't recognize her anymore.

"But why?" Donna Mimma says, weeping. "Flavietta, you used to look at me with your big eyes full of love. And you, my little Ninì, don't you remember me anymore? Donna Mimma? I'm the one who went to buy you in Palermo, with papà's money, me, with the ivory litter! My little ones, come here!"

The children don't want to come near. Surly and hostile, they eye her from a distance, her and that horrendous black hat on her knees. So Donna Mimma, after trying in vain to wipe the tears from her cheeks, but only making things worse, puts on her horrendous hat again and walks away.

Despite what Donna Mimma thinks, her horrendous black hat isn't the only reason the whole village has turned against her. If it weren't for her anger and spite, she could throw away the hat. But the science? Alas, the science, which tore from her head her beautiful sky-blue scarf and imposed instead this horrendous black hat. The science learned late and badly. The science that took away her vision and gave her glasses. The science that cheated her out of thirty-five years of experience. The science that cost her two years of martyrdom. No, that she can never throw away. And that is the real irreparable evil! Because this evening it happens that a neighbor, married barely a year and already about to become a mother, cannot find a place, not one single place in the four rooms of her house, where she can quiet the craving that is devouring her. She goes out onto the little terrace and looks . . . but all those stars twinkling in the sky are staring strangely at her. She feels their sharp sting, feels her flesh tingle with chills. And she starts to cry and moan that she can't take it anymore! You can wait, they say to her, you can wait until tomorrow. No, she says, if it keeps on like this, I'll be dead before dawn, and so, since the other one, the Piedmontese, is engaged elsewhere and has sent word that she's terribly sorry but she can't come tonight, seeing that now there are two of them in the village who practice the same profession, well yes, they can call Donna Mimma.

What? Who? Donna Mimma? And who is Donna Mimma? A rag to plug the leaks? She doesn't want to "substitute" for the Piedmontese! But in the end she gives in to their pleading. She places her hat on her head and off she goes. But oh, is it possible that Donna Mimma will not seize the opportunity to show that she has studied at the university for two years, just like the Piedmontese, and that now she knows how to do things exactly as she does, better than her, with all the rules of science and the precepts of hygiene? Poor wretch! She wants to show the woman all these rules of science, one by one, and one by one she wants to apply the precepts of hygiene. Well, with so much showing and applying, at a certain point they have to send urgently for the Piedmontese, and now for the doctor as well, if they want to save the poor mother and her little creature, who—impeded, suffocated, strangled by all those rules and precepts—might die.

And now it's really finished for Donna Mimma. After that, no one—and rightly so—wants any more to do with her. Embittered against the entire village, her horrendous hat on her head, she goes into the piazza every day now and causes a scene in front of the pharmacy, calling the doctor an ass and that thieving Piedmontese who came to steal her bread a slut. Some say she has taken to drink, because on her way home after these outbursts, Donna Mimma weeps, weeps inconsolably. And this, everyone knows, is a sure effect of wine.

■ ■ ■

The little Piedmontese, meanwhile, sky-blue silk scarf on her head and long calico shawl pulled tight around her slim figure, rushes from one house to the next, her eyes modestly lowered, and every now and then gives a little mischievous glance and a little smile that reveals those adorable dimples on her cheeks. She says regretfully that it's a real shame that Donna Mimma, after returning to the village, has fallen so, because she had hoped for some relief, given as how these blessed Sicilian papàs have far too much money to spend on children, and make her travel unceasingly, day and night, on her litter.

That very first day, Bartolino Fiorenzo had heard his future wife say:

"Actually, Lina, no . . . My name isn't Lina, it's Carolina. The Dearly Departed decided to call me Lina, and it stuck."

The Dearly Departed was Cosimo Taddei, her first husband.

"There he is!"

Bartolino's future wife had even pointed Taddei out to him. He was still there, smiling and waving his hat (a very animated snapshot, enlarged), on the wall facing the settee where Bartolino Fiorenzo was seated. And Bartolino instinctively nodded back.

It didn't even occur to Lina Sarulli, Taddei's widow, to remove his portrait from the living room. It was his house, after all. Cosimo Taddei, an engineer, had built it from square one, furnished it elegantly, and, in the end, left it to her, along with his entire estate.

Sarulli went on, without taking the least notice of her future husband's embarrassment.

"I wasn't happy about changing my name. But then the Dearly Departed said to me, 'And if instead of Carolina I called you *cara Lina*—dear Lina? Would that be better? It's almost the same, but so much more!' Okay?"

"Fine, yes, yes, that's fine!" Bartolino Fiorenzo replied, as if the Dearly Departed had asked his opinion.

"So, *cara Lina*, we agree?" Sarulli concluded with a smile.

"Yes, yes, we agree . . . ," the bewildered Bartolino Fiorenzo stammered, confused and ashamed that her grinning husband was watching and waving from the wall.

■ ■ ■

When—three months later—the Fiorenzos, now husband and wife, left for their honeymoon in Rome, having been escorted to the train station by family and friends, Ortensia Motta, a close friend of the Fiorenzo and Sarulli households, commented to her husband:

"So, poor Bartolino's taken a wife? I'd say he's been given a husband, rather!"

Ortensia Motta, mind you, did not mean to imply that Lina Sarulli, formerly Lina Taddei and now Lina Fiorenzo, was more man than woman. No. Too much woman, in fact, dear Lina was! But there really wasn't any doubt that, of the two of them, Lina had much more experience and far better judgment than Bartolino did. Ah, Bartolino—blond hair, ruddy round face—was like a big baby. An odd one, though: balding, but his baldness seemed fake, as if he'd shaved the top of his head himself, in order to erase his babyish look. Without succeeding, though, poor Bartolino!

"What do you mean, poor! Why poor?" old Motta, young Ortensia's husband, mewed in a nasal, irritated voice. Motta had orchestrated Bartolino and Lina's marriage and didn't want anyone speaking ill of it. "Bartolino's no fool. A very talented chemist he is . . ."

"Of course! First rate!" his wife sneered.

"Quite first rate!" Motta retorted.

A very talented chemist indeed, and had he wanted to publish the innovative, profound, and unquestionably original research he'd been carrying out since his youth, and till then the sole, exclusive passion in his life, undoubtedly, well, who knows . . . who knows which prestigious university of the realm would have awarded him a professorship on the first go. Erudite he was, highly learned. And now he would make an exemplary husband. He'd embarked on his conjugal life pure, a virgin at heart.

"Well, as for that . . . ," Ortensia remarked, as if, when it came to his virginity, she was disposed to concede even more.

The fact is, before Bartolino's marriage to Sarulli was decided, whenever she heard her husband advise Bartolino's uncle about the need to "marry off" the young man, she would burst out laughing. Oh, the laughs she had over it . . .

"Yes, my lady, marry him off!" her husband would snap at her.

Ortensia would stop laughing suddenly:

"Then go ahead, my dears, marry him off! I'm laughing to myself, about what I'm reading."

She was reading, in fact. While her husband played his regular game of chess with Mr. Anselmo, Bartolino's uncle, she would read some French novel to the elderly Mrs. Fiorenzo, whose paralysis had confined her to a chaise for the last six months.

Oh, how gay those evenings were! Bartolino, shut up in his chemistry lab; the elderly aunt, pretending to listen to the novel even though she no longer understood a thing; and those two old men, intent on their game of chess . . . they needed to "marry off" Bartolino in order to bring a bit of gaiety into the house. And now they'd married him off for real, poor boy!

Ortensia, meanwhile, imagining the young couple on their honeymoon, laughed at the thought of Lina tête à tête with that big bald baby, so inexperienced, a virgin at heart, as her husband said. Lina, who had spent four years with her dear engineer Taddei, so worldly, so vivacious, jovial, and enterprising . . . perhaps even too much so!

The young widow bride had probably noted the difference between them by now.

■ ■ ■

Just as the train shuddered in preparation for departure, Uncle Anselmo had said to his new niece:

"Don't forget, Lina . . . you will need to guide him!"

He'd meant guide him around Rome, where Bartolino had never been.

She had been there, though, with the Dearly Departed, on her first honeymoon; and she preserved the memory of even the smallest things, the most minor episodes—a highly detailed, crystalline memory, as if it had been only six months, rather than six years, since she'd been there.

The train ride with Bartolino took forever: the curtains didn't close. As soon as they pulled into the station in Rome, Lina said to her husband:

"Just leave everything to me now, please. Put those suitcases down!" And, to the porter who came to open the door:

"Here: three suitcases, two hatboxes, no, three hatboxes, one portmanteau, another portmanteau, this bag, here, another bag . . . What else? Nothing, that's everything. Hotel Vittoria!"

On the way out of the station, after having claimed their trunk, she nodded to the omnibus driver, whom she recognized. And once they were on board, she said to her husband:

"You'll see, a modest hotel, but very comfortable, good service, clean, decent prices, and centrally located too!"

The Dearly Departed—she recalled, without meaning to—had been very happy with it. And now, undoubtedly, Bartolino would be even happier. Oh, such a good boy! He didn't say a word.

"A bit dazed, are you?" she said. "Rome had the same effect on me, the first time . . . but you'll see, you'll like Rome. Look, look . . . Piazza delle Terme . . . The Baths of Diocletian . . . Santa Maria degli Angeli . . . and that there! Turn around! There in the distance, that's Via Nazionale . . . magnificent, isn't it? We'll go by there later . . ."

Getting off at their hotel, Lina felt right at home. She would have liked for someone to recognize her, just as she recognized almost everyone: the old manservant over there, for example . . . Pippo, yes; the same one they'd had six years ago.

"What's our room number?"

They had been given room number 12, on the second floor: a nice room, spacious, with an alcove for the bed, nicely arranged. But Lina said to the old manservant:

"And room number 19, Pippo, on the third floor? Could you see if it's free by any chance?"

"Right away," he replied with a bow.

"Much more comfortable," Lina explained to her husband. "With a small room next to the bed alcove . . . More air too, and less noise. We'll be much more comfortable there . . ."

She recalled that the Dearly Departed had done the same thing: he'd been given a room on the second floor and had it changed for one on the third.

The manservant returned a short while later to tell them that room number 19 was indeed free and at their disposal, should they prefer it.

"Of course, of course!" Lina hastened to say, clapping her hands joyously.

And upon entering, she was overjoyed to see that same room, with the same wallpaper, the same furniture, in the same place . . . Bartolino did not share her joy.

"Don't you like it?" Lina asked, unpinning her hat in front of the familiar mirror over the chest of drawers.

"Yes . . . it's fine . . . ," he said.

"Oh, look! I can see in the mirror . . . that little painting wasn't there before . . . There used to be a Japanese plate . . . it must have broken. But tell me, don't you like it? No no no no no! No kisses, not now . . . not with that dirty nose. You can wash up here, and I'll go to my little washroom . . . Farewell!"

And off she ran, exuberant.

Bartolino Fiorenzo looked around, feeling rather mortified. He went over to the alcove, lifted the curtain, and looked at the bed. It had to be the same one in which his wife had slept with Taddei for the first time.

And Bartolino could see—off in the distance, in the portrait on the wall in his wife's living room—the other man waving to him.

■ ■ ■

For the entire length of their honeymoon, not only did he lie down in that same bed, but he lunched and dined in the same restaurants where the Dearly Departed had taken his wife; and, like a little puppy, he traipsed around Rome after the Dearly Departed, who guided them through his wife's memories; he visited the antiquities and museums and galleries and churches and gardens, seeing and observing all that the Dearly Departed had shown his wife.

Bartolino was timid, and in those early days he didn't dare reveal how humiliated, how mortified he was beginning to feel having to follow, in each and every thing, the experiences, advice, tastes, and inclinations of her first husband.

His wife didn't mean to hurt him, though. She just didn't—couldn't—realize it.

At eighteen, lacking any discernment, any real notion of life, she had been completely taken with that man, who had shaped her and educated her, who had made her a woman. She was, in short, Cosimo Taddei's creation; she owed everything, absolutely everything to him, and she didn't think or feel or speak or move if not according to his ways.

So why, then, did she take another husband? Because Cosimo Taddei had taught her that tears are no remedy for calamities. Life is for the living, death for whom it takes. If she had died, he undoubtedly would have taken another wife; and so . . .

So now Bartolino had to do everything her way—Cosimo Taddei's way, that is, their master and guide: don't think about anything, don't worry about anything, just laugh and have fun, now is the time for it. She didn't mean to hurt him.

Yes, well, but a kiss at least . . . a caress, something, anything, that was not exactly as he had done . . . Was there nothing, nothing at all special that he, Bartolino, made her feel? Nothing uniquely his that might steal her away, even for a moment, from the dead man's power?

Bartolino Fiorenzo searched and searched . . . But his shyness prevented him from dreaming up new caresses.

Or rather, he dreamt them up, but to himself. Passionate caresses they were, yet all it took was his wife, on seeing him turn bright red, to ask:

"What's wrong?"

And all the passion drained away. He'd pull a monkey face and say:

"What do you mean, what's wrong?"

■ ■ ■

When they returned from their honeymoon, they were met with unexpected, upsetting, sad news: Mr. Motta, the author of their marriage, had died suddenly.

Lina Fiorenzo, who, when Taddei had died, had Ortensia at her side, offering all the comfort and care of a sister, now rushed to offer her the same.

She didn't imagine that consoling her would be a very difficult task: after all, Ortensia couldn't be too terribly afflicted by the calamity; a good man, poor Motta, yes, but extremely annoying, and much older than his wife.

Thus, on going to see her friend ten days after the tragedy, Lina was dismayed to find her truly inconsolable. She suspected that her husband had left her in dire financial straits. She ventured a polite inquiry.

"No, no!" Ortensia hastened to reply amid her tears. "But . . . you can understand . . ."

Understand what? All this suffering? Seriously? No, Lina Fiorenzo did not understand. And she confessed as much to her husband.

"Well!" Bartolino said, shrugging his shoulders and turning red as a shrimp at his worldly wife's thoughtlessness. "After all . . . I mean . . . Her husband died . . ."

"Oh, really, now!" Lina exclaimed. "Husband . . . ? He was practically old enough to be her father!"

"And does that seem like nothing to you?"

"But he wasn't that, either!"

Lina was right. Ortensia was weeping too much.

During the three months of Bartolino's engagement, Ortensia had noticed how distraught the poor young man was at the ease with which his future wife spoke of her first husband in front of him; he couldn't reconcile her constant, living, persistent memory of him with the fact that she was about to take a new husband. He'd talked about it with his uncle, who had tried to reassure him, saying her talk was actually proof of his wife's openness; that he shouldn't take offense, for the very fact that she was remarrying should persuade him that Taddei's memory was no longer rooted in her heart, but merely in her mind, since she had no qualms about speaking of him, even in front of her new husband. Ortensia knew that Bartolino was not assuaged in the least by this logic. And she had reason to believe that the young man's unease over his wife's so-called openness had only increased since their honeymoon. So when the couple came to offer their condolences, she had wanted to show herself inconsolable not so much to Lina as to Bartolino.

Bartolino Fiorenzo was so pleasantly impressed by the widow's grief that for the first time he dared contradict his wife, who did not want to believe in Ortensia's suffering. His face burning, he said to her:

"Excuse me, but didn't you weep too, when your . . ."

"What does that have to do with anything?" Lina interrupted him. "First of all, the Dearly Departed was . . ."

"Still young, yes," offered Bartolino, so she wouldn't have to say it.

"And yes, I wept, of course I wept," she continued.

"But not much?" Bartolino hazarded.

"A great deal . . . but in the end I made my peace with it, so there! And believe me, Bartolino, all that weeping on Ortensia's part, it's too much."

But Bartolino didn't want to believe her. In fact, after their conversation, he felt his vexation sharpen, not so much with his wife as with the late Taddei, because by now he realized that this way of thinking and feeling were not his wife's but rather the fruit of the teachings of her first husband, who must have been a tremendous cynic. Didn't he greet Bartolino with a smile and a wave every day, when he walked into the living room?

■ ■ ■

Oh, that portrait! He couldn't stand it anymore! It was torture! Taddei was always there, staring him in the face. On his way to his lab? There was Taddei's picture, smiling and waving, as if to say:

"Go ahead, go right ahead! I had my engineering study there too. You've set up your chemistry lab there now? Good work! Life is for the living, death for whom it takes."

Or to their bedroom? Taddei's image tormented him there as well. He would laugh and wave.

"Help yourself! Go on, help yourself! Good night! Are you happy with my wife? Ah yes, I taught her well . . . Life is for the living, death for whom it takes!"

He couldn't stand it anymore!

The entire house was full of that man, as was his wife. And he, so peaceable before, was now constantly seized by agitation, even though he tried to hide it.

Finally he began to act strangely, so as to upset his wife's habits.

Except that Lina had developed these habits as a widow. The vivacious Cosimo Taddei didn't have any habits, and had never wanted any. So when Bartolino first began acting strangely, his wife scolded him:

"Oh God, Bartolino, just like the Dearly Departed?"

He didn't want to give in though. He forced himself to come up with new whims. But whatever he tried, it seemed to Lina that the Dearly Departed, who'd gotten up to all sorts of mischief, had done the same.

Bartolino lost heart. Even more so because Lina seemed to

discover a liking for his whimsies. If he kept it up, she really would think she was seeing the Dearly Departed all over again.

And so . . . so Bartolino, to give vent to the anxiety mounting inside him from day to day, devised a distressing plan.

In truth, he didn't intend to betray his wife so much as to avenge himself on the man who had taken all of her, and who held her still. He was convinced that his wicked idea had come to him spontaneously; but actually, it must be said in his defense that it was practically suggested to him, insinuated, infiltrated by the woman who, when he was still a bachelor, had tried in vain many times to tempt him away from his overzealous study of chemistry.

For Ortensia Motta it was sweet revenge. While appearing profoundly sorry to betray her friend, she let Bartolino know that even before he had taken a wife, she . . . oh, it was practically inevitable!

It didn't seem so inevitable to Bartolino, and yet, good boy that he was, he felt disappointed, cheated almost, by how easily his plan had worked. Left alone for a while there in good old Motta's bedroom, he repented of his wicked deed. At a certain point his eyes fell on something shimmering on the rug, on Ortensia's side of the bed. A gold locket and chain, which must have slipped off her neck. He picked it up, with the idea of giving it back to her, but as he waited he fingered it nervously and, without meaning to, opened it.

He was astounded.

■ ■ ■

Even there, a tiny portrait of Cosimo Taddei, laughing and waving.

TWO DOUBLE BEDS

On her first visit to her husband's tomb, the widow Zorzi, in blackest mourning, was accompanied by attorney-at-law Signor Gàttica-Mei, an old friend of the deceased and a widower himself these past three years.

Gold-rimmed glasses; an eyeglass chain, also gold, that looped over his ears and onto his shoulders, and was pinned under his impeccable frock coat collar; a large pointy chin, shiny and clean-shaven; curly hair, a little too black perhaps, parted all the way down to his neck, which fanned out behind his ears; high shoulders and a rigid neck: all lent an austere, solemn gravity—suitable for the sad occasion—to the lawyer's demeanor, and made him seem stricken with grief.

He got off the San Lorenzo streetcar first. Then, assuming a vaguely military pose, he held out his hand to help the widow Zorzi down.

They were both carrying large bouquets of flowers, she for her husband, he for his wife.

But stepping off the streetcar, Zorzi had to hold her dress as well as her bouquet, and, hindered by the long black crepe veil that hid her face, couldn't see where to place her feet, couldn't see the black-gloved hand that the lawyer was offering and that she, moreover, would not have been able to take. Spilling down the steps, she nearly tumbled right on top of him.

"Idiot! Can't you see? My hands are full . . . ," Zorzi hissed furiously under her long veil.

"But I offered you my hand . . . ," he apologized, mortified, without even looking at her. "You just didn't see it!"

"Quiet. That's enough. Which way do we go?"

"Here, this way . . ."

Recomposed now, rigid and erect, each holding a bouquet of flowers, they made their way toward the Pincetto.[1]

■ ■ ■

Three years earlier, Gàttica-Mei had had a family tomb built for his wife and himself there: two plots, side by side, marked by two handsome stone slabs, rising slightly toward the head, with two little columns, each holding a lamp; the whole ensemble ringed by flowers and fake lava.

How poor Signor Zorzi, friend to Gàttica-Mei and his late wife, had admired that tomb the year before, on the Day of the Dead!

"Oh, nice! It looks like a double bed! Nice, very nice!"

And, as if presaging his own approaching end, he'd wanted to have another one built nearby, just like it, right away, for his wife and himself.

A double bed, exactly! And as a matter of fact, Gàttica-Mei, precise in all things, had accommodated his late wife on the left

---

1. The Pincetto is part of the Verano Monumental Cemetery in Rome.

side, so that he, when his turn came to be laid there, could give her his right, just as he had in their conjugal bed.

And on the stone he'd had the following epitaph carved, this also highly praised by that good soul Signor Zorzi for its moving simplicity:

HERE

MARGHERITA GÀTTICA-MEI

EXEMPLARY WIFE

LOST TO THE LIVING ON XV MAY MCMII

AWAITS IN PEACE

HER SPOUSE

Gàttica-Mei had then prepared another epitaph for himself, which one day would figure nicely on the second stone, a worthy complement to the first. It did not, in fact, state, as was customary, that attorney Anton Maria Gàttica-Mei HERE LIES or DIED, etc., etc. but rather that ON (dot dot dot) of YEAR (dot dot dot) he JOINED HIS SPOUSE.

And he almost would have liked to know the exact date of his death so as to complete the inscription, thus leaving everything in perfect order.

But given—yes—given the convention for childless couples' tombs, the epitaphs had to correspond in this way, out of necessity, so as not to disturb the harmony of the whole.

Having assumed, as was his duty, the sad task of organizing the funeral rites, transportation, and interment of his poor friend Zorzi, Gàttica-Mei had hit on a variant for his epitaph, one that—

by Jove!—if only he'd thought of it earlier . . . But that's the way it always is: everything improves over time, upon reflection . . . That "awaits in peace her spouse" of his wife's epitaph seemed too cold to him now, too simple, too dry, compared to Gerolamo Zorzi, who, on the right-hand side of his tomb, lies

AWAITING HIS FAITHFUL COMPANION
TO COME SLEEP BESIDE HIM

How much better that sounded! How pleasing to the ear!

He couldn't wait to reach the tomb, so as to receive the praises, which, in all good conscience he believed he merited, of the widow Zorzi.

But she, after first kneeling and reciting a prayer and placing the bouquet of flowers at the foot of the stone, and then lifting her long veil and reading the epitaph, turned to look at him, her face pale, frowning, and severe, and her chin, right where a large hairy wart stood, twitching, as it did in moments of fierce irritation.

"I think it's . . . it's satisfactory . . . isn't it?" he dared to ask, perplexed, afflicted, intimidated.

"Later, at home," Zorzi snapped. "We certainly cannot discuss it here, now."

Then she took another look at the tomb, shaking her head slightly for quite some time, before dabbing her eyes with a black-bordered handkerchief. She was crying for real, shaking all over in fact, a violent fit of barely suppressed sobs. So Gàttica-Mei, using two fingers, also extracted his perfumed handkerchief from his cuff, and with his other hand removed his glasses, and ever so slowly, and repeatedly, dried first one eye, then the other.

"No! Don't you cry!" the fitful widow shouted furiously, suddenly recovering from her weeping. "You, no!"

And she furiously blew her nose.

"Wh-why?" Gàttica-Mei stammered.

"Later, at home," Zorzi snapped again.

The lawyer hunched his shoulders and tried to explain:

"I thought that . . . I don't know . . ."

And looking again at the epitaph, his eyes came to rest on that "faithful companion" that . . . yes, of course . . . but good God! Such a patent expression, consecrated by custom . . . One said "faithful companion" as one would "large vase" or "frugal meal" . . . He simply hadn't thought about it, there.

"Perhaps . . . I can understand, but . . ."

"I said at home," Zorzi repeated for the third time. "However, since he cared so much about it too, poor Momo did, about this masterpiece here . . . allow me to note: two columns, two lamps . . . but why? One would have been sufficient."

"One? How? Well!" Gàttica-Mei was stunned. He spread his arms, smiling futilely.

"For the symmetry, right?" Zorzi asked bitterly. "But without any children, without any other relatives: as long as one of us is still alive, to come light the candle for the other . . . but who will come light it for me then, afterwards? And for you, over there?"

"I see . . . ," the shaken, befuddled Gàttica-Mei admitted, instinctively placing his hands on the nape of his neck, to fan out those two wings of hair behind his ears, a habitual gesture he repeated whenever he lost—even for an instant—self-control (in truth, something that happened rather frequently around the widow Zorzi). "But wait," he said, recovering himself, "allow me to also note: then . . . may that day never come! . . . then both lamps, here and there, will remain unlit, and . . ."

And the symmetry would be preserved. But the widow Zorzi did not want to give in.

"And so? So one, that one, will always be new, untouched, never lit, pointless. Therefore, it could have been done without, one would have been sufficient."

"The same is true for mine," Gàttica-Mei said. "And," he added, lowering his voice as well as his gaze, "were we to die together, Chiara . . ."

"You'd come light a candle for me here, or I for you, there, is that right?" asked Zorzi, even more acrimonious. "Oh, thank you, dear, thank you! But this is a discussion we shall have at home."

And waving her hand as if to dismiss him, she sent him to place his bouquet of flowers on his wife's tomb.

While she, tilting her head and resting the corner of her mouth on the outstretched index finger of her right hand, stayed and stared silently at her husband's tombstone, a half-withered rose next to the little column, trembling slightly in the soft breeze, seemed to bow its head bitterly on behalf of the good Momolo Zorzi buried there.

■ ■ ■

But it wasn't, as Gàttica-Mei had naively supposed, for that conventional phrase that the widow Zorzi had dug in her heels.

She knew, knew perfectly well, that epitaphs are written not to honor the dead, who are devoured by worms, but solely for the vanity of the living.

Thus it was not for the pointless offense to her dead husband that she had grown indignant, but for the offense that that epitaph held for her, still living.

What were Signor Gàttica-Mei's intentions? With whom did he think he was dealing? Had he imagined, in dictating that epitaph, that she—alive—and he—alive—should remain bound, slaves to the stupid order, the stupid symmetry of those two double beds there, beds made for death? That the falsehood, which . . . which yes, could have a certain decorative value for death, should persist and, from those two stones, impose itself on life? Just who did he take her for? Did he suppose that she, because of that "awaits in peace her spouse" on his family tomb, and that "awaiting his faithful companion, etc." of her husband's, would graciously agree to carry on being his convenient lover, in order to then go, as "faithful companion," to lie—or "sleep" rather—next to her spouse, and he next to his "exemplary wife"?

Oh no! Oh no, my dear attorney!

Those pointless falsehoods were fine there, carved on the dead. But not here, in life. Here one was compelled to employ useful lies, and to endure necessary ones. And she, an honest woman, had endured one (God knows with what sorrow!) for three years, while her husband was alive. Enough now! Why should she have to endure it any longer, this falsehood, now that its necessity had ceased with Signor Zorzi's death? Because of the bond of those stupid tombs? A bond that he, Gàttica-Mei, immediately safeguarding himself, had, with that new epitaph, hastened to reaffirm?

Oh no! Oh no, my dear attorney! A useless falsehood it was at this point, that "faithful companion."

She, an honest woman, could, out of necessity, deceive her husband when he was alive; did Signor Gàttica-Mei want her to continue to deceive him even now that he was dead? For no reason, or for the mere ridiculous fact of those twin tombs? Really now! True, when he was alive, she couldn't do without that falsehood; but now that he was dead, no, she didn't want to go on deceiving her husband. Her honesty, dignity, and decorum would not allow it. Signor Gàttica-Mei had been free for three years, and now she was free too. Either each alone, honestly, or honestly united, before the law and before an altar.

The discussion was long and harsh.

To start, Gàttica-Mei confessed candidly that nothing, absolutely nothing that she, with such malicious spirit, suspected had even crossed his mind when dictating that epitaph. If she had entered even slightly into the spirit of the convention for childless couples' tombs, she would have realized that those epitaphs there had practically written themselves, naturally, as inevitable consequences. The convention is ridiculous? Oh no, not true, not true . . .

"Ridiculous, ridiculous, ridiculous," the widow Zorzi reaffirmed with fiery vexation. "Just think, that exemplary wife of yours, who is waiting there in peace for you . . . Don't make me say what I would prefer not to! I know well, and you even better, what you went through with her . . ."

"What does that have to do with anything?"

"Let me speak! When in the world did poor Margherita ever understand you? Since she tormented you all the time? And you would come here to vent, with Momo and me?"

"Yes, but . . ."

"Let me speak! And why did I love you? I, who, in turn, did not feel understood by poor Momo? Oh, God, nothing makes one rebel more than injustice . . . but you wanted to remain faithful to Margherita till the end, and you dictated that lovely epitaph. I admired you then; yes, I admired you more the more you esteemed your wife, who was unworthy of your faithfulness. But then . . . yes, it's pointless, pointless to talk about it . . . I didn't know how to refuse you. I should never have done it, though! Just as you didn't, as long as your wife was alive. I too should have waited, till Momo died. But as things stand, only *I* have not fulfilled my duties. Well, yes, you too, but only toward a friend: as a spouse, you were true! And this, you see, now that your wife and my husband are both gone, and only you remain here with me, this is what weighs on me the most. And this is the reason I'm speaking! I am an honest woman, like your wife; honest, like you, like my husband! And I want to be your wife, do you understand? Or nothing! Ah, you're too taken with your lovely convention? But imagine me now, lying next to my husband, his 'faithful companion' . . . How comical, how excruciatingly comical! Anyone who knows, as well as those who don't know anything, seeing those two tombs there, will say, 'Oh, look at these two, well, just admire that, such peace among those spouses!' And no wonder, they're dead! A charade, what a charade."

And her hairy wart twitched for more than five minutes on her highly irritated chin.

Gàttica-Mei was wounded to his very soul by her lengthy harangue, but even more by her derision. Serious and composed as he was, he certainly could not allow his friend or anything that was his to be trifled with; just as he could not, when his wife was alive, have allowed betrayal.

Zorzi's wish to wed ruined everything for him. Never mind those two tombs waiting there; what about his new arrangement as a widower, to which he had adapted so well! Why now, a new upheaval in his life? There was no reason for it, really, no reason. As long as poor Zorzi was alive, he understood her scruples, her suffering, her remorse, but now, why? If there had been a divorce, a previous marriage, well then yes, to repair the deception done to someone else, that theft of honor, those subterfuges, which nevertheless had been so enticing; but why now? Now that no one was being betrayed, and — both of them free, widowed, of a certain age — neither of them needed to explain anything to anyone if they continued their tranquil relationship? Decorum? On the contrary, now that there was nothing wrong . . . Is this how she wanted to repair past harm? But poor Momolo wasn't here any more! To herself? Why? What harm was there to repair, to her or to him? Is love harmful? And then . . . well, by God, yes, why not think about it? Did she also want to lose the pension that her husband had left to her, about one hundred and sixty *lire* a month? A real shame!

The attorney tried in every way possible to convince her that it was spitefulness, foolishness, deplorable hardheadedness.

But the widow Zorzi was unshakable.

"Wife or nothing."

Hoping that her fixation would fade with time, he told her that it was pointless, cruel even, to be so severe with him now, since the law prescribed that she could not marry again until nine months had passed, and that they would speak about it again at that point, if at all. In vain.

"No, no, and no. It's wife or nothing."

■ ■ ■

And for eight months the widow Zorzi held out. He, poor man, tired of begging her every day, of wringing his hands, resigned himself in the end. A week passed, then two, three. A month and more, without his showing himself again.

And for four days now she, extremely agitated, had been debating whether she should try to meet him, as if by chance, on the street, or write to him, or even go confront him at home, when one of his servants came to announce that his master was gravely ill, of pneumonia, and that he beseeched her to pay him a visit.

She ran to him, tormented by remorse for her hardness, which perhaps was the cause of some disturbance in his life, and consequently, of that illness; she ran, overcome by the darkest presentiments. And in fact, she found him collapsed in bed, rattling, suffocating, death on his lips: unrecognizable. Forgetting every societal consideration, she remained at his side night and day, wrestling with death, without a moment's peace.

On the seventh day, when the doctors declared him out of danger, Zorzi, worn out after so many sleepless nights, wept, wept with joy, resting her head on the edge of the bed; and he was the one who, lovingly caressing her hair, said that he would make her his wife, right away, as soon as he was well.

But, having left his bed, he first had to learn to walk again. He couldn't stand up any more. Once so solidly and rigidly built, now curved and shaky, he seemed like a shadow of his former self. And his lungs . . . oh, his lungs . . . what a cough! With each new fit, panting, suffocating, he would pound his chest and say to her, as she looked at him in distress:

"It's nothing, nothing."

He improved a little during the summer. He wanted to leave the house, get a bit of air, first in the carriage, then on foot, supported by her and a cane. Finally, having regained some of his strength, he wanted her to hasten to prepare what was necessary for the wedding.

"I'll get better, you'll see . . . I feel better already, much better."

His conjugal home had remained intact: he'd merely removed the double bed from the bedroom, or rather, separated the two twin brass beds and had the one on which his wife had slept taken away. But Zorzi's conjugal home was also still fully intact.

Now, upon marrying, which of the two houses should they keep? She didn't want to upset him, infirm as he was, and knowing him to be methodical and a creature of habit; yet she really didn't feel like living there, in his house, as his wife: everything there spoke of Margherita; she couldn't even open a drawer without feeling a strange restraint, an indefinable consternation, almost as if every single object there jealously guarded the memory of the one who had used them. But he, too, would certainly feel strange among her belongings, in her house. Should they find another house, a new one, with new furniture, and sell the old? That would be best . . . And had he been healthy, the man he'd been before, she undoubtedly would have coaxed her lover in this direction . . . But now she had to resign herself to satisfying his needs, to changing things as little as possible. The double bed, in the meantime: that had to be new, of course. Then, disposing of her first husband's home, she would have her most precious possessions moved here; a selection of the items in best condition in both houses would be made, and whatever remained would be sold.

Which is what they did. And then they married.

The wedding ceremony seemed to bring good luck, because for about three months, until the middle of the autumn, he felt fairly good: his face had color, a bit too much perhaps, and his cough was gone. But then, with the first cold days, he got worse, and so he knew it was all over for him.

All that long winter, which he spent miserably between the bed and an armchair, savoring death, which hung over him, he was tormented till the end by one thought, one insoluble problem: those twin tombs in the Pincetto, there in the Verano cemetery.

Where was his wife going to bury him now?

And between the slow burn of his fever and the agonizing agitation of his illness, a deep, dull anger seized him and exasperated him more and more against his wife, who had wanted at all costs this pointless, foolish, wretched marriage. Yet he knew that for her, what had been foolish was his idea of building those two tombs like that; but he didn't want to admit it. Besides, what an idle discussion this was now, the only effect of which could be to sharpen his anger. The question was another. Could he now, as her husband, go and lie there next to his first wife? And could she, someday, having become the wife of another man, lie next to her first husband?

He refrained for as long as he could, but in the end he had to ask her.

"What are you going and thinking about now!" she yelled at him, without even letting him finish.

"But it needs to be thought about, and in time." He grumbled darkly, throwing her hateful glances. "I want to know, yes, I want to know!"

"Are you mad?" she shouted back. "You'll get better, you'll get better . . . wait and get better!"

Convulsing, he tried to get up from his chair.

"I won't make it till the end of the month! What will you do? What will you do?"

"We'll see, then, Antonio, please! Please!" she burst out, and began to cry.

Gàttica-Mei, seeing her cry, fell silent for a while, but then started mumbling again, gazing at his blackened nails.

"Then . . . sure . . . she'll see, then . . . such expense . . . such care . . . all for nothing . . . all muddled . . . But why? . . . Everything could have remained just the way it was . . . so good . . ."

He was alluding to the epitaph, preserved there in the desk drawer, that epitaph from four years earlier that he had prepared for himself, the one with ON (dot dot dot) of YEAR (dot dot dot) he JOINED HIS SPOUSE.

She found it, in fact, a few days later, rummaging around in the drawer, in her frenzy to make the funeral arrangements, this twice-widowed wife.

She read it, reread it, then threw it away, indignant, stamping her foot.

There, next to his first wife? Oh no, absolutely not, no, no, and no! He had been her husband now, and she simply could not tolerate having him go and lie next to that other one.

But where, then?

Where? There, in Zorzi's tomb. Both of them together, her two husbands, both for her alone.

So the "faithful companion" whom the good Momolo Zorzi was "awaiting" to come "sleep beside him" turned out to be attorney-at-law Gàttica-Mei. And in the other double bed, Margherita, the exemplary wife, still

AWAITS IN PEACE

HER SPOUSE

And she will go there, she, the double widow, as late as she possibly can.

Meanwhile, on the other tomb, both lamps on their little columns are lit, whereas both on this one are dark.

■ ■ ■

In this, at least, the symmetry had been preserved. Gàttica-Mei should be pleased.

After the station stop in Sulmona, Silvestro Noli was alone in the grimy second-class car.

He gave one last glance at the smoky lamp—the jerking of the train made the oil spatter and slosh about in the concave glass, nearly extinguishing the feeble, flickering flame—and closed his eyes, hoping that sleep (he was tired, having been traveling for a day and a night) would lift him out of the despair he was drowning in, deeper and deeper, as the train carried him closer to his place of exile.

Never again! never again! never again! For how long had the cadenced rumble of the wheels been repeating those same two words?

Never again. Yes—never again—the gay life of his youth—never again—the lighthearted company of his friends under Turin's crowded porticos, his hometown—never again—the comfort of his old family home with its warm, familiar scent—never again—his mother's affectionate coddling, or the tender smile of his father's protective gaze.

His dear old parents, whom he might never see again! Mamma, mamma especially! Oh, and in what a state he'd found her, after being away for seven years! All shrunken and hunched over, in so

few years, waxlike, and all her teeth gone. Only her eyes were still
alive. Those poor, dear, beautiful, blessed eyes!

Watching his mother and father, listening to them talk, wan-
dering from room to room and peering about, it really did seem that
life had come to an end, not only for him, but for his family too.
Life had ended for them as well when he left the first time, seven
years ago.

Had he taken it with him, then? What had he done with it?
Where was the life in him now? They'd let themselves believe he'd
taken it with him; but he knew that, departing, he was leaving life
behind. So when he couldn't find it there in that emptiness, when
he was told he wouldn't find anything there anymore because he
had taken it all with him, he had felt the icy hand of death.

And now, that chill still in his heart, he was returning to
Abruzzo. The fifteen days' leave granted him by the superintendent
of the boys' school in Città Sant'Angelo—where he had been teaching drawing for the last five years—was up.

Before Abruzzo, he'd taught in Calabria for a year, in Basili-
cata for another. In Città Sant'Angelo, crushed and blinded by a bitter longing for some affection to fill the emptiness engulfing him,
he had committed the folly of taking a wife, thus chaining himself
there forever.

His wife—born and raised in that high, humid, little village
without water but with all the disturbing prejudices, petty narrow-
mindedness, surliness, and inertia of provincial life, slow and sense-
less—rather than offering him companionship, had exacerbated
his loneliness, constantly reminding him how far he was from the

familiar intimacy that should have been his, and which his thoughts and emotions had never managed to penetrate.

A child had been born, and even his son—how dreadful!—felt alien to him, from the very first day, as if he belonged wholly to his mother, and not at all to him.

Perhaps, had he been able to wrest him from that house, from that village, the boy would have become his. Perhaps even his wife would have become a true companion, and he would have known the joy of having a family and a home of his own—had he only been able to accept a transfer. But he was denied even that hope of future salvation, because his wife, who had not wanted to leave her village even for a brief honeymoon, even to go to Turin to meet his parents and relatives, threatened to leave him were he to be transferred.

Stay, then. Stay there and rot, waiting in dreadful solitude for his spirit to gradually crust over. He loved the theater, music—all the arts—so much that it was practically all he talked about. But now he would thirst forever for such things, as for a glass of fresh, pure water! Oh, their crude, coarse water, gritty from the well, he couldn't stand it. People said it was safe to drink, but he'd had a stomachache for a while now. Merely his imagination, of course! Insult to injury.

Silvestro Noli's eyes filled with tears, which his closed lids could no longer hold back. He bit his lip, as if to keep a sigh from bursting forth as well, and took out his handkerchief.

He hadn't realized how blackened his face had become from the long journey. He stared at the handkerchief, offended and annoyed at the filthy impression his weeping had left. Seeing his life in that soot, he tore at it with his teeth.

The train finally came to a stop at Castellamare Adriatico.

For another twenty minutes' journey, he had to wait more than five hours. Such was the fate of passengers on the night train from Rome who needed to connect to the Ancona or Foggia lines.

Thank goodness the station café was open all night: spacious, well lit, with tables laid, one could while away the long, sad, tedious wait in its bustling brightness. Yet painted on the travelers' pale, puffy faces, filthy and forlorn, was a dreary distress, an oppressive annoyance, a bitter disgust at life that, far from family and friends and all one's usual habits, turned out to be vacuous, inane, unbearable.

A good many of them, perhaps, felt a lump in their throat at the mournful sound of the train whistling in the night. Perhaps they were thinking how there is no respite for human troubles, even at night. And since those troubles seem especially futile at night, stripped as they are of the illusions of the day, and combined with that distressing feeling of precariousness that keeps the traveler bewildered and in suspense, perhaps they were all sitting there thinking how it is human folly that lights the fires in the black engines, and how, at night, under the stars, those trains, racing across dark plains, clattering over bridges and barreling through tunnels, moan desperately, now and then, at being forced to pull the weight of human folly like that, through the night, along iron rails laid to give vent to man's inexhaustible, vain restlessness.

Silvestro Noli, after slowly sipping a cup of milk, got up and made for the door at the far end of the café. He wanted to breathe in the night air by the seashore, at the far end of the sleeping city's wide main street.

Except that, as he passed a table, he heard someone call his name: a petite, pale little woman, slender, and in full mourning dress.

"Professor Noli . . ."

He stopped, surprised and perplexed.

"Signora. . . . Oh, is that you, Nina? Here?"

It was the wife of his colleague Prof. Ronchi, whom Noli had met six years ago, at the technical school in Matera. Dead, yes, yes, he knew that—he died a few months ago, in Lanciano. Still young. Noli had read with grievous surprise the announcement in the bulletin. Poor Ronchi, who, after countless disappointments, had only just taken up his post at the high school, had died suddenly of a fainting fit: excessive love, people said, of that tiny little wife of his, whom he, like a big, brutal, stubborn bear, lugged with him everywhere.

And now here she was, the little widow, dabbing her lips with a black-bordered handkerchief and gazing at him with beautiful, black eyes sunk in dark, puffy sockets as, with a slight wobbling of her head, she spoke of her recent, horrible tragedy.

Seeing two large tears trickle from those beautiful black eyes, Noli invited her to accompany him along the deserted avenue toward the sea, so they could speak more openly.

The pitiful little creature quivered nervously all over. She jolted along beside him, gesticulating jerkily with her shoulders, arms, and long, bony hands. Her words came in torrents, and her temples and cheekbones were soon marred with red splotches. She had a habit of doubling certain consonants at the beginning of a word, which made it sound as if she were snorting, and she kept wiping the tip of her nose and upper lip—beaded in sweat from her rapid speech—with her handkerchief, while her abundant saliva occasionally drowned out her voice.

"Ah, Noli, don't you see? Here, Noli, he left me here, all alone with three little ch-ch-children, I don't know a soul here, I only just arrived, two months ago . . . alone, all alone . . . Oh, what a terrible man, Noli! He ruined himself, and me as well, ruined my health, my life . . . everything . . . Right on top of me . . . Did you know that, Noli? He died on top of me."

Her long shudder ended in what sounded like a whinny.

She started in again: "He took me away from my hometown, I've no one left there other than my sister, who's married off, on her own now . . . why would I go back there? I don't want to make a spectacle of my poverty in front of the very people who used to envy me . . . But here, alone with three ch-ch-children, a c-c-complete stranger . . . what am I to do? I'm desperate . . . I feel so lost . . . I went to Rome, to press for some assistance . . . But I'm not entitled to anything, it seems: only eleven years of teaching, so only eleven months' pension, a mere few thousand *lire* . . . which they still hadn't paid me! I screamed so much at the Ministry, they took me for c-c-crazy . . . My dear lady, he says to me, c-c-cold shower, c-c-cold shower! . . . How true! Maybe I really will go c-c-crazy . . . It hurts, here, all the time, like a gnawing, at the back of my head, Noli . . . and it's as if I were angry, yes, yes, I am angry still . . . as if I were burning inside . . . as if my whole body were on fire . . . on fire . . . Oh, how c-c-cool you are, Noli, so c-c-cool!"

And as she spoke, there, in the middle of the deserted, humid street, under the feeble electric streetlamps, which, spaced too far apart, gave off only a faint, opaline glow, she hung on his arm, buried her head—in its crepe widow's bonnet—on his chest, and sighed longingly.

Noli—astounded, dismayed, moved—instinctively pulled away from her. He realized that this poor woman was so desperate that she would have clung madly to the first male acquaintance who came her way.

"There, there," he said. "Cool? Ah, yes, I am cool! I'm already married, my lady."

"Ah," the little lady replied, immediately pulling away. "Married? You got married?"

"Four years ago, my lady. I have a son, too."

"Here?"

"Nearby. In Città Sant'Angelo."

The little widow let go of his arm now, too.

"But aren't you from Piedmont?"

"Yes, from Turin."

"And your wife?"

"Oh no, my wife is from here."

The two came to a stop under one of the electric streetlamps. They looked at each other: a comprehending, commiserating look.

She was from Bagnara Calabra, the farthest edge of Italy.

They saw themselves there, lost in the night on that long, lonely street leading to the sea, surrounded by the sleeping houses of that melancholy city, so far from their true affections, yet so close to where cruel destiny had fixed their abodes. And the deep sympathy they felt for one another, rather than draw them closer, bitterly convinced them to keep their distance, each locked in their own, inconsolable misery.

Silently they made their way toward the sandy shore.

The night was calm, the air off the water cool and refreshing.

They couldn't see the endless sea, but they could feel it, alive and pulsating in the infinite, black abyss of the tranquil night.

Except that, off in the distance, they glimpsed something sinister, blood-red, glimmering through the mist and trembling on the horizon. Perhaps it was the waning moon, wrapped in fog.

The foamless waves spread and flattened across the shore like silent tongues, scattering here and there on the smooth, shiny, sodden sand a seashell or two, which immediately disappeared when the wave went out.

All that enchanting silence was pierced by the incessant, brilliant blaze of countless stars, so alive they seemed to want to say something to the earth, in the profound mystery of the night.

The two continued silently for a long stretch across the soft, soggy sand. Their footprints lasted only an instant: the first would disappear just as the next was forming. The only sound was the rustle of their clothes.

They were drawn to a white glow in the darkness: a dinghy, pulled up on the shore and turned over. They sat—she on one side, he on the other—and stared silently at the placid waves as they spread like glass across the soft, dull, gray sand. Then the woman lifted her beautiful black eyes to the sky, baring to him and to the stars her pale, tortured brow and her throat, choked with anguish.

"Noli, don't you sing anymore?"

"Me . . . sing?"

"Yes, of course, you used to sing, on those fine nights. . . . Don't you remember, in Matera? You used to sing. . . . I can still hear the lilting sound of your voice . . . such a sweet, passionate falsetto . . . don't you remember?"

Suddenly recalling that distant memory, he felt the very depths of his being heave, as shivers of ineffable tenderness ran over his scalp and down his spine.

Yes, yes . . . it was true: he used to sing, then . . . even there, even in Matera he still held those sweet, passionate songs of his youth in his soul, and on fine evenings, strolling beneath the stars with his friends, those songs still blossomed on his lips.

So it was true. He had taken it away with him, the life from his parents' house in Turin; and if he sang in Matera, then he clearly still had it there, with this poor little friend—whom he may have even flirted with a little, in those distant days, oh, all in good fun, nothing mean-spirited—when he'd needed some affection, a woman's gentle tenderness.

"Do you remember, Noli?"

And staring into the darkness of the night, he whispered, "Yes . . . Yes, I remember."

"Are you crying?"

"I'm remembering . . ."

They fell silent again. Peering now into the night, both felt their unhappiness evaporate a little. It no longer belonged just to them, but to the whole world, to all beings and all things, to that somber, sleepless sea, to those stars shimmering in the sky—to all of life, which cannot know why it must be born, why it must love, why it must die.

The calm, cool night, embroidering the sea with stars, enveloped their grief, which exhaled into that night pulsating with stars, and then slowly, softly abated, as monotonous as those waves on the silent shore. The stars, too, flashing light into the abyss, asked why; the sea, with its weary waves, asked; as did the tiny shells scattered here and there on the sand.

Little by little the darkness dissipated, and the first cold, pale light of dawn began to spread across the sea. And now, whatever evanescent, mysterious, velvety aspect there may have been to their grief—those two perched on either side of an overturned dinghy in the sand—it contracted and crystallized, harsh and naked, as did the features of their faces in that bleak, dim dawn.

He felt himself engulfed once again by the habitual misery of his home, to which he would soon return. He saw it again in his mind's eye, as if he were already there: the house, with all its contours and colors, his wife and little boy inside, both of whom would rejoice at his return. And she too—the little widow—no longer saw so dark and desperate a fate: she had several thousand *lire* in her purse, so her livelihood was assured for a while; she would find a way to provide for herself and her three little children. She arranged her locks on her forehead and said smilingly to Noli: "I must look a sight, my friend, right?"

And they made to head back to the station.

■ ■ ■

The memory of that night was locked in the deepest recess of their souls, perhaps—who knows?—to resurface now and then, a distant memory, with that dark, placid sea and all those shimmering stars—a flicker of arcane poetry and bewildering bitterness.

Nené was a year and a few months old when her papà died. Ninì wasn't born yet, but he was on the way.

So. Had it not been for Ninì, perhaps his mamma, young and beautiful though she was, would not have thought of remarrying, but would have devoted herself entirely to little Nené. With her dowry and the small house her husband left her, she had enough to get by on her own, modestly.

But the thought of a boy to raise—knowing how inexperienced she was, and with no guidance or advice from relatives near or far—persuaded her to accept the proposal of a good young man, who promised to be an affectionate father to her poor fatherless children.

Nené was about three and Ninì a year and a half when their mamma remarried. Maybe because she was so concerned about Ninì, she didn't give much thought to the possibility of having more children with this new husband. But less than a year later, she almost died giving birth to twins. The doctors asked whom they should save, the mother or the tiny babies. The mother, of course! And the two infants were sacrificed. But in vain, for after a month or so of atrocious suffering, their poor unfortunate mamma died as well.

■ ■ ■

So Nené and Ninì were motherless now, left with someone whose name they didn't know, or even what he was doing there, in their house.

As for his name, had Nené and Ninì really wanted to know, the answer was easy: he was called Erminio Del Donzello, and he was a teacher: a French teacher in the technical school. But as for what he was still doing there, ah, not even he knew!

His wife was dead, his twin babies dead even before they were born, the house wasn't his, the dowry wasn't his, and those two children were not his. What *was* he still doing there? He asked himself the same question. But could he really leave?

Eyes red and dazed from weeping, he also asked all his neighbors, who, immediately after the tragedy, had entered the house as if they owned it, self-appointed tutors and protectors of the two little orphans. For which he might even have been grateful, had their manner not been so insulting.

He knew, of course, that, unfortunately, many people judge by appearances alone, and that the judgments they'd formed of him were most likely downright wicked, for his physical appearance didn't really help him much. His extreme scrawniness made him seem inconsequential. His neck was too long and—what's more— was equipped with a formidable Adam's apple, the only thing of any size amid all that scrawniness. His whiskers were coarse; his hair, combed in a fan behind his ears, was coarse; and his eyes were armored with frames since his nose was not fit for a more elegant pince-nez. Nevertheless, he was convinced—good God!—that he brought forth a most charming voice from that long neck, and that he accompanied his sweet, suave speech with gracious looks, smiles, and gestures, all while invariably wearing Lisle cotton gloves, which he never removed, not even at the technical school, while teaching French to the boys, who laughed about it, naturally.

Of course not! No compassion, no consideration for him in the entire neighborhood, for his double tragedy. It seemed, in fact, as if they all considered the death of his wife and twin babies a just and well-deserved punishment.

Their compassion was all for the two little orphans, whose fate they pondered in the abstract. So now their stepfather would, without a shadow of a doubt, take another wife: a shrew, obviously, a tyrant; with her he would have who knows how many offspring, whom Nené and Niní would be forced to wait upon until, from repeated abuse and torture, first one and then the other would be done away with.

Shudders of indignation and shivers of horror at such thoughts assailed the neighborhood men and women. And in this and that house, the two little children were hugged impetuously and bathed in tears.

For every morning now, in order to ingratiate himself with the hostile neighborhood and demonstrate his care and concern for the two little orphans, Erminio Del Donzello would, after carefully bathing and dressing them and before going to school, take them, one in each hand, and leave them now with this, now with that family of the many who offered to help.

In every family, each more charitable and concerned about the children's fate than the next, there was—naturally!—at least one marriageable young woman. And all of them, without exception, would make zealously affectionate mammas to those two little orphans. Only one would prove to be a perfidious tyrant, a ruthless shrew: whichever one Erminio Del Donzello chose.

For it was an inescapable necessity that Erminio Del Donzello marry again. The entire neighborhood was expecting it from one day to the next, and in truth, he was giving it serious thought as well.

How long could this go on? Those families offered with such zealous charity in order to entice him, no doubt about it. If he pretended for too long not to understand that, they would soon slam the door in his face — no doubt about that either. What then? Could he really care for those two little ones on his own? With school every morning, private lessons every afternoon, and homework to correct every evening . . . ? Take in a servant? Regardless of his appearance, he was young and warm-blooded. An old maid? But he had taken a wife because the bachelor's life of going around begging for love did not seem compatible with his age or dignity as a teacher. And now, with those two little ones . . .

No, really, it was an inescapable necessity, it truly was.

The embarrassment of choice, meanwhile, increased from day to day, and from day to day exasperated him even more.

And to think that, at first, given the circumstances, he had feared he would have a hard time finding a second wife! He needed a wife? He instantly found ten, twelve, fifteen of them, one more eager and impatient than the next!

Yes, okay, he was a widower, but, all things considered, only just barely; he'd hardly had time to be married, you could say. And as for the children, yes, they were there, but they weren't his. The house, meanwhile, at least until the children, who were still so young, came of age, was for him, as was the fruit of the dowry, which, together with his teaching salary, made for quite a nice little income.

Every neighborhood mother and young woman had done the math quite well. But Erminio Del Donzello was certain he would incur the wrath of hell if he chose a wife from among them.

He feared the mothers-in-law above all, and with good reason. Because, inevitably, all the disenchanted mothers would become his mothers-in-law; they would all appoint themselves posthumous mothers of his poor dead wife, and grandmothers of those two little orphans. And what sort of mother, what sort of grandmother, what sort of mother-in-law would Mrs. Ninfa in the house across the way be, for example? She who, more than all the others, had made and continued to make the most urgent display of every sort of service, together with her daughter Romilda and her son Toto!

They would come, all three of them, almost every morning and snatch the children from the house, to prevent him from taking them somewhere else. Come now, at least one of them! He had to give them at least one, either Nené or Ninì. Better Nené, oh, sweet girl! But Ninì too, sweet boy! And endless kisses and candies and caresses.

Erminio Del Donzello didn't know how to defend himself. Distressed, he would smile and turn this way and that, holding his gloved hands in front of his heart and twisting his neck like a stork:

"You see, my dear lady . . . my dear miss . . . I would not want to . . . I would not want to . . ."

"But let me say, Signor Del Donzello, let me say! You can rest assured that no one treats them as well as we do! My Romilda is crazy about them, you know, both of them? And look at my Toto! There he is . . . How about a piggyback ride, Ninì? My darling boy, how handsome you are! Toto, my dear! To', my love!"

Forced to give in, Erminio Del Donzello would walk away as if treading on thorns, turning this way and that and smiling, as if in apology to the other women in the neighborhood.

But while he, wearing his Lisle gloves, was teaching French to the boys at the technical school, what were the neighborhood women, in particular Signora Ninfa with her daughter Romilda and her son Toto, teaching Nené and Ninì? What prejudices, what suspicions did they insinuate in their little souls? And what fears?

Already Nené—who had grown into a pert, pretty little doll of a girl, with dimpled cheeks, a perky little mouth, sparkling eyes, and a sharp, cunning gaze, all jumps and starts and nervous giggles, her wild black hair always falling in her eyes however often she would toss it back with a quick, angry shake of her head—was determined to face boldly her future stepmother's imaginary threats, ill treatment, and abuses, with which the neighborhood women incensed her. And shaking her little fist, she would cry:

"I'll kill her!"

"Oh dear! My little love! What an angel! Yes, dear, you do that! Because it's all yours, you know? The house is yours, your mamma's dowry is yours, yours and your little brother's, understand? And it's up to you to defend him, your little brother! And if you need help, we're here to make them do what's right, her as well as him, don't you worry, we're here for you and Ninì!"

Ninì was a real teddy bear, big and placid, slightly bow-legged, and still stumbling over his words. When Nené raised her fist and cried, "I'll kill her!" he would slowly turn and stare at her, then ask in a hollow, placid voice: "You'd really hill her?"

And at this question, more outbursts of frenetic affection on the part of all those good neighborhood women.

■ ■ ■

Erminio Del Donzello realized all too well the fruits of these lessons when, after a year of hesitations and anguished perplexity, he finally chose a chaste old maid named Caterina—niece of a parish priest—married her, and brought her home.

The poor woman seemed to be reciting her prayers even when, with lowered eyes, she spoke about the shopping or the laundry. Yet every morning before leaving for school, Erminio Del Donzello would say to her:

"Remember, my dear Caterina. I know, I know how gentle you are. But please, try not to give all these vipers around here the least incentive to spit their venom. Make sure these little angels do not scream or cry for any reason. Remember."

Fine. But Nené's hair was snarled. Was she not supposed to comb it? Ninì, the little glutton, had a dirty snout, and dirty knees as well; was she not supposed to wash them?

"Nené, my little love, come here so I can comb your hair."

And Nené, stamping her foot:

"I don't want my hair combed!"

"Now now Ninì, at least you be good and come over here, my dear. Show your sister how you let me wash your face."

And Ninì, placid and dull, clumsily imitating his sister:

"I don't wanna be washed!"

And if Caterina forced them, even slightly, or went near them with comb or basin, their shrieks could be heard in the heavens!

And immediately the neighborhood women:

"Here it comes! Ah, those poor creatures! God have mercy, listen, listen! What is she doing? Ouch, yanking the girl's hair! And hear how she slaps the little one! Oh, what a disaster! God, God have pity on those poor innocent creatures!"

And if Caterina, so as not to make them scream, let Nené go around with her hair a mess and Nini all dirty:

"Would you look at what a state those two little loves are in: a disheveled puppy and a piglet!"

Some mornings Nené would sneak out of the house in her nightgown and bare feet. She would sit on the front steps, crossing her little legs and shaking her rebellious locks out of her eyes, laughing and announcing to everyone: "I'm being chastised!"

Shortly afterward, bow-legged Nini, he too in a nightshirt and bare feet, would slowly make his way down the stairs, holding his little tin chamber pot by the handle. He would place it on the step, sit down next to his sister, and, frowning, repeat in a serious yet baby voice:

"I'm be catsized!"

Imagine the indignant neighbors' cries of commiseration and outrage!

Here they are, naked, naked! What barbarity, and with this cold! They could die of bronchitis, or pneumonia, poor little creatures! How could God allow such a thing? Ah, really, they snuck out? They snuck out of bed, did they? And why did they do that?

A sign that these two little children, who knows how they're being treated! Ah, right, nothing . . . Churchgoing people, just imagine! Let's torment them without making them scream! Oh God, she's crying now, crocodile's tears!

A saint, even a saint would have lost her patience. That poor woman felt her heart tighten in her chest, not only for the cruel injustice, but also for the agony of watching that adorable little Nené growing into a devil, brought up by those vulgar, perfidious gossips, with no respect for anyone.

"This house is mine! The dowry is mine!"

Good Lord, the dowry! A little girl, only knee-high, screaming and shaking her fists and stamping her feet over a dowry!

Erminio Del Donzello seemed to have aged ten years in a few months.

He looked at his poor wife, who wept despairingly to him, but he didn't know what to say to her, just as he didn't know what to say to those two wild little devils.

Was the teacher at a loss for words? No. He didn't speak because he didn't feel well. And he didn't feel well because . . . because such is the destiny those two little ones bring with them, that's why!

Their father had died. And their mamma, in order to provide for them, had remarried. And died. And now . . . now it was his turn.

Of this Erminio Del Donzello was thoroughly convinced.

Now it was his turn!

Soon poor Caterina, his widow, in order to provide Nené and Ninì some guidance and support, would, in turn, marry again, and then she would die as well; and her second husband would then be compelled to take another wife. And so on and so on. An infinite succession of substitute parents would pass through that house in no time.

The fact that he already felt quite unwell was obvious proof.

It was destiny. There was nothing to do, nothing to say.

His wife, seeing that there was no way to shake him from that stupefying fixation, went to her uncle, the parish priest, for advice. He of course compelled her to obey her duty and her own conscience, without worrying about the vile protests of all those wicked neighbors. If those two little children could not be brought to reason with goodness, then by all means, she should use force!

Wise advice. But alas, its only effect was to hasten the end for the poor French teacher.

The first time Caterina put it into practice, Erminio Del Donzello, returning from school, saw Signora Ninfa's Toto, his face in his hands, coming toward him, followed by all the neighborhood women, shouting with raised arms.

His wife had had to barricade herself in the house. And there were guards and carabinieri at the door.

The entire neighborhood had signed a petition to present to police headquarters, in protest over the way those two little angels were being tortured.

The shame and trepidation at such an enormous scandal, and the anger at the persistent, ferocious iniquity, were such that Erminio Del Donzello, suffering a terrible and sudden excess of bile, arrived at death's door in a matter of days.

Before closing his eyes forever, he called his wife to his bedside and said in a faint voice:

"Let me give you some advice, my dear Caterina. Marry, my dear, marry Toto, Signora Ninfa's son. Don't worry; you will soon come join me. Leave it to him, then, him and another wife, to provide for those two little ones. You can be certain, dear, that he will soon die as well.

Nené and Ninì, meanwhile, at a neighbor's house, had found a tame little kitten and a small embalmed parrot, with which they were playing, happy and unaware.

"Meow, I'll strangle you!" said Nené.

And Ninì, tripping over his tongue, turned and said:

"You'd really tangle him?"

A BREATH OF AIR

Vivacious little Tittì, with her sparkling eyes, blond hair, slender arms, bare little legs, and an urge to laugh that, catching in her throat, explodes in short shrill cries, burst into the room and raced over to the balcony to open the glass door.

She'd barely managed to turn the handle. A hoarse, harsh growl, like that of a wild beast surprised in its sleep, stopped her suddenly. She swung around, terrified, and peered into the room.

Darkness.

The interior shutters were still half-closed.

Blinded by the light from the hallway, she couldn't see anything, but could feel, frighteningly, in the darkness the presence of her grandfather in his chaise: that tremendous obstacle bundled in gray checked shawls, coarse, hairy blankets, and pillows; the stench of old age, bloated and overripe, in the inertia of paralysis.

But it wasn't his presence that terrified her. What terrified her was the fact that she could have forgotten for a moment that there in this darkness of eternally closed shutters was her grandfather, and that, without even thinking about it, she could have transgressed her parents' strictest command, issued long ago and always observed by all, never to enter that room without first knocking and asking permission—what was it she was supposed to say?—*May I,*

Grandfather dear?—right, like that, and then, slowly slowly, on tiptoe, without making the least noise.

Her urge to laugh when first entering the room faded instantly to a gasp, and was about to swell into sobs.

So, quiet as a mouse, the tiptoeing, trembling little girl, thinking she couldn't be seen, never imagining that the old man, accustomed to the dark shadows, could see her, crept toward the door. She'd almost made it when her grandfather called her over with an imperious, severe "Here!"

Dismayed, holding her breath, and still tiptoeing, the little girl anxiously approached him. She, too, was finally beginning to make things out in the darkness. Catching sight of her grandfather's piercing, wicked eyes, she immediately lowered her own.

Vigilant with terror and burning with mute, ferocious resentment, the old man's soul, having been driven out of the rest of his body, which death had already invaded and rendered immobile, seemed concentrated in those eyes with their swollen, watery lids, the dull redness of which made one think with disgust of the slimy touch of a tarantula.

The only thing he could still move—and that just barely—was one hand, the left one, and only after staring at it for a long time with those eyes of his, as if to instill it with movement. The effort of will, upon reaching his wrist, scarcely managed to lift his hand off the covers slightly, and only for a second; then it would fall back again, inert.

The old man persisted in that exercise of will because this slight, momentary movement which he could still elicit from his body was for him life, all there was of life, in which others moved about freely and participated fully, in which he too could still participate, but just that much—no more.

"B . . . but why . . . the balcony? . . ." babbled his tongue-tied little granddaughter.

He didn't answer. She continued to tremble. But in that trembling the old man perceived something new: it wasn't her usual trembling with fear, which the little girl barely suppressed whenever her father or mother forced her near him. There was fear, but something else too, beneath it, suffocated by the fear that his harsh, sudden call had caused: something else, which turned her trembling into a quiver. A strange quiver.

"What's wrong?" he asked her.

The little girl, hardly daring to raise her eyes, answered:

"Nothing."

But the old man perceived something unusual in her voice now too, even in her breath. He repeated, with more rancor:

"What's wrong?"

A sudden burst of sobs. And the little girl immediately threw herself to the floor, convulsing, shouting, and writhing amid her sobs, with a violence and fury that oppressed and irritated the old man even more, for they, too, struck him as unusual.

His daughter-in-law ran into the room, shouting:

"Oh god, Tittì, what happened? What now? Here? What's come over you? Now, now . . . enough! Come here, come to mamma . . . How did you get in here? What are you saying? Bad? Who? Ah . . . Grandfather's bad? You're bad . . . Grandfather, Grandfather who loves you so much . . . What happened?"

The old man, to whom this last question was addressed, glared ferociously at his daughter-in-law's smiling red lips, then at her beautiful golden-blond bangs, which the little girl, now writhing in her mother's arms, tousled with her hand, insisting that they leave the room right away.

"Tittì, ouch! My hair . . . oh God . . . you're pulling out all mamma's hair, bad girl! See? Look . . . look at all mamma's hair in your hand . . . mamma's hair . . . look, look . . ."

And as she disentangled first one and then another and then another gold strand from her daughter's tiny fingers, she kept saying:

"Look . . . look . . . look . . ."

The little girl, instantly upset to think she really had pulled out all her mother's hair, gazed at her hand, eyes brimming with tears. Not seeing anything, but hearing instead her mother's full, gay laugh, she grew furious again, more furious, and forced her to flee the room.

The old man was breathing heavily. A question was gurgling up inside him, sharpening his rancor.

What's wrong with them? What is wrong?

He had perceived something unusual, out of the ordinary, in his daughter-in-law's eyes, her voice, in her laugh even, as well as in the way she had disentangled her hair from her daughter's tiny fingers.

No, they weren't the same as every other day, neither the little girl nor his daughter-in-law. What was wrong?

And his rancor increased even more when, lowering his eyes to the blanket spread across his legs, he spotted a golden-blond strand, which, carried perhaps on the breath of her laugh, had come to rest ever so lightly there, on his dead legs.

He insisted for a long time, impelling the hand on his legs to move closer, little by little, in small fits and starts, to that hair, which was as odious to him as a jeer. And this was how—breathless from the vain effort, which, lasting half an hour already, had exhausted him—he was found by his son, who, before leaving the house to go about his business every morning, would come to his father's room to greet him.

"Good morning, papà!"

The old man lifted his head. His eyes widened with a dark look of frightful astonishment. His son, too?

The young man, who thought his father was looking at him like that to let him know that he had not appreciated his granddaughter's disobedience, hastened to say:

"A little devil, isn't she? She disturbed you. Do you hear that? She's still crying out there . . . I scolded her, yes, I did. Goodbye, papà. I'm in a rush. See you later, okay? Nerina will be right in."

And he left.

The old man's eyes, still full of astonishment and fear, followed him to the door.

Him too, his son! He'd never used that tone of voice before: "Good morning, papà!" Why? What did he want? Were they all conspiring against him? What had happened? That little girl, who'd come in first, all stirred up . . . then her mother, with that laugh . . . about her hair being yanked out . . . and now his son, his son even, with that cheery *"Good morning, papà!"*

Something had happened, or was going to happen, that day, something they wanted to conceal from him. But what?

They had appropriated the world, his son, daughter-in-law,

and granddaughter had, the world he had created, into which he'd brought them. And not only that; they'd appropriated time as well, as if he too were not in time! As if time weren't also his, as if he didn't see it, breathe it, think about it too! He was still breathing, he saw everything and more—more than them—and he thought about everything!

A muddle of images and memories tossed and turned inside him, as if in a tempestuous flash. La Plata, the *pampas*, the salty swamps of lost rivers, the countless herds champing, bleating, grazing, bellowing. He had built his fortune there, out of nothing, in forty-five years, making use of every means and every art, seizing the moment, or astutely setting snares and then sitting tight: first as a gaucho, then as a farmer, then as a hired hand on big railroad contracts, and finally as a builder. After the first fifteen years, returning to Italy, he had taken a wife, and then, right after the birth of his only son, had gone back there, alone. His wife died without his ever seeing her again; his son, given into the care of his mother's relatives, grew up without his knowing him. Four years ago he repatriated, a half-dead invalid: horribly bloated with dropsy, oxidized arteries, ruined kidneys, a ruined heart. But he didn't give up: even like that, his days—maybe even his hours—numbered, he had wanted to purchase some land in Rome, to build some new buildings, and he broke ground right away, having himself carried there in a wheelchair so he could live amid the workers, in the chaos of construction: as rough as a rock, bloated, enormous. Every fifteen days he would have liters of serum extracted from his stomach, then back to the construction site, until an attack of apoplexy, two years ago, had struck him down, right in his chair, but without finishing him off. It had not been granted to him to die with his boots on. His whole body was shot, he was wasting away, awaiting the final end, full of rancor for that son, so different from him, a stranger practically, who, without needing to, after winding up the construction projects and investing his father's vast wealth, carried on with his modest legal affairs, almost as if to deny him even the smallest satisfaction, and to vindicate his mother's as well as his own long abandonment.

No communion of life, ideas, or sentiments with that son of his. He hated him, and he hated his daughter-in-law, and the little girl too: yes, yes, he hated them, hated them because they left him out of their lives and didn't . . . they didn't even want to tell him what had happened that morning, the reason all three of them seemed so different from usual.

Large tears oozed from his eyes. Completely unmindful of what he had been for so many years, he gave himself over to weeping, like a baby.

■ ■ ■

Nerina, the servant, took no notice of his weeping when she came in a short while later to look after him. The old man was full of water: nothing wrong, then, if he shed a bit though his eyes. And with that thought in mind, she unceremoniously dried his face and then picked up the bowl of milk, dipped a ladyfinger in it, and started feeding him.

"Eat, eat."

He ate, but kept stealing glances at her. At a certain point he heard her sigh, but not with tiredness or boredom. He immediately looked up and stared her in the face. There, she was about to sigh again, that coquette. Seeing herself stared at, instead of sighing, she blew air out her nose, shaking her head as if vexed. And why did she turn red like that, all of a sudden? What was wrong with her today?

So all, all of them, then, were acting unusual today? He didn't want to eat any more.

"What's wrong?" he angrily asked her too.

"Me? What?" Nerina said, stunned by his question.

"You . . . all of you . . . what is it, what's wrong?"

"Nothing . . . I don't know . . . what is it you see?"

"You're sighing!"

"Me? I sighed? No! Or maybe I did, but without meaning to. I really don't have anything to sigh about."

And she laughed.

"Why are you laughing like that?"

"Like what? I'm laughing because . . . because you said I sighed." And she laughed harder now, uncontrollably.

"Go!" the old man shouted.

■ ■ ■

Late in the day, when the doctor arrived for his usual visit and the old man's daughter-in-law, son, and granddaughter came back in the room, the suspicion he'd been harboring all day, even during his sleep, that something had happened, something they all wanted to keep from him, became crystal clear, a certainty.

They were all in agreement. To distract his attention, they talked of incomprehensible things; but their secret understanding was perfectly obvious in their looks. They had never looked at each other that way before! Their gestures, voices, and smiles did not at all match what they were saying. All that heated discussion about wigs, wigs! which were coming back into style!

"Excuse me, but green? Green, violet?" his daughter-in-law, all red, shrieked with feigned anger, so feigned that she couldn't keep her mouth from laughing.

Her mouth was laughing all on its own, it was. And her hands rose on their own to caress her hair, as if her hair wished to be caressed by her hands.

"I see, I see," the doctor replied, beatitude painted on his entire, full-moon face. "It would be a sin to hide hair like yours under a wig."

By now the old man could barely contain his fury. He would have liked to throw them out of the room with a bestial roar. But as soon as the doctor took his leave and the daughter-in-law, holding the little girl's hand, saw him out, his fury broke on his son, who had stayed there with him. He assailed him with the same question he had vainly asked his granddaughter and the servant:

"What's wrong? Why are you all like this today? What has happened? What are you hiding from me?"

"Nothing, papà! What would we be hiding from you?" the son replied, stunned and distressed. "We're . . . I don't know, we're just how we've always been."

"That's not true! There's something new, I can see it, I can feel it! Do you think—because I'm like this—I don't see anything, don't feel anything?"

"Truly, papà, I don't know what you think you see in us. Nothing has happened, I swear, I double swear! Come on, relax!"

His son's sincere tone calmed him down a little, but he still wasn't convinced. There was something new, it was undeniable. He could see it, feel it in them.

But what?

When he was alone in the room, the answer came to him suddenly, silently, from the balcony.

In early evening, the balcony door, the handle of which had remained unlatched since the little girl turned it this morning, now opened slowly, just a little, with a breath of air.

At first the old man didn't notice; but then he smelled the whole room filling with a delightful, intoxicating perfume that rose up from the garden and encircled the house. He turned and saw a ribbon of moonlight on the floor, like the luminous trace of that perfume, in the dark shadows of his room.

"Ah, that's it . . . that's it . . ."

The others couldn't see it, couldn't feel it themselves, because they were still inside life. But he, nearly outside it now, had seen it, had felt it in them. So that's why, that's why, this morning, the little girl wasn't just trembling, but quivering all over; that's why his daughter-in-law laughed and was so delighted with her hair; that's why the servant was sighing; that's why all of them had that unusual, new air about them, without even being aware of it.

■ ■ ■

Spring had entered his room.

FAITH

Into that priest's humble little room full of light and peace, with its old Valenza bricks that here and there had lost their glaze and on which a rectangle of sunlight from the window stretched silently and softly through gold-flecked dust motes, bricks stamped with crisp shadows of the embroidered curtains and even the green cage hanging from the shelf with the canary hopping about inside, there wafted the smell of just-baked bread from the oven in the little courtyard below, a warm breath that melded with the damp odor of incense from the nearby chapel and the pungent scent of lavender sprigs tucked among the linens in the old highboy.

It seemed as if nothing more could ever happen in that little room. The sunlight was still; still, the peace; still, the blades of grass between the gray cobblestones in the small courtyard below the window; still, the stalks of hay fallen from the feeding trough in a corner beneath the roof of blood-red tiles, and the tiny pebbles that had tumbled down from the steep, rough slope above.

Inside, small, tidy old chairs, painted black, sat on either side of the highboy. With small silver crosses on their backs, they seemed like little old nuns, content to stay there, sheltered and safe and untouched, and happy to gaze on the priest's modest little iron bed with the black cross and fine, old yellowed ivory crucifix on the whitewashed wall above the headboard.

Most notable was the large wax Baby Jesus on top of the high-boy, in a sky-blue silk-lined basket, protected from the flies by a thin veil, also sky blue. A tiny hand under his chubby little cheek, he seemed to be making the most of the silent sunlight to sleep his rosy sleep amid those mingling scents of incense, lavender, and warm, homemade bread.

Don Pietro was sleeping too, his bald, shriveled head tilted pathetically against the back of the small jute armchair at the foot of the bed. But his was a very different sleep. The slack-jawed sleep of a sick old man. His thin eyelids seemed to lack the strength to close over the hard, aching globes of his clouded eyes. His nostrils narrowed with the weary whistle of his irregular breathing, which revealed the infirmity of his heart.

In his sleep, his haggard, yellow, angular face had assumed a nasty, vulgar expression: a betrayal, it seemed, as if, during his momentary absence, his miserable and desperately exhausted body were trying to avenge itself on his spirit, which, for so many years and with such an austere will, had tortured and reduced it to servitude. With that vulgar abandon, that drool dangling from his saggy lip, his body was trying to say it couldn't take it anymore, and so manifested its repugnant, bestial suffering.

Don Angelino, after bursting into the room, had halted immediately, then continued forward on tiptoe. He'd been silently contemplating the sleeping figure for ten minutes now, but with an exasperated anguish that was gradually turning to rage, his fists opening and closing so tightly that his fingernails sunk into his flesh. He would have liked to cry out, waking him up:

"I've made up my mind, Don Pietro: I'm leaving the priest-hood!"

But he forced himself to hold his breath, for fear that, if that saintly old man awoke, he would suddenly find him there in all his infuriated anguish, which must show in his eyes and his disgusted expression. He was even tempted to swat the birdcage hanging from the shelf and send it flying out the window, so fearful was he that the annoying rasp of the canary's tiny feet on the zinc bottom would wake him.

■ ■ ■

For more than four hours the day before, pacing back and forth in that little room, gesticulating wildly, thrashing his whole frame, kicking at his priest's cassock, as if to strip it off or keep it from touching his rebellious little body, he had argued fiercely with Don Pietro about his resolution to abandon the priesthood. Not because he had lost his faith. No. But because, with all his studies and medi-tations, he was sincerely convinced he had acquired another faith, freer and more alive, and thus could no longer accept or endure the dogmas, obligations, and mortifications the old one imposed on him. The argument had grown heated, on his side only—not over Don Pietro's replies as much as his own increasing self-contempt at his unsurmountable, absurd need to confide in this aged saint who had been his teacher and then his confessor for so many years, even though he knew he was incapable of comprehending his torments, anguish, and desperation.

And as a matter of fact, Don Pietro had let him vent, half

closing his eyes now and then and smiling ever so slightly with those white lips of his—a good-natured, ironic little smile for which his lips were no longer suited—or murmuring indulgently, without the least hint of scorn: "Vanity . . . vanity . . ."

Another faith? What other faith, as there is only one? Freer? More alive? Ah, so that was where the vanity lay. Something he would come to realize all too well, after his youthful impulse had passed, his diabolical fervor was spent, and the blood in his veins cooled. His impudent eyes would no longer burn and, white-haired or bald, he would not be so handsome, or so proud. In short, Don Pietro had treated him like a child. Yes, like a good boy who would not create the scandal he was threatening to, partly for the sorrow it would cause his elderly mother, who had sacrificed so much for him.

At the thought of his mamma, Don Angelino's eyes stung with tears again. But it was precisely for her, precisely for his elderly mother that he had come to this resolution, so as to stop deceiving her. And also because it was agony to see her venerate him like some minor saint. What cruelty, what a cruel spectacle, the old man's sleep was! There, in the infinite privation of that worn-out, neglected body was the clearest proof of the new truths that had revealed themselves to him.

But just then, the door to the little room opened and Don Pietro's elderly sister entered: tiny, waxen, dressed in black, with a black wool kerchief on her head, and even more stooped and trembling than her brother. It was as if Don Angelino's own mother— tiny, waxen, and dressed in black, just as this woman was—had entered the room, summoned by his tears. He looked at her in despair, not understanding at first her gesture, which seemed to ask: "Is he sleeping?"

Don Angelino nodded.

"And you, why are you crying?"

But the old man opened his blank eyes now. Mouth still agape, he lifted his head from the back of the chair.

"Ah, Angelino, is that you? What is it?"

Don Pietro's sister approached and, bending over his chair, whispered a few words in his ear. Don Pietro struggled to his feet, shuffled over to Don Angelino, and rested a hand on his shoulder.

"Would you do me a favor, my son? An old widow has arrived from the countryside, and she's asking for me. As you see, I can barely stand. Would you like to go in my place? She's down in the sacristy; you can take the back stairs here. Go, go, you've always been a good son to me. And may God bless you!"

Don Angelino left without saying a word. Perhaps without even fully understanding. In Don Pietro's dark, narrow spiral staircase he stopped and rested his head on his hand, which he'd been running along the wall as he descended, and wept again like a child. A suffocating sob that burned his eyes. A sob of humiliation, rage, and pity all together. When he reached the sacristy, he suddenly felt alienated from everything. It seemed different, as if he were entering it for the first time. Frigid, bleak, and brightly lit. He found the old woman sitting there, but didn't quite understand what she was waiting for. She almost didn't seem real to him.

A decrepit peasant, bundled up and filthy, her bloodshot eyelids hideously turned out. She mumbled endlessly, her pointy chin bouncing and almost touching her nose. In one hand she clutched two young cocks by their feet, and resting in the palm of the other were three silver *lira* coins, saved for who knows how long. Her feet were buried in a pair of enormous, shabby men's shoes, and near them on the floor sat a dirty knapsack full of dried almonds and walnuts.

Don Angelino looked at her in disgust.

"What do you want?"

Straining to see him, the old woman babbled something, her tongue tangling between toothless gums in her flabby, hollow cheeks.

"What did you say? I can't hear you. Your name is Zia Croce[1]?"

Yes, Zia Croce. She was Zia Croce. Don Pietro knew her well. Croce Scoma, whose husband had died many years ago, drowned in the Naro River. She'd walked here, with that knapsack on her back, from the Cannatello plains. More than seven miles. And with this offering of two cocks and a knapsack full of almonds and walnuts and the three *lire* for mass, she intended (Don Pietro knew) to placate Saint Calogero, saint of all mercy, who had cured her son of a deadly disease. As soon as he was healed, however, he had gone off to America. He had promised to write, and to send her enough to live on, every month. Sixteen months had passed. No word of him. She didn't even know if he was alive or dead. If she could at least know he was alive, well, never mind then that he never sent her anything. But no letter, not even one line! Nothing. Everyone told her it was because she had not fulfilled her vow to Saint Calogero

---

1. *Croce* means cross, and *Zia* or "Aunt" is a typical title for elderly women in southern Italy.

right after her son's recovery. Of course that's why, even she realized that. But (Don Pietro knew) that was because her son's illness
had stripped her of everything. She barely had eyes left to weep. To
weep blood, yes, blood! Then, with her son gone, old and without
any help as she was, how was she to save up the offering and those
three *lire* for mass, when she barely earned enough to keep from
dying of hunger every day? Sixteen months it had taken her, and
with what sacrifices, only God knows! But now, here were the two
cocks, and here were the three *lire*, and the almonds and the walnuts. The merciful San Calogero would be placated, and soon, no
doubt about it, she would receive news from America that her son
was alive and well.

While the old woman talked, Don Angelino paced back and
forth in the sacristy, casting his ferocious eyes this way and that and
opening and closing his hands. He was tempted to grab her by the
shoulders and shake her furiously, shouting in her face:

"This is your faith?"

But no. Other people, maybe, but not this poor old woman.
He would have liked to grab his fellow priests by the shoulders and
shake them, his fellow priests who held so many poor people in
such abjectness of faith, and who made money off that abjectness.
Oh God, how could they accept this old woman's three *lire* to say
mass, or her cocks or almonds and walnuts?

"Take your knapsack and get out of here!" he shouted, trembling all over.

She stared at him, astounded.

"You can go, I'm telling you," Don Angelino added, growing
even more furious. "San Calogero doesn't need your cocks or your

dried figs! If your son has something to say to you, you can be sure he will write. As for the mass, Don Pietro is ill. Go! Go!"

The old woman seemed stunned by his furious language.

"What are you saying? Don't you understand that this is a vow? A vow!"

There was such bewilderment in that word, simple though it was, incredulity almost, at his incomprehension, that Don Angelino was forced to fix his attention on it. He checked himself, remembering that he was there in place of Don Pietro. In less ferocious language, he tried to persuade the old woman to take back her cocks and almonds and walnuts, and told her that, as for the mass, well, if she really wanted, perhaps he could say it instead of Don Pietro, but only on the condition that she kept her three *lire*.

The old woman turned and looked at him, in terror almost, and said again:

"But how? What are you saying? What sort of vow would it be then? If I don't give what I promised, what is my vow worth? Excuse me, but who am I talking to? Aren't I talking to a priest? So why do you treat me this way? Or maybe you think I'm not giving everything I promised San Calogero with all my heart? Oh God! Oh God! Because I told you how much I struggled to gather it?"

She began to weep desperately, with those horrible, bloodshot eyes.

Moved and full of remorse, Don Angelino repented of his severity, suddenly overcome by such respect for that old woman weeping over her offended faith that he felt humiliated, ashamed. He went over and comforted her, told her that was not what he was thinking, and that she should leave everything, yes, even the three *lire*. And that in the meantime he would go into the church and say mass for her, right away.

He called the sacristan and ran to the washbasin. While the sacristan helped him robe, he contemplated how, after mass, he would find a way to give her back her three *lire* and her cocks and her knapsack of walnuts. But now, in order for her offering to be worthy enough to be acceptable to that poor old woman, did it not also require something from him, something he no longer felt he had? What offering would it be—three *lire*—if, after all the hard-ships and sacrifices that old woman had endured to fulfill her vow, he did not celebrate mass with more sincere and ardent fervor? An unworthy pretense, for three *lire* of alms?

Don Angelino, robed now, chalice in hand, uncertain and op-pressed by anguish, stopped for an instant on the threshold of the sacristy and peered into the deserted church. Was it advisable to approach the altar, devoid of faith as he was? But then he saw the old woman prostrate before it, forehead to the floor, and he felt his entire breast lift, as if from a breath not his own, and his back was pierced by a strange, new sensation. Oh, why had he always imag-ined faith to be beautiful and radiant like the sun? Here was faith, here, in the misery of that kneeling pain, in the wretched poverty of that prostrate fear!

Don Angelino approached the altar as if propelled, exalted by such faith that his hands trembled. His entire soul trembled, just as it had the first time he drew near it.

Eyes closed, entering into the soul of that old woman as into a dark, narrow temple where the altar of faith burned, he prayed for that faith. In that temple he prayed to God, whatever he was, whatever he might be, yet surely the sole good, sole consolation for such misery.

■ ■ ■

And when the mass was over, he did not return the three *lire* and the offering, so as not to diminish with a small gift the great gift of faith.

Every year it was a disgraceful display of power, a shameful high-handedness on the part of the entire peasantry of Montelusa toward the poor priests of our glorious Cathedral.

The statue of Our Lady of the Immaculate Conception, kept all year in a cabinet in the sacristy of the Church of Saint Francis of Assisi, on December 8 would be adorned with gold and gems and a silver-starred, blue silk mantle and, after solemn ceremonies inside the church, carried on a litter through the steep streets of Montelusa, past crumbling houses crowding against each other, up, up to the Cathedral at the top of the hill, to be left there for the night, the guest of Montelusa's patron saint, Saint Gerland.

Our Lady of the Immaculate Conception was supposed to remain in the Cathedral from Thursday evening till Sunday morning: two and a half days. But as this seemed too brief, custom was to let her stay that first Sunday after her feast day, waiting till the following Sunday to transport her, with even greater pomp, back to the Church of Saint Francis.

Except that, nearly every year, bad weather prevented the procession from taking place that second Sunday, so it had to be postponed till the following Sunday, and, from Sunday to Sunday, sometimes for several months.

Now, this prolonged hospitality, in and of itself, would not have been an issue had not Our Lady of the Immaculate Conception, by ancient right, enjoyed a prebend[1] for the entire length of her stay in the Cathedral. Every day she was there, it was as if the Cathedral Chapter had another canon: she earned as much as a canon, on obsequies and everything else; and the deputies of the congregation kept close watch to make sure she was not shortchanged, so that, with the fruits of her prebend, the feast day in her honor would, with each passing year, become more splendid. This, in addition to all the other expenses relating to her stay which weighed on the Chapter, expenses and labor: masses every day, a sermon every day, firecrackers and rockets, and, for the poor sacristan, lengthy bell ringing every morning and every evening.

Perhaps, for love of the Blessed Virgin, the Cathedral canons might have tolerated in peace and decrease the labor and the expense, had the belief not taken root among the peasantry of Montelusa that the Immaculate Conception wanted to remain in the Cathedral for a month or two precisely to spite the canons, who every year lifted their hands to the heavens and prayed it would not rain, at least on the Sunday of the second procession.

It so happened that, at this same time of year, the peasants were perennially dissatisfied with the amount of water the heavens sent for their crops; and so, if some year it really didn't rain, blame fell on the Cathedral canons, who couldn't wait to be relieved of the Immaculate Conception.

Well then, in the long run, the Cathedral canons, from hearing it said over and over, did, in fact, grow spiteful. Not with the Virgin

---

1. The stipend that a beneficed canon of a cathedral receives.

exactly, but with those churlish boors, and even more with those upstarts in the congregation who, not content to fan the peasants' shameful belief in their spitefulness for the Virgin, grew so insolent as to send, every Saturday as evening was setting in, three or four of the cheekier ones to the piazza, to stroll past the Cathedral, hands behind their backs and noses in the air, waiting for a canon to come out. Whom they would then ask, with a foolish grin:

"Excuse me, Canon, sir, what do you think? Will it rain tomorrow, or not?"

■ ■ ■

It was, as you can see, an intolerable irreverence.

Monsignor Partanna should have put a stop to it, at all costs. All the more so as everyone knew that those congregation friars, in their frenzy to make money any way they could, went so far as to speculate shamefully on the Blessed Virgin, pawning at the Catholic Bank of Saint Gaetano the gold, gems, and even the starry mantle she had received from her faithful followers.

The Lord Bishop should have ordered that the Immaculate Conception was to be returned to the Church of Saint Francis no later than the second Sunday after her feast day, regardless of the weather, rain or no rain. After all, there was no danger of her getting wet under the magnificent baldachin that the most robust seminary students took turns carrying.

It was the peasants' wives, rather, the women of Montelusa or—as the reverend canons of the Chapter kept saying—the trollops, the trollops who were afraid of getting wet, saying it was the Virgin Mary! They didn't want to ruin the silk dresses they donned for the procession, a sacrilegious, vain spectacle: all of them posing like the Immaculate Conception, their hands—rings on every finger—open in front of their hearts, silk shawls pinned to their shoulders, eyes turned heavenward, and all their pendants and big teardrop earrings and brooches and bracelets jiggling with each step.

But the Lord Bishop refused to see.

Perhaps, now that he was old and decrepit, he too was afraid of getting wet and catching something, walking bareheaded in the rain behind the litter; and little did he care that the poor Chapter vicar, Monsignor Lentini, who had delivered so many sermons that year—one a day, all on the same topic—had been reduced to such a state that even the church pews felt sorry for him.

It had already been eleven Sundays now, eleven, since December 8, when, as his elderly housekeeper Piconella, who brought him his coffee in bed every morning, entered, the poor man lifted his head from his pillow and asked, mournfully:

"Is it raining?"

Piconella didn't know what to say anymore. Because it truly did seem that the weather enjoyed tormenting that good man, and with unbelievably refined cruelty. Some Sundays would start off sunny, so Piconella, jubilant, would run to tell the Lord Bishop the news:

"Sun, Lord Bishop, sun! sun!"

And the sacristan would festively peal the bells, *din don dan, din don dan*, for the Immaculate Conception would certainly be gone before noon.

Except that, after people had begun pouring into the piazza for the procession; and even the seminary staircase's iron door, through which the Blessed Virgin would exit every year, had been opened;

and the seminary students had arrived, two by two in their embroidered gowns; and firecrackers had been placed all around the piazza, here came the thunder and lightning as a new storm blew in suddenly from the sea.

The sacristan, to avert it, rang the bells again over the furor of the crowd, who in the meantime had taken to protesting, incensed that the canons rashly sought to send away the Blessed Virgin in this impending threat.

Yelling and hissing and tongue-lashing in front of the Bishop's palace, until, to restore the peace, the Lord Bishop had one of his secretaries announce that the procession would be postponed until the following Sunday, weather permitting.

■ ■ ■

Five Sundays out of eleven, the scene was repeated.

That eleventh Sunday, as soon as the piazza had emptied out, the Chapter canons all burst into the vicar's home. A remedy had to be found—at all costs, at all costs—for this brutal abuse of power!

Poor Monsignor Lentini, holding his head in his hands, gave them a dazed look.

The yelling and hissing and threatening had been hurled more at him than at them. But that wasn't the reason he looked dazed. Another week of sermons on the Immaculate Conception, after eleven already! That was all he could think about just then, and the thought made his head spin.

Monsignor Landolina, the dreaded rector of the Oblate School, finally came up with the remedy. It was enough to utter a name to set their troubled minds to rest.

"Mèola! We need Mèola! My friends, we need to call on Mèola!"

Marco Mèola, the ferocious anticlerical tribune who, four years earlier, had sworn to save Montelusa from the threat of invasion by the Redemptorist Fathers, had by now lost all his popularity. Though it was true, on the one hand, that he had kept his promise, on the other it was no less true that the ways and means he used, and then the kidnapping, and the riches he received as a result, did not lend credence to his claim that his had been a heroic sacrifice. Though Monsignor Partanna's niece, the girl he kidnapped from the convent, was, in fact, an ugly hunchback, the dowry the Bishop was forced to provide was beautiful and bountiful. And all things considered, the Montelusa clergy bigwigs, who'd never really swallowed their Bishop's promise to bring back the Redemptorist Fathers, had, even after the elopement, or rather because of it, continued secretly — not an open friendship exactly — to look favorably on Marco Mèola.

Nevertheless, it certainly must have pleased him that, without risk of losing his secret friends, he now had an opportunity to win back the esteem of his old comrades as well as his prestige as an anticlerical tribune.

So — two trustworthy friends would have to be sent furtively to Mèola, to propose, in the name of the entire Chapter, that, this coming Sunday, he give a lecture against religious holidays in general, and sacred processions in particular, using as a pretext the deplorable chaos of the previous Sundays: all that yelling, hissing, and tongue-lashing in order to keep the Immaculate Conception from returning to the Church of Saint Francis.

Once word of the lecture had spread throughout the town, the Bishop would be easily persuaded to publish an indignant protest against the patent violation of religious freedom that the liberals of Montelusa—enemies of the faith—had in mind, and a sacred invitation to all the faithful of the diocese for the coming Sunday, *whatever the weather, rain or no rain,* to gather in the Cathedral piazza in order to defend from every possible abuse the venerated image of the Immaculate Conception.

The Chapter canons unanimously accepted and approved Monsignor Landolina's proposal.

Only that saintly vicar Monsignor Lentini dared to invite his colleagues to consider if it were not imprudent to cause trouble on the other side, to stir up that hornet's nest. But once it was suggested to him that he could base the coming week's sermons on Mèola's lecture, preaching against an intolerance that strove to prevent the faithful from manifesting their devotion to the Virgin, after several "I see, but . . . I see, but . . ."s, he finally gave up.

■ ■ ■

Monsignor Landolina's brilliant idea had a far greater impact than the Chapter canons ever intended.

After four years of silence, Marco Mèola hurled himself into the fray like a starved lion. After just two days of scuttlebutt in the civil servants' clubs, and in the Pedoca café, he managed to cause so much unrest that the Lord Bishop really was forced to respond with a fierce pastoral, and in his sacred invitation for the coming Sunday he called on all the faithful not only of Montelusa, but also of nearby towns.

The invitation concluded: *"Even were it to pour, we are confident that the fiercest storm will not dampen in the least your sacred
and most fervent ardor. Even were it to pour, this coming Sunday
the Immaculate Conception will leave our glorious Cathedral and,
escorted and protected by all the faithful of our diocese, return to her
residence."*

■■■

But lo and behold, after such a long stretch of bad weather, that
twelfth Sunday brought the laughter of springtime, the first of the
season, and with it such sweetness that every turbulence suddenly
vanished from people's minds, as if by magic.

At the festive peal of the bells, all of Montelusa came out into
the bright air, to drink in the sensual warmth of the first sun of the
new season; a liquid smile of bliss on everyone's lips, and a delicious
languor in every limb, a heartfelt desire to give in to warm, frater-
nal embraces.

So the Chapter vicar, Monsignor Lentini, who from Monday
to Saturday of that twelfth week had had to deliver six more sermons on the Immaculate Conception, quietly gathered the Chapter canons around him and asked if it were not possible to somehow
prevent the — by now — pointless scandal of Mèola's anticlerical lecture, which was like a thorn in his side.

It was certain not to rain, not that day, not for months. Couldn't
Mèola get sick and put off his lecture for some other time, the following year perhaps, the second Sunday of rain after December 8?

"Oh, right! Of course!" the canons understood immediately.
"That way the remedy won't be wasted!"

The same two trustworthy friends were hurried off to Mèola. A cold, constipation, an attack of gout, a sudden bout of laryngitis:

"Seeing as it's not raining . . ."

Mèola was recalcitrant, outraged. Cancel? Postpone? Oh no, for God's sake, they were asking too much of him, now that he'd managed to win over Montelusa's liberals again!

"Okay," his two friends said. "If it were raining . . . But seeing as it's not raining . . ."

"Seeing as it's not raining," Mèola thundered, "what is the Provincial Prefect doing? Only he, only he can prohibit the lecture now, for the sake of public order! So, seeing as it's not raining, go to the Prefect then, right away, and I, in bed with a raging fever, could receive the prohibition order in an hour!"

■ ■ ■

And so, on February 25, without any disturbance, the Immaculate Conception returned to the Church of Saint Francis of Assisi after spending twelve Sundays in the Cathedral. And the people's rejoicing over how the good weather had defeated the liberals of Montelusa was truly extraordinary that year.

A "GOY"

My friend Mr. Daniele Catellani, with a handsome head of curly hair and a big nose—the hair and nose of his race—has one bad habit: he laughs deep in his throat. It's so irritating that people are often tempted to slap him.

All the more so because, immediately afterward, he agrees with what you're telling him, agrees with a nod and a hasty "Right, right! Right, right!"

As if it weren't your very words that had just provoked such disrespectful laughter in him.

You're still irritated and disconcerted, naturally. But rest assured that Mr. Daniele Catellani will do as you say. It's never the case that he objects to other people's opinions, proposals, or observations.

But first he laughs.

Maybe because, having been caught unawares in some abstract world of his, so different from the one you suddenly call him back to, he has the same sensation a horse has at times, when it flares its nostrils and neighs.

■ ■ ■

Besides, there exists abundant proof, the sincerity of which I believe it would be a sign of inordinate diffidence to doubt, of Mr. Daniele

Catellani's submissiveness and goodwill to agree with the world of others without creating a conflict.

Let's begin with the fact that, in order not to offend with his Jewishness, too blatantly revealed by his surname (Levi), he discarded it and took that of Catellani instead.

But he did more than that.

He married into a Catholic family, one of the holiest of holier-than-thou families, forming a so-called mixed marriage, albeit on the condition that his children (and he has five already) would all be baptized, like their mother, and thus irremediably lost to his faith.

Yet people say that my friend Mr. Catellani's highly irritating laugh started at the exact same time as his mixed marriage.

Though not, apparently, because of his wife—a most decent woman, and very good to him—but rather because of his father-in-law, Mr. Pietro Ambrini, nephew of the late Cardinal Ambrini and a man of the most intransigent clerical principles.

Why on earth, you must be wondering, did Mr. Daniele Catellani get himself mixed up with a family fortified by such a formidable future father-in-law?

Well!

It's obvious that, once he'd conceived the idea of a mixed marriage, he wanted to carry it through in no uncertain terms; and who knows, perhaps he even deluded himself that the very act of taking a wife from such a notoriously devout Catholic family would make it clear to all that he considered his being born a Jew an accident that should not be taken into account in the least.

He had to endure bitter fights as a consequence of his marriage.

But it's a fact that our greatest hardships in life are always those we face in order to erect the gallows with our own hands.

But perhaps — at least according to what people say — my friend Catellani would not have managed to hang himself without the help of the not completely disinterested Millino Ambrini, his wife's younger brother, who ran off to America two years later over a very delicate matter, about which it is best not to speak.

The fact is that his father-in-law, yielding *obtorto collo*[1] to the marriage, imposed on his daughter the binding condition not to deviate one iota from her holy faith and to respect with utmost zeal all its precepts, without neglecting any of its practices. He also insisted that it be his sacrosanct right to oversee that all precepts and practices were scrupulously observed, one by one, not only by the new Mrs. Catellani, but also and even more so by the children who would be born to her.

Yet even after nine years, despite his son-in-law's submissiveness, blindingly obvious proof of which he gave and continues to give his father-in-law, Mr. Pietro Ambrini will not relent. Cold, cadaverous, and cosmeticized, his clothes always new-looking despite years of wear, and with that ambiguous odor of powder that women apply under their arms and elsewhere after a bath, he has the nerve, on seeing his son-in-law go by, to wrinkle his nose, as if, to his ultra-Catholic nostrils, Mr. Catellani still has not shed his highly noxious *foetor judaicus*.[2]

---

1. "Against his will." The phrase *obtorto collo* means "taking by the neck or collar," referring to the practice allowed by Roman law of a plaintiff dragging a reluctant defendant to court.

2. Literally, "stench of Judaism."

■ ■ ■

I know because we've often spoken about it together.

Mr. Daniele Catellani laughs in his throat the way he does not so much because his proud father-in-law's vain obstinacy in regarding him as an enemy of the Catholic faith seems comical to him, as because of what he has been perceiving for a while now in himself.

But really, is it possible, in an age such as ours, in a country such as ours, that one such as he must become the target of religious persecution, one released since childhood from any active faith, and disposed to respect that of others, Chinese, Indian, Lutheran, Islamic?

And yet that's exactly how it is. There's not much to say: his father-in-law persecutes him. It may seem ridiculous, unbelievably ridiculous, but there is real religious persecution in that house. It may only be one-sided, and of a poor defenseless soul, or rather, of one who deliberately entered unarmed, intent on surrendering; but it is a real religious war that his blessed father-in-law starts anew every day in his home, at all costs, with inflexible, fierce, hostile determination.

Now, let's put aside the fact that—beaten down day after day— due to the bile already beginning to rise up in him, bit by bit the *homo judaeus* within starts to revive and re-form, without his wanting to admit it. Let's put that aside. Yet my friend Mr. Daniele Catellani cannot help but perceive the increasing lack of consideration and respect he receives from people because of his entire family's excessive religious practices, which his father-in-law flaunts so deliberately, not out of any sincere sentiment, but out of spite for him and with the manifest intention of gratuitously offending him. And that's not all. His children, those poor children, so oppressed by their grandfather, have also started to perceive confusedly that the cause of the continual oppression inflicted on them by their grandfather must be in him, in their father. They don't know what it is, but it must be in him. By now it's clear that the good Lord Jesus (yes, good Jesus especially), and also the saints — today this one, tomorrow that one — to whom they pray with their grandfather every day in church, need all their prayers, because he, their father, certainly must have done them who knows what enormous evil. Good Jesus especially! And when their grandfather drags them by the hand to church, they turn, those poor little creatures, and cast on their father looks of such deep, perplexed anguish and distressed rebuke that my friend Mr. Daniele Catellani would have the right to shout who knows what curses, if . . . if he did not prefer instead to throw back his curly-haired, big-nosed head and burst into his usual throaty laughter.

Yes, really! Otherwise he would actually have to admit that he had committed a pointless act of cowardice in turning his back on the faith of his fathers, in renouncing in his children his chosen people: '*am olam,* as the Rabbi says. And he would have to feel himself truly a goy, a stranger in the midst of his own family; and finally face up to his idiotic, highly Christian father-in-law and force him to open his eyes and consider that, yes, it is not right to insist on seeing his son-in-law as *deicidal,* when the Christians, who should consider themselves brothers all in Christ, in the name of this God killed by the Jews two thousand years ago, butchered each other happily for five years in a war that, without taking away anything from those to come, is unprecedented in history.

No, no, really! Laugh, go ahead and laugh. Are these truly things to think and say in this day and age?

My friend Mr. Daniele Catellani knows well what the world is like. Jesus, yes, he does. Brothers, they all are. And then they slaughter each other. Naturally. And it's all completely logical: each side is in the right, so that in taking this side, you can't help but agree with what that side refutes.

Agree, agree, always agree.

But first perhaps — and why not? being caught unawares — have a good laugh. But then agree, agree, always agree with everything.

Yes, sir, even war.

■ ■ ■

And yet (God, what an interminable laugh that time!) and yet, well, during the last year of the Great War, Mr. Daniele Catellani wanted to play a practical joke on his father-in-law, one of those sorts of joke you'll never forget.

For you should know that, despite the widespread carnage that year, Mr. Pietro Ambrini had with remarkable insolence thought to celebrate Christmas with more pomp than ever, for the sake of his dear little grandchildren. And so he had had made a great many little terracotta shepherds, who bring their humble offerings to the manger in Bethlehem, to the just-born Baby Jesus: straw baskets of pure white ricotta, and panniers of eggs and raviggiolo cheese; and flocks of fluffy lambs and little donkeys laden with even richer offerings, followed by farmers and peasants. And on camelback, the Three Kings, solemn in their capes and crowns, who arrive with their retinue from far, far away, from beyond the shooting star, which has come to rest over the cork grotto, where the rosy Baby Jesus, made of wax, lies on a bit of real straw between Mary and Joseph, who holds a flowering staff, and behind him are the ox and little donkey.

The good grandfather had wanted the nativity scene to be plenty big that year, and all in proper perspective, with hillocks and crags, palm trees and agave plants, and country paths on which all those shepherds could be seen, in various sizes, arriving with their little flocks of sheep and donkeys, and the Three Kings.

He'd worked on the nativity scene for more than a month, in secret, with the help of two laborers who built the platform for it. And he wanted it to be illuminated by garlands of tiny blue lights; and for two pipers from the Sabine Hills to come play the *piffero* and jaw harp on Christmas eve.

His grandchildren were to know nothing about it.

They were to discover his marvelous surprise on coming home from midnight mass, chilly and all bundled up: the sound of the *piffero*, the smell of incense and myrrh, and the nativity scene, like a dream, illuminated by all those garlands of tiny blue lights. And all the neighbors, along with the friends and relatives who had been invited to the feast, would come see this great wonder, which had cost Grandfather Pietro so much effort and money.

Seeing him going about the house, all absorbed in mysterious matters, Mr. Daniele had laughed; he'd heard the hammering of the two workmen erecting the platform in there, and had laughed.

The devil, who had been dwelling in his throat for so many years, decided to give him no peace for Christmas that year: and so, laughter, endless laughter. In vain had Mr. Daniele raised his hands to signal the devil to calm down; in vain had he warned him not to exaggerate, not to go too far.

"No, we won't exaggerate!" the devil inside of him had replied. "Rest assured, we won't go too far. There's no denying that these little shepherds with their little baskets of ricotta and panniers of eggs and raviggiolo cheese are a precious joke. All on their way to the grotto in Bethlehem! Well then, don't you worry, we shall go along! We'll play a joke too, no less precious. You'll see."

And so Mr. Daniele let himself be tempted by his devil, let himself be won over, above all, by this specious consideration: that he would go along with the joke.

On Christmas eve, as soon as Mr. Pietro Ambrini and his daughter and grandchildren and all the servants left for midnight mass, Mr. Daniele Catellani, trembling all over with crazed joy, entered the room where the nativity scene was. In great haste, he removed the Three Kings and the camels, the little sheep and don-keys, the little shepherds with their raviggiolo cheese and panniers of eggs and baskets of ricotta—characters and offerings to the good Jesus that his devil considered unsuitable for Christmas in a war-torn year such as this. And what—more suitable—did he put in their place? Oh, nothing, just some other toys: little tin soldiers, lots and lots of them, armies of tin soldiers, of every nationality, French and German, Italian and Austrian, Russian and English, Serbian and Romanian, Bulgarian and Turkish, Belgian and Ameri-can and Hungarian and Montenegrin, all with their rifles leveled at the grotto of Bethlehem, and then lots of little lead cannons, whole batteries of them, of every shape and size, all pointed—from above, below, every which way—at the grotto of Bethlehem. It must really have made a new and very charming spectacle.

Then he hid behind the platform.

■ ■ ■

I'll leave it to your imagination how he laughed from the back of the nativity scene when, after midnight mass, Grandfather Pietro and his grandchildren and daughter and the whole host of guests came to see the marvelous surprise, as the incense smoked and the pipers sounded their instruments.

Passengers arriving on the night train from Rome had to wait at the Fabriano station until dawn in order to continue their journey to the Marche on a slow local train.

At dawn, a woman so undone by grief that she could barely stand was practically carried into a filthy, second-class compartment where five of the six seats were already occupied.

In the early-morning light, the sheer squalor and oppressive closeness of the dirty compartment, reeking of smoke, made that unwieldy, pitiful tangle of clothing, hoisted with much puffing and moaning first from the platform and then from the footboard, seem like a nightmare to the five other passengers, who had spent a sleepless night.

The puffs and moans that accompanied and supported from behind all that exertion came from her husband, who eventually emerged, gaunt, haggard, and as pale as a cadaver, but with small, lively eyes that pierced his pallor.

His distress at seeing his wife in such a state did not keep him from being punctilious despite his grave embarrassment; yet evidently his efforts had left him mildly irritated as well, fearful, perhaps, of not having given those five other passengers sufficient proof of his strength in supporting and maneuvering that heavy bundle of a wife into the compartment.

Once seated, however, after extending his apologies and thanks to his traveling companions, who had immediately moved aside to make room for the hapless lady, he could now show himself ceremonious and considerate with her as well; he straightened her clothes and adjusted the collar of her cape, which had ridden up over her nose.

"Are you all right, dear?"

The wife not only did not respond, but angrily pulled her cape up again—higher, so that now it hid her entire face. He gave a distraught smile and sighed:

"Oh . . . what a world!"

He felt it necessary to explain to his traveling companions that allowances should be made for his wife: she was in such a state because of their only son's sudden and imminent departure for the war. For the last twenty years they had lived only for him. The year before, they'd moved from Sulmona to Rome so he would not embark on his university studies alone. When war broke out, their son, called to enlist, had enrolled in an accelerated course for cadets; three months later, appointed second lieutenant and assigned to the 12th Infantry Regiment, Casale Brigade, he had gone to join the depot in Macerata, where, he assured them, he would be for at least a month and a half, training recruits. But no. Instead he's being sent to the front, after only three days. They'd received a telegram in Rome the day before, announcing his surprise departure. And so they were on their way to say goodbye, to see him off.

The wife stirred under her cape, shuddered, writhed, even growled like a wild beast several times, exasperated by her husband's long explanation. He seemed not to realize that their plight—which may have befallen many, perhaps all of them — rather than arousing any special sympathy would probably irritate and incense their five traveling companions who, unlike her, did not appear to be despondent or vanquished by grief, even though they probably had one or more sons off at war. Yet perhaps her husband was deliberately explaining and offering all that information about their only son and his sudden departure after just three days, etc., so that the others would repeat coldly, harshly all the things he had been saying to her for months now, in other words since their son had enlisted; and not so much to console her as well as himself as to persuade her spitefully to resign herself, which was impossible.

And in fact, the others greeted his explanation coldly.

"You should thank God, my good man, that your son is on his way to the front only now!" one of them said. "Mine has been there since the day the war started. And he's been wounded, I'll have you know, twice already. Lightly, as luck would have it, once in the arm, once in the leg. A month's leave, but then it was right back to the front again."

"I have two sons there," another added. "And three nephews."

"Yes, but an only son . . . ," the husband proffered.

"Not true, don't say that!" the man rudely interrupted. "You may spoil an only child, but you don't love him more! It's one thing — when you have more than one child — to divide a piece of bread among them all, but you don't divide up paternal love. A father gives all the love he can to each of his children. And so if I'm suffering now, it's not half for one, half for the other. I feel for both."

"True, yes, how true," the husband admitted timidly, with a pitiful, embarrassed smile. "But now — since we're already talking about it, mere speculation of course, knock on wood—let's take the case of . . . not you, my dear sir, good heavens, no . . . but the case of a father who has more than one son at war: if—God forbid!—he loses one, at least he still has the other!"

"Yes, of course," the man agreed with a frown. "A son for whom he must go on living. Whereas you . . . well, not you, but a father who has only one son, let's say, and if it happens that his only son dies, if, now that his son is dead, he doesn't know what to do with his life anymore, well, he can take it, and farewell. While I, do you understand? I have to go on living, for my other son, the one I still have. So my situation is still worse!"

"What sort of talk is this!" Another traveler jumped in now, a fat, red-faced man who looked around the compartment with bulging, watery, bloodshot eyes.

He was gasping for breath, and his eyes looked as if they would pop right out of his head from some frantic, inner violence, some exuberant vitality, which his massive, disheveled body could no longer contain. As if suddenly remembering he was missing two front teeth, he held a giant paw in front of his mouth, but then for-getting again, he continued, indignantly:

"Do we have children for our own sakes?"

The others leaned forward and looked at him in dismay. The man who'd spoken first, the one whose son had been at the front since the first day of the war, sighed:

"Well no, for the fatherland . . ."

"Well, my good sir," the fat traveler remarked, "if you say it like that—'for the fatherland'—it sounds like a grievance!"

"My son, I gave birth to you
not for myself, but for the fatherland . . ."[1]

"Rubbish! Since when? Do you really think about the fatherland when a son is born to you? Nonsense! Sons come into this world not because we want them but because they must, and they take life with them, not only their own, but ours as well. That's the truth. We are here for them, not they for us. And when they turn twenty . . . but just think, they're exactly the same as you and I were at that age. There were our mothers and fathers, but there were plenty of other things as well: pleasures, a girlfriend, the latest friendships, longings, cigarettes, and yes, the fatherland, that too, when we were twenty, and didn't have children of our own; the fatherland, which, now tell me, had it called us, wouldn't it have meant more to us than our fathers and mothers? Now we're fifty, sixty, my dear sir. Sure, there's still the fatherland, but of course, in-side us is also — and it's more powerful — our affection for our chil-dren. Which one of us, if he could, would not go, would not want to go and fight in place of our sons? All of us, for sure! Don't we want to consider what our sons are feeling now that they're twenty? Our sons who, when the time comes, must, of course, feel more af-fection for the fatherland than for us? Obviously I'm talking about

---

1. These are the closing lines of "La madre e la patria," a poem by Italian poet and politician Giovanni Prati, which takes the form of a dialogue between a mother and a son. This theme was prevalent in nationalist literature of the Risorgimento.

good sons, and I say 'of course' because, for them, we too become sons before the fatherland, old sons who are no longer agile and so must stay home. If there is a fatherland, if fatherland is a natural necessity, like the bread we all must eat so as not to die of hunger, then someone has to go defend it, when the time comes. And so they go, at age twenty, they go because they must, and they don't want tears. Because, even if they die, they die happy and filled with passion. (I'm still talking about good sons, of course!) Now, when one dies happy, without having seen all of life's ugliness and irritation, the troubles that this miserable life holds, the bitterness and disillusions, what more could we ask? We should laugh, not cry . . . or cry as I do, yes indeed, I cry happily because my son sent word that his life—*his* life, mind you, the life we must see in our sons, not *our* lives—that he'd lived his life as best he could, and that he'd died happily, and that I shouldn't dress in black. And as you can see, I haven't."

And as he spoke, he tugged on his light-colored jacket in proof. His bruised lips trembled atop his missing teeth, and his eyes welled up with tears. In closing, he let out two sharp laughs that could have been sobs.

"Well . . . well."

The mother, hidden under her cape, had for three months now searched, in everything that her husband and others said to console and persuade her, for one word, just one, that, in the deafness of her dark distress, might resonate, might make her understand how it could be possible for a mother to resign herself to sending her son, not even to his death, but merely to a probable risk of life. But she'd never found one, not one word, among all those that had been said to her. So she had assumed that if the others spoke, if they were able to speak to her that way, about resignation and consolation, it was simply because they did not feel what she felt.

But this traveler's words had astounded her. All of a sudden she realized that it wasn't that the others did not feel as she did, but on the contrary, that she was unable to feel something that everyone else did, and that allowed them to resign themselves, not only to the departure but even to the death of their sons.

She raised her head and drew herself out of the corner of the compartment in order to listen to the answers the traveler was giving to his companions' questions about when and how his son had died. On hearing that all the others not only understood but actually admired the old man, and were congratulating him for being able to speak so about the death of his son, she was dumbfounded, and felt as if she'd been dropped into a world hitherto unknown to her, which she was seeing now for the first time.

Except that she suddenly saw the same bewilderment on those other travelers' faces that must be on hers, as soon as she, without actually meaning to, as if she still hadn't heard or truly understood anything, sat up and asked:

"So . . . so your son is dead?"

■ ■ ■

The old man turned and looked at her with those dreadful eyes, open so impossibly wide. He looked and looked at her, and then suddenly, as if it were only now, faced with that incongruous question, that inappropriate amazement, that he finally understood, at last, that his son really was dead, gone forever. His face puckered, he grew flustered, quickly pulled a handkerchief from his pocket and, to the astonishment and dismay of the other passengers, burst into piercing, excruciating, uncontrollable sobs.

It happened one evening, a Sunday, after a long walk.

Tullio Buti had been renting the room for about two months. His landlady, Mrs. Nini, a nice, old-fashioned little lady, and her daughter, now a withered old maid, never saw him. He left early every morning and came home late every evening. They knew he worked at one of the ministries, that he was a lawyer, but nothing more.

His little room, narrow and modestly furnished, bore no trace of his presence. It seemed as if he intentionally, deliberately wanted to remain detached, as in a hotel. True, he had placed his underwear in the bureau and hung a few suits in the closet. But on the walls or other furniture, nothing—not a box, not a book, not a portrait. Never a ripped-open envelope on the desk, never a piece of clothing—a collar or a tie—tossed on a chair, no sign that he felt at home.

The Ninis, mother and daughter, feared it wouldn't last. They'd had a hard time renting that little room. Plenty of people had come to see it, but no one wanted it. In truth, it wasn't very comfortable or very cheery, with just that one window, which gave onto a private narrow alley, through which neither light nor air ever came, suffocated and hemmed in as it was by the house across the way.

Mother and daughter would have liked to compensate their

long-awaited lodger with gestures of kindness and courtesy; how many they had planned and prepared as they waited: "We'll do this for him; we'll say this to him," and so on and so forth. Especially Clotildina, the daughter: so many charming favors, so many special "civilities," as her mother would say. Oh, just like that they'd prepared them, without any ulterior motive. But how could they possibly put them into practice if he never let himself be seen?

Had they seen him, they might have realized right away that their fears were unfounded. That sad little room, dark and suffocated by the house across the way, perfectly matched their lodger's mood.

Tullio Buti always went around by himself, without even a cigar or a cane, those two companions of even the shiest, most solitary soul. His hands buried in the pockets of his overcoat, shoulders hunched up, face frowning, hat pulled low over his eyes, he looked to be harboring the blackest bitterness against the world.

In the office, he never exchanged a word with any of his colleagues, who had not yet decided which nickname — Bear or Owl — fit him best.

No one had ever seen him set foot in a café in the evening, though many had seen him hurriedly dodge the busier streets, so as to be swallowed up by the shadows of the long, straight, solitary streets in the better neighborhoods; had seen him step away from the wall every time he came upon a lamppost, skirting the circle of light it cast on the sidewalk.

Never a spontaneous gesture, nor even the tiniest variation of his facial features, or the slightest sign with eyes or lips ever betrayed the thoughts that seemed to absorb him so, the dark gloom in which he was always enveloped. The devastating effect that those thoughts and gloom must have had on his soul was abundantly obvious in the haunting fixedness of his clear, piercing eyes, the pallor of his haggard face, and the premature graying of his unkempt beard.

He never sent or received letters, never read the newspaper, never stopped or even turned to look at whatever was happening on the street that attracted others' curiosity; and if, now and then, the rain caught him by surprise, he simply kept on walking at the same pace, as if nothing had changed.

What he was doing living like this, no one knew. Perhaps not even him. There he was. . . . Perhaps he couldn't even imagine that one could live differently, or that, by living differently, his boredom and sadness would weigh upon him less.

He'd never had a childhood, he'd never been young, ever. The savageness he had witnessed growing up, from a most tender age, of his father's brutality and ferocious tyranny, had extinguished every spark of life in his soul.

His mother died young, the result of her husband's atrocious tortures, after which the family broke up: one sister became a nun, a brother ran off to America. He too fled the family home, a wanderer who, through unbelievable hardship, managed to raise himself up to his current position.

He no longer suffered now. He seemed to be suffering, but even the sensation of pain had been deadened in him. He always seemed lost in thought, but in truth, he didn't even think anymore. It was as if his spirit were suspended in some sort of dumbstruck gloom that was more like a faint, vague bitterness in his throat. Walking the deserted streets at night, he would count the streetlamps, nothing more. Or study his shadow, or listen to the echo of his footsteps, or, from time to time, stop in front of a villa garden and contemplate the cypresses, dark and closed, like him, more nocturnal than night itself.

■ ■ ■

That Sunday, tired of the long walk along the old Appian Way, he decided, quite remarkably, to go home. Still too early for dinner, he would wait in his little room for the day to fade and dinnertime to arrive.

This was a most welcome surprise for the Ninìs, mother and daughter. Clotildina even clapped her hands with glee. Which of the many kindnesses and courtesies, so carefully planned and prepared, which of the many favors and "civilities" should they offer him first? Mother and daughter confabulated. All of a sudden, Clotildina stomped her foot and slapped her forehead. Good heavens, the lamp! First she had to bring him a lamp, the good one, of porcelain with painted poppies and a frosted glass globe, put aside just for him. She lit it and knocked discreetly on the lodger's door. She trembled so with emotion that the globe teetered on its base, turning nearly black with smoke.

"May I? The lamp."

"No, thank you." Buti answered from behind the door. "I'm about to go out."

The spinster made a little face and lowered her eyes, as if the lodger could see her. She insisted.

"But I have it right here. So you won't have to sit in the dark."

"No, thank you," Buti repeated harshly.

He was sitting on the little sofa behind the desk, staring blankly at the gathering gloom of his little room, while the last glimmer of twilight slipped sadly from his windowpanes.

How long did he stay like that, perfectly still, eyes wide, without thinking, without even noticing that the shadows had already enshrouded him?

All of a sudden, he could see.

He looked around in astonishment. Yes, the little room had suddenly grown brighter, illumined with a gentle glow, which seemed to be carried on some mysterious breeze.

What was it? How had it happened?

Ah, there. The light in the other house. A lamp had just been lit in the house across the way: the breath of some stranger's life entered and dispelled the darkness, the emptiness, the desert of his own existence.

He sat for a while, gazing at that faint light as if it were something miraculous. He was seized by an intense anguish as he noticed how sweetly it caressed his bed, the wall, his pale hands resting limply on the desk. And in that anguish arose the memory of his suffocated childhood, of his mother. And it seemed to him as if the light of some distant dawn had breathed into the dark night of his soul.

He stood up, went to the window, and furtively, behind the glass, peered into the house across the way, into that window where the light shone.

He saw a family gathered around the dinner table: three little boys and the father, already seated, the mother still standing, serving them, and trying—as he inferred from her gestures—to check the impatience of the two older boys who brandished their spoons and squirmed in their chairs. The youngest one stretched his neck and twisted his little blond head: evidently they had tied his bib too tight. But if his darling mother quickly served him his soup, he would no longer notice how tight it was. There, there, see? How hungrily did he gulp it down, sticking the whole spoon in his mouth! And his papà laughed through the steam rising from his plate. Now mamma sat down too, there, right across from him. When Tullio Buti saw that, in sitting, she lifted her eyes to the window, he instinctively made to step back, but then realized that he couldn't be seen in the dark, so he stayed on, watching that little family eat dinner, forgetting completely about his own.

■ ■ ■

From that day on, every evening upon leaving the office, instead of setting out on his usual solitary walk, he would take the road home. And every evening he would wait for the darkness of his little room to brighten sweetly with the light from the other house. Like a beggar, he would stay there behind the windowpanes, savoring with infinite anguish that sweet and tender intimacy, that familiar comfort those others enjoyed, and that he too had enjoyed as a child on those rare evenings of tranquility when mamma . . . his mamma . . . like her . . .

And he would weep.

Yes. The light in the other house worked this wonder. The dumbfounded darkness in which his soul had been suspended for so many years dissolved in that sweet, soft light.

Tullio Buti never wondered, all this time, what strange suppositions his staying there in the dark must have kindled in the minds of his landlady and her daughter.

Twice more Clotildina had offered him a lamp, but in vain. He could have a candle, at least! But no, not even that. Did he not feel well?, Clotildina, her voice tender, had dared ask through the door the second time she'd taken him the lamp. "No," he had answered, "I'm fine like this."

In the end . . . well, yes, but good gracious, it was completely excusable! In the end, Clotildina had spied on him through the keyhole and had seen, to her surprise, the lodger's little room suffused by the faint glow of the light in the other house—yes, the Masci house. And she had seen him, erect behind the windowpanes, peering intently into the Masci home.

All in a tumult Clotildina had run to her mother, to reveal the great discovery: "He's in love with Margherita! With Margherita Masci! In love!"

A few evenings later, as he was watching through the window the little family eating dinner as usual—though without papà that evening—Tullio Buti, much to his surprise, saw his landlady, Mrs. Ninì, and her daughter Clotildina enter the room across the way and be greeted like old friends.

At a certain point, Tullio Buti leapt back from the window, breathless with anxiety. The darling mother and her three little ones had raised their eyes toward his window. Without a doubt, those two women were talking about him.

And now? Now it would all be over! The next evening that mother, or her husband, knowing he was hovering mysteriously in the dark in the little room across the way, would close the shutters.

And so, from then on, that light for which he lived, that light which was his innocent pleasure and his only comfort, would shine on him no more.

■ ■ ■

But that's not what happened.

That same evening, when the light across the way was extinguished and he was plunged into darkness, he waited for the family to go to bed. When, after a little while, he cautiously went to open his window to let in some air, he saw that the window across the way was also open; a little later he saw—and trembled with fear at the sight—the woman appear at her window. Perhaps her curiosity had been roused by what the Ninìs, mother and daughter, had said about him.

Those two tall buildings, whose windows—like eyes—gazed so closely at each other, did not permit even a glimpse of blue sky above or dark earth below, where the garden was closed by a gate. They never permitted a ray of sunlight or a moonbeam to filter down.

So the woman across the way could only have come to the window for him, for undoubtedly she had realized that he, too, was at his darkened window.

They could barely discern each other in the dark. But he had known for some time that she was beautiful; he already knew the gracefulness of her gestures, the sparkle of her dark eyes, the smile on her red lips.

But that first time, more than anything else, he felt pain—pain at the surprise that threw everything into confusion and took his breath away in an almost unbearable, anxious throb. It took a tremendous effort not to withdraw, but to wait until she withdrew first.

That dream of peace, love, and sweet, tender intimacy, which he imagined that family enjoying, and which he, indirectly, had also enjoyed, would crumble if that woman came furtively to the window in the dark for a stranger. Yes, for this stranger, for him.

And yet, before she withdrew, before she closed the window again, she whispered to him, "Good evening!"

What had the Ninìs dreamed up about him to inflame this woman's curiosity so? What strange, potent attraction had the mystery of his reclusive life worked on her if, from the very first, she left her little ones alone and came to him, as if to keep him company for a while?

As they faced one another, even though each avoided the other's gaze and they almost pretended to themselves that they were there at the window for no reason, both of them—of this he was certain—had trembled with the same unformed expectation, both daunted by the spell that drew them together in the dark.

When, late that night, he closed his window again, he was certain that the next evening, she, having put out her lamp, would once again come to the window for him. And that's exactly what happened.

From then on, Tullio Buti no longer waited in his little room for the light in the other house to be lit. Instead he waited impatiently for it to be put out.

The passion of love, never felt before, now burned fiercely, voraciously, in the heart of that man who had spent so many years cut off from life. And it crashed over, broke, and swept away that woman, as if in a whirlwind.

The same day that Buti moved out of his little room at the Ninìs, the news exploded like a bomb that Mrs. Masci, the woman on the fourth floor of the house across the way, had abandoned her husband and three children.

The little room that had housed Buti for nearly four months remained empty, and for several weeks the room across the way, where the family used to gather every evening for dinner, remained shrouded in darkness.

But then the light was relit on that sad dining table, at which the father, dazed by the disaster, stared at the bewildered faces of three boys who did not dare turn their eyes to the door where every evening their mother used to come in carrying a steaming soup tureen.

The lamp that illuminated that sorry scene once again brightened, though with a ghostly glow, the little room across the way, now empty.

■ ■ ■

Did Tullio Buti and his lover, months after their cruel folly, remember?

One evening the Ninìs were startled to see their strange lodger appear before them, greatly distressed. What did he want? The little room, the little room, if it was still available! No, not for himself, not to live there! But to visit, for just an hour, even for just a minute, every evening, secretly! For pity's sake, pity for that poor mother who wanted to see her children, from afar, without being seen! They would take every precaution, they would even disguise themselves, they would come in when the stairs were empty; he would pay double, triple the rent, just for one minute a day.

No. The Ninìs were not willing to consent. However . . . as long as the room remained unrented, they would concede, every now and then . . . But for heaven's sake, only on the condition that they were not found out! And only now and then . . .

Like two thieves, they came, the following evening. Gasping for breath, they entered the dark room and waited, waited until it brightened again with the light from the other house.

That was the light by which they had to live now. Like this, from afar.

There it was!

Tullio Buti could hardly bear it at first. But she drank it in, as if dying of thirst. Sobs catching in her throat, she hurled herself at the window, her handkerchief pressed against her mouth. Her little ones . . . her little ones . . . her little ones . . . there, there they were . . . at the dinner table . . .

■ ■ ■

He rushed to the window to support her, and there they stayed, clinging to each other, transfixed, spying.

Who Swift was, and who Swallow, neither I nor anyone in that little mountain village where they came to make their nest for three months every summer really knew.

The young miss at the post office, scrutinizing the very rare letters they received, swears she never once managed, in all those years, to extract a human sound from the combination of k's and h's and w's and all the f's of his or her last name. But even if the young miss at the post office had managed to sound out those two names, what more would we really know?

So much the better, I thought. Better to call them *Swift* and *Swallow*, as everyone in that little mountain village did: not only because they returned every summer, from who knows where, to their old nest; not only because they moved about, or rather fluttered restlessly, from morning to evening the whole time they were there, but also for another slightly less poetic reason.

No one in that village might ever have thought of naming them so if he, a foreigner, hadn't arrived that first year in a long black twill morning coat with fluttering tails and white trousers; and if, in looking for a secluded little vacation house, he hadn't chosen the small villa belonging to the village doctor and mayor, so small it was like a swallow's nest, tucked among the chestnut trees on top of a precipice known as the Bastion.

The villa was so very small, and he so very large! Oh, a big, beefy gentleman, with gold-framed glasses and a black, tousled beard that imperiously overran his cheeks, almost up to his eyes, without, however, making him seem the least bit cruel or gloomy, because he exuded, from his whole vigorous frame, a sincere and smiling cordiality.

His head high on his Herculean torso, he always seemed ready to respond, with childlike verve, to some mysterious, far-off call that only he could hear: up some mountain peak, or down some never-ending valley, heading now this way, now that. And he would come back all sweaty, red-faced and panting, yet smiling, a small fossil of a shell in his hand, or a little flower in his mouth, as if it were that very shell or that very flower that had suddenly called to him from miles and miles away, from up on the mountain or down in the valley.

And seeing him head off like that, with his black morning coat and white trousers, how not call him *Swift?*

■ ■ ■

The first year, Swallow arrived about fifteen days after him, after he'd found and prepared the nest up there among the chestnut trees.

She had arrived out of the blue, without his knowing anything about it, and she'd had trouble making it understood that she was looking for that foreign man, that she wanted to be taken to his house.

Every year Swallow would arrive two or three days after Swift, and always like that, out of the blue. Only one year did she arrive a day before him. Which proves that they hadn't arranged things, and that some grave obstacle must have prevented them from receiving news of each other. Clearly, as could be gleaned from the stamps on their letters, back in their home country they lived in two different cities.

Right from the start, suspicion arose that she was married, and that every year, set free for three months, she came to see her lover, to whom she couldn't even communicate the exact day of her arrival. But how to reconcile such impediments and such rigorous surveillance with the complete liberty she enjoyed for three months of summer in Italy?

Perhaps the doctors had told Swallow's husband that she needed the sun's restorative powers; and her husband granted her those three months of vacation every year, unaware that Swallow, in addition to—or rather, more than—those of the sun, went to Italy for the restorative powers of love.

She was tiny and diaphanous, as if made of air; clear blue eyes, shaded by long lashes, and timid-looking, dumbstruck almost, set in her delicate face. It seemed that even a puff of wind would carry her away, or that she would break at the slightest touch. It was somewhat distressing to imagine her in the arms of that big, impetuous man.

But into the arms of that big man, who, trembling like a tamed beast, waited impatiently for her up there in the little villa, she, so tiny and delicate, ran every year, happily throwing herself into them, not afraid of breaking, not even of being hurt slightly. She knew all the sweetness of his strength, all the reassuring, firm lightness of his force, and she gave herself passionately to him.

∎∎∎

Swallow's arrival every year was a celebration for the village.

At least that's what Swallow believed.

The celebration was within her, of course, and so, naturally, she saw it all around her. Of course, why not? All the tiny old houses, which time had dressed in its distinctive rusty coats, opened their windows to her arrival, the water in the fountains laughed, the birds seemed giddy with joy.

Swallow, of course, understood the birds' conversations better than the villagers'. Those, in fact, she didn't understand at all. But the birds, it seemed she really did, because she would smile happily, turning here and there toward the chattering sparrows hopping among the branches of the tall oak trees that flanked the steep road from Orte to the mountain village.

The coach, laden with suitcases and bags, would climb slowly, and the coachman couldn't help but turn around now and then and smile at tiny Swallow, who was returning, as she did every year, to her nest, and gesture with his hands that he was already there: yes, her Swift was up there, arrived three days ago, he was there, he was there.

Swallow would lift her eyes to the distant peak, where the chestnut trees, still in shadow, were steeped a deep blue, and she would strain her eyes to make out the little rosy dot of the villa.

She couldn't see it yet; but there was the ancient, iron-colored castle that overlooked the village; and there, lower down, the hospice for old beggars, with the cemetery right next door, as if it were an antechamber where they could wait for Lady Death to receive them.

The grove of majestic black holm oaks that hung over the road at the base of the village made Swallow feel cold and dismayed every time she passed under it. But the feeling didn't last long. And as soon as she was beyond it, she could see the villa up on the Bastion.

How they lived together up there no one really knew, but it was easy to imagine. An elderly maid would go clean every morning, when Swift and Swallow fled their nest and fluttered about tirelessly here and there, as if drunk with joy, up the mountain or down in the valley, through the countryside, or over to a nearby village. There are those who say they'd sometimes seen Swift hold his little Swallow in his arms, like a child.

Everyone in the village would smile happily seeing them go by, so filled with joy and love, when, tired from their long jaunts, they would come to the trattoria to eat. Everyone had grown accustomed to seeing them, and felt that some charm, some pleasure would be lost to the village if Swift and Swallow were not to return to their nest some summer. The doctor wouldn't consider renting the villa to anyone else, convinced by now that after so many years, they would not fail to return.

She would leave first, toward the end of September. Then, two or three days later, he would leave as well. But in those final days before their departure, they never left their nest, not even for a moment. It was understood that they had to prepare for a separation that would last the whole year, had to hold each other close, for a long time, before parting for the whole year. Would they see each other again? Would she, so tiny and delicate, survive so many cold months without the flame of his love, without his great strength to support her? Perhaps she would die during the winter; perhaps he, returning to their nest the following summer, would wait for her in vain.

The summer would come, and Swift would arrive and wait anxiously one, two, three days; and on the third day, here was Swallow, but each year ever more delicate and diaphanous, her eyes ever more timid and dumbstruck.

Until the seventh summer . . .

■ ■ ■

No, it wasn't Swallow who failed to return. She arrived, late. But he hadn't; it was a great disappointment for the entire village.

"What do you mean, he's not coming? Hasn't he arrived yet? Will he come later?"

The doctor, besieged by questions, shrugged his shoulders. How was he to know? He too was sad that the village was without the happy spectacle of the lovebirds, but he was also more than a little annoyed that his villa had gone unrented.

"So much for trust . . ."

"But something must have happened, of course."

"Maybe he died?"

"Or maybe she died?"

"Or maybe her husband found out . . ."

And they all looked sorrowfully at the rosy villa, the empty nest on top of the Bastion, amid the chestnut trees.

June came and went, then July; August was about to go too when the news suddenly spread throughout the entire village:

"They're coming! They're coming!"

"Both of them together, Swift and Swallow?"

"Yes, together, both of them!"

The doctor ran, as did all those who'd been sitting in the pharmacy, and all the vacationers in the café in the piazza. But it was another disappointment, and greater than the first one.

Yes, inside the coach making its way slowly up from Orte was Swallow (there, so to speak!) but that certainly was not Swift next to her. It was someone else, a dreadful, squat, blond man with a square, placid, hard face.

Her husband, perhaps. What do you mean, perhaps? Who else could it be? Her husband, him! He seemed to be legitimacy personified. And legitimacy was what he seemed to say with every look of his bespectacled, oval eyes; *legitimacy, legitimacy*, with every step, as soon as he got down from the coach and made his way over to the doctor, who was also the mayor, to beg him, in French, if he could please let them have a litter so as to transport a poor sick woman, unable to stand on her own two feet, up to a certain villa, situated, so he'd been told, up on . . .

"But of course, I know it well: the villa belongs to me!"

"No, I beg of you, sir: situated, so I've been told, and I repeat, so high that it is impossible to reach by coach."

Oh, how clearly Swallow's eyes, from inside the coach, said that she was dying because of this dignified, respectable man, who knew how to speak so politely! Only her eyes were still alive — no longer timid, but shining with joy at being able to see those places again, and shining too with a new touch of mischievousness, which death (too late!), now so close, had taught them.

"Laugh, all of you laugh, laugh out loud, all together, laugh along with me," her mischievous eyes said to all the people gathered around the coach, dismayed and disoriented with sorrow, "laugh out loud at this dignified and respectable man, who knows how to speak so politely and precisely! His respectability, his sensible, scrupulous precision will be the death of me! But don't despair, I beg of you, for I have been granted the mercy of dying here; avenge me instead by laughing loudly at him. I can only laugh softly now, and for only a little while longer, and only with my eyes, like this. Do you see the state your Swallow has been reduced to? She who used to fly now has to be taken up to the villa in a litter."

"And Swift? Your Swift?" the eyes of those gathered around the coach asked anxiously. "What has become of your Swift, who never came? Did he not come because of the state you're in? Or are you in this state because he is dead?"

Swallow's eyes may have understood their anxious questions, but her lips could not reply. And so her eyes closed in pain.

Eyes closed, Swallow looked dead.

■ ■ ■

Something certainly must have happened; but what, no one knows. Assumptions can be made, one can easily invent things. But this much is certain: Swallow came to die, alone in that villa up there, and what happened to Swift no one ever knew.

But really now, can you believe this? It's enough to drive you truly insane, not being able to tell which one of them is mad, this Mrs. Frola or that Mr. Ponza, her son-in-law. Only in the ill-fated city of Valdana do such things happen, magnet for all sorts of eccentric outsiders.

Either she's mad, or he is, there's no middle ground: one of them has to be mad. Because that's what we're dealing with, nothing less . . . But wait, it's best to set things out in order.

What dismays me most, I swear, is the anguish the inhabitants of Valdana have endured these past three months; I really don't care about Mrs. Frola and Mr. Ponza, her son-in-law. Because, while it is true that they have suffered a grave affliction, it is no less true that at least one of them had the fortune to go mad as a result, and the other played along, and continues to play along, so that it is impossible, I repeat, impossible to know which of the two is truly mad. Undoubtedly there is no greater comfort they could offer one other. But really, to draw an entire city into this nightmare, does that seem a small matter to you? Denying it any basis for rational judgment, so that it is no longer possible to tell the difference between fantasy and reality? An endlessly alarming agony. We see them every day, those two; we look them in the face, knowing that one of them is mad; we study them, scrutinize them, spy on them, but all for naught! We still can't tell which one it is, where reality ends and fantasy begins. Naturally, the pernicious suspicion begins to take hold that reality and fantasy amount to the same thing, and that every reality might just as easily be fantasy, and vice versa. Does that seem a small matter to you? If I were in the Prefect's shoes, I would not hesitate, for the health and well-being of its inhabitants, to banish Mrs. Frola and Mr. Ponza, her son-in-law, from Valdana.

▪ ▪ ▪

But let's proceed in an orderly fashion.

   This Mr. Ponza arrived in Valdana three months ago, to serve as Secretary of the Prefecture. He found lodging in the new build-ing on the edge of town, the one people call The Honeycomb. Yes, there. A small apartment, on the top floor. With three windows facing out to the countryside—tall, dreary windows (even though the building is new, that side, with the north wind blowing, and all those dull, drab fields, has already grown dreary, who knows why)— and three facing in to the courtyard, wrapped by a narrow balcony with grated partitions. Little baskets hang from the railing up there, ready to be lowered by a cord should they be needed.

   At the same time, however, to everyone's amazement, Mr. Ponza rented another small apartment in the center of the city, 15 Saints Street, to be exact: a kitchen and three rooms, furnished. He said it was for his mother-in-law, Mrs. Frola. And in fact, the lady arrived five or six days later. Mr. Ponza, alone, met her at the sta-tion, accompanied her to the apartment, and left her there, alone.

   Now really, it's understandable that a daughter, when she gets married, leaves her mother's home in order to go and live with her husband, even in another city. But that this same mother, unable to bear being apart from her daughter, leaves her home and city to be close to her daughter, and yet—in a city where both women are strangers—goes to live in a different house, this is not so readily understandable. Unless one assumes that the incompatibility between mother and son-in-law is so fierce as to make living under the same roof absolutely impossible, even in such circumstances.

That's what everyone in Valdana thought at first, naturally. And of course, the one vilified in everyone's eyes was Mr. Ponza. As for Mrs. Frola: while some did allow that she too might bear some blame—a lack of human compassion, or some form of stubbornness or prejudice—they all respected her maternal love, which drew her to her daughter even though forced to live apart from her.

Appearances, it must be said, played a significant role in the high regard for Mrs. Frola and the impression immediately stamped in everyone's mind of Mr. Ponza: harsh, cruel even. Squat, no neck, as black as an African, with thick, bristly hair on a low forehead, a single, severe bushy eyebrow, a cop's shiny mustachio, and dark, glowering eyes—practically no whites—which can barely contain a violent, exasperated intensity, who's to say whether from dreary distress or annoyance at the sight of other people, Mr. Ponza certainly is not one to inspire affection or familiarity. Mrs. Frola, on the other hand, is a pale, elderly lady, frail, with noble features and a melancholy air. Yet such an unimposing melancholy, vague and courteous, that it does not prevent her from being amiable with everyone.

Now, Mrs. Frola immediately offered proof of this amiability, which comes so naturally to her, and as a result, in everyone's mind the aversion to Mr. Ponza grew immediately. Her character was apparent to all: not merely mild, submissive, and tolerant, but also remarkably charitable for the hurt her son-in-law causes her. What's more, it was discovered that it isn't enough for Mr. Ponza to relegate that poor mother to a separate apartment. His cruelty goes so far as to forbid her even to visit her daughter.

Except that when she calls on the women of Valdana, Mrs. Frola, genuinely distraught that people could think such a thing about her son-in-law, raises her tiny hands and protests immediately that no, it is not cruelty, not cruelty. And she hastens to sing his praises and say every good thing imaginable about him: such love, such care, such attentiveness, and not only for her daughter, but also for herself, yes, yes, for her too; considerate . . . selfless. No, not cruel, good heavens, no! It's merely that he wants his little wife all to himself, Mr. Ponza does, to the point that even the love she clearly bears (and which he allows, of course) for her mother, he wants it to come to her not directly but rather through him, by means of him, that's all. Yes, it may seem cruel, this way of his, but it's not; it's something else, something else that she, Mrs. Frola, understands perfectly well, and is distressed not to be able to explain properly. It's his nature . . . or perhaps some sort of illness, as it were? Goodness me, all you have to do is look into his eyes. They may create a bad impression, at first, those eyes of his. But to someone like herself, who knows how to read them, they say it all: they speak of the enclosed fullness of his love, an entire, amorous world in which his wife must dwell, without leaving, even for an instant, and in which no one else, not even her mother, can enter. Jealousy? Perhaps. But that would be to define too simplistically this private plenty of love.

Selfishness? But a selfishness that gives itself entirely — a whole world — to its beloved! All things considered, it would be selfishness on her part were she to try and break open this enclosed world of love, insert herself by force, when she knows how happy her daughter is, how adored . . . For a mother, that is enough! Besides, it isn't actually true that she doesn't see her daughter. She sees her two or three times a day. She enters the courtyard, rings the bell, and her daughter immediately appears up on the balcony.

"How are you, Tildina?"

"Just fine, mamma. You?"

"As God wills, my child. Now, lower the basket!"

And inside the basket is always a letter, a few words with the day's news. There, that's enough for her. They've been living this way for four years now, and Mrs. Frola has grown accustomed to it. Resigned, she is. It hardly bothers her anymore.

■ ■ ■

It is easy to see how Mrs. Frola's resignation, her accustoming herself — or so she claims — to her martyrdom, comes at the expense of Mr. Ponza, her son-in-law. All the more so as she bends over backward to excuse him with her endless justifications.

It is thus with outright indignation and — I would add — fear that the women of Valdana who had received a visit from Mrs. Frola receive word the following day of another unexpected visit, by Mr. Ponza, who begs, if it is not too inconvenient, they grant him a mere two minutes of their time for a "necessary declaration."

Mr. Ponza — face flushed, eyes glowering more than ever, hand clutching a white handkerchief, which contrasts sharply, as do his cuffs and collar, with his dark skin, hair, and suit—continually wipes his low forehead and chafed purple-red cheeks, which are dripping with sweat, not so much from the heat but rather the effort—painfully obvious—he is making to control himself, so that even his big hands with their long fingernails are shaking. In one sitting room to the next, facing those women who stare at him in near terror, he first asks if Mrs. Frola, his mother-in-law, had been to see them the day before; then, with sorrow and strain and ever-increasing agitation, if she spoke to them about her daughter; and if she told them that he forbids her from seeing her altogether, or from entering their home.

As is easy to imagine, the women, seeing him so agitated, hasten to respond that yes, it's true, Mrs. Frola did tell them about the prohibition to see her daughter, but also every good thing imaginable about him, to the point not only of excusing him but of refusing to blame him in the slightest.

But rather than calming him down, the women's responses make Mr. Ponza even more agitated. His eyes grow darker, harsher, more glowering; his sweat drips more heavily. Finally, struggling even more violently to contain himself, he arrives at his "necessary declaration."

Which, simply, is this: Mrs. Frola, poor thing, may not seem mad, but she is.

Yes, for four years now. And her madness consists precisely in believing that he does not want her to see her daughter. But what daughter? Her daughter is dead; she died four years ago. And Mrs. Frola was so grief-stricken that she went mad. And a good thing too, for madness was her way of escaping her inconsolable grief.

Naturally, the only way of escape is to believe it's not true that her daughter is dead, but rather that it is he who does not want her to see her anymore.

Mr. Ponza, purely out of obligation to be charitable to a sorrowful soul, has been indulging this pitiful madness for four years now, with many a solemn sacrifice: though beyond his means, he maintains two homes: one for himself, and one for her. And he obliges his second wife, who, thank goodness, charitably complies, to indulge this folly as well. Charity, obligation—fine, but only to a point: in his capacity as a civil servant, Mr. Ponza cannot allow the people of Valdana to believe something so cruel and implausible about him, namely that, be it jealousy or something else, he forbids a poor mother to visit her own daughter.

His declaration made, Mr. Ponza bows before the bewildered women and takes his leave. Their bewilderment barely has time to fade, however, when here comes Mrs. Frola again, with her sweet air of vague melancholy, asking their forgiveness if, because of her, these good women took fright at her son-in-law Mr. Ponza's visit.

Mrs. Frola in turn declares, with all the sincerity and simplicity in the world, though in strict confidence, for heaven's sake! since Mr. Ponza is a civil servant, which is precisely why she refrained from telling them earlier, because, well, yes, it could seriously jeopardize his career: Mr. Ponza, poor thing—an excellent, excellent, impeccable Secretary of the Prefecture, well-mannered, precise in every deed and thought, brimming with good qualities—Mr. Ponza, poor thing, on this one point only. . . . no longer reasons clearly. The truth is: he is the one who is mad, poor thing. And his madness consists precisely in believing that his wife died four years ago and in going around saying that she, Mrs. Frola, is the one who is mad for believing her daughter is still alive. No, he doesn't do it to justify somehow his practically maniacal jealousy and his cruel forbiddance to visit her daughter. No. He believes, he actually believes, poor thing, that his wife is dead, and that the woman living with him now is his second wife. Such a pitiful case! Because previously, this man had actually risked destroying—killing—his delicate young wife with his excessive love, to the point that she had to be taken away from him in secret and, unbeknownst to him, confined to a convalescent home. Well, the poor man, whose mind was already gravely affected by his amorous frenzy, went mad as a result. He became convinced that his wife truly had died, and the idea so fixed itself in his mind that there was no hope of canceling it, even when his little wife, restored to health after about a year, returned to him. He was so sure she was someone else that, with the help of friends and relatives, they had to stage a fake wedding, which had the effect of restoring the equilibrium of his mental faculties.

Now Mrs. Frola believes she has reason to suspect that her son-in-law fully regained his sanity a while ago, and that he is pretending, merely pretending, to believe that his wife is his second wife, in order to keep her all to himself, not share her with anyone, perhaps because every so often the fear seizes him that she could be taken from him in secret again.

Yes, of course. How else to explain all his care and concern for her, his mother-in-law, if he truly believes that the woman he lives with is his second wife? He wouldn't feel obliged to show such regard for someone who, in fact, is no longer his mother-in-law, would he? Mrs. Frola says this, mind you, not as a further demonstration that he is the one who is mad, but rather as proof, even to herself, that her suspicion is well-founded.

"And meanwhile," she concludes with a sigh that shapes her lips into a sweet, sad smile, "meanwhile, my poor daughter must pretend to be someone else. And I too am obliged to pretend to be mad, believing that my daughter is still alive. It doesn't cost me much, thank God, because my daughter is up there, healthy and full of life. I see her and speak to her, albeit condemned never to live with her, and to see her and speak to her only from afar—all so that he can believe, or pretend to believe, that my daughter, God forbid, is dead, and that the woman he lives with is his second wife. But let me say again, what does it matter if, with this ruse, we have managed to give them both their peace of mind back? I know that my daughter is adored and happy. I can see her and speak with her. For love of her and of him, I have resigned myself to living like this, and to be taken for mad. Patience, my dear lady . . ."

■ ■ ■

So now I ask you, don't you think all of us in Valdana should be taken aback, eyeing each other like fools? Who to believe? Which one of them is mad? Where is the line between reality and fantasy?

Mr. Ponza's wife could say. But you can no more believe her if, in his presence, she says she is his second wife, than if, in Mrs. Frola's presence, she confirms she is her daughter. You would have to take her aside and make her tell the truth in private. But that is not possible. Mr. Ponza—mad or not—truly is extremely jealous and does not allow anyone to see his wife. He keeps her under lock and key up there, as if in prison—which undoubtedly speaks in Mrs. Frola's favor. But Mr. Ponza claims he is forced to do so, that his wife actually compels him, for fear that Mrs. Frola would suddenly enter their house. That might be just an excuse. But the fact remains that Mr. Ponza does not have a single servant in his home. He says it is to save money, obliged as he is to pay rent on two homes. He, meanwhile, has taken it upon himself to do the shopping every day, while his wife, who according to him is not Mrs. Frola's daughter, has taken on, out of pity for a poor old woman who was once her husband's mother-in-law, all the housework, even the most menial tasks, depriving herself of the help of a servant. Everyone finds it rather far-fetched. But it is also true that this state of affairs can be explained, if not by pity, then by Mr. Ponza's jealousy.

The Prefect of Valdana, meanwhile, is satisfied with Mr. Ponza's declaration. Yet Mr. Ponza's appearance and even more so his conduct certainly do not work in his favor, at least according to the women of Valdana, who are all more inclined to give credence to Mrs. Frola. As a matter of fact, she is so considerate as to show them the affectionate letters that her daughter lowers down to her in the basket, as well as many other personal documents, the validity of which, however, Mr. Ponza negates, insisting that they were issued in order to substantiate the piteous ruse.

This much is certain, at any rate: both of them exhibit a marvelous spirit of sacrifice toward each other, which is deeply moving. And each has for the other's presumed madness the most exquisitely piteous consideration. They both come across as clearheaded, so much so that it never would have occurred to anyone in Valdana to say that one of them was mad had they not said so themselves: Mr. Ponza about Mrs. Frola, and Mrs. Frola about Mr. Ponza.

■ ■ ■

Mrs. Frola goes often to see her son-in-law at the Prefecture, to ask his advice on some matter, or waits for him at the door so that he can accompany her shopping. And he, for his part, goes very often to see Mrs. Frola during his free time, and visits her every evening in her furnished apartment. And whenever they happen to run into each other on the street, they immediately and with the utmost courtesy fall into step together, he giving her his right side and, if she is tired, offering her his arm. And off they go together, amid frowns of irritation, astonishment, and consternation as we study them, scrutinize them, spy on them, but all for naught! We still have no way of knowing which one of them is mad, where reality ends and fantasy begins.

So far so good. A comedy. Nothing new to baffle or annoy the audience. And well crafted. Among the characters: a distinguished Prelate—a Red Eminence, that is, a Cardinal—who has taken in his Sister-in-Law (a poor widow with whom, in his youth, before embarking on his ecclesiastical career, he had been in love), and the widow's Daughter, already of marrying age, whom His Eminence would like to marry to a young Favorite of his, raised in his own home since he was a babe, ostensibly the son of one of his former secretaries, but in truth . . . But really, now—a youthful error, one for which the distinguished Prelate could not now be rebuked with the bluntness of a quick synopsis, when it is, in fact, the crux of the entire second act: a dramatic scene with his Sister-in-Law, in the dark. Or rather, on a moonlight-bathed veranda, since His Eminence, before beginning his confession, orders his faithful servant Giuseppe: "*Giuseppe, dim the lights.*" So far so good. The actors, each enamored of his role, are ready. Yes, even Gàstina. Very pleased to be playing the poor, fatherless niece, who naturally is not the least bit interested in marrying His Eminence's Favorite, and whose fits of proud rebellion little Gàstina relishes, because she expects thunderous applause.

To make a long story short, on the eve of opening night, my friend Faustino Perres, in anxious anticipation of the success of his new play, could not have been more pleased.

Except for the bat.

Yes, a damned bat, which, every evening that season at our Arena Nazionale, either came in through an opening in the pavilion roof, or at a certain hour stirred from the nest it must have made up there amid the hoists, pins, and bolts, and began to flit about madly, not over the audience's heads, since the house lights of the enormous arena are lowered during a performance, but—attracted by the footlights, spotlights, and running lights—there, on stage, right in the actors' faces.

Little Gàstina was absolutely terrified of bats. She'd nearly fainted three times during rehearsal, seeing it fly so close to her face, her hair, right in front of her eyes, and the last time—God, how disgusting!—that flap of screeching, viscous membrane nearly brushed her lips. It was a miracle she didn't scream. The strain it put on the frightened Gàstina to stay there and act while her eyes inevitably tracked the flight of that revolting creature, or—unable to bear it any longer—to run off the stage and lock herself in her dressing room, exasperated her to the point that she finally declared that if they couldn't find a way to keep that bat from flitting around the stage during the play, then she could no longer be responsible for her reactions, and there was no telling what she might do one of these evenings.

Proof that the bat was not coming in from outside but had, in fact, chosen to nest in the rafters arrived the evening before opening night. The roof openings had all been kept closed, and yet, at the usual hour, the bat swooped toward the stage in a furious flutter. Faustino Perres, panic-stricken for the fate of his new play, begged and beseeched the impresario and the theater director to send two, three, four workers up to the roof, at his own expense even—to find the nest and drive out the insolent creature. But they told him he was crazy. The theater director in particular flew into a rage at the idea, because he was sick and tired, yes, sick and tired of Signorina Gàstina's absurd fears about her gorgeous hair.

"Her hair?"

"Yes, yes, her hair! Haven't you realized that yet?" She'd been led to believe that, were the bat to strike her head, its wings are covered in some sort of sticky substance, so the only way to untangle it would be to cut her hair. "Don't you see? That's what she's afraid of! Instead of getting into character and living her part, at least enough to stop worrying about such nonsense!"

Nonsense, a woman's hair? Little Gàstina's gorgeous hair? The theater director's outburst multiplied a hundredfold Faustino Perres's terror. Oh God! Oh God! If that's really what little Gàstina is afraid of, his play is ruined!

■ ■ ■

Little Gàstina intended to spite the theater director. Before the start of dress rehearsal, legs crossed, one elbow resting on her knee and her chin in her hand, she asked Faustino Perres in a serious voice if His Eminence's line in the second act—"*Giuseppe, dim the lights*"—could perhaps be repeated at other points in the performance, since the only way to get rid of a bat that flies into a room at night is to turn out the lights.

Faustino Perres went cold.

"No, no, I'm serious! Because—excuse me, Perres—don't you want to give a perfect illusion of reality with your play?"

"Illusion? No. Why do you say illusion, Signorina? Art creates its own reality."

"I see. Then I say to you that art creates it and the bat destroys it."

"What? Why?"

"Because it does. Let's suppose that one evening, in real life, during a quarrel between a husband and wife, or a mother and daughter, what do I know! or some other sort of conflict, by chance a bat flies into the room. Fine: what then? I assure you that the quarrel will break off temporarily because of the bat; they will either turn out the lights, or move to another room, or maybe someone goes and gets a stick, climbs on a chair, and tries to hit it, knock it to the floor; then the others, believe me, will instantly forget their quarrel and, grinning in disgust, run to see what the odious creature looks like."

"Of course! But that is in ordinary life!" poor Faustino Perres objected, a wan smile on his lips. "But I did not include a bat in my work of art, Signorina."

"You didn't include it, but what if it intrudes anyway?"

"You simply have to ignore it!"

"Does that seem natural to you? I, who must live the part of Livia in your play, can assure you that it is not; because I know, far better than you, how terrified of bats Livia is! Your Livia—mind you—not me. You never thought about it, because you couldn't have imagined a situation in which a bat flies into the room while she is proudly rebelling against her mother and His Eminence. Yet you can be certain that the bat will fly in tonight. So let me ask you, for the sake of that same reality you so desire to create, does it seem natural to you that, given her fear and loathing of bats, which makes her squirm and scream at the mere thought of coming in contact with one, she just stands there, as if it were nothing? A bat flits in front of her face and she pretends not to notice? You must be joking! Livia runs off, I tell you; she runs off the stage, or hides under a table, screaming like a madwoman. Therefore, I advise you to consider if it might not be better to have His Eminence call Giuseppe and repeat—"*Giuseppe, dim the lights*"—Or . . . wait! Yes! even better! This would be the perfect solution!—he tells him to get a stick, climb on a chair, and . . ."

"Oh, sure! Interrupt the scene halfway through? To the uproarious delight of the entire audience."

"But it would be the height of naturalness, my dear! Believe me. For the sake of your play, since that bat—like it or not—intrudes on the scene: *a real bat!* And if you don't take it into account, your play, with Livia unfazed and the other two not even noticing and carrying on as if it weren't there, will inevitably come off as fake. Don't you see?"

Faustino Perres is exasperated.

"Good God, Signorina. If this is a joke . . ."

"No, no! I mean it," Gàstina retorted. "I'm serious. Perfectly serious!"

"Well then, I say you're mad," Perres said, getting to his feet. "In order for me to take into account that bat, and to make my characters do so as well, it would have to be part of the reality I created; it would have to be a fake bat, in other words, not a real one! Because a random element from real life cannot simply insert itself by chance, from one moment to the next, in the created, essential Reality of a work of art."

"And what if it does?"

"But it's not real! It can't be! That bat is not inserting itself into my play, merely onto the stage where you perform."

"Fine! But the stage is where I perform your play. It's one or the other, then: on that stage, either your play — or the bat — is alive. And the bat, I can assure you, is very much alive. I've already explained that, with a live bat on stage, Livia and the other characters will not seem natural if they have to carry on as if it weren't there when it clearly is. Conclusion: it's either the bat or your play. If, my dear Perres, you deem it impossible to eliminate the bat, then put your play in the hands of God. I will prove to you that I know my part, which I shall perform enthusiastically, because I like it. But I will not answer for my nerves tonight."

■ ■ ■

Every author, every real author, even a mediocre one, to anyone observing him in moments such as opening night for Faustino Perres, appears to be moved or, if you prefer, ridiculous, in the way he — more than anyone else, at times he and no one else — is carried away by what he has written, and laughs and cries and, with bated breath, unconsciously imitates the actors' expressions, gesturing now with this hand, now with that, as he argues or affirms.

I, who observed Faustino Perres on opening night, who kept him company in the wings, amid stage hands and on-duty firemen, can assure you that, for the entire first and the beginning of the second act, Faustino Perres did not even think about the bat, so absorbed was he in his play. Which is not to say that he didn't think about the bat because it hadn't yet made its usual appearance on stage. No. He didn't think about it because he couldn't. So much so that when, toward the middle of the second act, the bat finally did appear, Perres didn't even notice it. He didn't understand why I elbowed him, but merely turned and gave me a dumb look:

"What?"

He only started thinking about it when his play began to take a turn for the worse — not because of the bat or the apprehensions it caused the actors, but because of the obvious defects of the play itself. In truth, the first act had earned only mild, tepid applause.

"Oh my God, look, there it is . . . ," the poor man began to mutter. In a cold sweat, he began to lift one shoulder, lean back, tilt his head now this way, now that, as if the bat were flitting around him and he had to dodge it. He wrung his hands, covered his face. "Oh, God, oh God, it seems mad . . . Look, it practically flew in Rossi's face! . . . Why is it doing this? Why? And Gàstina is about to make her entrance!"

"Be quiet, for heaven's sake!" I urged him, grabbing him by the arms and shaking him, trying to pull him away.

But I couldn't. Gàstina entered from the opposite wing. Perres, trembling all over, stared at her as if bewitched.

The bat circled above, flitting around the eight-globed chandelier hanging from the roof. Gàstina, clearly flattered by the expectant silence that greeted her appearance, seemed not to notice. The scene continued in the same silence, which evidently pleased her.

Ah, if only the bat hadn't been there! But it was! It was! The audience, all intent on the performance, hadn't noticed it either; but there it was, there it was. It seemed to target Gàstina on purpose now, she who, poor thing, was doing everything possible to salvage the play, holding out against her ever-increasing terror of that damned, disgusting bat and its relentless persecution.

Faustino Perres suddenly saw the abyss open before his very eyes right there on stage. He buried his face in his hands as Gàstina shrieked unexpectedly and sank into His Eminence's arms.

I tried to drag Faustino away while the actors, meanwhile, carried off the swooning Gàstina.

No one, amid all the initial confusion and chaos on stage, gave a thought to what was happening in the audience. There was a ruckus in the distance, but no one paid it any heed. Ruckus? What ruckus! It was applause. What? Yes! Applause! Applause! Delirious applause! The entire audience was on its feet, clapping frenetically for four minutes now, calling for the playwright and the actors to come to the front of the stage so they could proclaim that fainting scene, which had been acted with extraordinary believability, a triumph, for they had taken it seriously, as if it were part of the play.

What to do? The theater director, flying into a rage, grabbed the trembling Faustino Perres by the shoulders and shoved him onto the stage. Perres, gaping in puzzlement, was greeted with a resounding ovation, which lasted more than two minutes. And he had to appear another six or seven times to thank the audience, who, seeming not to tire of clapping, clamored for Gàstina as well.

Gàstina! Gàstina!

But how? Gàstina was in her dressing room, still in the grips of a nervous fit, to the dismay of all those hovering around trying to help.

The theater director had to take the stage and announce, regretfully, that the acclaimed actress was unable to appear, and thank the gracious audience because the faint, acted with such intensity, had provoked a sudden illness, and as a result the rest of the evening's performance would have to be suspended.

■ ■ ■

At this point, one cannot help but ask if that damned bat could have done Faustino Perres a worse turn.

It might have been a comfort somehow to attribute the failure of his play to the bat. But to owe it this triumph, a triumph dependent merely upon the frenetic flight of those disgusting wings!

Perres, recovered slightly from his initial astonishment, though still more dead than alive, ran over to the theater director, who had so mercilessly shoved him onstage to thank the audience. Hands in his hair, he shouted: "And tomorrow night?"

"What was I supposed to say? What was I supposed to do?" the furious theater director yelled back. "Was I supposed to tell the audience that their applause was all for the bat and not for her? So fix it! Immediately! Make sure they clap for her tomorrow night!"

"Right! But how?" poor Faustino Perres anguished, foundering again.

"How? How? You're asking me?"

"But Commendatore,[1] that fainting fit is not in my play!"

"Then you need to put it in, my dear man, at all costs! Didn't you see what a success it was? All the newspapers will be talking about it in the morning. You can't do without it. And don't worry,

---

1. *Commendatore* is used for a member of an honorary order of chivalry. Here the title suggests that he is a bigshot.

don't worry, my actors will know how to fake with the same believability what tonight they did unintentionally."

"Right . . . but, don't you see," Perres tried to make him understand, "it all went so well tonight because the performance had to be suspended after she fainted! But if tomorrow it has to carry on . . ."

"That's exactly the remedy you need to find, for God's sake!" the theater director yelled in his face.

But just then, little Gàstina appeared, recovered from her faint.

"But how? How?" she asked, her hands, aglitter with rings, fixing a fur hat on her gorgeous head of hair. "Do you really not understand that it is up to the bat, and not you, sirs, to say?"

"Stop with that bat!" snapped the theater director, menacingly puffing out his chest.

"Me, stop? You are the one who must stop, sir!" Gàstina smiled serenely, sure she would spite him even more now. "Look, sir, let's be reasonable. I may be able to command a fake faint in the second act if Signor Perres takes your advice and includes it. But then you must command the real bat not to make me faint again, for real, in the first or third act, or even in the second, after the fake one! Because, believe me, gentlemen, feeling it hit my face, here, here, on my cheek, I fainted for real! And I will not perform tomorrow night, no, no sir, I won't, because neither you nor anyone else can force me to perform with a bat hitting me in the face!"

"Oh no! We shall see about this! We shall see!" the theater director said, shaking his head vigorously.

But Faustino Perres—fully convinced that the only reason for the applause that evening was the sudden and violent intrusion of an extraneous, random element, which, rather than wrecking, as it should have, art's pretense, had miraculously inserted itself, conferring on it then and there, in the illusion of the public, proof of its marvelous believability—withdrew his play and never spoke about it again.

One day, idle shepherds, climbing the crags of Mìzzaro, surprised a large male raven brooding peacefully on a nest.

"Hey, bozo, what're you doing? Just look at you, brooding! That's your wife's job, you bozo!"

It's impossible not to think that the raven would have squawked his reasons. He squawked them alright, but in raven language, so naturally he wasn't understood. The shepherds played at tormenting him all day long; then one of them took the raven home to the village, but the next day, not knowing what to do with him, he tied a little bronze bell around his neck as a memento, and set him free.

"Enjoy!"

■ ■ ■

What impression that sonorous pendant made on the raven as he flew through the air with it around his neck only he really knew. But judging from the way he flew now, far and wide, no longer mindful of his wife or nest, he seemed delighted with it.

Din dindin din dindin . . .

The peasants, stooped over, intently working the land, on hearing that incessant ringing, would straighten up and look around, across the expanse of fields baking in the sun.

"Where are those bells coming from?"

There wasn't even a hint of wind, so from what far-off church could that festive pealing be coming?

The last thing they could have imagined was that it was a raven, ringing a bell like that above their heads.

"Spirits!" thought Cichè, who was working all alone on a farm, digging wells for fertilizer around the trunks of almond trees. And he crossed himself. Because he believed in Spirits, Cichè did! He'd even heard them call him sometimes, in the evening, coming home late from the countryside, along the main street, near the abandoned kilns where, so everyone said, they lived. Call him? How? Like this: *Cichè! Cichè!* And his hair would stand on end under his cap.

He'd first heard the ringing in the distance, then closer, then in the distance again. There wasn't a soul around, just countryside, trees, and shrubs, which didn't talk and didn't hear, and whose indifference increased his alarm. Then, when he went to get his lunch, which he'd brought from home that morning—half a loaf of bread and an onion—in his knapsack, hung, along with his jacket, on an olive tree a ways away, yes sir, the onion was there, inside the knapsack, but the bread was nowhere to be found. Three times, in the space of a few days, the same thing.

He didn't breathe a word to anyone because he knew that when the Spirits pick on someone, it's no good complaining: they'll go at you however they want, and they'll have their way with you.

"I don't feel good," Cichè would say to his wife when, returning home from work in the evening, she'd ask him why he looked so bewildered.

"You sure can eat, though!" she'd note a little later, seeing him down two and three bowls of soup, one after the other.

"Right, I can eat!" Cichè, who'd fasted since morning and was furious that he couldn't confide in her, would say, chewing on his words.

Until news spread through the countryside of that thieving raven, who went around ringing his bell in the sky.

Cichè's mistake was that, unlike all the other peasants, who'd also been uneasy, he couldn't bring himself to laugh about it.

"I'll make him pay, I promise, I swear!"

So what did he do? In his knapsack, along with his half a loaf and onion, he brought four dried fava beans and four lengths of twine. As soon as he got to the farm, he unsaddled his donkey and led him to the shore, to graze on what stubble remained. Cichè talked to his donkey, the way peasants are wont to do; and the donkey, pricking up now this ear, now that, would snort every now and then, as if to answer him somehow.

"Go on, Ciccio, go," Cichè said to him that day. "Now you just watch, we're going to have some fun!"

He made holes in the fava beans and strung them together with the four pieces of twine, which he tied to the saddle, and then arranged the beans on top of his knapsack, which he'd placed on the ground. Then he headed off and began hoeing.

An hour passed, then two. Now and then Cichè would interrupt his work, thinking he'd heard the tinkle of a bell in the sky. He'd straighten up and cock his ear. Nothing. So he'd go back to his hoeing.

Lunchtime arrived. Unsure as to whether he should go get his bread or wait a little longer, Cichè finally went; but then, seeing the trap so perfectly laid on top of his knapsack, he didn't want to ruin it; meanwhile, he clearly heard a tinkling in the distance. He looked up.

"Here he is!"

And, heart in his throat, he crouched down and hid quietly in the distance.

But the raven, as if he were enjoying the sound of his bell, circled higher and higher, and did not come down.

"Maybe he sees me," Cichè thought, and he got up and hid farther off.

But the raven kept flying high in the sky, without showing any sign of wanting to land. Cichè was hungry, but he wasn't ready to give up. He went back to his hoeing. He waited and waited: the raven still high in the sky, as if on purpose, and Cichè starving, his bread right there, just two feet away, good sirs, without his being able to touch it! Cichè was eating himself up inside, but still, he stubbornly held out.

"You'll come down! You'll come down! You must be hungry too!"

But the raven, meanwhile, seemed to respond spitefully with his bell:

"Neither you nor me! Neither you nor me!"

And so the day passed. Cichè, exasperated, vented on his donkey. He saddled him up again, the four fava beans dangling from the saddle like some new kind of decoration. And riding home,

Cichè angrily gnawed his bread, which had tormented him all day long. With each mouthful he cursed the raven—scoundrel, thief, traitor—because he hadn't let Cichè catch him.

But the next day, things worked out.

Cichè, having prepared the trap again with the same care, had only been working for a little while when he heard an agitated ringing nearby and a desperate cawing amid a furious beating of wings. He rushed over. There was the raven, caught by the twine, which was sticking out of his beak and strangling him.

"Ah ha! So you fell for it!" Cichè shouted, grabbing him by his damn wings. "Was it good, that fava bean? Now it's my turn, you ugly beast! Try this!"

Cichè cut the twine and, for starters, planted two punches on the raven's head.

"This is for scaring me, and this for starving me!"

The donkey, who'd been pulling up stubble along the coast, was frightened by the raven's caw and bolted. Cichè ordered him to stop. Then he showed him the ugly black bird.

"Here he is, Ciccio! We got him! We got him!"

Cichè bound the raven's feet, hung him on a tree, and went back to work. As he hoed, he got to thinking about how he would take his revenge. First he would clip the raven's wings, so he couldn't fly anymore; then he would give the bird to his children and the other kids in the neighborhood, so they could torture him to death. And he laughed to himself.

When evening came, Cichè adjusted the saddle on his donkey's back, took the raven from the tree branch and hung him by his feet from the rump strap of the saddle, mounted, and headed off.

The bell, still tied to the raven's neck, started tinkling. The donkey pricked up his ears and stopped dead in his tracks.

"Giddyup!" Cichè shouted, tugging on the halter.

The donkey started up again, though far from convinced by the strange sound that accompanied his slow plodding along the dusty road.

As he rode, Cichè was thinking that from that day on, no one would have to hear that raven ringing his bell in the air above Mìzzaro anymore. Cichè had him right there, that wicked bird, who no longer showed any signs of life.

"What're you doing?" Cichè asked, turning and smacking the bird on the head with the halter. "Are you asleep?"

"Crah!" the raven said in response to the blow.

The donkey, hearing that unexpected, awful voice, stopped suddenly, neck tense, ears pricked. Cichè burst out laughing.

"Giddyup, Ciccio! What, are you scared?"

And he hit the donkey on the ears with his rope. A little while later, he asked the raven again:

"Are you asleep?"

And another blow, harder now. And so the raven, louder now:
"Crah!"

But this time, the donkey leapt like a goat and took off. Cichè, straining his arms and legs, tried to hold him back, but in vain. The raven, banged about by that furious flight, was cawing desperately, but the more he cawed the faster the frightened donkey ran.

Crah! Crah! Crah!

Cichè was screaming in turn, and yanking, yanking on the halter; but by now those two creatures were crazed, each terrorizing the other, one cackling and the other fleeing. The night resounded for a while with the fury of that desperate flight, then a loud thud, and then, nothing.

The next day, Cichè was found at the bottom of a ravine, broken to bits under his donkey, also broken to bits: a ghastly grave steaming in the sun and swarming with flies.

■ ■ ■

The raven of Mìzzaro, black against the beautiful blue morning sky, was once again ringing his bell in the air, blissful and free.

As Mèndola's carriage passed the little church of San Biagio on the main street, on the way back from his farm, he decided to go up the hill to the cemetery, to see just how much truth there was to the complaints the Town Hall had been receiving about the custodian, Nocio Pàmpina, also known as Sacrament.

Town councilor for about a year now, Nino Mèndola had been feeling poorly right from the first day he took office. Dizzy spells. Without wanting to admit it to himself, he was afraid he'd be struck down any day now with apoplexy, an illness that had prematurely taken his entire family. So he was always in a wretched mood, as the poor little horse hitched to his carriage knew all too well.

But that whole day, out in the countryside, he'd felt good. The physical activity, the relaxation . . . So, as if to face his secret fear, he decided then and there to go inspect the cemetery, something he'd promised his colleagues on the town council he would do but had been putting off for days.

"As if the living weren't enough!" he thought to himself as he went up the hill. "Even the dead make for work in this lousy town! It's the living who always cause the real problems, though! The dead don't know worth a damn whether they're well looked after or not. Well, maybe, maybe not. It's upsetting to think that when we're dead we'll be entrusted to that drunken fool Pàmpina, who'll treat us poorly . . . That's it, I'm going to take a look."

All lies.

Nocio Pàmpina was the ideal cemetery custodian. A cadaverous-looking creature whom a mere breeze could carry away, with pale, lifeless eyes and a voice as feeble as a mosquito's, he seemed to be one of the dead himself, come up from below to carry out a few little domestic chores as best he could.

And besides, what was there to do? All decent folk there, and—by now—all peaceful.

Okay, the leaves. A few fallen leaves, from the hedges, littered the sidewalks. And the mischievous sparrows, unaware that lapidary style does not call for punctuation, had, along with all the other riches their droppings provide, bestowed a few too many commas and exclamation points on the tombstone inscriptions.

Mere trifles.

But just as he was stepping inside the custodian's tiny store-room, to the right of the gate, Mèndola stopped suddenly.

"What's that?"

Nocio Pàmpina's miserable mouth widened into a shadow of a smile and whispered:

"A coffin, your Excellency."

A very handsome coffin, in fact. Of finely polished chestnut wood, gilded, with brass knobs. Clearly money was no object. It was just sitting there, right in the middle of the tiny storeroom.

"Thank you, I can see that," Mèndola retorted. "I mean, why is it here?"

"It belongs to Cavalier Piccarone, your Excellency."

"Piccarone? What for? He's not dead, is he?"

"No, no, your Excellency! And may he never die!" Pàmpina replied. "But you probably know, your Lordship, that his wife died last month, poor gentleman."

"And so?"

"So he accompanied her up here, walked the whole way, old as he is. Yes, indeed. Then he called me over and said, 'Listen, Sacrament, in less than a month you'll have me up here too.' 'What are you saying, your Lordship!' I answered. 'Hush,' he says. 'Now listen to me, my son, this coffin cost me more than twenty *onze*. And it's a beauty, as you can see. No expense spared for the Dearly Departed, you realize. But now that the impression has been made,' he says, 'what is the Dearly Departed going to do underground with this beautiful coffin? It's a shame to waste it,' he says. 'So this is what we'll do. We'll bury the Dearly Departed,' he says, 'with just the inner zinc one, and this one here we'll put aside for me, and I'll use it too. I'll send for it one of these days, at dusk.'"

Mèndola had heard and seen enough. He couldn't wait to go about town spreading news of the coffin that Piccarone had set aside for himself.

■ ■ ■

Gerolamo Piccarone, lawyer and — under Bourbon rule — Knight of San Gennaro, was notorious in town for his stinginess and guile. And what a miserable paymaster! The stories people told about him made your jaw drop. But this — Mèndola thought as he merrily tapped his poor horse's reins—this takes the cake. And it was true, as true as true can be! He'd seen the coffin himself, with his very own eyes.

He was so busy imagining the laughs his story would get, told in Pàmpina's tiny voice, he didn't even notice the commotion and clouds of dust his carriage was kicking up in its mad flight, until all of a sudden—"Whoa! Whoa!"—he heard voices shouting wildly at him from Hunter's Tavern, which a certain Dolcemàscolo ran there on the main road.

Sitting under the pergola out front were Bartolo Gaglio and Gaspare Ficarra, avid hunters who were shouting like that because they were afraid their friend Mèndola had lost control of his horse.

"Lost control? I was galloping . . ."

"Oh, so that's how you gallop, is it?" Gaglio asked. "Do you have a spare neck at home?"

"If only you knew, my friends!" Mèndola exclaimed breathlessly, dismounting cheerfully. And so, beginning right with these two friends, he told the story of the coffin.

At first, to show their surprise, they feigned disbelief. So Mèndola swore—word of honor—that he'd seen the coffin with his own eyes, in Sacrament's tiny storeroom.

The two friends, for their part, began recounting other, well-known anecdotes about Piccarone. Mèndola was anxious to get back in his carriage, but they wanted him to drink and had already asked Dolcemàscolo for a glass for their friend the town councilor.

But Dolcemàscolo, like a bump on a log, didn't budge.

"Hey, Dolcemàscolo!" Gaglio yelled.

The tavernkeeper, jacketless, shirt sleeves rolled up revealing his hairy arms, and his boat-shaped fur cap cocked over one ear, shook off his torpor with a sigh. "Pardon me," he said, "but I'm getting real riled up, I am, listening to your stories. Just this morning, Cavalier Piccarone's dog Turk, that nasty beast that comes and goes as it pleases between his owner's farm in Cannatello and his villa up here . . . you know what that beast did to me? Stole more than twenty links of sausages, that I'd had hanging on that shutter there. I hope they poison the beast! But lucky for me, I've got two eyewitnesses!"

Mèndola, Gaglio, and Ficarra burst out laughing. "Forget about it, my friend!" Mèndola said.

Dolcemàscolo raised his fist, and his eyes flashed fire. "Oh, no, he'll pay for those sausages! For the love of God! He'll pay me, he'll pay all right," he insisted over his customers' incredulous laughter and obstinate denials. "You'll see, gentlemen. I've figured out a way. I know what he's made of."

And with that sly, habitual gesture of his, he pulled down the lower lid of one eye and winked with the other.

What exactly he'd figured out, he wouldn't say. He did say he was waiting for the two peasants who were there that morning, during the sausage theft, to return from the countryside, and that sometime before evening they'd all go to Piccarone's villa together.

Mèndola got back in his carriage without having his drink. Gaglio and Ficarra settled their bill and, after advising the tavernkeeper, for his own good, to forget about getting paid, headed off.

■ ■ ■

Gerolamo Piccarone, lawyer and Knight of San Gennaro at the time of "King Bomb,"[1] had spent more than twenty years building that one-story house of his on the avenue on the outskirts of town, and rumor had it that it hadn't cost him a cent.

The scandalmongers said it was made with rocks Piccarone had found along the road, and which he'd rolled there himself with his foot, one by one.

Yet he was also a most learned scholar of jurisprudence, a high-minded man with a profound philosophical spirit. It was said that a book of his, on Gnosticism, and another on Christian philosophy, had even been translated into German.

But Piccarone was one who cooked his mallow three times. In other words, he was the bitterest enemy of anything new. He still went around dressed in the style of 1821, and with a fringe beard. Gruff, shoulders hunched, brows knitted, eyes half closed, he scratched his chin constantly and grunted approvingly at his secret thoughts.

"Uh . . . uh . . . Italy! They united Italy. . . . How nice . . . Italy . . . roads and bridges . . . uh . . . Street lights. . . . Army and navy . . . uh . . . uh . . . compulsory schooling . . . what if I want to go on being a jackass? Oh, no sir! Compulsory schooling. . . . Taxes! And Piccarone has to pay . . ."

---

1. When Sicily declared independence during the 1848 revolutions, Ferdinand II ordered a naval flotilla to shell the city of Messina for eight hours, even though the city's defenders had already surrendered. This attack, which killed many civilians, earned the Bourbon king the nickname "Re Bomba" or King Bomb.

In truth, he paid little or nothing by dint of quibbling over the tiniest matters, which exhausted and exasperated even the most enduringly patient. He would always conclude by saying: "What does this have to do with me? The railway? I never travel. Electricity? I never go out at night. I don't expect anything, thank you very much, and I don't want anything. Except a bit of air to breathe. Did you make the air as well? Must I pay for the very air I breathe?"

He had, in fact, retired to his little villa as well as from his profession, which until a few years earlier had earned him rather handsome profits. He must have put aside quite a bit. Who would he leave it all to when he died? He had no relatives, near or distant. The banknotes, well, yes, those he could probably take down with him, in that beautiful coffin he'd had set aside for himself. But the villa? And his farm down in Cannatello?

When Dolcemàscolo, together with the two peasants, showed up at Piccarone's gate, Turk, the nasty guard dog, hurled himself furiously against the bars, as if he knew the tavernkeeper was there for him. The old servant realized it was no good trying to hold him back or shoo him away. Piccarone, who was reading in the gazebo in the middle of the lawn, had to whistle for him and then hold him by the collar until the servant could chain him up.

Dolcemàscolo, who knew what's what, had put on his Sunday best. Clean-shaven, he seemed even more prosperous and gentlemanly than usual standing between those two poor peasants who had come back from the fields tired and covered in clay; a sight to see, he was, his face all peaches and cream, and quite fetching with that little curly-haired wart on his right cheek, near his mouth.

He entered the gazebo and exclaimed with feigned admiration: "What a handsome dog! What a fine-looking beast! And quite the guard dog! Worth his weight in gold."

Piccarone, brow knitted and eyes half closed, grunted a few times, nodding at the praise, and then said, "So what is it you want? Have a seat."

And he pointed to some iron stools scattered about the gazebo. Dolcemàscolo drew one up to the table and said to the peasants, "Sit over there. I've come to you, sir, for some advice, given as you are a man of the law."

Piccarone opened his eyes.

"I don't practice law anymore, my friend, haven't for quite a while."

"I know," Dolcemàscolo added hastily. "But you are an authority on the law, sir. And my father, bless his soul, always used to say to me, 'Listen to the authorities, my son!' Besides, I know how conscientious you were in your practice, sir. I don't have much faith in these young lawyers today. Not that I want to pick a fight with anyone, mind you! I'd be mad . . . I came here for some simple advice, which only you, sir, can give me."

Piccarone closed his eyes again.

"Go on, I'm listening."

"You know, sir—" Dolcemàscolo began. But Piccarone snorted irritably. "Of course I know! I know as much as you! I know, you know . . . Get to the point, my friend!"

Dolcemàscolo didn't take this well, but he smiled anyway and started again.

"Yes, sir. What I wanted to say is that you, sir, know that I have a tavern on the main street . . ."

"Hunters' Tavern. Yes, I know. I've passed it many times."

"On your way to Cannatello, of course. So you certainly will have seen how I always hang some provisions under the pergola: bread, fruit, prosciutto."

Piccarone nodded his head yes, then added mysteriously, "Seen, and even tasted, now and again."

"Tasted?"

"They taste of sand, my son. Being near the road, you realize . . . But enough. Get to the point."

"Right, sir." Dolcemàscolo swallowed. "Let's suppose I've hung out some . . . some sausages, for instance. Now, sir . . . maybe you . . . oh! I was about to say it again! It's a habit of mine . . . Well, sir, maybe you don't know, but it's quail season. So on the main street, it's hunters and dogs all the time. I'm getting to the point! So this one dog goes by, sir Cavalier, and jumps up and grabs my sausages right off the shutter."

"A dog?"

"Yes, sir, a dog. So I dive after it, me and these two poor peasants here, who had stopped to buy something to go with their bread before heading out to work the fields. Isn't that the truth? So all three of us run after the dog, but we can't manage to catch it. Besides, even if we did, sir, tell me, what could I have done with those sausages, all bitten and dragged along the road . . . It wouldn't even be worth picking them up! But I recognized the dog, I know who it belongs to."

"Uh, just a minute—" Piccarone interrupted now. "The owner wasn't there?"

"No, sir!" Dolcemàscolo answered right away. "He wasn't with the hunters. It's clear the dog had run off. Good sniffing dogs can smell the hunt, and they can't stand being locked up at home. So they run off. That simple. But like I said, I know who the dog belongs to. And so do these two friends of mine, who were present at the theft. Now, sir, as a man of law, you merely need to tell me if the dog's owner is obliged to pay the damages, that's all!"

Piccarone didn't hesitate.

"Of course he's obliged, my son."

Dolcemàscolo leapt for joy, but then checked himself right away. He turned to the two peasants.

"Did you hear that? The honorable lawyer says that the owner of the dog is obliged to pay me damages."

"Unquestionably obliged, unquestionably," Piccarone confirmed. "I didn't tell you no, did I?"

"No, sir," Dolcemàscolo replied, overjoyed, clasping his hands. "But you must pardon me, sir, if, poor ignorant soul that I am, I took such a roundabout way to get to the point of saying that you, sir, must pay me for the sausages, because the dog that stole them from me was yours, Turk."

Piccarone stared at Dolcemàscolo for a while, dumbfounded. Then, all of a sudden, he lowered his gaze and started reading the big book that lay open in front of him on the table.

The peasants looked each other in the eye. Dolcemàscolo raised a hand, signaling for them to keep quiet.

Piccarone, still pretending to read, scratched his chin with one hand, grunted, and then said, "So, it was Turk, was it?"

"I swear, sir Cavalier!" Dolcemàscolo stood up and crossed his heart, in solemn oath.

"And so you came here," Piccarone continued, in a deep, calm voice, "with two witnesses, right?"

"No, sir!" Dolcemàscolo countered right away. "Just in case you didn't believe me."

"Ah, is that why?" Piccarone grumbled. "But I believe you, my friend. Sit down. You're a good man. I believe you and I'll pay you. Am I known for not paying, then?"

"Who would say such a thing, sir?"

"Everyone! And you think so too, right? Come on. Two . . . uh . . . two witnesses . . ."

"I swear, for you as much as for me!"

"Good, fine, just as you say, for me as much as for you. I have no interest in paying unfair fees, my friend. But I'm happy to pay what's fair, always have been. Turk stole your sausages? Tell me how much, and I'll pay you for them."

Dolcemàscolo, who had come prepared to fight who knows what battle against the old toad's quibbles and snares, now, faced with such submissiveness, suddenly went limp with mortification.

"A trifle, Cavalier. Probably twenty links, more or less. Almost not worth talking about."

"No, no," Piccarone replied resolutely. "Tell me how much it is. I owe you money and I intend to pay you. Right away, my son! You work, you suffered a loss, so you must be compensated. How much?"

Dolcemàscolo shrugged his shoulders, smiled and said, "Twenty links, big ones. . . . Two kilos. . . . One *lira* twenty per kilo . . ."

"That's all you sell them for?" Piccarone asked.

"But sir," Dolcemàscolo answered, his voice all honey now. "You didn't eat them, you see. So I'm charging you . . . I wouldn't want . . . I'm charging you what they cost me."

"Nothing doing!" Piccarone insisted. "I didn't eat them, but my dog did. So, you said, two kilos, give or take. Is two *lire* a kilo all right?"

"As you please."

"Four *lire*. That's fine. Now tell me, my son, twenty-five minus four, how much is that? Twenty-one, if I'm not mistaken. Fine. Give me twenty-one *lire* and we'll call it even."

At first Dolcemàscolo thought he'd heard wrong.

"Excuse me?"

"Twenty-one *lire*," Piccarone repeated placidly. "Here we have two witnesses, for me as much as for you, right? You came here to ask my advice. Well, my son, for advice, legal consultations, I charge twenty-five *lire*. That's my fee. I owe you four for the sausages, so if you give me twenty-one, we're all settled up."

Dolcemàscolo stared him in the face, unsure whether he should laugh or cry. He didn't want to believe Piccarone was serious, but it didn't look as if he was joking.

"I . . . you?" he stuttered.

"It seems quite clear to me, my son," Piccarone explained. "You are a tavernkeeper, and I a humble lawyer. Now, just as I do not deny your right to be compensated, you will not deny mine for the illumination you requested and which I gave you. Now you know that if a dog steals your sausages, the dog's owner is obliged to recompense you. Did you know that before? No! Knowledge is something you pay for, my friend. I suffered and spent a lot to acquire it! Do you think I'm joking?"

"But sir!" Dolcemàscolo, tears running down his cheeks, conceded, opening his arms. "I won't make you pay for the sausages, sir Cavalier, I'm just a poor fool, forgive me, and let's call it even, truly."

"Oh no, oh no, my friend!" Piccarone exclaimed. "I don't forgive anything! The law is the law, for you as it is for me. I'll pay, I want to pay. Pay and be paid. I was sitting here studying, as you can see. You made me waste an hour of my time. Twenty-one *lire*. My fee. If you're not completely convinced, then listen to me, my friend. Go to another lawyer and inquire if this money is due me or not. I'll give you three days. If by the third day you haven't paid me, my friend, you can be sure, I will sue you."

"But sir Cavalier!" Dolcemàscolo entreated, hands clasped, but his expression suddenly altered.

Piccarone thrust out his chin and raised his hands. "No excuses! I'm suing you!"

Dolcemàscolo's eyes dimmed. He was overcome with rage. What was the harm? Nothing. But he couldn't help thinking about the jokes they'd make, he could already imagine them, just by looking at the amused faces of those two peasants. Jokes about him, who had thought himself so clever, and who had worked so hard to achieve victory, which was practically in his grasp. And now, when he least expected it, to see himself caught in his own trap, and transformed suddenly into a ferocious beast.

"Ah, so that's why," he said as he drew closer, arms raised, fists clenched, "so that is why your dog is such a thief? You trained him yourself!"

Piccarone rose agitatedly to his feet and lifted his arm.

"Get out! You'll also have to answer for insulting a gentleman who . . ."

"Gentleman?" Dolcemàscolo roared as he grabbed Piccarone's raised arm and shook it furiously.

The two peasants hurled themselves at Dolcemàscolo to stop him. But all of a sudden, just like that, the old man went limp, and hung there without moving, dangling by one arm from Dolcemàscolo's violent grip. And as soon as the bewildered Dolcemàscolo opened his hands, Piccarone fell, first onto the stool, then he spilled to one side, and then rolled to the ground, landing all in a heap.

Seeing the peasants' terror, Dolcemàscolo's face contracted, as if in a spasm of laughter. What? He hadn't even touched him!

The peasants kneeled over the body and moved one of his arms.

"Run! Run!"

Dolcemàscolo looked at them both as if in a daze. "Run?"

Just then they heard the gate creak and saw the coffin, which the old man had had set aside for himself, entering in triumph on the shoulders of two panting porters. They seemed almost to have been summoned, then and there, just for this.

Dolcemàscolo and the peasants were petrified at the apparition.

It didn't occur to Dolcemàscolo that Nocio Pàmpina, after the town councilor's visit and comments, would have hastened to comply with regulations by sending back the coffin. But he suddenly recalled what Mèndola had said that morning, there in his tavern. In that empty, waiting coffin, which had appeared at exactly the right moment as if mysteriously summoned, he saw the hand of destiny; destiny had made use of him, of his hand.

He clasped his head and started to shout. "Here it is! Here it is! It was calling to him! You are all my witnesses, I never even touched him! The coffin was calling to him! He had it set aside for himself! And here it is, he had to die!"

And he grabbed the two porters by their arms to shake them from their stupor.

"Isn't that the truth? Isn't it? Say it!"

■ ■ ■

But those two porters were not the least bit amazed. Since they were delivering the lawyer's coffin, for them it was the most natural thing in the world to find the lawyer dead. They merely shrugged their shoulders and said, "But of course, here we are."

ROMULUS

It's well known that in so-called civil societies, also called historical societies, legends can no longer be born. Among simple folk, however, a legend may and often is born, humbly, and then crawls along timidly, like a small snail, immediately withdrawing its tentacled eyes amid the worthless, bubbling trail of slime as soon as some history professor, with a stiff, ink-stained finger, reaches out and touches them.

The history professor believes that sacred truth lies in that stiff, ink-stained finger of his, and that it's a good thing to make the snail withdraw its eyes. Wretch! And even more wretched are those who come after him, who have their ancestors' and forefathers' deeds documented minute by minute, deeds which, had they been relegated to memory and the imagination, would perhaps have taken on the hazy hue of poetry, like all distant things.

History, history. Enough of poetry.

■ ■ ■

So here he is, without the she-wolf, without his brother Remus, or the flight of vultures: Romulus, just as the historians present him to us; just as I met him yesterday, still alive.

Romulus: the founder of a city.

And, looking him squarely in his wolf eyes, it must be said, it's a shame! One could easily believe a she-wolf had nursed him when he was a baby, some ninety years ago. And even though it wasn't his brother, he really did have a rival Remus opposite him. The only reason Romulus didn't kill him was that Remus took it upon himself to die first, in timely fashion, on his own. But don't go searching the maps for the city this Romulus founded. You won't find it. Posterity will find it for sure, though, three or four hundred years from now, marked, I'm sure, by one of those little circles that indicate the capital cities of a province, its worthy name next to it: *Riparo*, so everyone can imagine the fine things that will be there: streets, piazzas, buildings, churches, monuments, with Mr. and Mrs. Prefect, if such wise social orders even still exist then, and if (with the help of God, who chastises the ambitions of man) an earthquake has not shaken it to its very foundations. But let's hope not.

It's more than a hamlet now, a nice village already, and soon to have two little churches.

One is this one here. Formerly a stable, it was transformed into a church on Romulus's urging: just one small altar, old wood oiled by the hot stench of manure, and a print of the sacred heart of Jesus, simply tacked to the wall, of course, but what does it matter? Jesus feels right at home in this manger.

Every Sunday a priest on his molly mule comes from miles and miles away to say mass, all sweaty and caked in dust in summer, in winter bundled up to his eyeballs and holding a green silk umbrella, just like in the oleographs. The mule, tethered to the ring next to the door, waits, snorting and kicking at the flies on her haunches.

Look, here are her scuff marks. Poor beast, she doesn't know it's a divine duty. To her it seems like a huge nuisance, and a thousand years before it's over.

The other church, the new one, will be finished soon, and will be real elegant, bell tower, the whole works, three altars and a pulpit and the sacristy, everything, in other words: a real church, built as a church from square one, with so much a head from each villager.

Now, when this village becomes a city, not one of its many sons will know anything about their founding father Romulus; how and why the city was born; why here and not somewhere else. Once a city has risen up, it's impossible to see how the land, how the place was before it was there. It's hard to cancel out life, when life has expressed and imposed itself on a place with so much weighty clutter: houses, streets, piazzas, churches.

It used to be a desert here, nothing but blessed desert. Men whose lives unfolded far, far away passed through this desert as if unfurling a ribbon: a wide road. And little by little, carts started traveling this ribbon of road in solitude, and occasionally a man on horseback, armed, would peer around warily, dismayed to discover he's the only one seeing so much solitude, so far away and so unfamiliar to everyone. Surrounded by silence, under the sullen vastness of the sky.

When, four hundred years from now, electric tram bells and car horns will clamor and squeal amid the confusion of crowded streets illuminated by arc lamp posts, with the twinkling and sparkling of glass, of mirrors in the bulging windows of fancy shops, who will ponder that solitary light in the sky, the Moon, which in silence and solitude looked down from above on the white ribbon of road in the middle of the immense desert, or remember the crickets and tree frogs loudly chirping all alone here? Who, amid the empty chatter in the cafés, will think about the angry cicadas that, among the chopped stubble here, cut through the vast, still closeness of the dazzling, endless summer days?

■ ■ ■

Carts, men on horseback, a few others on foot. They'd come through here, and they'd all feel uneasy at the solitude that eventually became unbearably oppressive. What was this road to them? The length of their journey, the path to take. Who would have thought to stop?

One man. This old man here. About thirty years old at the time, absorbed in thoughts that drew him away from the company of other men to seek his fortune in solitude, he had the courage one summer day to stop the shadow of his own body in the middle of this road. Perhaps he felt that many others like him, on passing by, had felt or would feel the need for a little rest in that spot, a little comfort and assistance. Here, he said.

He looked around and observed what before he'd seen merely with the distracted gaze of one who is passing through and doesn't think about stopping; now he looked with the sense of his presence here, not just for a moment, but for good; and he tried to breathe the empty air, to see the things around him as if this were his air, his daily view. And with the courage that was rising up inside him to settle down and establish himself here, he compared the infinite sadness of that solitude—if, that is, he had the courage to resist and endure it, not now, but through the winter, when the cold and the frowning sky and the endless days of rain would seem more bleak and frightening.

■ ■ ■

The old man speaks by way of an apologia; he recounts that as a boy he had a sickly little sister, a poor eater, whose mother toiled to please her.

One day, while he was playing furiously in the street with his friends, his mother, sitting on the front stoop, called him over, a barely cooked egg in her hand. She wanted him to slowly, carefully drink off the white, which his sickly sister found disgusting.

Well, he was supposed to only sip off the white, but in the fury of his interrupted game, without intending to, he sucked out the entire egg, yolk and white, the whole thing, leaving his mother and little sister wide-eyed with surprise, and an empty shell.

■ ■ ■

It was the same thing now, here on the road.

When he said "here," he certainly didn't have in mind today's village or tomorrow's city. He figured it would always be just him offering assistance to all who came along. But there was enough air in that first breath of his in the middle of the road not just for one thatched roof, but for all of today's village and tomorrow's city. And his courage in raising that first thatched roof was so great that others couldn't help but be drawn to it.

But when an unexpected necessity meets with a delusion, the necessity seems like a betrayal.

This was it: after he, braving the horrors of solitude alone for months on end, had managed to get the passing carts to stop in front of his thatched roof, and then, after erecting little by little a stone house and bringing his wife and children there, had managed to sit the carters down under a pergola to drink some wine, a sample bottle of which hung like a sign from a branch over the door, and to eat out of rustic bowls the food his wife had cooked while he repaired a cartwheel or spring, or shoed a horse or mule, another man came along and built another house across from his, a bit further down the road.

Because this (the old man knows it now, and can speak from experience), this is how a village is born.

It's not true at all that men come together to offer each other comfort and assistance. They come together to wage war. When a house goes up somewhere, the next house doesn't place itself alongside it as companion or good sister; no, it stands opposite, like an enemy, to take away its air and its view.

Romulus didn't have the right to keep another house from rising up across the way. The land on which it was built didn't belong to him. But before he'd arrived, this land had been a desert. What life had there been there? He was the one who had given life to the place. The fraud and usurpation that the other man came here to commit was not of land, but of the life he had given the land.

"It's not yours!" was all the other man could say to him.

"Right. But what was there before you came?" was all he could shout in reply. "Would you ever have come if I hadn't come here first? When there was nothing? And now you come and rob me of what I built here!"

■ ■ ■

But—he had to admit—he had built too much for one man.

All the carts stopped there now for their usual respite, often a long line of them. His wife couldn't serve them all, and was so exhausted she could barely stand; and he, who had only the two hands God had given him, could barely feel them at night, they were so tired. So there was room enough and work enough not only for another, but maybe even for three or four others.

Now the old man says he would have preferred just that. With three or four others, they would have become companions, partners, and could have divvied up the work; and maybe his wife would not have worked herself to death. But just one other—of course he became his enemy, an enemy to drive away, even with a knife, from the life he had brought into being along that road; that life was his. Faced with three or four together, he would have tried, would have reached an agreement; and they certainly would have recognized and respected him as the first, the leader. But against just one other, he had to defend himself fiercely, so as not to let him take any of the life there, or only that little he could no longer hold in his own two hands. But the consequence was that his wife died from too much work.

"God!" the old man now says, pointing to the heavens.

And he leaves shrouded in the shadows past events and circumstances, in which he recognizes God's hand, and thus man's duty to accept them, obediently and resignedly, painful and cruel as they may seem. Events pass, and in the face of the certainty that God's justice triumphs always, it's pointless to recall them.

Romulus must reason this way. He must recognize that his wife's death was God's justice: that God, in other words, punished him with her death for his wanting too much. Because in the end Romulus must point out the triumph of divine justice in himself who—once Remus died—married Remus's wife. And why did Remus die? That too was divine punishment, a great fear God placed upon him; he died because he realized that the man he had set himself against, devastated now by the death of his wife, would unleash all his fury and desperation on him.

Could God allow for a punishment of his to become excessive and therefore unjust, allowing that other man to profit from that which Romulus had lost upon the death of his wife? God's punishment, which for Romulus was suffering, for the other was fear; so much fear that he died of it. Romulus doesn't elaborate.

He does, however add that in those two opposing houses, both filled with children who until then had never been allowed to approach each other or play together; in one of those two opposing houses was a man without a woman and in the other a woman without a man. And he, dressed in black, saw her, also dressed in black; and God made charity blossom in their hearts, a reciprocal need for help and comfort.

And the first war ended.

Romulus shakes his head and smiles.

He sees in his mind's eye how after the first two houses, others rose, and the children of each family grew up, some marrying among themselves, others bringing a spouse, be it a husband or a wife from afar.

Oh, those houses, one here, one there! Not enemies exactly.

No. But across, they were. They didn't turn their backs to each other, but one turned slightly this way, another that, as if they didn't want to look each other in the face. Until, with the passing of the years, a third house—a peacemaker—rose up in between and reunited them.

"This is why," Romulus says, "old roads in small villages are all crooked, why every house is skewed."

Yes, this is why. But then, oh Romulus, civilization arrives, with its urban development plans, which require houses to stand all in a row.

"Frontal war," you say.

Yes, but civilization means the recognition precisely of the fact that man, in addition to many other instincts that drive him to make war, also has what is called a social instinct, so that he lives only with his same kind.

■ ■ ■

"See then," you conclude, "if man can ever be happy!"

Bernardino Lamis, Professor of the History of Religion, half closing his sad, suffering eyes and, as was his habit on the most solemn of occasions, resting his skull-like head in his delicate, trembling hands, the fingers of which seemed tipped with shiny pink shells rather than nails, announced to the only two pupils who, with dogged fidelity, had enrolled in his course: "In the next class, gentlemen, we shall speak of the Cathar Heresy."

One of the two, Ciotta—a squat, brown-haired student from Guarcino, in the Roman Campagna—ground his teeth with ferocious glee and rubbed his hands together fervently. The other, Vannìcoli—pale, with bristly blond hair, a listless air, and light, languid eyes that grew even more despondent now—pursed his lips and pointed his nose, as if sniffing some unpleasant odor, to show he understood the distress the topic must cause his revered teacher, after all he had told him privately about it. (For Vannìcoli was convinced that, when he and Ciotta accompanied him home after class, Professor Lamis spoke exclusively to him, the only one who truly understood him.)

And as a matter of fact, Vannìcoli knew that about six months earlier, in Germany (Halle, Saxony-Anhalt), Hans von Grobler had published a mammoth monograph on the Cathar Heresy, which the critics had praised to the skies; and that three years prior, Bernardino Lamis had written two ponderous tomes on the same subject, which von Grobler clearly had not taken into account, mentioning them only once, in passing, in a brief and disparaging footnote.

It cut Bernardino Lamis to the quick. He was even more distressed and indignant about the Italian critics, who, in blindly lauding the German work, did not even remotely remember his two, earlier volumes; nor did they waste a single word on the German author's shameful treatment of their fellow Italian. He had waited more than two months for someone, one of his former students at least, to come to his defense. Then—even though he knew it was not ideal—he defended himself, noting, in a long and meticulous review peppered with biting irony, all the careless errors, large and small, which von Grobler had made, all the points he had appropriated from his own work without acknowledging him, and then reasserted, with new and incontrovertible arguments, his own views against those of the German historian.

Two journals had rejected his defense, however, as too long and of too little interest to most readers. A third had been sitting on it for over a month, and who knows how much longer it would continue to do so, judging by the less than courteous reply Lamis received from the editor when he'd prompted him.

So Bernardino Lamis really did have reason to vent bitterly that day as his two devoted pupils walked him homeward, as usual, after class. He spoke to them of the shameless charlatanism that had spread from the realm of politics to that of literature, and which now, unfortunately, was ruining the sacred and inviolable dominion of science; of the cowardly servitude rooted deep in the Italian character, for which anything from beyond the Alps or across the ocean was a precious gem, while everything produced in Italy was a contemptible fake; and finally, he hinted at stronger arguments against his adversary, to be developed in his next lecture. Ciotta, already savoring the pleasure of his professor's ironic and ill-tempered ideas, rubbed his hands together again, while the stricken Vannìcoli sighed.

At a certain point, Professor Lamis fell silent and adopted a distant expression: a signal to his two pupils that he wished to be left alone.

After every class, to unwind, he would stroll with his students down to Piazza del Pantheon, up to Piazza della Minerva, across Via dei Cestari, and onto Corso Vittorio Emanuele. Near Piazza San Pantaleo he would adopt a distant expression, because — before heading down Via del Governo Vecchio, where he lived — he would duck furtively (for that was his intention) into a pastry shop, emerging shortly after with a paper cone.

Professor Lamis's two pupils, who knew he was as poor as a church mouse, could not fathom that mysterious purchase three times a week.

Goaded by curiosity, Ciotta even entered the pastry shop one day, to ask what the professor purchased there.

"Amaretti, meringues, hazelnut pastries."

Who were they for?

His little nieces and nephews, said Vannìcoli. But Ciotta was convinced they were for the professor himself. Ciotta had surprised him once in the street, right as he was reaching in his pocket for a meringue, and he must have had one in his mouth as well, which explains why he didn't return Ciotta's greeting.

"Well, even if it were true, where's the harm in that? A sweet tooth!" Vannìcoli had replied, annoyed, his languid gaze following his feeble old professor as, slow and shuffling, he tottered away.

Not merely this little gluttony, but a great many more things could be forgiven this man who, for the sake of learning, had reduced himself so, his shoulders so hunched they seemed to want to slide off him, but were held on pathetically by his long neck, which protruded as if under a yoke. Professor Lamis's bald patch peaked out like a leathery half-moon between his hat and the nape of his neck, over which a silvery straggle of hair quivered, flopping here and there over his ears and turning, on his jowls and chin, into a beard.

Neither Ciotta nor Vannìcoli could ever have imagined that that paper cone Bernardino Lamis carried home contained his meal for the entire day.

Two years before, his sister-in-law, a real harpy, with seven children, the oldest of which was barely eleven, had descended on him from Naples, after his brother's sudden demise there. Professor Lamis, let it be noted, had never wanted to take a wife, so as not to be distracted in any way from his studies. So when, without any advance notice, he was met with this shrieking army, camped out on the landing in front of his door, straddling countless bales and bundles, he was aghast. Unable to escape down the stairs, he considered for a moment throwing himself out the window. The four tiny rooms of his modest abode were invaded; the discovery of a small garden, their uncle's only pleasant pastime, provoked a frenetic jubilation in the seven inconsolable orphans, as his fat Neapolitan sister-in-law called them. A month later, not a single blade of grass was left in that little garden. Professor Lamis had become a shadow of his former self; he wandered about his study, seeming to have lost his mind and holding his head in his hands, as if to keep it, too, from being carried off by the shrieking and crying and pandemonium that raged from morning to night. It had lasted a year, this torment, and who knows how much longer it would have gone on had he not realized, one day, that his sister-in-law, not satisfied with his salary, which he handed over to her in full the 27th of every month, would help her oldest child clamber up from the garden to the window of his study, the door to which he prudently kept locked, in order to steal his books:

"Big fat ones, Gennarie', big and fat and new!"

Half of his library had ended up at the used book sellers for practically nothing.

Incensed, in a rage, that very same day, after forbidding his sister-in-law to ever show her face to him again, Bernardino Lamis, with six crates of his remaining books, three rustic bookshelves, a large cardboard crucifix, a basket of linens, three chairs, a big leather easy chair, his tall desk, and a washstand, went to live— alone—in those two little rooms on Via del Governo Vecchio.

He sent her his pay through the university porter now, punctually every month, keeping only the bare minimum for himself.

He hadn't wanted to take a servant even half-time, for fear that she would come to some understanding with his sister-in-law. And besides, he didn't need one. He hadn't even brought his bed with him: he slept in his easy chair, wrapped in a wool blanket, a shawl over his shoulders. He didn't cook. A follower, in his own way, of Fletcher's theory of mastication, he ate little and chewed a lot. He would empty the contents of that notorious paper cone into his two large pants pockets, half in one, half in the other, and—as was his habit—while he stood reading or studying, he would nibble on an amaretto or a meringue or a hazelnut pastry. If he was thirsty: water. After a year of that inferno, this felt like paradise.

But then came von Grobler with his miserable book on the Cathar Heresy to spoil everything.

■ ■ ■

As soon as he got home that day, Bernardino Lamis set to working feverishly again.

He had two days to finish crafting the lecture that was so important to him. He wanted it to be formidable, every word a jab at that dreadful German von Grobler.

He was in the habit of writing his lectures out word for word, on foolscap, in a minuscule hand. Then, in class, he would read them in a slow, serious voice, knitting his brow, tilting his head back, and squinting in order to see through the lenses drooping off the tip of his nose, bristly little bushes of gray hairs protruding from the nostrils. His two faithful pupils had plenty of time to take notes, as if taking dictation. Lamis never used the raised professorial desk, instead sitting humbly at a small table below it. The pupils' desks were arranged, amphitheater style, in four rows. The room was dark, and Ciotta and Vannìcoli would sit in the last row, one on each end, so as to get the light from the two grated oculi high up on the wall. Lamis never saw them during class; all he would hear was the rasping of their frenzied pens.

Since no one had come to his defense, he would avenge himself of that damned German's insolence, delivering a memorable lecture right there in class.

First, he would succinctly and lucidly expound the origin, cause, essence, historical importance, and consequences of the Cathar Heresy, summarizing from his two volumes on the subject; then he would enter into the polemics, availing himself of his critical study of von Grobler's book. In command of the material as he was, and with his critical study at hand, his only concern now was to rein in his pen. Motivated by bitterness, he could have written two more volumes, heftier than the previous ones, in the space of two days.

Instead, he had to limit himself to a straightforward lecture of just over an hour: in other words, no more than five or six pages of foolscap in his minute handwriting. Two were already written. The remaining three or four were for disputation.

He wanted to reread the draft of his review of von Grobler's book before he set about writing. He took it out of his desk drawer, blew off the dust, and—glasses perched on the tip of his nose—stretched out in his leather chair.

Reading it, he was so gratified that it's a miracle he didn't stand up right in his chair. And, in less than an hour, he inadvertently ate all the meringues that were supposed to last him two whole days. Mortified, he turned his pockets inside out, to shake out the crumbs.

Of course he began writing with the intention to briefly summarize his critical study. However, as he wrote, he gradually allowed himself to be won over by the temptation to incorporate the whole of it, word for word, in his lecture, since nothing, not a single comma, seemed superfluous to him. How could he possibly eliminate certain witty and effective remarks? And certain pertinent, decisive arguments? And countless others that came to him as he wrote, even more coherent and convincing, and equally impossible to leave out.

When the third day dawned—the day of his lecture—on Bernardino Lamis's desk were not six but a good fifteen pages, covered in his tiny handwriting.

He was dismayed.

Extremely scrupulous in his duties, he was in the habit, at the beginning of every year, of providing an overview, to which he rigorously adhered, of all the material to be covered during the course. That year, because of von Grobler's ill-fated publication, he had already allowed one concession to his wounded pride, that of speaking in untimely fashion about the Cathar Heresy. He simply could not devote more than one class to it. Under no circumstances did he want it said that Professor Lamis, whether out of caprice or the need to vent, spoke inopportunely or unnecessarily about a subject that was, at best, only remotely related to the course material.

Thus it was absolutely necessary, in the few hours that remained, to reduce to eight or, at most, nine the fifteen pages he had written.

This cost him so much intellectual effort that he didn't even notice the violent storm—hail, thunder and lightning—that suddenly let loose over Rome. When he got to the front door of his building, his lecture bundled under his arm, it was pouring. What to do? Class was to begin in ten minutes. He went back upstairs, armed himself with an umbrella, and then set out in the downpour, protecting as best he could his "formidable" lecture.

He arrived at the university in a pitiful state, drenched from head to toe. He left his umbrella in the janitor's office, stamped his feet to shake off the rain, dried his face, and made his way up to the loggia.

The classroom—dark even in good weather—was like a catacomb in this hellish hurricane; you could barely see. Yet on entering, Professor Lamis, who was in the habit of never raising his head, was consoled to glimpse, out of the corner of his eye, an unusually large crowd, and in his heart he praised his two faithful pupils, who had evidently spread the word among their classmates of the special commitment with which their old professor was to deliver today's lecture, which had cost him so much trouble and labor and which, thanks to his supreme effort, contained so many treasures of wisdom, and captured so much wit.

Overcome with emotion, he put down his cap and, unusually, stepped up to the professor's desk. His delicate hands were shaking so much that he struggled more than a little to place his glasses on the tip of his nose. The room was perfectly silent. Professor Lamis unrolled his papers and began to read in a loud, resonant voice that even he marveled at. What pitch would he adopt once, having finished the expository part, he launched into the disputation, for which this tone of voice was not suitable? But Professor Lamis was no longer master of himself. As if bitten by the viper of his own style, he felt his kidneys suddenly split open from the thrill; his voice gradually grew louder, and he began to gesticulate. Yes, Professor Bernardino Lamis, always so rigid and reserved, was gesticulating! Too much bile had built up in him those six months; too much indignation, provoked by the servitude and silence of Italian scholars. This was his moment of revenge! All those fine young students, sitting and listening religiously to him, would talk about today's lecture, would tell how he had sat in the professorial chair to ensure that his contemptuous reply would travel with greater solemnity from the Atheneum of Rome not only to von Grobler, but to all of Germany.

He'd been reading like this, with increasing animation and vibrancy, for three-quarters of an hour when his pupil Ciotta— who, having been caught in the heavy downpour on his way to the university, took shelter in a doorway—appeared, a little frightened, at the entrance to the classroom. Being late, he'd been hoping that Professor Lamis would not have come to class in such dreadful weather. What's more, he'd found a note in the janitor's station downstairs from Vannìcoli, who begged him to apologize to their beloved professor: Having slipped in his doorway last night and tumbled down the stairs, dislocating his shoulder, he could not, because of his acute pain, attend class today.

So who was Professor Bernardino Lamis talking to with such fervor?

Ciotta, tiptoeing like a thief, stepped over the threshold and peered around. Still slightly dazzled by the light from outside, dim as it was, he too caught sight of numerous students, and was astonished. Is it possible? He strained to take a better look.

Twenty or so raincoats, draped here and there to drip in the dark, deserted classroom, formed Professor Lamis's entire audience that day.

Ciotta stared at them, dumbfounded. Seeing his professor lecturing so enthusiastically to raincoats, he felt his blood run cold. He stepped back, almost afraid.

Meanwhile, the hour being up, a horde of law students spilled noisily from a nearby classroom—the owners of the raincoats, apparently.

Ciotta, still catching his breath from the shock, immediately extended his arms and planted himself in the classroom door, preventing them from entering.

"Please! Don't go in! Professor Lamis is in there."

"What's he doing?" they asked, astonished at how distraught Ciotta was.

Ciotta, wide-eyed, placed a finger to his lips, then said quietly: "He's talking to himself!"

They burst into noisy, uncontrollable laughter.

Ciotto quickly closed the classroom door and again begged them:

"Be quiet, please, quiet! Don't humiliate him, the poor old man! He's talking about the Cathar Heresy!"

The students promised to keep quiet, but they wanted the door opened again so as to enjoy the spectacle of their poor raincoats, dripping there in the dark, listening to Professor Bernardino Lamis's formidable lecture.

■ ■ ■

". . . but Manicheism, gentlemen, what, in the end, is Manicheism? You tell me! Now, if, as our illustrious German historian Mr. Hans von Grobler claims, the first Albigensians . . ."

Without a doubt, Mr. Charles Trockley is right. In fact, I'm prepared to admit that Mr. Charles Trockley can never be wrong, because he and Reason are one and the same thing. Every move, every look, every word of his is so definitive and precise, so studied and certain, that surely everyone must agree that regardless of the circumstances, irrespective of the question posed or the situation that arises, it's impossible for Mr. Charles Trockley to be wrong.

Let me give you an example: he and I were born in the same year, in the same month, almost on the same day, he in England and I in Sicily. Today, June 15, is his forty-eighth birthday, whereas I will turn forty-eight on June 28. So—how old will we be next year, he on the 15th and I on the 28th of June? Mr. Trockley does not get flustered, does not hesitate, not even for a second: he responds confidently, decisively, that on June 15 and 28 of next year, we will both be one year older, in other words, forty-nine.

How could one possibly find fault with Mr. Charles Trockley's reasoning?

But time does not pass at the same rate for everyone. One day, one hour, might do more harm to me than ten years to Mr. Charles Trockley, given that rigorous self-discipline of his. Given the deplorable disorder of my spirit, I might live more than an entire lifetime in this year alone. And my body, weaker and far less cared-for than his, has undoubtedly, in its forty-eight years, worn itself out more than Mr. Trockley's will in the space of seventy. So much so that, despite his silver hair, there is not one wrinkle on that cooked-shrimp face of his, and he still fences with youthful agility every morning.

Well, yes, but what does any of that matter? For Mr. Charles Trockley, all such considerations, whether practical or theoretical, are idle, and far removed from reason. Reason tells Mr. Charles Trockley that, when all is said and done, on the 15th and 28th of June of next year, we will both be one year older, in other words, forty-nine.

That said, listen to what happened to Mr. Charles Trockley recently, and see if you are able to fault his reasoning.

■ ■ ■

Last April, following the usual itinerary for an Italian journey mapped out in the Baedeker, Miss Ethel Holloway, the very young and very lively daughter of Sir W. H. Holloway, the very wealthy and very authoritative Peer of England, arrived in Girgenti,[1] Sicily, in order to visit the marvelous ruins of the ancient Greek city there. Enticed by the enchanting valley, which, warmed by the breeze off the African sea, was all abloom that month with white almond flowers, she decided to stay more than one night at the grand Hôtel des Temples, which rises in a most agreeable spot in the open countryside, beyond the steep, impoverished modern little town.

Mr. Charles Trockley has been vice consul of England at Gir-

---

1. Girgenti is the Sicilian name for Agrigento.

genti for twenty-two years, and for twenty-two years, every day around sunset, he sets out from the upper town on the hill and walks with that elastic, measured gait of his to the ruins of the Akragan temples, airy and majestic on the rugged cliff that interrupts the descent of the neighboring hill, the Akrean hill, where a temple covered in sumptuous marbles once rose: the ancient city that Pindar extolled as the most beautiful of all earthly cities.

The ancients said that the Akragans ate every day as if they would die the next, and built their houses as if they would live forever. They don't eat much there now, because of the extreme poverty in Girgenti and the surrounding countryside, and, after numerous wars, seven fires, and as many sacks, nothing remains of the houses of the ancient city. In its place is a Saracen grove of almond and olive trees, hence known as the Grove of the Civitas. And the leafy, ashen-colored olive trees, which advance in formation right up to the majestic temple columns, seem to be praying for peace for those abandoned slopes. When it can, the River Akragas, whose banks Pindar lauded as being rich with flocks, runs below the cliff. A few small herds of goats still cross that rocky riverbed: they clamber up the craggy cliff and lie down, or ruminate in the meager pastureland, in the solemn shade of the ancient Temple of Concord, which still stands. The goatherd, beastly and sluggish as an Arab, lies down as well, on the steep steps of the pronaos, and produces mournful noises on his reed flageolet.

Mr. Charles Trockley has always found this intrusion of goats in the temple to be a terrible profanation, and he has filed countless formal complaints with the monuments' caretakers, but has never obtained any response other than a smile of philosophical indulgence and a shrug of shoulders. Mr. Charles Trockley, shaking with indignation, has grumbled to me about the smiles and shrugs on those occasions when I have accompanied him on his daily walk. It often happens that, either in the Temple of Concord or higher up, in the Temple of Hera Lacinia, or in the one commonly known as the Temple of the Giants, Mr. Charles Trockley bumps into parties of his compatriots, who have come to see the ruins. And to all of them, with an indignation that neither time nor habit have yet to placate or diminish in the least, he points out the profanation of those goats lying around or grazing in the shade of the columns. But in truth, not all the English visitors share Mr. Trockley's indignation. Many, in fact, find a certain poetry in those goats reposing among the temples, abandoned and alone in the middle of that great expanse of forgotten countryside. To Mr. Trockley's great dismay, more than one actually has seemed to appreciate and admire the sight.

More appreciative and admiring than all the others was, last April, the very young and very vivacious Miss Ethel Holloway. In fact, while the indignant vice consul was offering up some precious gem of archaeological information, which neither the Baedeker nor any other guide had come to appreciate yet, Miss Ethel Holloway committed the impropriety of suddenly turning her back to him in order to run after a darling little black kid, just a few days old, who, after caprioling among the reclining goats, as if midges of light were dancing in the air around him, seemed so bewildered by his own bold, ungainly leaps that now, in the still—to him—uncertain spectacle of life, the slightest sound, the gentlest breeze, the faintest shadow made him tremble and shiver bashfully.

I had accompanied Mr. Trockley that day, and delighted as I

was by young Miss Holloway, who immediately fell in love with the little goat, so much so that she wanted to buy it, at any cost, I was also pained by poor Mr. Charles Trockley's suffering.

"Buy the kid goat?"

"Yes, yes! Buy it right now!"

And just like that dear little creature, the young Miss Holloway trembled too, most likely never imagining, not even remotely, that no nastier trick could be played on Mr. Trockley, who has fiercely despised those goats for so long.

Mr. Trockley tried in vain to discourage her, to get her to consider the difficulties that would arise from such a purchase. But in the end he had to give in, and, out of respect for her father, he approached the savage goatherd and negotiated the sale of the little black kid.

Miss Ethel Holloway, after shelling out the money for the purchase, told Mr. Trockley that she would entrust her baby goat to the manager of the Hôtel des Temples, but that as soon as she returned to London she would telegraph for the dear little creature, which was to be sent to her as soon as possible, all expenses paid. Then she rode in her carriage back to her hotel, the bleating kid squirming in her arms.

I watched as that impassioned young lady, delicate and blond in her black carriage, rode off toward the sunset — a magnificent burst of clouds over the sparkling sea, glistening like an immense gold mirror — in a halo of blazing light; it was like a dream. It occurred to me then that the ability to conjure instantaneously such vivid yearning, such vivid affection for a little black goat, this far from her homeland and her usual ambiance and affections, means that she must have not even a crumb of that solid reason that governs with such gravitas the actions, thoughts, movements, and words of Mr. Charles Trockley.

So what did the young Miss Ethel Holloway have in place of reason?

Nothing but foolishness, according to Mr. Charles Trockley, who was barely able to contain his rage — a pitiful sight in a man like him, who is always so composed.

The reason for his rage lies in the events that followed upon the purchase of that little black kid.

■ ■ ■

Miss Ethel Holloway left Girgenti the next day. From Sicily she headed to Greece, from Greece to Egypt, from Egypt to the Indies.

It's a miracle that, having arrived safe and sound in London toward the end of November, after eight months and many adventures, which she certainly must have had on such a long journey, she still remembered the little black goat she bought so long ago in Sicily, amid the ruins of the Akragan temples.

As soon as she arrived, she wrote, as agreed, to Mr. Charles Trockley, to have her baby goat sent to her.

The Hôtel des Temples closes in mid-June every year and opens again in early November. The manager, to whom Miss Ethel Holloway had entrusted her baby goat before leaving that June, had, in turn, entrusted it to the hotel caretaker, but without any particular instructions; rather, he made it clear that he was more than a little annoyed at the trouble the beast caused and was continuing to cause him. The caretaker waited every day for Mr. Charles Trockley, the vice consul, to come and take the kid and send it off to England, as the hotel manager had said. But seeing as no one arrived, he had the brilliant idea of handing it over for safekeeping to the same goatherd who had sold it to Miss Holloway, promising to make him a gift of it if she, as seemed likely, no longer cared to have it, or — if the vice consul did, in fact, come ask for it — compensation for its care and pasture.

When, about eight months later, Miss Ethel Holloway's letter arrived from England, the manager of the Hôtel des Temples, together with the caretaker and the goatherd, found themselves in a sea of confusion: the first for having entrusted the kid to the caretaker, the caretaker for having entrusted it to the goatherd, and the goatherd for having given it in turn to another goatherd, with the same promises that the caretaker had made to him. But no one knew what had become of this second goatherd. The search lasted more than a month. Finally, one fine day, Mr. Charles Trockley was greeted in his vice consul office at Girgenti by a dreadful, smelly beast with horns and mottled rust-colored fur, all ratty and encrusted with dung and mud, who — head lowered menacingly — bleated hoarsely, loudly, as if demanding Mr. Trockley what it was he wanted of him, reduced inevitably to this state and finding himself in such a strange place, so far from his usual habitat.

Well, Mr. Charles Trockley, as is his wont, appeared not the least bit alarmed by such an apparition. Without a moment's hesitation, he calculated the time that had passed since the beginning of April till the end of December, and concluded that the darling little black kid of this spring reasonably could have grown into this foul creature. And without the least shadow of doubt, he replied to Miss

Holloway that he would send the goat on the first English merchant ship sailing home from Porto Empedocle. He hung a sign with Miss Ethel Holloway's address around the dreadful beast's neck and gave orders for it to be taken to the port. Then, seriously jeopardizing his dignity, he dragged the reluctant beast on a rope along the wharf, followed by a flock of young rascals. He loaded it onto the departing steamer and returned to Girgenti, convinced that he had scrupulously fulfilled his obligation, not so much to Miss Ethel Holloway in her deplorable lightness, as for the respect he owed her father.

■ ■ ■

Yesterday, Mr. Charles Trockley came to see me at home. He was in such a state, body and soul, that I was filled with consternation and immediately rushed to his side, made him sit, and called for a glass of water.

"For the love of God, Mr. Trockley, what has happened to you?"

Mr. Trockley, still speechless, extracted a letter from his pocket and handed it to me.

It was from Sir H. W. Holloway, Peer of England, and contained a string of insolent abuse aimed at Mr. Trockley for the insult that he dared deliver his daughter by sending her that foul, frightening beast.

This was the thanks Mr. Trockley received for all the troubles he'd gone through.

But what did the foolish Miss Ethel Holloway expect? Did she really expect that the same little black kid, which, all glossy and trembling with fear, had leapt about among the columns of an ancient Greek temple in Sicily, would be delivered to her in London eleven months or so later? Did she really? Mr. Charles Trockley couldn't stop thinking about it.

Seeing him in such a state, I tried to comfort him as best I could, and agreed that Miss Ethel Holloway really must be not only extremely capricious, but unreasonable beyond words.

"Foolish! Foolish! Foolish!"

"Let's say unreasonable, Mr. Trockley. But you see, my dear friend"—I allowed myself to add, timidly—"having left in April with the delightful image of that little black kid in her heart, she could not, let's be fair, resign herself (unreasonable as she apparently is) to you, Mr. Trockley, suddenly sending her that monstrous billy goat."

"Well, then?" Mr. Trockley asked, sitting up straight and eyeing me hostilely. "What, according to you, was I supposed to do?"

■ ■ ■

"I don't mean, Mr. Trockley"—I hastened to say, embarrassed—"I don't want to seem as unreasonable as the young Miss Holloway from your faraway country, but, in your place, Mr. Trockley, do you know what I would have done? I would have replied that the darling little black kid had died of longing for her kisses and caresses. Or I would have bought another little black kid, all tiny and glossy, just like the one she bought last April, and I would have sent it to her, confident that Miss Ethel Holloway would never consider that her baby goat could not remain unchanged during those eleven months. So I continue to maintain that Miss Ethel Holloway is, as you can see, the most unreasonable creature on this earth, and that you, my dear friend Mr. Trockley, are completely in the right."

As soon as the head groom left, cursing even more than usual, Smoke turned to Blackie, the new arrival who shared his feeding-trough, and sighed:

"So, I see! You're off to a good start, my friend! Trappings, ribbons, and plumes. First-class today."

Blackie turned his head away. He didn't snort, because he was a well-bred horse. But he didn't want to be on familiar terms with that Smoke.

Blackie came from a princely stable, so scrubbed you could see your reflection in the walls, beechwood troughs in every box, brass rings, leather-padded dividers, and posts with shiny knobs.

Oh well!

The young prince, all keen on those thundering carriages that—it's true!—make a terrible stink, spew smoke from behind, and run off on their own, and not satisfied with nearly breaking his neck three times already, had hastened to rid himself of Blackie and Raven, the only two horses left in the stable, whom he'd kept to pull his mother's landau, as soon as the old princess (who, bless her! never wanted anything to do with those devils) was stricken with paralysis.

Poor Raven: who knows where he'd ended up, after so many years of honorable service!

The old princess was forever confined to a chaise now. Good Giuseppe, the old coachman, had promised Blackie and Raven that he would intercede on their behalf when he, together with the other faithful servants, went to kiss her hand.

But oh! From the way good old Giuseppe, returning to the stables shortly afterward, had caressed their necks and flanks, they both understood that all hope had been lost, that their fate was sealed. They would be sold.

And in fact . . .

Blackie was still trying to figure out where he'd landed. It wasn't bad, exactly, no. It wasn't the princess's stable of course, but still, it was a decent place. More than twenty horses, all black and all rather old, but still good-looking, dignified, and quite serious. Maybe even a bit too serious!

Blackie doubted whether any of them had figured out exactly what their job was. They seemed to think about it endlessly, in fact, without ever coming to any conclusion. The slow swish of their tails and the occasional pawing of hooves were unquestionably gestures of deep-thinking horses.

Only Smoke was sure — absolutely sure — that he'd understood everything perfectly.

What a vulgar, presumptuous beast!

A regiment nag, declared unfit after three years of service because — or so he said — he'd bucked some boorish light cavalryman from Abruzzo. All he did was talk.

Blackie, his heart still heavy over his old friend Raven, couldn't stand Smoke. His confidential manner irritated him more than anything, as did his endless maligning of his stable mates.

God, what a mouth he had!

Not one of the twenty horses there was spared! This one was like this, that one like that . . .

"That tail . . . just look at it! Now tell me, please, is that a tail? And is that any way to move it? Quite the lively swish, hey?

"Take it from me, he was a doctor's horse.

"And that one there, that fine Calabrian trotter, just look how he flops his pig's ears, very elegant. And that forelock! And throat! Rather lively too, wouldn't you say?

"Every now and then he dreams he hasn't been gelded, and tries to make love to that mare over there, three places to the right, see her? With that old-lady head, low in the shoulders, belly practically grazing the floor.

"You call her a horse? More like a cow, I'd say. And you should see how she walks, straight out of riding school! Like she's crossing burning coal. But oh, wait till you see how she foams at the mouth, my friend! Right, because she's fresh, that one. Still has to cut her teeth, just imagine!"

■ ■ ■

Blackie tried in every way he could to let Smoke know he wasn't interested in hearing his talk. But Smoke just ranted all the more.

To spite him.

"You know where we are? A shipping company. There's all different kinds. This one here is called an 'undertaker.'

"You know what that means? It means pulling a black carriage, tall and strange-shaped, with four little columns holding up the roof, and all decked out with fringe and drapes and gold plating.

Real deluxe, in other words. But it's such a waste, you won't believe it! Because—you'll see—no one ever gets in.

"Just the coachman, very serious-looking, up on the box.

"And we go slow, always at a walk. No danger of working up a sweat, no need for a rub down afterward, or for the coachman ever to give us the whip or hurry us in any way!

"Slowly, slowly, slowly.

"Wherever it is we're going, we always get there in time.

"And humans—I've figured out—must have some special reverence for our carriage.

"Like I said, no one dares get in, and everyone, as soon as they see it pull up in front of a house, stand and stare with long, frightened faces, and some even encircle it with candles, and then, as soon as we pull away, lots more follow behind, without saying a word.

"And there's often a band in front of us. But the music it plays will tear your insides out, my friend.

"Now listen to me: you've got a nasty habit of snorting and jerking your head around. Well, you're just going to have to stop. If you already snort for nothing, just imagine when you hear that sad music!

"There's no denying that the work's light, but it takes composure and solemnity. No snorting, no jerking. It's already something that they let us swish our tails a bit.

"Because—I'll say it again—the carriage we pull is highly respected. You'll see how they all remove their hats when we go by.

"You know how I figured out it's a shipping company? Like this.

"About two years ago, I was standing there, hitched to one of our pavilion carriages, in front of an enormous gate, our usual destination.

"The gate's enormous, you'll see! Behind it are lots of dark, pointy trees, perfectly straight, two rows of them that go on forever, and on either side, lush green meadows, with the most delicious grass, but that's wasted too—you'll be in trouble if you stretch your neck to nibble some on the way by.

"So there I was, standing at the gate, when an old friend from my army days pulls up alongside me. Poor thing was in pretty bad shape, hitched to—can you imagine?—one of those long, low-slung wagons with iron supports and no springs.

"'Hey Smoke,' he says to me, 'just look at me, I can't take it anymore!'

"'What's your line of work?' I ask.

"And he says to me:

"'I transport boxes all day long, from the shipping office to the customs house.'

"'Boxes?' I say. 'What sort of boxes?'

"'Heavy ones!' he says. 'Full of things to be shipped.'

"It was like a revelation.

"Because you should know that we carry a box of sorts too, a long box. They slide it in the carriage real slowly (they always do everything real slowly), from the back, and meanwhile, they all remove their hats and stare in dismay. Who knows why! But since we deal with boxes too, we must be a shipping company, don't you think?

"What the devil's inside them, though? They're heavy, all right, you won't believe it! But luckily, we always only transport one at a time.

"Goods to be shipped, for sure. What sort of goods, though, I don't know. But of great importance, it seems, because there's always a lot of pomp and people involved.

"At a certain point, usually (but not always), we stop in front of some majestic structure, maybe it's the customs house for our line of goods. Some men come out the door, in black skirts and un-tucked shirts, the customs officials, I guess; the box is loaded off the carriage; everybody removes their hats again; and the officials mark the box with some sort of permit.

"Where all this precious stuff goes—that's what I still haven't been able to figure out. But I've got a hunch the humans don't really know either, which is some consolation.

"In truth, from the splendor of the boxes and all the pomp and solemnity, one could suppose they must know something about the shipments. But I see them all looking so dumbfounded, uncertain. And from my long familiarity with humans, my friend, I've man-aged to learn that men do lots of things without having any idea why they're doing them!"

■ ■ ■

That morning, it was just like Smoke had figured from the head groom's cursing: trappings, ribbons, and plumes. A coach and four. It really was first-class.

"See? Didn't I tell you?"

Blackie found himself hitched to the shaft, together with

Smoke. And Smoke, naturally, kept on annoying him with his endless explanations.

But that morning Blackie was also annoyed by the high-handedness of the head groom, who, whenever there was a four-in-hand, always put him in the wheel pair, never in the lead.

"What a dog! As you can see, those two up front, they're only for show. Pull? They don't pull worth a darn! We go so slowly, we're the ones doing all the pulling, while they get to have a nice little stroll, stretch their legs, all dressed up and all. And will you just look at what sort of beasts they choose over me! Recognize them?"

They were the horses Smoke had identified as the doctor's horse and the Calabrian trotter.

"That damn Calabrian! Good thing he's in front of you, though! Oh yes, my friend, you'll realize soon enough that it's not only his ears that are piglike, and you'll thank the head groom for giving him double rations. Some have all the luck. Don't snort, already! And stop wagging your head around! Keep it up, my dear boy, and he'll tug the reins so hard your mouth will bleed, I'm telling you. There's going to be speeches today. You'll hear how cheerful they are! One, two, three speeches . . . I did a high-class event once—five speeches! Enough to drive you mad. Standing still for three hours, covered in all this finery, which makes it hard to breathe: legs shackled, tail imprisoned, ears poking out two holes. Real cheerful, with flies biting you under your tail! So what are these speeches? Who knows! To tell you the truth, I haven't been able to figure out much. These high-class shipments must be real complicated. And maybe all those speeches are explanations. If one's not enough, they make

two; if two aren't enough, they make three. Like I told you, sometimes they even get up to five, and at that point even I feel like kicking left, right, and center, and then rolling on the grass. It could be
like that today. What fun! Did you see the head groom, all decked
out too? And the servants, and torch bearers. Say, are you skittish?"

"What do you mean?"

"Come on, do you spook easily? Because you'll see, in a little
while they'll start sticking those burning candles right under your
nose . . . Easy now, hey . . . easy! What's gotten into you? See?
There's a good tug on the reins . . . Did it hurt? You'll get a lot more
of that today, I'm telling you. What the heck are you doing? Are you
nuts? Don't go stretching your neck out like that! Good one, fool,
what do you think you're doing, swimming? Playing Odd or Even?
Be still . . . Oh yeah? Take that, then . . . Whoa, careful, I'm warning
you, that yanks my bit too! He's crazy! Good god, he's really crazy!
All this panting, snorting, snarling, neighing, arching his back . . .
what's going on? Well, look at that, he's prancing! He's nuts! Completely nuts! Prancing while pulling a first-class carriage!"

Blackie really had gone nuts: panting, neighing, champing at
the bit, trembling all over. The servants leapt off the carriage, in a
mad rush to hold Blackie still in front of the palace where they were
supposed to stop, amid a great throng of stiff-looking humans in
long coats and top hats.

Everyone was yelling. "What's happening?" "Oh, look, one of
the horses pulling the hearse is rearing up!"

A swirl of confusion. They all crowded around the carriage,
curious, astonished, scandalized. The servants still couldn't calm
Blackie down. The coachman had stood up and was tugging furi-

ously on the reins. In vain. Blackie kept on pawing, neighing, foaming, jerking his head toward the palace door.

He only quieted down when an old servant in livery suddenly appeared at the door. Thrusting the others aside, he took Blackie by the bridle and, with tears in his eyes, exclaimed:

"It's Blackie! It's Blackie! Oh, poor Blackie, of course you're acting up! It's my mistress's horse! The poor princess's horse! He recognized the palace, he can smell his old stable! Poor Blackie, poor Blackie . . . be good now, good boy . . . Yes, see? It's me, your old friend Giuseppe. Be good, now . . . poor Blackie, it's up to you to take her now, see? Your mistress. It's up to you, poor thing, you still remember her. She'll be happy it's you who's taking her, this last time."

Giuseppe turned to the coachman who, turning beastly because of the bad impression the funeral home was making in front of all those gentlefolk, was still yanking furiously on the reins, threatening to whip Blackie, and shouted:

"Stop it! That's enough! I'm in charge here. He's as meek as a lamb. Sit down. I'll drive the whole way. We'll go together, hey, Blackie? We'll take our good mistress there together. Slowly, slowly, just like we always used to, remember? Be good now, so as not to hurt her, poor old Blackie, you still remember her. They've already put her in the casket, Blackie, they're bringing her out now."

Smoke, who had been listening in astonishment, now asked:

"Your mistress, inside the box?"

Blackie gave him a sideways kick.

But Smoke was too stunned by this revelation even to feel it.

"Oh, so we . . . ," he said to himself, "so we . . . look, look . . .

I meant to tell you that . . . this old man's weeping, and I've seen lots of other people weeping too, other times . . . and so many distraught faces . . . and that slow, sad music. I get it now, I understand everything . . . So that's why we have such light work! It's only when people weep that we horses can be happy, and pull so gently . . ."

■ ■ ■

And he had the urge to prance himself.

THE FLY

Panting, out of breath, to get there as fast as they could—"this way, here, come on!"—when they reached the base of the village, they used their hands too, to scramble up the rough, chalky escarpment—"hurry up, hurry up!"—because—"goddamn!"—their hobnail boots kept sliding.

As soon as they appeared, red-faced, at the top, the women, clustered around the fountain on the edge of town and gossiping, all turned to look. Aren't those the Tortorici brothers? Yes, Neli and Saro Tortorici. Oh, poor things! Why in the world were they running like that?

Neli, the younger of the two, unable to go on, stopped for a minute to catch his breath and tell them, but Saro grabbed his arm and dragged him away.

"Giurlannu Zarù, our cousin!" Neli said over his shoulder, raising his hand in benediction.

The women exploded in exclamations of lament and horror.

"Who did it?" one of them asked loudly.

"No one." Neli yelled back from afar. "God!"

The brothers turned and ran to the little piazza, where the medical officer's house was.

■ ■ ■

The worthy doctor, Sidoro Lopiccolo, in shirtsleeves, his chest showing, a good ten days' growth of whiskers on his flabby cheeks, eyes swollen and bleary, shuffled aimlessly from room to room in his slippers, a sick little girl in his arms, all yellow, mere skin and bones, about nine years old.

His wife, bedridden these past eleven months; six children in addition to the oldest, in his arms, all of them ragged, filthy, half wild; and the whole house turned upside down, a real mess. Broken dishes, orange peels, piles of trash on the floor, broken chairs, armchairs losing their stuffing, beds left unmade for who knows how long, the bedspreads in tatters because the children amused themselves playing war on the beds: pillow fights, what darlings!

The only thing that remained intact, hanging on the wall in a room that had once been the parlor, was an enlarged photograph, a portrait: his portrait, Doctor Sidoro Lopiccolo, when he was still a lad, freshly graduated, nicely kempt, smart-looking, smiling.

It was to this portrait that he now made his way. He sneered softly, showing his teeth, bowed, and, holding up his sick little girl, introduced her.

"Here you are, Sisiné!"

Sisiné was his pet name, what his mother used to call him; his mother, who had great expectations for him, the favorite, the mainstay, the standard-bearer of the family.

"Sisiné!"

He welcomed the two peasants like a rabid dog.

"What do you want?"

It was Saro who spoke, still panting, cap in hand.

"Mr. Doctor, a poor soul, our cousin, he's dying . . ."

"Lucky him! Ring the bells, a joyous occasion!" the doctor shouted.

"Oh no, sir! He's dying, all of a sudden, nobody knows from what. In a stable in Montelusa."

The doctor took a step back and exclaimed ferociously:

"In Montelusa?"

It was a good seven miles' journey from here. And what a journey!

"Hurry, for heaven's sake, hurry!" Soro begged. "He's gone all black, like a piece of liver! And he's swelled up, it's terrifying. For heaven's sake!"

"Do you expect me to walk?" the doctor shouted. "Walk ten miles? Are you crazy? The mule, I want the mule, did you bring her?"

"I'll run and get her now," Soro hastened to say. "I'll borrow her."

"Well then," said Neli, the younger brother, "I'll just run and get a shave."

The doctor turned and looked at him, eyes burning.

"It's Sunday, sir," Neli, nonplussed, apologized with a smile. "I'm engaged."

"Ah, you're engaged?" the doctor sneered, beside himself. "Then take her, here!" he said, thrusting his sick daughter into Neli's arms. Then one by one he grabbed the other children, who were all hovering about, and pushed them furiously between Neli's knees.

"And this one! And this one! And this one! And this one! Beast! Beast! Beast!"

The doctor turned his back and seemed about to leave, but

then wheeled around again, gathered up his sick little girl, and shouted to the two brothers:

"Go! The mule! I'll be there in a minute."

Neli Tortorici's smile returned as he headed down the stairs behind his brother. He was twenty years old, his fiancée, Luzza, sixteen: fresh as a rose! Seven children? So few! He wanted twelve. And to support them, all he had were the two hands God had given him, but they were strong, and he was happy. Work and song, he was good at both. It wasn't for nothing that they called him Liolà,[1] the poet. And feeling loved by everyone, for his obliging kindness and constant good mood, he smiled even at the air he breathed. The sun hadn't managed to cook his skin yet, or to dry out his beautiful blond curls, which many women must have envied; and many women blushed, all flustered, if he looked at them in a certain way, with those clear, bright blue eyes of his.

All things considered, what was troubling him that day, more than his cousin Zarù's situation, was the way his Luzza, who'd been longing for Sunday for six days now, in order to spend a little time with him, was going to pout. But could he, in all good conscience, shirk his Christian duty? Poor Giurlannu! He was engaged too. What a tragedy, and so suddenly! He'd been harvesting almonds—beating the trees—down at the Lopes estate, in Montelusa. The morning before, Saturday, it'd looked as if it might rain, even though there didn't seem to be any imminent danger. Toward noon, however, Lopes said, "God can do a lot in an hour; I wouldn't want my almonds sitting on the ground in the rain, my children."

---

1. *Li' o la'* means "here or there."

And he ordered the women harvesters to go up to the storeroom and start husking. "You," he said to the men (including Neli and Saro Tortorici) who'd been knocking the almonds off the trees, "you can go up too, if you want, and help the women husk." "Sure," Giurlannu Zarù said, "but will I still get my daily wage, my twenty-five *soldi?*" "No, I'll pay you regular for half the day, the rest at half a *lira*, like the women."[2] "How generous of you! What, isn't there enough work for us men to do, and earn our whole day's pay?" It wasn't raining; in fact, it didn't rain all that day, or that night. "Half a *lira*, like the women?" Giurlannu Zarù said. "I wear pants. Pay me half a day at twenty-five *soldi*, and I'll be on my way."

But he didn't leave. He stayed and waited for his cousins, who contented themselves with husking for half a *lira*, with the women. But at a certain point he got tired of doing nothing but watching, and made his way to a nearby stable to catch some sleep, advising the crew to wake him when it was time to go.

They'd been beating almond trees for a day and a half, yet the harvest was slight. The women proposed husking them all that very evening, working late and then sleeping there the rest of the night, and heading back up to the village the next morning, rising before dawn. Which is what they did. Lopes brought fava beans and two flasks of wine. They finished husking at midnight, and all of them, men and women, lay down to sleep serenely on the threshing floor, where the straw was wet with dew, as if it truly had rained.

"Sing, Liolà!"

---

2. One *lira* was worth twenty *soldi*, so the women were paid less than half what the men earned.

And Neli burst into song. The moon, which came and went through a thick tangle of black and white clouds, had the face of his Luzza, who smiled and clouded over at the love stories, now happy, now sad, he sang about.

Giurlannu Zarù had stayed in the stable. When Saro went to wake him before dawn, he found him all black and bloated, with a raging fever.

This is what Neli Tortorici recounted to the barber, who, distracted at a certain point, nicked him with the razor. A tiny cut, near his chin, it was nothing, really! Neli didn't even have time to feel it, because right then Luzza appeared at the door of the barbershop with her mother and Mita Lumìa, Giurlannu Zarù's poor fiancée, who was screaming and sobbing desperately.

It took quite an effort to make that poor girl understand that she couldn't go all the way to Montelusa to see her fiancé: she could see him that evening, as soon as they brought him, as best they could, up to the town. Saro suddenly appeared, braying that the doctor was already in the saddle and couldn't wait any longer. Neli pulled Luzza aside and begged her to be patient: he'd be back before evening, and would say all kinds of sweet things to her.

Which are already sweet things, when two lovers say them while holding hands and gazing into each other's eyes.

■ ■ ■

What a forbidding road! At certain precipices, death passed before Dr. Lopiccolo's eyes, even though Saro and Neli, on either side of him, held the mule by the halter.

From that high road, the whole countryside spread out before them, all its plains and valleys, planted with olive and almond groves, and fodder, yellow now with stubble, and here and there little black smudges—the fires the farmers would light to burn back the fields—and in the distance the sea, a bitter blue. The mulberry, carob, cypress, and olive trees still kept their various shades of everlasting green, while the crowns of the almond trees had already been thinned.

All around them on this vast horizon, there seemed to be a veil of wind. But the heat was tiring, the sun so hot it split the stones. Every now and then a sparrow's shriek or a magpie's laughter would come from beyond the dusty hedges of prickly pear, which made the doctor's mule prick her ears.

"Evil mule,[3] evil mule!" the doctor would moan.

His eyes fixed on those mule ears, the doctor didn't even notice the sun glaring in his face, and left his ugly green parasol resting on his shoulder.

"No reason to fear, sir, we're right here," the brothers Tortorici would say to reassure him.

In truth, the doctor really had no reason to fear. But for his children, he said. He had to look out for his own skin because of those seven unfortunate creatures.

To distract him, the Tortorici brothers set to telling him what a lousy year it had been: grain was scarce, barley was scarce, fava beans were scarce; as for the almonds, well, as he knew, they don't always set: the trees are laden one year, bare the next; and the olives,

---

3. "Mula mala"—an untranslatable play of words that replicates the rhythm of the mule's hooves.

they weren't even worth mentioning: the fog had shriveled them early on; and there was no making up for things with the grape harvest, as all the vineyards in the area were diseased.

"How comforting!" the doctor would say every now and then, shaking his head.

Two hours into their journey, they'd already run out of things to talk about. The road ran straight for a good while, and now it was the mule's hooves and the brothers' hobnail boots that conversed on the thick layer of whitish dust. At a certain point, Liolà started to sing listlessly, under his breath, but he soon stopped. They didn't meet a soul, since—it being Sunday—all the peasants were up in the village, attending mass, or doing their shopping, or relaxing. Maybe no one had stayed down in Montelusa, at Giurlannu Zarù's side, maybe he was dying all alone, if he was even still alive.

As a matter of fact, they found him alone, stretched out on a low wall in the stinking stall, just as Saro and Neli had left him: bloated, black and blue, unrecognizable.

They could hear his death rattle.

The sun beating through the window grate near the feeding trough landed on an inhuman-looking face: nose swallowed by the swelling; lips black and horribly tumescent. And the exasperated rattle that escaped those lips, like a snarl. A piece of straw caught in his curly brown hair glistened in the sunlight.

Alarmed, all three stopped to stare at him, as if held back by the horror of that sight. The mule snorted and pawed at the cobblestones. Then Saro Tortorici went over to the dying man and called him tenderly.

"Giurlà, Giurlà, the doctor's here."

Neli went to tie the mule to the feeding trough, next to which was what looked to be the shadow of another beast, the donkey who'd lived in that stall and who had imprinted his image on the wall from rubbing against it so much.

When Saro called his name again, Giurlannu Zarù stopped wheezing and tried to open his blackened, bloodshot eyes, which were filled with fear. He opened his hideous mouth and groaned, as if burning inside:

"I'm dying!"

"No, no," the distraught Saro was quick to say. "The doctor's here. We brought him ourselves, see him over there?"

"Take me to the village!" Zarù begged breathlessly, unable to close his lips. "Oh mamma mia!"

"Sure, the mule's here!" Saro said right away.

"I'd even carry you there myself, Giurlà, in my arms!" Neli said, rushing to kneel next to him. "Don't lose heart!"

Giurlannu Zarù turned toward Neli's voice and fixed him with those bloody eyes, as if not recognizing him at first. Then he moved his arm and held him by the belt.

"You, handsome, you?"

"Yes, me, come on! Are you crying? Don't cry, Giurlà, don't cry! It's nothing!"

And he laid a hand on his cousin's chest, which heaved with sobs stifled in his throat. At a certain point Zarù shook his head furiously and then, raising his hand, grabbed Neli by the neck and pulled him close.

"Together . . . we were supposed to get married together."

"And we will, without a doubt!" Neli said, removing the hand clutching at his neck.

Meanwhile the doctor was studying the dying man. A case of anthrax, clearly.

"Tell me, do you recall being bit by an insect?"

Zarù shook his head no.

"Insect?" Saro asked.

The doctor explained the disease as best he could to those two ignoramuses. Some animal must have died of anthrax somewhere around there. Who knows how many insects had landed on its carcass, thrown in the bottom of some ravine. Then one of them must have flown here and transmitted the disease to Zarù, right in this stall.

Zarù turned his face to the wall as the doctor spoke.

No one knew it, but death was still there, in the stall: so small that they would barely have noticed, even if they had seen it.

On the wall was a fly. Seemingly motionless at first, but, on closer inspection, it could be seen to extract its tiny proboscis and pump it up and down, then quickly clean its slender front feet, rubbing them together, as if in satisfaction.

Zarù caught sight of it and fixed his eyes on it.

A fly.

It could have been that one, or another one. Who knew? Because now, hearing the doctor talk, he seemed to remember. Yes, the day before, when he'd thrown himself down there to sleep, waiting for his cousins to finish husking Lopes's almonds, a fly had pestered him. Might it be this one?

He watched it take flight all of a sudden, and turned to follow it with his eyes.

There, it landed on Neli's cheek. And from his cheek it moved oh so lightly, in two bounds, to his chin, to the razor nick, attacking it voraciously.

Giurlannu Zarù stared at it for a while, intent, engrossed.

"A fly, maybe?"

"A fly? Why not?" the doctor said.

Giurlannu Zarù didn't say anything more. He went back to staring at that fly, which Neli, seemingly stunned by the doctor's words, did not brush away. Zarù paid no more attention to the doctor's talk, enjoying instead how he so captured his cousin's attention that he stood as still as a statue, unaware of the bother of the fly on his chin. Oh, if only it were the same one! Then yes, they really would marry together! Zarù had been seized by a dark envy, a veiled but ferocious jealousy of his handsome, healthy young cousin—so full of promise, so alive—while he was to die so suddenly.

All of a sudden Neli, as if finally feeling the bite, lifted a hand and brushed away the fly. Then he started feeling his chin, right along the little cut. He turned to Zarù, who was staring at him, and was a little disconcerted to see that his cousin had opened his hideous lips in a monstrous smile. The two cousins stayed like that for a while, eyeing each other. Then Zarù said, almost without wanting to:

"The fly."

Neli, not understanding him, bent his ear to his cousin.

"What did you say?"

"The fly," Zarù said again.

"What fly? Where?" Neli asked, dismayed, looking at the doctor.

"There, where you're scratching yourself. I'm sure of it!" Zarù said.

Neli showed the doctor the nick on his chin.

"What's this here? It itches."

The doctor frowned at him. Then, as if wanting to get a better look, he led him out of the stable. Saro followed them.

Then what happened? Giurlannu Zarù waited, waited a long time, anxiety gnawing at his insides. He could hear them talking confusedly outside. All of a sudden Saro stormed back inside, grabbed the mule, and, without even turning to look at Zarù, left again, moaning, "Ah, my Neluccio! Ah, my Neluccio!"

Was it true, then? They deserted him there, like a dog. He tried lifting himself on one elbow, and called out twice:

"Saro! Saro!"

Silence. No one was there. Unable to hold himself up any longer, he fell back and rooted about for a while, so as not to hear the terrifying silence of the countryside. The doubt suddenly came to him that he'd been dreaming, that in his fever he'd dreamed it all. But then, turning to the wall, he saw the fly again.

There it was.

■ ■ ■

It extracted its tiny proboscis and pumped it up and down, then quickly cleaned its two slender front feet, rubbing them together, as if in satisfaction.

ON THE MARK

Raffaella Òsimo knew that the medical students were supposed to come to the hospital again that morning, so she begged the ward sister to take her to the chief physician's room, where the medical semiotics lessons were held.

The sister gave her a disapproving look.

"You want to show yourself to the students?"

"Yes. Please choose me."

"You know you look like a lizard?"

"I know. But I don't care! Choose me."

"Well, what cheek! What is it you think they're going to do to you in there?"

"What they did to Nannina, right?"

Nannina, who'd been discharged the day before, had had the bed next to hers. As soon as she'd returned from the chief physician's room, she showed Raffaella her body, which was all marked up like a map: lungs, heart, liver, and spleen, each marked with a dermographic pencil.

"You want to go?" the sister concluded. "Fine by me, I'll take you. But keep in mind that the marks won't come off for days, not even with soap."

Òsimo shrugged and said with a smile:

"Just take me, and don't worry."

A bit of color had returned to her face, but she was still so thin: nothing but eyes and hair. Those eyes — black and beautiful — shined keenly again now, though her minute, girlish body was lost amid the folds of the blankets on that small hospital bed.

■ ■ ■

For the ward sister, as for all the other sister nurses, Raffaella Òsimo was an old acquaintance.

She'd already been in the hospital twice before. The first time for . . . well, blessed girls! They let themselves be led down the garden path, and then who pays the price? A poor little innocent creature, who ends up in the foundling hospital.

In truth, Òsimo, too, had paid bitterly for her mistake; about two months after giving birth, she'd returned to the hospital, more dead than alive, with three mercuric chloride pills in her stomach. This time it was anemia; she'd already been there a month. By dint of iron injections, she was getting better, and would be released in a few days.

They were very fond of her in the ward, the shy, smiling grace of her inconsolable goodness earning their pity and compassion. For not even her despair expressed itself in tears or gloom.

The first time, she'd smiled and said that all that was left for her now was to die. But victim though she was of that fate shared by far too many girls, her somber threats did not arouse any particular dread. It's well known that every girl who has been seduced and betrayed threatens suicide: you can't take it seriously.

But Raffaella Òsimo said it and did it.

In vain, then, had the good sisters tried to comfort her with religion; she had responded just as she did now, listening attentively, smiling, and saying yes; but it was clear that the lump in her heart neither melted nor lightened as a result of their exhortations.

Nothing could entice her to let hope into her life again; she knew she had deluded herself, that the real deception came from her inexperience, from her passionate, credulous nature, more than from the young man to whom she had given herself, and who never could have been hers.

But resign herself? No, she couldn't.

If, to other people, there was nothing unique about her story, that didn't make it any less painful for her. How she had suffered! First, the agony of seeing her father perfidiously murdered. Then the irreparable loss of all her aspirations.

A poor seamstress now, she'd been betrayed like many others, abandoned like many others; but someday . . . True, many others said the same thing: *But someday* . . . They were lying, though. Because the need to lie rises spontaneously in the oppressed hearts of the vanquished and destitute.

But Raffaella wasn't lying.

She was still young; surely she would have obtained her teaching certificate had her father, who had lovingly supported her studies, not died suddenly, in Calabria: assassinated during election season, not out of direct hatred, but at the hand of an unknown killer undoubtedly in the pay of the faction opposing Baron Barni, whose zealous and faithful secretary he was.

Once elected to parliament, Barni, aware that she was also

motherless and alone, took her into his home: a charitable gesture intended to show himself in a good light to his electors.

Which is how she came to Rome in an ambiguous role: they treated her like a member of the family, but meanwhile, she figured as governess to the baron's younger children, and occasionally as the baroness's lady-in-waiting. All without being paid, of course.

She worked; Barni was credited for his charity.

But what did it matter to her, at that point? She'd poured her heart into her work, in order to earn the paternal goodwill of the man who had taken her in, and in the secret hope that her loving cares—her unpaid services, that is—would be sufficient, considering her father's sacrifice, to win over any objection the baron might have when his oldest son, Riccardo, declared to him his love for her, as he had already promised to do. Oh, Riccardo was quite sure that his father would willingly acquiesce; but he was only nineteen, still in high school; he didn't have the courage to make such a declaration to his parents; better to wait a few years.

Wait . . . was it possible to wait? there? in that house, together all the time, with all his sweet talk, and after so many promises and vows . . .

She had been blinded by passion.

When, finally, her error could no longer be kept hidden, thrown out! Yes, thrown out, she could say, with no mercy, with no consideration for her condition even. Barni had written to an elderly aunt of hers, to have her come and take her away, immediately, back to Calabria, promising an allowance; but the aunt had implored him to wait until she delivered at least, so as not to have to face the scandal in a tiny village; and Barni had given in, but on the condition that his son would know nothing about it, and would think she had already left Rome. Yet after giving birth, Raffaella didn't want to return to Calabria; the baron, furious, had threatened to terminate her allowance—which he did, in fact, after she tried to kill herself. Riccardo left for Florence. She—it was a miracle she survived—took up work as a seamstress's assistant, to support herself and her aunt. A year passed; Riccardo returned to Rome, but she didn't even try to see him again. Having failed in her violent attempt, she got it in her head to let herself die little by little. One fine day her aunt lost her patience and went back to Calabria. A month ago, after fainting in the house of the seamstress for whom she worked, she was brought to the hospital, where she was being treated for anemia.

The other day, from her hospital bed, Raffaella Òsimo had seen the medical students walk through the ward on their way to symptomatology class. There was Riccardo—she'd hadn't seen him for two years—with a young woman at his side, another student probably, blond, beautiful, and foreign-seeming. It was clear from the way he looked at her—there was no fooling Raffaella!—that he was in love. And how she smiled at him, gazing adoringly into his eyes. . . .

She had followed them with her gaze to the far end of the ward; then she just stayed there, wide-eyed, propped up on her elbow. Nannina, in the bed next to her, had started to laugh.

"What did you see?"

"Nothing . . ."

She had smiled too, sinking back onto her bed, her heart beating so hard it seemed about to jump out of her chest.

Then the ward sister had arrived and invited Nannina to get dressed; the professor wanted her in his room, for the lesson.

"What are they going to do to me?" Nannina had asked.

"Eat you! What do you think?" the ward sister had replied. "Today it's your turn, the others will have theirs as well. After all, you're leaving tomorrow."

At first Raffaella had trembled at the thought. So fallen and forlorn, how would she show herself to him again? When beauty fades, there's no pity or sympathy for certain errors.

Riccardo's classmates, seeing her in such a deplorable state, would undoubtedly mock him:

"Really? With that little lizard?"

It wasn't out of revenge. She did not want to avenge herself.

But when, about half an hour later, Nannina had returned to her little bed and had explained what they'd done to her, and showed her her body, all marked up, Raffaella had suddenly changed her mind; and now here she was, trembling impatiently, waiting for the students to arrive.

■■■

Finally, around ten, they arrived. The foreign girl was at Riccardo's side, just like the other day. They were looking at each other and smiling.

"Shall I get dressed?" Raffaella asked the ward sister, sitting up excitedly in bed as soon as they appeared at the far end of the ward.

"Aya, how eager you are! Lie down," the ward nurse insisted, "and wait till the professor gives the order."

But Raffaella, for whom it was as if the sister had said, "Get dressed!" did so in secret.

She was ready and waiting under the covers when the ward nurse came to get her.

Deathly pale, her whole miserable little body convulsing, her hair falling every which way, but smiling and eyes sparkling, she entered the room.

Riccardo Barni was talking with his foreign-looking classmate so didn't notice her right away, while she—flustered by so many students—searched for him with her eyes. So she didn't hear the chief physician and professor of semiotics say to her:

"Come here, my child!"

At the sound of the professor's voice, Barni turned and saw Raffaella, who was staring at him now, her face all red. Appalled, he whitened, and his vision clouded.

"Well, now!" the professor shouted. "Here!"

Raffaella, hearing all the students laugh, roused herself, more bewildered than ever; she watched Riccardo withdraw to the far end of the room, near the window; she looked around, smiled nervously, and asked:

"What do I have to do?"

"Here, here, lie down here," the professor, who was standing at the head of a table on which was spread a sort of quilt, ordered her.

"Yes, sir, here I am!" Raffaella hurried to obey, but it was too hard to pull herself up to sit on the table. She smiled again and said: "I can't reach."

A student helped her up. Once she was seated, before lying

down, she looked at the professor—handsome, tall, clean-shaven, with gold eyeglass frames—and, pointing to the foreign-looking girl, said:

"If she could draw on me . . ."

More laughter from the students. The professor smiled too.

"Why? Are you ashamed?"

"No, sir. But I would be happier."

And she turned to look toward the window at the far corner of the room, where Riccardo had retreated, his back to the room.

The blond student instinctively followed Raffaella's gaze. She had already noted Barni's sudden agitation. When she realized that he had retreated, she, too, grew agitated.

But the professor called to her:

"Come on, then, Miss Orlitz. Let's make our patient happy."

Raffaella lay down on the table and looked at the young woman, who lifted her veil. Ah, how beautiful she was, fair-skinned and delicate, with the sweetest, light-blue eyes. She removed her cloak, took the dermographic pencil the professor held out to her, bent over Raffaella, and, with uncertain hands, uncovered her bosom.

Raffaella Òsimo squeezed her eyes shut with shame for her meager breasts, now exposed to the gaze of all those young men. She felt a cold hand on her heart.

"It's beating too hard," the young woman immediately said in a thick, exotic accent, withdrawing her hand.

"How long have you been in the hospital?" the professor asked.

Raffaella, eyelids flickering, answered nervously without opening her eyes.

"Thirty-two days. I'm almost recovered."

"Check for an anemic murmur," the professor said, handing the student a stethoscope.

Raffaella felt the cold instrument on her skin, then heard the young female voice:

"Murmur, no . . . palpitations, yes. Too many."

"Come now, the percussion exam," the professor enjoined.

At the first taps, Raffaella leaned her head to one side, clenched her teeth, tried to open her eyes, then closed them again right away; she was making a tremendous effort to contain herself. Now and again, when the young woman stopped tapping in order to make a small mark on Raffaella's skin, dipping the pencil in a glass of water another student held for her, Raffaella would blow anxiously through her nose.

How long did the torture last? And he, at the window the whole time . . . why didn't the professor call him back? Why didn't he invite him to see her heart, which his blond companion was slowly tracing on her miserable bosom, so shriveled because of him?

There, the percussion exam was finally over. Now the student connected all the dashes, completing the drawing. Raffaella was tempted to take a look at her heart, outlined there; but suddenly she couldn't bear it any longer. She burst into sobs.

The professor, cross, sent her back to the ward, ordering the head nurse to send in another patient who was less hysterical and foolish than this one.

Òsimo peacefully endured the ward nurse's scolding, and returned to her little bed to wait, all atremble, for the students to leave the room.

Would he seek her out with his eyes, at least, as he crossed the ward? But no, no, what did he care about her anymore? She wouldn't even raise her head to let him catch a glimpse of her. He wasn't supposed to see her again. It was enough that she made him aware of how haggard she'd become, because of him.

She grasped the edge of the sheet in her trembling hands and pulled it up over her face, as if she were dead.

■ ■ ■

For three days Raffaella Òsimo diligently checked that the outline of her heart had not faded from her breast.

■ ■ ■

Once released from the hospital, standing before a small mirror in her bare little room, she drove a sharp dagger, held firm against the wall, right in the middle of the mark that her oblivious rival had drawn for her.

THE LITTLE FAN

The shabby little public park, dry and dusty and drowsy in the middle of a vast piazza hemmed in by tall, yellowish apartment buildings, was practically deserted in the mugginess of that scorching August afternoon.

Tuta entered the park, her baby in her arms.

A skinny old man, lost in a gray alpaca suit, sitting on a bench in the shade, had placed a handkerchief on his head. And on top of the handkerchief, a small, yellowed straw hat. His sleeves carefully rolled up past his wrists, he sat reading a newspaper.

Next to him, on the same bench, an out-of-work laborer slept sideways, his head on his arms.

Every now and then the old man would stop reading and cast an anguished look at his neighbor, whose greasy, plaster-spattered hat was about to fall off. Evidently that ugly old hat—who knows how long it had been poised like that—should I fall or not?—was beginning to exasperate him. He would have liked to nudge it back onto the man's head, or knock it off with his finger. He snorted, then glanced around; who knows, maybe he could find another bench in the shade. But there was only one, a ways off, occupied by a fat old lady dressed in rags, who, every time the old man turned to look, broke into a gaping, toothless yawn.

Tuta, smiling and on tiptoe, slowly made her way to the bench. She put a finger to her lips for silence, then gently picked up the sleeping man's hat and placed it back on his head.

The old man followed her movements with his eyes, first with surprise, then with chagrin.

"With yer good grace, mister," Tuta, still smiling, said, and curtsying now, as if she had done him and not the sleeping work-man the favor. "How 'bout a penny for this here poor creature."

"No!" the old man snapped in vexation (who knows why?) and went back to his paper.

"We're doin' the best we can!" Tuta sighed. "God will provide."

And she went to sit on the other bench, next to the tattered old woman, with whom she immediately struck up a conversation.

Tuta was barely twenty: short and shapely, with pale white skin and shiny black hair parted in the middle, combed across her fore-head, and woven into thick braids at the nape of her neck. Her eyes sparkled with an almost aggressive cunning. Every now and then she bit her lip and wiggled her slightly crooked, turned-up little nose.

She told the old lady her bad-luck story. Her husband . . .

Right from the start the old lady gave her a look that set the terms of their conversation: she was willing to let Tuta vent, but not to dupe her. That, no. So there.

"Is he really your husband?"

"We was married in church."

"Oh, well, just in church."

"What's that mean? Ain't he my husband?"

"No, my girl, it doesn't count."[1]

"What do you mean, it doesn't count?"

"You know, it doesn't count."

Ah, yes, the old lady was right. It didn't count. In fact, her husband had been trying to get rid of her for a while now, and had sent her off to Rome to find work as a wet-nurse. She hadn't wanted to come; she knew it was too late, since the baby was already nearly seven months old. She'd spent two weeks in the home of a broker, whose wife, in order to recoup her expenses and cover the cost of Tuta's lodging, had finally dared to propose that she . . .

"Can ya imagine? To me!"

Her indignation had made her milk dry up. And now she didn't have any left, even for her own baby. The broker's wife had taken Tuta's earrings, and even kept the little bundle of things she'd brought from her village. She'd been out on the street since this morning.

"For real, ya know!"

She didn't want to go back to her village, and anyway, she couldn't; her husband would never take her back. So now what was she going to do, with a baby in her arms? She'd never even find a job as a servant this way.

The old lady listened diffidently, because as Tuta said all this,

---

1. After Italian unification, the new civil code stipulated that only civil marriages were valid. This remained the case until 1929, when Mussolini signed the Lateran Pact, ending decades of hostility between Italy and the Vatican.

she didn't sound desperate at all. In fact, she was smiling and kept repeating, "For real, ya know!"

"Where are you from?" the old lady asked.

"Cori."

And for a minute it was as if she were seeing, in her mind's eye, her far-off village. Then she roused herself, looked at her baby, and said:

"And now where'm I gonna leave him? Right here on the ground? Poor sweet little thing."

She lifted him up and kissed him hard several times.

"You made him? You keep him," the old lady said.

"Me make him?" Tuta turned. "Well, I made him, and God punished me for it. But he's suffering too, poor innocent creature! What did he ever do wrong? Really, God don't do things right. And if He don't, just imagine the rest of us. But we're doin' the best we can."

"That's the way of the world!" the old lady sighed, struggling to her feet.

"Life's a hardship," another old lady who happened to pass by added with a shake of her head: a corpulent asthmatic leaning on a cane.

The first old lady produced a filthy pouch that hung from her waist, hidden among her tattered clothes, and took out a crust of bread.

"Here, want this?"

"Yes, may God reward you," Tuta hastened to reply. "I'll eat it. Can you believe I haven't had a thing since morning?"

She broke it in two: the bigger piece for herself, and the other she jammed in her baby's rosy little fingers, which didn't want to open.

"Have a little nibble, Nino, it's good! A real luxury! Eat, eat!"

Dragging her feet, the tattered old lady headed off with the lady with the cane.

The park had livened up a bit. The custodian was watering the plants. But not even the watery gusts seemed to rouse them from the dream—an infinitely sad dream—in which those poor trees were lost, rising out of sparse flower beds blooming with orange peels, eggshells, and scraps of paper, and shielded by twigs and random rocky outcroppings or rings of artificial stone with seats carved in them.

Tuta studied the shallow round pool in the center, the greenish water stagnating beneath a dusty film that would break whenever—plop!—any of the people sitting around the pool tossed in an orange peel.

The sun was already starting to set, and now nearly all the benches were in the shade.

A lady of about thirty, dressed in white, came and sat on one nearby. Her copper hair was tousled, her face freckled. As if unable to stand the heat, she kept trying to shove a sullen-looking boy with waxy yellow skin and a sailor suit off her lap, while glancing about impatiently and winking nearsightedly, as if she were expecting someone. And every now and then she would try to push the boy away again—Go find someone to play with. But the boy didn't budge. He stared at Tuta eating her bread. And Tuta stared back, intently observing the lady and boy. All of a sudden she said:

"With good grace, lady, if sometime ya were needin' a woman to do the washin' or give ya a hand . . . No? Oh well!"

Then, seeing that the sickly boy never took his eyes off her and didn't respond to his mother's repeated hints to move, she called him over: "Ya wanna see the little one? Come take a look then, deary, come on."

After a violent shove from his mother, the boy approached her. He looked at Nino for a while, eyes glazed over like a cat that's been lashed. Then he grabbed the piece of bread out of his tiny fist. Nino shrieked.

"No! poor puppy!" Tuta exclaimed. "Ya took his bread? He's cryin' now, see? He's hungry . . . at least give'm a little piece."

Tuta looked up to call the boy's mother, but didn't see her on the bench: she was at the far end of the park, talking excitedly with a bearded beast of a man who listened distractedly, hands behind his back, a strange smile on his lips, an ugly white hat on the back of his neck. The baby was still screaming.

"Well," Tuta said. "I'll tear a piece off then . . ."

So now the boy started to scream too. His mother came running, and Tuta, *with good grace*, explained what had happened. The boy clutched the bread to his chest with both hands, refusing to give it back, even at his mother's exhortations.

"Do you really want it, Ninnì? Will you eat it?" the red-haired lady asked. "He doesn't eat a thing, you know, not a thing. I'm desperate! If only he really wanted it . . . but it's probably just a whim . . . Let him have it, please."

"Well, sure, of course," Tuta said. "Here, sweetie, you eat it . . ."

But the boy ran over and threw the bread in the pool.

"For the fishies, hey Ninnì?" Tuta exclaimed with a laugh. "And my poor little puppy, who's starvin'? . . . I don't got no milk, no home, no nothin' . . . For real, lady, you know . . . nothin'!"

The lady was eager to return to the man waiting for her in the distance. She took two coins out of her purse and gave them to Tuta.

"God'll repay you," Tuta said to the woman's back as she hurried off. "Come on, my little boy, I'll buy you a sweet, I will! We made two *bajocchi*[2] with that old lady's bread. So hush now, my little Nino, we're rich . . ."

The baby quieted down. Tuta stood there, clutching the two coins in one hand and looking at the people filling the park: children, wet-nurses, nursemaids, soldiers . . .

It was one big commotion.

Vendors selling lupini beans, doughnuts, and other treats made their rounds amid girls jumping rope, boys chasing one another, babies screaming in the arms of their wet-nurses, who chatted calmly among themselves, and nursemaids flirting with the soldiers.

Every now and then Tuta's eyes lit up and her lips formed a strange smile.

Really, no one wanted to believe she didn't know what to do, where to go? She had trouble believing it herself. But that's the way it was. She'd entered the park in search of a little shade, and had been there about an hour already. She could stay till evening. And then? Where was she going to spend the night, with that creature in

---

2. A *bajocco* is a small copper coin issued by the Papal States through 1865.

her arms? And the next day? And the one after that? She didn't have anyone, not even back home, except for the man who didn't want anything more to do with her. And besides, how would she even get back there? So? Was there no way out? She recalled that old witch who had taken her earrings and bundle. Go back to her? She flew into a rage. Gazing at her little boy, who had fallen asleep, she said:

"So, Nino, the river for both of us? That way . . ."

She raised her arms, as if to throw him in. And she, right after him. "No, no!" She lifted her head and smiled, eyeing the people going by.

The sun had set, but the suffocating heat persisted. Tuta undid the button at her throat and tucked her collar under, revealing a little of her pure white chest.

"Hot?"

"I'm dyin'!"

In front of her was an old man with two paper fans stuck in his hat, two more, open and gaudy, in his hand, and a basketful on his arm, all jumbled together, red, yellow, light blue.

"Two *bajocchi!*"

"Go on!" Tuta said, shoving him with her shoulder. "What're they made of? Paper?"

"What do you expect? Silk?"

"Hmmm, and why not?" Tuta replied, smiling defiantly. Then she opened her hand, which grasped the two coins, and added:

"These two *bajocchi*'s all I got. Will you give me it for one?"

The old man shook his head, dignified. "You got to be kidding!"

"Damn you then! Gimme it. I'm dyin' of heat. The little one's sleeping . . . We're doin' the best we can! God'll provide."

■ ■ ■

She handed him the two coins, took the fan, and opened her blouse even further. She began fanning, fanning, fanning her nearly bare breasts, laughing, and, with shining, inviting, provocative eyes, looked brazenly at the soldiers going by.

Those black holm oaks, two rows of them, planted around the vast rectangular piazza, to provide shade in summer. But in winter, what were they for? To splatter passersby, at every little gust of wind, with the water that collected in the leaves after a rain. And to make Papa-Re's[1] kiosk rot a little more. That's really what they were for.

But without the bad—remediable, moreover—that the trees caused in winter, could the good—the cooling in summer—exist? No. And so? So if something works for Man, he accepts it without thanking anyone, as if it were his due. All it takes, though, is for something to go wrong, and he gets upset and starts screaming. An irritable, ungrateful beast, Man is. Good Lord, all he'd have to do is avoid walking beneath the oaks just after a rain.

Yet it's true that Papa-Re, inside his kiosk there, did not enjoy the summer shade those holm oaks offered. He couldn't because he was never there during the daytime, in summer or in winter. It was a mystery what he did all day, where he went. He'd arrive every day from Via San Lorenzo, from somewhere far off, a grim expression on his face. The kiosk was closed all day, and Papa-Re, though he

---

1. Until Italian unification, the Pope (*Papa*) was the sovereign ruler of the Papal States and therefore often referred to as the Pope-King or *Papa-Re*. Here the nickname conveys the character's allegiance to the old order.

hardly ever enjoyed it, nevertheless paid the tax that was levied on all fixed property.

It might have seemed a mockery to consider Papa-Re's kiosk as "fixed": with all the woodworms living inside it, in place of its always-absent owner, it could practically have walked by itself. But the taxman isn't interested in woodworms. Even if the kiosk were to start strolling across the piazza or down the streets on its own, Papa-Re would have had to pay the tax on it, just as for any truly *fixed* property.

Behind the kiosk, a bit further back, was a purported café or — with all due respect to the owner — a hovel, made of wood and pretentiously decorated in the floral style, where certain so-called cabaret singers, accompanied on an out-of-tune piano whose yellowed keys were like the teeth of a poor soul who fasts for a living, shrieked late into the night . . . But no, how could they shriek, poor creatures, when they didn't even have the strength to say, "I'm hungry"?

And yet, that *café chantant* was jam-packed every night with customers who, choking on smoke and the smell of tobacco, reveled, as if it were Carnival, at the coarse, pathetic expressions and consumptive-monkey movements of those unfortunate females who, unable to lift their voices, would lift their arms — and more often their legs — to the seven heavens (*"Brava! Bis! Biiis!"*). The customers favored now this one, now that, applauding and booing with such fervor and tenacity that the police had to intervene more than once to calm their violent quarrels.

It was for these distinguished customers that Papa-Re, dying of cold and dozing off, waited in his kiosk every night, past the final bell, his goods spread out in front of him: cigars, stearin candles, boxes of matches, wax tapers for climbing the stairs, and the few evening papers that remained after his usual round through the neighborhood.

He would arrive at his kiosk just as evening drew near, and wait for a little girl—his granddaughter—to bring him a large terracotta brazier. He would take it by the handle and, with outstretched arm, swing it back and forth to rekindle the fire, which he would then cover again with ashes he kept in the kiosk, then set it down and let it smolder, not even bothering to lock the door. Without that brazier, Papa-Re, old and decrepit as he was, wouldn't have been able to endure the nighttime cold for so many hours.

And oh, without two sturdy legs, without a loud voice, how could he keep peddling newspapers? But it wasn't just the passing of time that had reduced him so, nor were his limbs the only part of him enfeebled by the years; his soul too, poor Papa-Re, enfeebled by his many misfortunes. His first misfortune: the dethroning of the Holy Father, of course;[2] then the death of his wife; then that of his only daughter, an atrocious death, after the disgrace and shame, in a vile hospital where her little girl, for whom he continued to live and suffer, had come into the world. If it weren't for that poor innocent creature to support . . .

The destiny that oppressed and overwhelmed Papa-Re in his old age could be seen in that ugly old hat of his, crumpled and lumpy, so big that it sunk over his eyes and onto his neck. Who gave

---

2. On September 20, 1870, Rome was captured by Italian nationalists, marking the final defeat and dissolution of the Papal States under Pope Pius IX.

it to him? Where in the world did he find it? When Papa-Re, standing under that hat in the middle of the piazza, half closed his eyes, he seemed to be saying: "Here I am. See? If I want to go on living, I have no choice but to stand here under this hat, which weighs on me and makes it hard for me to breathe."

If I want to go on living! Papa-Re didn't want to go on living for anything in the world: he was all shriveled up, and barely earned a thing anymore. Before, the distributor would give him newspapers by the dozen. Now, out of charity, he'd pass him a few copies at most, whatever was left after supplying all the other peddlers who would set on him, shouting that they needed theirs first, so they could start in on their rounds. So as not to be crushed by the throng, Papa-Re would hold back, waiting until even the women peddlers got theirs. Often some boor would hurl a bundle at him, and he'd take it without a fuss, stepping to one side so as not to be run over by those who, heads down and in a blind fury, bolted every which way as soon as they got their papers. Sighing, teetering on his poor, crumpled legs, he'd watch them blast off like rockets.

"Here you go, Papa-Re, two dozen tonight, a real splurge. There's a revolution in Russia."

Papa-Re shrugged his shoulders, half closed his eyes, grabbed his stack of papers, and headed off after the others, doing his best to run on those wobbly legs of his and straining his clucking voice to yell:

"The *Tribuuuune!*"

Then, in a different tone:

"Revolution in Russiaaa!!!"

And then, almost to himself:

"Big news tonight, the *Tribune*."

Good thing that two doormen on Via Volturno, one on Via Gaeta, and another on Via Palestro still waited loyally for him. The rest he'd try to sell as best he could, roaming the entire Macao neighborhood. At about ten, tired and out of breath, he'd hole up inside his kiosk, where he would wait, dozing, for customers to come out of the café. He'd had it up to here with this miserable job! But when you're old, what alternative is there? Try as you might, you won't come up with one. Well maybe one: the towering wall of the Pincian Hill.[3]

■ ■ ■

Every time, around sunset, he saw his young granddaughter appear—barefoot, her ragged dress worn and tattered, and bundled, poor creature, in an old wool shawl that a neighbor had given her—Papa-Re regretted even the minor expense of that little fire, which was yet so essential for him. The only good things left in his life were the child and the brazier. Seeing them arriving together in the distance, he would smile and rub his hands. Then he would kiss his little granddaughter's forehead and start swinging the brazier to rekindle the coals.

The other night—either his soul was more enfeebled than usual, or he was more tired, but as he swung the brazier back and forth, it suddenly slipped from his hand and smashed to smithereens in the middle of the piazza. *Bam!* Much laughter from those

---

3. He could jump to his death from the high wall.

who happened to be passing by as the brazier soared and crashed, laughter for the face Papa-Re made on seeing his faithful, cold-night companion slip out of his hand, and for the naïveté of the little girl, who had instinctively run after it, as if to catch it in mid-air.

Grandfather and granddaughter looked each other in the eye, dumbstruck. Papa-Re, his arm still outstretched, as if still swinging the brazier — eh, he'd swung it too far! — and the coal, sizzling there among the potsherds in a puddle of rainwater.

"Hurray for happiness!" he said finally, snapping out of his stupor and shaking his head. "Laugh, go ahead and laugh. Tonight I'll be happy too. Go on, my little Nena, go. Maybe it was just as well, in the end."

And he set off for his newspapers.

That evening, instead of holing up in his kiosk around ten, he made a bigger round than usual through the Macao neighborhood. His nocturnal lair would be cold, and, sitting still, he'd feel it even more. In the end though, he grew tired. But before entering his kiosk, he went to look at the spot in the piazza where the brazier had shattered, as if a bit of warmth might still emanate from it. From the purported café came the strident notes of the little piano, and every now and then a roar of applause and whistles. Papa-Re, the collar of his filthy overcoat pulled up over his ears, hands numb with cold, and clutching to his chest the few newspapers he had left, paused to peer through the fogged glass door. It must be nice in there, with some warm punch in your belly. Brrr! The north wind had picked up again; it sliced his face and turned the cobblestones in the piazza white. Not a cloud in the sky; even the stars seemed to tremble from the cold. Papa-Re, looking at his dark kiosk under the black holm oaks, sighed, tucked the newspapers under his arm, and went to remove the shutter in front.

"Papa-Re!" A hoarse voice called out from inside the kiosk.

The old man started and leaned in to look.

"Who's there?"

"Me, Rosalba. The brazier?"

"Rosalba?"

"Vignas. Don't you remember me? Rosalba Vignas."

"Ah," said Papa-Re, who mixed up the strange names of all those cabaret singers past and present. "Why don't you go inside where it's warm? What're you doing in there?"

"Waiting for you. Aren't you coming in?"

"What do you want from me? Let me see you."

"I don't want to let myself be seen. I'm tucked under the counter here. Come in, we'll be cozy."

Papa-Re circled the kiosk, holding the shutter, then stooped and stepped through the little door.

"Where are you?"

"Here," the woman said.

He couldn't see her, hidden as she was under the counter where Papa-Re laid out his newspapers, cigars, boxes of matches, and candles. She was sitting where he, perched on his high stool, usually rested his feet.

"The brazier?" She asked again, from under the counter. "Don't you use it anymore?"

"Hush, it broke, today. Flew out of my hand when I was waving it back and forth."

"Oh, great! So you're dying of cold? I was counting on that brazier of yours. Come on, Papa-Re, sit down, I'll warm you up myself."

"You? What do you want to go warming me up for, now? I'm old, my child. What is it you want from me?"

The woman let out a shrill laugh and grabbed him by the leg.

"Come on, calm down!" Papa-Re said, shielding himself. "You stink of booze. Have you been drinking?"

"A little. Sit down. We'll fit. Come on, right here . . . up on your stool. Now let me warm your legs. Or maybe it's another brazier you want? Well then, here."

And she placed a bundle — so warm! — in his lap.

"What's this?" the old man asked.

"My daughter."

"Your daughter? You brought your daughter along too?"

"I've been kicked out of my house, Papa-Re! He's left me."

"Who?"

"Him, Cesare. Threw me out on the street. With my babe in my arms."

Papa-Re climbed off his stool, bent down, and, crouching in the dark, handed the woman back her daughter.

"Here, my child, here, now go. I've got my own troubles. Leave me in peace!"

"It's cold," the woman said, her voice hoarser now. "Are you going to throw me out too?"

"What do you want to do, take up residence in here?" he asked bitterly. "Are you mad? Or just drunk?"

The woman didn't answer, but she didn't move either. She

might have been crying. In the silence could be heard, faint as a shadow, the tickle of a mandolin, coming from the far end of Via Volturno. It gradually drew nearer, but then suddenly started to fade, drifting off and dying in the distance.

"Let me wait here for him, please," the woman started in again, gloomily, after a bit.

"Wait for who?" Papa-Re asked.

"I already told you. Cesare. He's there, in the café. I saw him through the window."

"So go join him then, if you know he's there! What do you want from me?"

"I can't, not with the *baby*. He's left me! He's in there with another woman. You know who? Mignon! That's right, the famous Mign . . . right, who's going to start singing tomorrow evening. He's introducing her, can you believe it? He had the maestro teach her the songs, paid by the hour. I just came to say two words to him, when he comes out. To him and to her. Let me stay here. Where's the harm in that? On the contrary, I'm warming up the place, Papa-Re. Outside, with this cold, my poor little creature . . . Besides, it won't be long now, half an hour more or less. Come on, Papa-Re, be good! Sit down and hold my baby on your knees. There's no room for her down here. Besides, you'll both be warmer. She's sleeping, poor thing; she won't be any trouble."

Papa-Re sat down again, muttering as he took the baby in his lap.

"Well, would you look at this! So I have myself another brazier tonight. But what is it you want to say to him?"

"Nothing. Just two words," she said again.

They were silent for a good while. From the station came the mournful whistle of a train arriving and then departing. Stray dogs wandered through the vast, empty piazza. In the distance, two night watchmen, all bundled up. In the silence, even the hum of the electric street lamps could be heard.

"You have a granddaughter, don't you, Papa-Re?" the woman, rousing herself, asked with a sigh.

"Nena, yes."

"No mother?"

"No."

"Look at my daughter. Isn't she beautiful?"

Papa-Re didn't answer.

"Isn't she beautiful?" the woman insisted. "Now what will become of her, my poor little babe? But I can't . . . I can't go on like this. Someone has to take pity on her. You know I won't be able to find work, not with her in my arms. Where am I going to leave her? And besides, who's going to hire me? Nobody's going to take me in, not even as a maid."

"Shut up!" the old man interrupted her, starting violently and beginning to cough.

He was thinking about his daughter, who'd also left him with a little baby girl, just like this one on his knees. Tenderly, slowly, he drew her to his chest. Those caresses weren't for her, though, but for his little granddaughter, whom he suddenly remembered once being as tiny, as good and quiet, as this one.

Applause and indecorous shouting burst from the café.

"Vile man!" the woman muttered through clenched teeth. "He's having a grand time in there with that ugly monkey, more shriveled than death. So, he usually comes by here in the evening, doesn't he? To buy a cigar, right after he leaves the café?"

"I don't know," Papa-Re said, shrugging his shoulders.

"What do you mean, you don't know? Cesare, the Milanese. Tall, blond, big guy, beard parted on his chin, jaunty. Oh, so handsome! And he knows it, the scoundrel, and uses it to his advantage. Don't you remember he took me in last year?"

"No." The old man was annoyed. "How am I supposed to remember if you won't even let me see you?"

The woman gave a mocking laugh, like a sob, and then said grimly:

"You wouldn't recognize me anymore. I'm the one who used to sing little duets with that idiot Peppot. Peppot, remember him? *Monte Bisbin?* Yeah, him. But it doesn't matter if you don't remember. I'm not like I was. He's ruined me, done me in, in just one year. And you know something? At first he said he wanted to marry me. What a joke! Imagine!"

"Imagine!" Papa-Re repeated, already half asleep.

"But I never believed him," the woman continued. "Just as long as he keeps me now, I'd say to myself. Because of this little creature here I'd conceived, who knows how, maybe because I was too taken with him. God's way of chastising me. Besides, what did I know? But then things got worse. You think it's nothing to have a child! Gilda Boa. . . . Remember Gilda Boa? She used to tell me to throw the baby away. Throw her away? How? That's what he wanted to do—throw her away for real. He had the nerve to say she didn't look like him. But just look at her, Papa-Re: his spitting image! Oh, vile man! He knows perfectly well she's his, that I never could have gone with anyone else, I was crazy for him . . . I could barely see straight, I was so attracted to him! But I became worse than a slave for him, you know? He'd beat me—I never said a word. Starve me to death—I never said a word. It was agony, I swear—not for me—for this little one here, because I was so famished I didn't have any milk. But now . . ."

She went on like that for a while, but Papa-Re wasn't listening anymore. Exhausted, comforted by the warmth of the little bundle he'd found instead of his brazier, he'd fallen asleep, as usual. He woke with a start when the door to the café was flung open and noisy customers began spilling out, the last applause still sounding in the hall. But where was the woman?

"Hey! What are you doing?" Papa-Re asked sleepily.

She'd opened the door with one hand and was waiting, hiding between the legs of his stool, crouched and panting, like a beast ready to pounce.

"What're you doing?" Papa-Re repeated.

A shot rang out.

"Keep quiet, or they'll arrest you too!" the woman yelled as she dashed outside, slamming the door behind her.

Papa-Re, terrified by the screams, curses, and tremendous confusion behind the kiosk, hunched over the little baby, who had jumped at the sound of the gun, and, trembling, pulled her tight to his chest. A carriage raced up and, a second later, galloped away toward Saint Anthony's hospital. A furious knot of people passed the kiosk, yelling, and then headed off toward Piazza delle Terme. Some stayed around, though, talking about what happened. Papa-Re was all ears, but he didn't move, afraid the baby would start to cry. After a while, one of the waiters from the café came to buy a cigar.

"Hey, Papa-Re, did you see that pathetic little tragedy?"

"I . . . I heard," he stammered.

"And you didn't even move, eh?" the waiter laughed. "Always with that brazier of yours, right?"

■ ■ ■

"Right, with my brazier," Papa-Re said, still hunched over, his mouth opening into a miserable, toothless grin.

Shouting, suitcase in hand, I threw myself at the train, which was already juddering to depart. I just managed to grab hold of a second-class car and, with the help of a furious conductor who had come running, opened the door and hurled myself inside.

Phew!

In the car were four women, two small children, and a baby girl, not yet weaned, who was rather exposed just then: little legs in the air, on the knees of an enormous, clumsy wet-nurse who was tranquilly wiping her bottom in utmost liberty.

"Mamma, look, another nuisance!"

So was I received (and deservedly so) by the older of the two children—a scrawny little boy, probably about six years old, big ears, hair standing straight up, and an upturned nose—who addressed the woman reading in the corner. An ample, greenish veil lifted over her hat made a deceptively appealing frame for her pale, thin face.

The woman was annoyed, but pretended not to hear and continued reading. Foolishly, because the boy—as one can easily imagine—announced again, in the same tone of voice:

"Mamma, look, another nuisance."

"Hush, you impertinent child!" the woman snapped. Then, turning to me with ostentatious mortification:

"Forgive me, sir, please."

"But of course," I exclaimed, smiling.

The boy looked at his mother, surprised by her scolding. "But why?" he seemed to ask; "you said it yourself!" Then he looked at me with such a bewildered yet mischievous smile that I couldn't help but add:

"Well, son? I would have missed the train, and lost my connection, otherwise."

The little boy grew serious, stared intently, and then, rousing himself with a sigh, asked me:

"How could you have lost it? You can't lose a train. It runs on boiling water, along a *train treck*. It's not a coffeepot. A coffeepot doesn't have wheels, so it can't go anywhere on its own."

The boy's logic seemed impeccable to me. But his mother scolded him again, with a tired, irritated air. "Don't talk nonsense, Carlino."

The other child, a girl about three years old, was standing on the seat close to the big wet-nurse, staring out at the fleeting countryside. Every now and then she would wipe her breath from the glass with her little hand, marveling silently at the illusory flight of trees and bushes.

I turned to contemplate my other traveling companions, who sat facing each other in the corner: two women, both dressed in black.

Foreigners: Germans, I ascertained, after hearing them speak a little.

One—the young one—seemed to be suffering from the journey, and was clearly unwell. Very pale, she kept her eyes closed, and her blond head fell back against the headrest. The other one, older, a stout woman with olive skin and rigid posture, seemed oppressed by the nightmare of her insipid little hat with its stiff, straight brim; balanced on what remained of her hair, gray and twisted and bunched in a black hairnet, it seemed some sort of punishment.

She sat perfectly still, never for a moment taking her eyes off the young woman, who must have been her mistress.

At a certain point, I saw two giant tears stream from the young woman's closed eyes. I looked quickly at the old woman, who pressed her lips together, turning the corners down in an evident attempt to check a wave of emotion, and batted her eyes several times to hold back tears.

What unknown drama was sealed up in those two women dressed in black, journeying so far from their home? For whom, for what was she crying, that pale young woman so wrought with grief?

The sturdy, robust old woman seemed consumed by her inability to comfort her. But in her eyes was not the desperate acquiescence to grief one usually has when faced with a death, but rather a harsh, fierce rage, perhaps against one who was making that adored creature suffer so.

I don't know how many times I must have sighed while daydreaming about those two. I do know that from time to time, my sigh would rouse me and I would look around.

The sun had set a while ago. The last gloomy glimmer of twilight still lingered in the sky: an agonizing moment for travelers.

The two children had fallen asleep. The mother had lowered her veil and may have been dozing as well, her book resting in her lap. Only the baby girl hadn't managed to fall asleep. She wasn't crying, but she flailed about restlessly, rubbing her face with her tiny little fists, while the wet-nurse puffed and cooed repeatedly:

"Hush little darling, don't you cry, and I will sing you a lullaby."

And then, as if sighing impatiently, she listlessly hummed the motif from a country dirge: *Aoo'h! Aoo'h!*

There, in the dark shadows of the impending night, from the lips of that coarse peasant woman, the melancholy dirge unfurled in a soft voice of improbable sweetness and ineffable, mesmerizing bitterness:

> *I watch, I watch over you, sing me the dirge,*
> *He who loves you more than me, my child, deceives you.*

Observing the young woman slumped there in the corner of the car, I felt my throat tighten with a distressing urge to weep, I don't know why. And she, hearing the sweet song, opened her beautiful blue eyes, fantasizing in the dark. What was she thinking? What was she regretting?

I understood a moment later, when I heard the vigilant old woman ask in a low voice suffocated by emotion:

Willst Du deine Amme nah?

"Would you like your wet-nurse near you?" And she rose and went and sat next to her, drawing that blond head to her shriveled bosom. The young woman wept silently as her wet-nurse kept repeating in the dark:

■ ■ ■

> *He who loves you more than me, my child, deceives you.*

A first-class carriage, with festooned and feathered horses, a coachman, and groomsmen in wigs: his relatives certainly wouldn't have gone for that, not for him, anyway. But a second-class carriage, well, yes, if only for appearances' sake.

Two hundred and fifty *lire*: the going rate.

And the coffin, well, even if it wasn't pine or walnut or beech, they certainly wouldn't have left it bare exactly (again, for appearances' sake).

Lined in red velvet, even if of the poorest quality, with gilded upholstery nails and handles: four hundred *lire*, at least.

Then: a generous tip for whoever washed and dressed him once he was dead (what a job!); the outlay for the silk skullcap and cloth slippers; the outlay for the four large candles, one for each corner of the bed; a tip for the gravediggers for carrying the coffin to the hearse, and then from the hearse to the grave; the outlay for a funeral wreath, good Lord, one, at least; never mind the village band, which could be done without; but a couple dozen candles for the little orphan girls at the *Boccone del povero*[1] to carry, who

---

1. A religious institute in the province of Agrigento; the name means "Mouth of the Poor."

survived on the fifty *lire* they were always given to accompany the city's dead; and who knows how many other unexpected expenses.

Matteo Sinagra's relatives would be saved all this by his going on his own two feet to kill himself, economically, at the cemetery, right in front of the little gate to his family tomb. In such a way that, right there, after the arrival of the magistrate, they could toss him in on four bare planks with very little expense, without even giving him a brushing, and lower him down to where his father, mother, first wife, and their two little children had been resting now for a while.

The dead have an air of believing that death's advantage is the loss of life, that it all ends there. And for them it does, no doubt about it. But they never think of the dreadful burden of their body, which stays there on the bed, all rigid, for a couple of days, or of the trouble and expense for the living, who, even though they weep over the dead, also need to liberate themselves of him. Knowing how much this liberation costs, in a case such as his—a dead man in good health—he, a willing dead, could kindly make the short walk to the cemetery and accommodate himself there tranquilly on his own.

There. By now, Matteo Sinagra had nothing else to think about. Life suddenly seemed drained of all meaning. He could barely even remember anymore what it was he'd done in his life. Oh sure, all those foolish things people usually do. Without realizing it. Thoughtlessly, easily. Yes, because he'd been pretty lucky, he had, until three years ago. Nothing had ever seemed terribly hard to him, and he'd never hesitated, not for a minute, never puzzled over whether he should do something, or go this way or that. He'd cheerfully and confidently thrown himself into everything he'd attempted; he'd explored every path, and had always succeeded, over-coming obstacles that to others might have seemed insurmount-able.

Until three years ago.

Then, who knows how, who knows why, the form of inspira-tion that had aided and propelled him forward, sure-footed and eager, for so many years suddenly vanished; his cheerful confidence crumbled, and along with it the endeavors that until now he had sustained with means and skills but that now, all of a sudden, and much to his dismay, he no longer knew how to account for.

Just like that, from one day to the next, everything had changed, grown dark on him, even the look of things and of people. He'd sud-denly found himself face to face with another self, whom he didn't recognize in the least, in another world, which he was discovering for the first time: a harsh, dull, opaque, inert world.

At first he was in a sort of daze, like that which silence provokes in people who are used to living amid the constant din of machines when they're suddenly turned off. Then he thought not only of his own ruin, but that of his second wife's father and brother, who had entrusted him with large sums of money. But perhaps his father- and brother-in-law, despite suffering serious setbacks, could pick themselves again. His ruin, on the other hand, was absolute.

He holed himself up at home, crushed not so much by the gravity of the calamity as the awareness of how irreparable the mys-terious breakdown was that, like lightning, had upset the workings of his life.

Move? Why? Leave the house? Why? Every action, every step was futile now, even speaking.

Mute, all beard and hair now, he just huddled in a corner, numbly observing his wife's desperate fits and tears.

Until his brother-in-law stormed in and kicked him out, after first forcefully shearing him.

There was something he could do, to earn ten measly *lire* a day: he could be an errand boy for a small agrarian bank that had just opened. What was he doing there, brooding on that chair? Out! Out! Hadn't he done enough harm already? Did he expect to live off his victims, his wife and two little children? Out!

Out. So here he was. He'd left his home a few days ago. He'd taken the errand boy job for the small agrarian bank. Threadbare cap, faded suit, worn-out shoes, the look of a conceding fool.

No one recognized him anymore.

"Matteo Sinagra, him?"

To tell the truth, he didn't recognize himself anymore either. And finally, that morning . . .

It had taken a friend of his, a dear friend from the good old days, to clarify the situation for him.

Who was he now, anyway? No one. Not only because he'd lost everything he had; not only because he'd been reduced to the miserable, humiliating state of messenger boy, in a faded suit, threadbare cap, and worn-out shoes. No, no. He was truly no one now, because there was nothing left to him, apart from the outer appearance (and even that, so changed, unrecognizable!) of the Matteo Sinagra he had been until three years ago. He didn't feel himself to be, nor did others recognize him in this errand boy who had recently left home. And so? So who was he? Someone else, someone who hadn't yet come to life, who needed to learn, if anything, to live another life, a meager, tormented life, on ten lousy *lire* a day. Was it worth it? Matteo Sinagra, the real Matteo Sinagra, had died, died definitively, three years before.

This is what the eyes of his friend, whom he'd chanced to meet that morning, said, with the most innocent cruelty.

Having returned to the village after an absence of six years, the friend knew nothing of Matteo Sinagra's calamity. Passing him on the street, he hadn't even recognized him.

"Matteo? Really? You're Matteo Sinagra?"

"That's what they say . . ."

"Really?"

And those eyes of his simply stared at Matteo, stared in such bewilderment—a mixture of pity and disgust—that he suddenly saw himself in them: dead, completely dead, without so much as a crumb remaining of the life Matteo Sinagra had once lived.

And so, as soon as his friend, unable to find a word, an expression, or even a smile to offer this shadow of a man, had turned his back to him, he had the strange impression that everything truly had been drained of all meaning, that all of life was in vain.

But only since then? No . . . for God's sake! Three years it's been like this . . . he'd been dead for three years, for a good three years . . . and yet he was still here, still standing? Still walking, breathing, seeing? But how? . . . if he wasn't anything anymore! If he wasn't anyone anymore! Still in that same suit, from three years ago . . . those shoes, from three years ago, still standing . . .

Oh come on, wasn't he ashamed? A dead man, still walking? Go lie down, there, in the cemetery!

Once this dead man was out of the way, his relatives would look after his widow and two little orphan girls.

Matteo Sinagra felt his waistcoat pocket for his revolver, his faithful companion for so many years. And there he was, on the road leading to the cemetery, for sure.

It's quite amusing, really, an unprecedented pleasure.

A dead man, making his way on his own, on his own two feet, slowly, slowly, taking his own sweet time, walking to his destiny.

Matteo Sinagra knows perfectly well he's a dead man: an old dead man, even: having been dead for three years, he'd had all the time in the world to empty himself of every regret of his lost life.

He's light now, light as a feather! He has found himself again, has assumed his proper role, as his own shadow. Free of all obstacles, exempt from every affliction, liberated from every weight, he's going to lay himself to rest comfortably.

Here it is: the road that leads to the cemetery, which he's now traveling for the last time, as a dead man—no return—appears to him in a new light, fills him with the joy of liberation, that he's truly already outside of, beyond, life.

The dead take this road in a coach, closed and soldered in a double coffin of zinc and walnut. But he is walking, breathing. He can turn his head this way and that, can still look about.

And he sees with new eyes those things that are no longer for him, that no longer have any meaning for him.

The trees. . . . oh, look! Is that what trees were like? And those mountains over there . . . why? Those blue-colored mountains, with that white cloud up above . . . the clouds . . . how strange they are!

. . . and there, in the distance, the sea . . . was it always like that? Is that really the sea?

And the air that fills his lungs, what a new flavor it has, such a cool sweetness on his lips, his nostrils . . . the air. . . . ah, the air . . . how delightful! He breathes it in . . . ah, he drinks it in now, in a way he never did back then, back when he was alive; now he can drink it in, as no one who's still alive can! Air for air's sake, not a breath in order to live. All of this infinite, enveloping delight—the other dead can't have it, they who travel that road in a coach, stiff, stretched out flat and plunged in darkness inside a coffin. Not even the living can have it, the living who don't know what it means to enjoy it *afterward*, like this, once and for all: living, present, trembling eternity!

The road is still long. But he could just as well have stopped here: he has entered eternity, he's walking in it, breathing it in, a divine drunkenness, unknown to the living.

"Do you want me? Take me with you . . ."

A pebble. A pebble along the road. And why not?

Matteo Sinagra bends down and picks it up, weighs it in his hand. A pebble . . . is this what rocks were like? Yes, look: a little landslide, some rocks have shattered, a piece of living earth, of this whole living earth, of this shattered universe . . . And here it is, in his pocket: the pebble will come with him.

And that little flower?

Of course, that too, here, here, in the buttonhole of this dead man, who, so extraneous, so serene and happy, is making his way on his own, on his own two feet, to his grave, as if going to a party, with a flower in his buttonhole.

There's the cemetery entrance. Another two dozen steps, and the dead man will be home. No tears. He's coming on his own, at a brisk pace, a flower in his buttonhole.

They make quite a sight, these cypress trees guarding the gate. Oh, a modest home, on the top of a hill, amid some olive trees. There must be a hundred family tombs here, more or less, artless and unpretentious: chapels with a little altar, a gate, and a few flowers here and there.

For the dead, it's an enviable abode, this cemetery, far from the village. The living rarely come here.

Matteo Sinagra enters and greets the old custodian sitting in front of his tiny house to the right of the gate, a dull gray wool shawl over his shoulders and his official cap on his nose.

"Hey, Pignocco!"

Pignocco is asleep.

Matteo Sinagra stands there contemplating the sleep of that one living being among so many dead, and—as a dead man—he feels upset, mildly irritated.

That's easy to say. It does the dead good to think that a living soul watches over their sleep and busies himself on the land that covers them. Sleep above, sleep below: too much sleep. He should wake Pignocco, and say to him:

Here I am, I'm one of yours now. I came on my own, on my own two feet, to save my relatives a little money. And this is how you take care of us?

Oh come on! Care? Poor Pignocco! What sort of care do the dead need? Once you've watered the flower beds here and there; once you've lit a few lamps on this or that tomb, lamps that don't illuminate anyone; once you've swept the dead leaves from the paths—what else is there to do? No one says a word in here. The buzz of the flies, then, and the slow rustle of forgotten olive trees on the hill persuade him to sleep. He's waiting for death too, poor Pignocco. Just look at him: while he waits, he sleeps on top of all those dead who are sleeping forever below.

Maybe he'll wake up in a little while, at the sharp sound of the pistol. But maybe not even then. It's so small, his pistol, and Pignocco is sleeping so profoundly . . . Later, toward evening, when he makes his final round before locking the gate, he'll find a black obstacle there at the end of the path.

"Oh, what's this here?"

Nothing, Pignocco. Someone who has to go below. Call, call for a bed to be made up for him down there, as best as can be, without too much fuss. He came on his own, to save his relatives the expense, and also for the pleasure of seeing himself like this, beforehand, a dead man among the dead, at home, arrived at his destiny in good health, eyes open, mind alert. Leave the pebble in his pocket, it too was fed up with sitting there on the road all alone. And leave that flower in his buttonhole, the dalliance of a dead man. He picked it himself, and offered it to himself, on his own, for all the funeral wreaths that his friends and relatives won't be offering him. He's here, above the earth, but it's really as if he'd come up from below after three years, curious to see what effect these family tombs make up here on this hill, these flower beds, these gravel-lined paths, these black crosses and tin wreaths in the section for the poor.

A nice effect, really.

And ever so quietly, on tiptoe, Matteo Sinagra, without waking Pignocco, steps into the cemetery.

■ ■ ■

It's early yet, for going to sleep. He'll wander the paths until late, take a look around (as a dead man, naturally). He'll wait until the moon rises, and then, good night.

He set himself free in his sleep, though how, he doesn't know; perhaps it's like when you sink underwater, sensing that your body will surface again on its own; yet all that surfaces is the sensation, a floating shadow of the body that has remained below.

He was sleeping, and is no longer in his body; he can't say he woke up, and he doesn't really know where he is now; it's as if he's suspended, floating in the air of his closed room.

Alienated from his senses, the memory of them lingers beyond their functioning; already detached, but not yet far off: his hearing, there, where even the faintest noise in the night is; his sight, here, where a flicker of light is; and the walls, the ceiling (which from here seems dusty), and below, the floor and the rug, and that door, and the fading fear of that bed with the green duvet and yellowish blankets, under which one assumes there is a body, lying inert; his bald head, sunk in the rumpled pillows; eyes closed and mouth open between the reddish hairs of mustache and beard—thick hairs, metallic almost—a dry, black hole; and one eyebrow hair so long that, if he doesn't keep it in place, it falls over his eye.

Him, that! One who is no longer. One whose body had become a burden. An effort just to breathe! His entire life, restricted now to this room; feeling himself gradually losing everything, keeping himself alive by staring at this or that object, afraid of falling asleep. And then, in fact, in his sleep . . .

How strange they sound, there in that room, life's last words:

"Given my current condition, do you think it's worth attempting such a risky operation?"

"At this point, frankly, the risk . . ."

"It's not the risk. I mean, is there any hope?"

"Ah. Little."

"Well, then . . ."

The rosy lamp, hanging in the middle of the room, has been left on in vain.

■ ■ ■

But now, in the end, he has set himself free, and he feels rancor, rather than aversion, for his body there.

He could never understand why other people identified that image as the thing that was most him.

It wasn't true. It isn't true.

He was not that body there; on the contrary, there was so little of him there. He was, in life, in the things he thought, which stirred inside him, in everything he saw outside himself, no longer seeing himself. Houses roads sky. The whole world.

Fine. But now, without his body anymore, it's the pain he clings to, the dread of disintegrating and diffusing into everything else in order to hold on to himself, but in clinging to it, the fear returns, not of falling asleep, but of disappearing into something that will remain there, in and of itself, without him: an object: the clock on the nightstand, the picture on the wall, the rosy lamp hanging in the middle of the room.

He is now those things; but they are no longer what they were when they still meant something to him; those things that have no meaning in and of themselves, and are therefore nothing to him now.

This is what it is to die.

■ ■ ■

The wall of the villa. But how, is he outside already? The moon shines down on it; and there below, the garden.

The trough, roughhewn, extends from the outer wall, which is dressed in the green of climbing roses.

The water falls in trickles into the trough. Now a plash of bubbles, now a strand of glass, clear and fine and still.

How crystal clear the water is, as it falls! It turns green as soon as it reaches the trough. At times the strand is so fine, the drops so scant, that the turbid depths look like an oceanic eternity.

Small green and white leaves, slightly yellowed, float on the water. The mouth of the iron drainpipe, level with the surface, would drink the overflow in silence were it not for the thronging leaves drawn to it. The sucking of the clogged drain is like a gruff rebuke at these silly, scurrying fools, who seem in a rush to be swallowed up, to disappear, as if it weren't wonderful to swim, so bright and buoyant, in the dark green, glassy water. But they fell! How buoyant they are! And you, mouth of death, decide their destiny!

To vanish.

To grow, surprisingly, becoming infinite: the illusion of the senses, already scattered, little by little empties itself of things that seemed to be there but were not: sounds, colors — not there; all is cold, all is silent; it was nothing; and death, this nothing of life as it once was. That green . . . oh, how he had longed to be grass once, at dawn, along a river bank, gazing at the bushes and breathing in the fragrance of all that greenery, so fresh and new! A tangle of live, white roots clinging to the black earth, sucking its juices. Ah, life is earthy! It doesn't want the sky, if not to let the earth breathe! But now he is like the fragrance of the grass, dissolving with this very breath, this discernible vapor that disperses and then disappears, but without coming to an end, without anything surrounding it anymore. Yes, pain perhaps, which, even if he can still manage to perceive it, is already far away, beyond time, in the infinite sadness of an empty eternity.

One thing: to continue to consist in just one thing, something small even, insignificant, a stone, almost nothing. Or a flower even, which quickly fades, like this geranium . . .

■ ■ ■

"Oh, look, down in the garden, that red geranium. It's radiant! But why?"

■ ■ ■

Sometimes, in the evening, a flower suddenly glows like that, in a garden. And no one knows why.

ITALIAN TITLES AND PUBLICATION DATES

The following list gives the English title, Italian title, and date of first publication for each story in this collection.

The Revenge of the Dog ◾ La vendetta del cane, 1913

The Cat, a Goldfinch, and the Stars ◾ Il gatto, un cardellino e le stelle, 1917

The Jar ◾ La giara, 1909

Donna Mimma ◾ Donna Mimma, 1917

The Dearly Departed ◾ La buon'anima, 1904

Two Double Beds ◾ Due letti a due, 1909

Night ◾ Notte, 1912

Nené and Ninì ◾ Nené e Ninì, 1912

A Breath of Air ◾ Filo d'aria, 1914

Faith ◾ La fede, 1922

Seeing As It's Not Raining . . . ◾ Visto che non piove . . . , 1912

A "Goy" ◾ Un "goj," 1916 (as "Il presepe di quest'anno," or This Year's Nativity Scene)

When You Understand ◾ Quando si comprende, 1916

The Light in the Other House ◾ Il lume dell'altra casa, 1909

Swift and Swallow ◾ Rondone e Rondinella, 1913

Mrs. Frola and Her Son-in-Law Mr. Ponza ◾ La signora Frola e il signor Ponza, suo genero, 1915

The Bat ▪ Il pipistrello, 1920

The Raven of Mìzzaro ▪ Il corvo di Mìzzaro, 1902

The Waiting Coffin ▪ La cassa riposta, 1907

Romulus ▪ Romolo, 1915

The Cathar Heresy ▪ L'eresia catara, 1905

The Little Black Goat ▪ Il capretto nero, 1913

Prancing ▪ La rallegrata, 1913

The Fly ▪ La mosca, 1904

On the Mark ▪ Nel segno, 1904

The Little Fan ▪ Il ventaglino, 1903

The Brazier ▪ Lo scaldino, 1905

Dirge ▪ Nenia, 1901

On His Own ▪ Da sé, 1913

In the Evening, a Geranium ▪ Di sera, un geranio, 1934

ACKNOWLEDGMENTS

I am grateful to the many people who helped me bring Pirandello's stories into English. Paola Inzillo, Rita Fabbrizio, Rosaria Riccioli, Roberto Polillo, Gianni Marizza, Marinetta Piva, Deborah Miller, and Margaret Brucia and her Italian relatives offered insights about Pirandello's language and life in Sicily. Patricia Caprotti, who bequeathed me her dictionaries and so much more, unflaggingly explained and interpreted enigmas. Angelo De Gennaro guided me through the intricacies of Pirandello's syntax. Rebecca Stewart was my midwife for "Donna Mimma." Giuseppe Mazzotta offered inspiration. Karl Kirchwey gifted me his friendship and wise counsel. Dana Prescott and the Civitella Ranieri Foundation granted me time and space to work. Mark Seymour provided important historical background, astute advice, and precious moral support. Kim Hastings, Joe Solodow, and Bruce Coffin were patient and generous readers, whose suggestions greatly improved my translation. Geo Calhoun sustained me in more ways than he knows.

Sincere thanks to Ted and Cecile Margellos for their vision in creating this series, and to John Donatich for his encouragement and forbearance. Ann-Marie Imbornoni, Danielle D'Orlando, and Abbie Storch guided the project through Yale University Press, and Anne Canright carefully edited the manuscript.

Luigi Pirandello (1867–1936) is Italy's most important modern playwright and one of the most significant literary figures of the last century. An intense and prolific writer, Pirandello composed plays, poetry, novels, essays, and short stories. His groundbreaking 1921 play *Sei personaggi in cerca d'autore* (Six Characters in Search of an Author) upended conventional notions of author, actor, and audience, and revolutionized the very concept of theater. He was awarded the Nobel Prize in 1934.

Pirandello was born in Agrigento, Sicily, to an anti-Bourbon family actively engaged in Italian unification. The family moved to Palermo when he was thirteen, and Pirandello later studied in Rome and Bonn before returning to Rome to teach and write.

The central themes of *Sei personaggi in cerca d'autore*—identity, the relation of self to others, the ambiguity of truth, and the tension between appearance and reality—also animate his magnificent collection of short stories. It is in these ironic, bitter tales that Pirandello reveals himself as a master storyteller, with a remarkable ear for dialogue, a keen sense of the crushing burdens of class, gender, and social conventions, and a fine observer of the drama of daily life.

Virginia Jewiss is a translator of Italian literature and cinema. Her literary translations include Roberto Saviano's *Gomorrah* and Melania Mazzucco's *Vita*. She has adapted into English the screenplays for numerous films, including Matteo Garrone's *Tale of Tales*, Paolo Sorrentino's *Youth* and *This Must Be the Place*, as well as the scripts for his HBO series *The Young Pope* / *The New Pope*. She received her PhD in Italian literature from Yale, where she is Senior Lecturer in the Humanities and Director of the Yale Humanities in Rome program.